ADVENTURERS WANTED

Other Books by M. L. Forman

ADVENTURERS WANTED, BOOK ONE:
SLATHBOG'S GOLD

ADVENTURERS WANTED, BOOK TWO:
THE HORN OF MORAN

ADVENTURERS WANTED, BOOK THREE:
ALBREK'S TOMB

BOOK TWO

ADVENTURERS WANTED

THE HORN OF MORAN

M. L. FORMAN

For Daniel, who makes every day an adventure

Visit us at ShadowMountain.com

First printing in hardbound 2011.
First printing in paperbound 2012.

Library of Congress Cataloging-in-Publication Data

Forman, Mark, 1964–
The Horn of Moran / M.L. Forman.
p. cm.— (Adventurers wanted ; bk. 2)
Summary: Sixteen-year-old wizard-in-training Alex Taylor and his band of fellow adventurers battle a goblin army, navigate an enchanted forest, and try to solve the sphinx's riddle in their quest to find the lost Horn of Moran and return it to Alusia before the nation erupts in war.
ISBN 978-1-60641-226-8 (hardbound : alk. paper)
ISBN 978-1-60908-911-5 (strippable paperback)
[1. Fantasy. 2. Adventure and adventurers—Fiction. 3. Wizards—Fiction. 4. Magic—Fiction. 5. Orphans—Fiction.] I. Title.
PZ7.F7653Ho 2011
[Fic]—dc22 2010037531

Printed in the United States of America
R. R. Donnelley, Crawfordsville, IN

10 9 8 7 6 5 4 3 2 1

CONTENTS

ACKNOWLEDGMENTS

There are a lot of people who deserve special thanks for making this story happen, especially the fans who insisted that it be published and who sent me letters and e-mails and posted on my blog. My thanks to you all.

Also, I want to thank my friends at Shadow Mountain who worked long and hard to make this book happen.

First on the list is Lisa Mangum, my editor. She's the one who makes me look like I know what I'm doing when I write. She keeps the story on track even when I wander off and basically cleans up the many little messes that I make. I may go crazy when I first see the edits, but I'm always glad that Lisa is there to fix things.

Special thanks to Chris Schoebinger, my go-to guy at Shadow Mountain. I'm sure he has a fancy job title, but in the end he's the guy who gets things done and makes all of this possible. Thanks to him for all the time and energy he's put into this story.

Credit should also be given to illustrator Brandon Dorman, whose outstanding work creates a face for the story and helps bring the words to life.

Special credit goes to Richard Erickson, Art Director. He puts it all together and helps makes the book shine. I'm not sure how he does it, but I'm glad he does.

And to those I've missed mentioning, know that I remember you in my heart.

And finally, a few words of motivation from Sir Winston Churchill that have helped keep me going when, from time to time, it all seemed hopeless:

"Never give up. Never, never give up."

Chapter One

Wizard in Training

A cool breeze stirred the curtain by the open window. Alex watched the slow, swaying movement of the cloth for a moment before forcing his tired mind to focus. Standing up with some difficulty, he stretched, then turned off the lamp on the table he used as a desk. It had been a long day, but as tired as he was, Alex didn't want to sleep.

"Foolish," Alex said as he moved toward his bed.

It was foolish not to sleep, foolish not to let his body rest. There was nothing to fear, not here at home. He knew his dreams—even his nightmares—might be important, but he didn't know what, if anything, they meant.

"The dreams won't come tonight," Alex told himself as he dropped onto his bed.

He only half-believed his own words. The dreams had been random, waking him at least once a week. The last one had been only three days before, and Alex hoped for an uneventful night. Reaching out, Alex turned off the light beside his bed. He let himself relax, clearing his mind of worries, and slowly let sleep take him.

Almost immediately, Alex found himself walking along a

familiar, narrow, dark corridor. Shadows danced in the flickering light of the few torches that were hanging from the walls, creating the illusion of movement. For a moment Alex felt that he was inside some living thing, the walls moving around him like some giant creature was breathing. But the dream was entirely silent, and that troubled him.

He knew where he was—this dimly lit corridor had haunted his dreams for months—and he knew where he had to go. Slowly Alex started forward, following the line of torches deeper into the unknown. He walked for what felt like hours, and with each step the silence pressed a little closer, making it harder for him to breathe.

Eventually, a chamber appeared in front of him just as it always did, empty except for an enormous mirror in the center of the room. Reluctantly Alex moved toward the mirror, afraid of what it would show him yet knowing he would look anyway. A reflection appeared slowly, as if it, too, was afraid to look out of the mirror.

This time, though, it wasn't a single image that appeared in front of him, but two. Alex's breath caught in his throat, and he had to force himself to breathe. The two images were both of him, but one image was true, reflecting him as he was, while the other image was different, an older version of Alex. After a moment the two reflections separated, the older to the left side of the mirror, the younger disappearing to the right, out of his line of sight.

Alex stepped closer to the mirror, trying to see where the images had gone, but the surface was blank. He lifted his hand, and as he touched the mirror, the glass rippled like water under his fingers. Without thinking he pushed himself through the liquid surface of the mirror. As he stepped through, he discovered that the mirror was still in front of him, but now he was surrounded by other mirrors as well.

Panic clawed at the back of Alex's mind, but he couldn't run, he could only turn and look into the mirrors around him. Most were empty, reflecting only darkness back at him, but two mirrors held images of himself. On his left, the older Alex walked slowly away. To his right, his true reflection looked back at him.

Alex faced his true reflection and reached out to touch the mirror. His hand passed through the watery surface, and at his touch all the mirrors around him collapsed, the water dropping to the stone floor and vanishing into the cracks.

Doors appeared on either side of the chamber, and a large double door seemed to emerge out of the floor at the far end.

Alex moved to the middle of the room. Standing with his eyes partly closed, he listened for any sound, anything that would help him understand why he was there or know what to do next. A cold breeze blew across his face. It came from the direction of the double doors, and he took it as a sign. He moved to the doorway, reaching out for the glimmering, gold doorknob. Then he stopped, his hand shaking slightly. He could feel evil and hate waiting behind the doors. Not just waiting, waiting for *him.*

Alex froze. He didn't want to know what was behind those doors, and yet a sudden need filled him, an urgency and the knowledge that time was running out. He feared whatever was waiting for him behind the doors, but something in his mind told him that he had to face his fears. He had to confront the evil that was waiting for him. If he turned back now—if he gave in to his fear—then his future would vanish like the water from the mirrors. It took all the strength he had to lift his hand and push open the doors.

Everything went dark as he moved through the doorway, and his feet found only emptiness. Alex tumbled into the darkness, his voice screaming that it wasn't fair, anger and frustration racing through his mind. Laughter answered his protests, a laughter that filled his mind with rage and his bones with ice. There were no answers here; there was only the laughter and the endless falling into darkness.

Alex woke with a start.

For a moment he was lost, and then he had to fight to get free of his blankets. Alex fumbled with the lamp beside his bed, knocking things over in his hurry to turn on the light. Finally, feeling panicked that he was really still asleep, the light came on.

Rubbing his eyes, Alex twisted around and sat on the edge of his bed. He glanced at the clock on the wall and saw that it was 4:30 A.M. For a minute he sat there, looking around the room, making sure that he wasn't in another dream.

Staggering to his feet, Alex moved to his desk. He dropped into the swivel chair, turned on the lamp, and pulled a large notepad toward him. Checking his calendar, he scribbled the date on the notepad, followed by the time. For a long moment he paused, and then he slowly started to write everything he could remember about the nightmare he'd just had.

Alexander Taylor was not what he appeared to be. Most people thought Alex was a normal sixteen-year-old boy, but they were wrong. Alex was—among other things—an adventurer.

Six months ago, Alex had indeed been what people expected him to be: normal. But that had all changed when he had accidentally wandered into the adventure shop belonging to Mr. Cornelius Clutter. After entering Mr. Clutter's shop, Alex had become part of a great adventure, and that experience had changed everything he thought he knew. While on his adventure he had learned all kinds of new things, but perhaps the strangest thing of all was that he had learned he was an untrained wizard.

When Alex had come home from his first adventure—on the same afternoon that he had left—he was shocked to learn that his stepfather, Mr. Roberts, knew all about adventures and magic. Not only that, but Mr. Roberts told Alex that his father had been an adventurer as well.

That had been six long months ago, and almost everything in Alex's life had changed. His stepbrother, Todd, had gone off to college, and Alex no longer had to wash dishes or help in the kitchen, or even clean up once the customers at the tavern had left. In fact, the only things Alex really had to do were study and practice magic.

Learning magic sometimes required open spaces in order to keep things from getting out of hand. Alex smiled as he remembered the first time he'd tried to summon a magical wind.

He'd ended up blowing everything in his old bedroom into a giant mess. To make things easier for Alex, and to help prevent problems like the mess in his bedroom, Mr. Roberts had cleared the third floor of the tavern and given the space entirely to his stepson.

This morning Alex was grateful for the privacy. He leaned back in his chair and reviewed the details he had written down about his dream. His teacher, Whalen Vankin, had told Alex that the dreams he was having might be warnings. "Dreams are often more than they appear to be," Whalen had said in his letters. "As your power grows, you will have many dreams, and many nightmares. You would be wise to pay attention to both."

Alex wondered when he would be able to meet the great wizard face to face. Whalen was perhaps the greatest wizard alive, and he had agreed to take Alex as his apprentice. Unfortunately, Whalen was currently on an adventure of his own, so Alex was stuck at home waiting, learning magic by magical mail.

Whalen had sent Alex several books about magic—some of which could only be read by moonlight—and several small magical objects as well. He had also sent a letter instructing Alex about what he should do and what he should try to learn. Whalen had warned him not to join any more adventures, at least not until they had met in person.

Alex was learning a lot, but he hated waiting for a new adventure. It was hard for him to imagine what was taking Whalen so long. And apart from waiting, there were other things that annoyed him. Though his first adventure had taken a year and a half, he'd come home as his fifteen-year-old self. He wasn't as strong as he remembered being, or as tall, or anything else. He felt trapped in his own small, weak body.

Being smaller and weaker than he remembered wasn't the worst thing about being home. What really annoyed him was the way people treated him. On his adventure, Alex had been treated as an equal. His fellow adventurers were always willing to listen to his opinions and ideas. Here, at home, there were few people who even pretended to listen to a sixteen-year-old. Some people would smile politely and nod, but if anything that was more frustrating than the people who simply ignored him.

Alex tried hard to push his frustrations away, but it wasn't always easy. He often found himself becoming angry for almost no reason at all. Whalen had warned him it would be hard to control his emotions—anger most of all—and Alex was working hard to keep his emotions from running away with him.

Sighing, Alex realized he wasn't going to be able to go back to sleep. At least not for a while. Pushing aside the notepad, he reached for his magic bag and whispered into the top. As soon as he had finished speaking, a second magic bag appeared in his hand, a bag that had once belonged to his father. Setting his own bag aside, he whispered the password that would allow him to enter his father's bag.

After returning home from his first adventure, Alex had spent a lot of time searching the bag and, with Mr. Roberts to answer his questions, he felt like he was finally getting to know his father.

There were the things he'd expected to find in his father's bag: stored food, a bedroom, clothes, a treasure room that was at least as large as his own, and lots of other things that adventurers would find helpful or useful. But then there were the things he had not expected to find. His father had a surprisingly large library, sculptures of different creatures, maps of places Alex had never heard of or even read about, a kitchen big enough to cook for a hundred people, and a room that was set up like a blacksmith shop.

"Your father was a gifted smith," Mr. Roberts had said when Alex had questioned him about the workroom. "He won lots of awards for the weapons and armor he made. He also made all kinds of jewelry—rings, necklaces, brooches, and such. Never sold any of it as far as I know; he used to give the pretty things away to friends, or sometimes to people who helped him on an adventure."

Once inside the bag, Alex headed directly for the workroom. Whalen had suggested, more than once, that he find a hobby; something to take his mind off waiting. Something that had nothing at all to do with magic. Making things with his hands, not with magic, seemed like a perfect hobby. There were plenty of books in the workroom to get him started, as well as piles of his father's notes.

Alex was walking past the large stone dragon statue that stood next to the workroom door, when he noticed something he was sure he had never seen before. A golden chain was dangling from the dragon's mouth.

Curious, he looked at the chain for a minute, wondering where it had come from. He could feel magic near the dragon's head, an old spell with little power. He'd never felt magic like that before, so he carefully reached out and touched the chain.

Nothing happened. He pulled gently on the chain, ready to let go of it if he felt the magic change, and he heard something move inside the dragon's mouth. As the chain moved inch by inch, the mouth of the dragon slowly opened. A pendant attached to the chain dropped out of the dragon's mouth where a rolled-up piece of paper now appeared.

Slowly Alex reached for the paper, half afraid that the mouth would snap shut on his hand, or worse, close before he could get the paper out. The dragon's jaws didn't move, and the old magic he had felt was fading, its purpose fulfilled. Carefully unrolling the paper, his jaw dropped open as he started to read.

> *My son,*
>
> *I cannot tell you all that I would wish in this short note. I have left this pendant for you, not to wear, but to study. The ancient symbol on the pendant is an important one, with great meaning to those who know what it is. All I can say is that you may freely trust any person who wears this symbol or a pendant like this one. Do not wear this pendant yourself, but remember it. Do not ask questions about the symbol unless you meet a person who wears it. I hope, in time, that you will learn more and understand why I cannot explain more to you.*
>
> *Your loving father,*
> *Joshua*

Alex was dumbfounded. He looked at the pendant, and then read the note again just to make sure he wasn't imagining things. He looked at the dragon, whose mouth remained open as if it had always been that way. His head spun with excitement, and for several minutes he wasn't sure what to do.

Wildly at first, and then with more control, Alex sent his magic searching. If his father had left him one magically hidden message, maybe he had left others. He searched every corner of the bag, and then to make sure he hadn't missed anything, he searched again. There was no magic to be found, no hidden compartments or doors, nothing. If there were other messages for him, his father had hidden them very well, and all he could do was wait until they were ready to be discovered.

Disappointed that he hadn't found more, Alex turned his attention to the pendant in his hand. It was made of gold and silver, and it looked like a small flower or a blossom of some kind. He tried to remember if he'd ever seen anything like it before. Nothing came to mind, but he had never paid much attention to the jewelry that others wore. He focused on the pendant for a few more minutes, promising himself that he would remember it if he ever saw it again.

Finally, Alex looped the chain over the dragon's head, letting the pendant hang around the neck of the statue. His father had left him a message, and he would remember it. He had questions, and in time he hoped he would find the answers, but he wasn't going to find them in his father's bag, and he wasn't going to find them today.

"You look tired," Mr. Roberts commented when Alex sat down for breakfast.

"Another nightmare," Alex replied.

"I guess that goes with being a wizard."

"It's not so bad," said Alex, trying to be casual.

"Bad enough, it would seem. What does Whalen have to say about it?"

"He says that dreams can sometimes be warnings and that I should try to remember them."

"Well, it's good to have a warning, even if you lose some sleep."

"It would be, if I knew what the nightmare was about," Alex replied in a resentful tone. "The dreams are always so mixed up, it's hard to know what any of it means. Or even if it means anything at all."

"Don't let it get to you, Alex. I'm sure you'll understand the dream in time," said Mr. Roberts. "It takes time to understand most things after all."

"I just hope the warning isn't for something that's going to happen today," said Alex.

"I doubt it," Mr. Roberts replied with a chortle. "Why don't you have some breakfast and then get a few more hours of sleep. If a dragon turns up, I'll be sure to wake you."

It was nearly noon when Alex woke up again. He still felt a little tired, but he rolled off the bed and stretched just the same. There were things he needed to do, and he wasn't going to let his bad dreams stop him.

Sitting down at his table, Alex looked at the notepad he'd used the night before. What he remembered from the nightmare didn't make any more sense to him now than it had when he'd written it down. He was sure it must be a warning, but the broken bits of his dream were impossible to piece together no matter how hard he tried.

"Just have to pay attention and keep my eyes open," Alex said to himself as he tossed the pad back onto the table.

A small popping sound and a loud ding interrupted his thoughts.

Looking around, Alex saw a yellow bowling-pin shaped creature with a red zigzag line around its middle standing on the far edge of the table. The geeb was balancing on its single birdlike leg, waiting for him to say something.

"Hello," said Alex in surprise.

"Ding," the geeb replied, its head changing into the shape of a small bell.

"Do you have a message for me?" Alex questioned.

"Ding!"

"Can I have the message, please?"

"Ding," replied the geeb and an envelope appeared from what Alex always thought of as the geeb's mouth.

"Thank you," said Alex.

"Ding!"

"Have you been paid?"

"Honk." The geeb's head took the shape of a small bicycle horn.

"Hang on a moment," said Alex as he opened the letter. "Let me see what this is, then I'll pay you."

"Ding!"

Alex recognized Whalen's handwriting on the front of the envelope, and he felt certain that this would be another long letter explaining magic, answering questions, and telling him what he should study next. To his surprise, however, the envelope contained only a short message and no instructions at all.

Dear Alex,

Have just heard about a new adventure our friend Silvan Bregnest is putting together. He is in a bit of a rush and has asked me for permission to take you along. As the adventure is happening in Norsland, I thought you might like to go.

I will expect you to keep up with your studies while you're away and to keep me informed of your activities. If you promise to send me a report every two weeks, I think you should join Bregnest on this adventure.

Yours in fellowship,
Whalen

P.S. I believe Bregnest will be sending you a geeb shortly. Good luck, and remember to keep me up to date.

Alex was stunned for a moment. His chest felt like a large balloon had inflated inside of him, and he thought he might float away with happiness. He had been waiting for months, and now Whalen had said he could go on another adventure. Better yet, Whalen had even picked an adventure for him to join. And best of all, his friend Bregnest would be leading the adventure. It was much more than Alex had dared to hope for. He was so distracted that he almost forgot about the geeb standing on the edge of his table.

"Ding!"

"Oh, sorry. Can you take a reply back to Whalen?" Alex asked as he reached for a piece of paper.

"Ding!"

Alex thought for a moment, and then wrote a quick reply to Whalen. He reviewed the page once before folding it and putting it in a new envelope, writing Whalen's name as neatly as he could on the outside.

"Can you take this to Whalen Vankin?" Alex asked the geeb again, wanting to make sure it would deliver the message to the right person.

"Ding," the geeb answered, but made no move to accept Alex's letter.

"Oh, yes, your payment. Sorry about that."

Alex retrieved a small ruby from his magic bag and tossed it in the general direction of the geeb. The geeb hopped into the air, catching the ruby with ease before landing back on the table. Once on the table the geeb produced eight gold coins and seven silver coins as change for the ruby.

Alex held his letter out for the geeb to take. "If you require more payment, please return."

"Ding." The geeb accepted the letter and then disappeared with a single hop on its birdlike leg and a small popping sound.

Almost immediately, a second geeb appeared with a loud ding.

"Do *you* have a message for me?" Alex asked, surprised.

"Ding!"

"May I have it, please?"

"Ding!"

"Thank you," said Alex, picking up the envelope that the geeb had dropped and tearing it open. He had trouble unfolding the letter and getting it right side up, but once he did, a smile spread across his face.

Master Alexander Taylor, Esq.

Dear Alex,

As you may have already heard from our friend, Whalen Vankin, I am putting together another adventure. I've written to Whalen and asked if you might come along. Whalen seems to think that it would be good for you to join the adventure, so I thought that I should send you a message and ask you to at least listen to the details.

This won't be a great quest like our last adventure, but there is a large reward involved. If you are interested in coming, please send me a message. I'd like to meet as soon as possible at Mr. Clutter's Adventure Shop to discuss details and the bargain.

Your friend,
Silvan Bregnest

P.S. Andy has informed me that our friends Skeld and Tayo have both decided to get married, and they want you at the weddings. This won't be a problem for our adventure, and shouldn't cause us any delay.

Alex read the letter through twice, wondering when Bregnest wanted to meet at the adventure shop. He bit his lip, worried. Now that he thought about it, he didn't remember seeing Clutter's shop when he'd been in Sildon Lane only a few days ago. In fact, he didn't remember seeing it at all since he'd gotten home. If the shop wasn't still there, how was he going to meet Bregnest and go on this adventure?

"Can you take a reply back?" Alex questioned.

"Ding!"

Alex thought about Bregnest's note and the fact that their friends Skeld and Tayo were both getting married. Missing the weddings was unthinkable; he had to go. If worse came to worst, he would ask Whalen how to travel to Telous using magic.

"Here's your payment for delivering the message," Alex said to the geeb, who was waiting patiently on the table.

He tossed a small diamond in the air. The geeb caught the jewel easily as it fell through the air, and once again left a handful of gold and silver coins as change.

"Please take this message to Silvan Bregnest."

"Ding," the geeb answered, and accepted the message Alex had just written.

The second geeb of the day vanished, and Alex added the coins to his magic bag. He was wondering if he should go ahead and ask Whalen about getting to Telous with magic now, or if he should wait until after he'd tried to find the adventure shop, when another popping sound made him jump. Alex had never seen so many geebs in so short a time, and he wondered what this one might be bringing him.

After asking the geeb for the message and to wait for a reply, Alex sat down and opened the newest envelope. He could see from the writing that it was a second note from Whalen.

Dear Alex,

I've received your promise and intend to hold you to it. I had hoped to meet with you before you went on another adventure, but that has proven impossible. My current adventure is taking much longer than expected, and I have no idea when I'll be able to return.

I know you've been working hard to learn everything you can, and I promise you that much of what you have already learned will come in handy on this new adventure. I will warn you, however, not to become overconfident. There are many magical places and people in the known and the unknown lands, and many of them are not as friendly as they might be. To be honest, there are people and powers that would like nothing more than to control you, or failing that, to destroy you.

This is a dangerous time for you, as you are not yet fully trained; and yet, you are able to use great power when you need to. I must warn you again to be careful when using your powers and remind you to not let your emotions get the best of you. Emotions are powerful things, Alex, and you need to learn to keep them under control. Study hard and keep your eyes open for danger. Remember, you are a wizard in training.

I will write when I can but will expect a message from you at least every other week.

Be careful and have fun.

Yours in fellowship,
Whalen

Alex thought Whalen sounded worried in his letter, and he wondered what exactly Whalen had meant by saying it was a dangerous time for him. His concerns about the note didn't last long, and thoughts of a new adventure filled his mind.

His first adventure had been so exciting, and he'd had so much fun with his friends. Slowly, however, his happy memories turned to darker thoughts. He considered what new dangers he might have to face. Were the nightmares he'd been having warnings about Bregnest's new adventure? Whalen had said that Bregnest was in a rush to put the company together, and Bregnest had wanted to meet as soon as possible. It seemed that time might be running out, but running out on what, Alex couldn't guess.

Chapter Two

The Adventure Begins

Later that night, after the customers had left the tavern, Alex had a long talk with his stepfather. He told him about the invitation to join a new adventure and that he needed to look for the adventure shop the next morning.

"Do you think the shop will still be there?" Alex asked, remembering the times he had walked past the building thinking it was just an old bookstore.

"It'll be there," said Mr. Roberts with confidence. "Always was when I went looking for it."

"But if it's not there, what will I do?"

"You'll be all right. Adventurers always seem to find it, and since you're an adventurer . . ." Mr. Roberts trailed off, looking at Alex with understanding. "I know this is only your second adventure, Alex. Nobody expects you to know everything."

"I know, but . . ."

"But you're a wizard in training," Mr. Roberts said slowly. "You think they will expect more of you. You think that it is your job to keep the company safe with your magic, to sense danger coming and help your friends avoid it."

Alex nodded. "I have magic, so I should be able to do more. I should be . . ."

"Be what?" Mr. Roberts questioned. "If you think it's your job to do everything on this—or any—adventure, you're wrong. You will be part of a team. You can't do everything by yourself, even with your magic. Do as much as you can, Alex. But you have to let the others do what they can as well."

"I like the idea of being part of a team," said Alex.

"Good," said Mr. Roberts. "Being part of the team is a hard lesson for a lot of young adventurers to learn. I had a hard time learning about teamwork, at least at first. Can you tell me what kind of adventure you are joining? Where will your company be going? Can you give me any details at all?"

Alex shook his head. "All I know is that Whalen mentioned it would be in Norsland. And Bregnest said there would be a reward."

"Well, if nothing else, I expect you to win some honor," said Mr. Roberts. "After all, to an adventurer, honor is worth more than treasure."

Alex nodded. He had learned a great deal about adventurers from his stepfather and had a much better understanding about the true meaning of honor.

As Alex climbed into bed, his mind was buzzing with all that had happened that day: the nightmare he'd had, the hidden message from his father, a new adventure, and Whalen's warning about it being a dangerous time. All of it crowded his mind, but quickly slipped away as sleep overcame him.

Alex skipped breakfast the next morning and left the tavern with only a quick good-bye to his stepfather. He was so excited to be on his way that he almost walked past the adventure shop before he even noticed it.

Like the last time he was here, there was a large cardboard sign in the front window of the shop. "Adventurers Wanted," the sign said in bright red letters. Without waiting for the sign to change, as it often did whenever he looked away from it, Alex opened the door and stepped inside.

"Well, hello," a cheerful voice said as soon as the shop door closed. "So good to see you again."

"Hello, Mr. Clutter."

Cornelius Clutter looked exactly as Alex remembered him, right down to the shockingly pink bow tie that he always seemed to wear. Today he wore a tan shirt under his dark green apron, and his round smiling face was just the same as it had been the last time Alex had seen him.

"Looking for a new adventure, are you? I've had some interesting proposals in the last few weeks. I'm sure most companies would love to have you along, if you're interested."

"Actually, I'm looking for Silvan Bregnest," said Alex, as Mr. Clutter started sorting through papers on the counter.

"Ah, well, that is something," said Mr. Clutter, setting down his papers and looking up at Alex. "Master Bregnest happens to be here this morning. He's interviewing a potential candidate for his new adventure."

"I'll wait."

"Very good then. I'll get you some tea—or would you prefer something else?"

"Something cold if you have it."

Mr. Clutter nodded and hurried off without another word. Alex was surprised—usually Mr. Clutter never stopped talking. After a few minutes he reappeared, carrying a large silver tray in both hands and humming softly to himself.

"I've seen the details of Master Bregnest's new adventure, and I have to say I'm quite impressed," he said, offering a glass to Alex. "Yes, quite a good quest this time, and the payment is more than fair."

"Can you tell me about the quest?" Alex questioned as he sniffed at the glass.

"Oh, no," Mr. Clutter replied, returning to his pile of papers. "I'll leave that for the leader of the adventure. It's not my place to be telling, after all. Still, I think you will be interested, and if you're not . . . Well, there are several other adventures getting started right now, and most of them sound exciting."

Alex took a sip from the glass. The liquid turned out to be lemonade, but tasted both sweeter and a bit more sour than any he had ever had before. He took a cake from the tray and ate it while he waited.

It wasn't long before he heard a door close at the back of the shop. He turned toward the curtains that divided the back of the shop from the front, his excitement growing as he waited.

"The task seems simple enough, but that doesn't really mean anything," Alex heard Bregnest saying. "And it may take some time to find what we are looking for."

"And what are you looking for?" Alex questioned, as Bregnest stepped through the curtains.

"Alex!" Bregnest exclaimed. "I mean, Master Taylor."

"It's good to see you again, my friend," Alex replied as he allowed Bregnest to pull him into a friendly hug.

"It is very good to see you. I've been explaining this new adventure to Master Valenteen," said Bregnest, nodding toward a thin man who had followed him through the curtains. "He's agreed to join the company, so we only need one more member before we can start."

Alex glanced at the man standing behind Bregnest, surprised by what he saw. The man was extremely thin, almost skeletal, but what caught Alex's attention was that it looked as if the whole left side of the man's face was badly bruised.

"Perhaps you had better tell *me* about this adventure," Alex said, looking back to Bregnest.

"I was hoping you would ask," said Bregnest with a grin. "You don't mind waiting here for a bit do you, Val?"

"Not at all. Take your time. I'm sure Mr. Clutter won't mind if I look around a bit."

"Oh, no, not at all," said Mr. Clutter to Val. "Would you like some lemonade?"

"Come on then," said Bregnest, nudging Alex's shoulder and nodding toward the back of the shop.

Alex turned to look at Val more closely as he passed by. Up close, he couldn't see any trace of the bruises he thought he'd seen before. He wasn't sure what to think, but after a moment he decided it must have only been a shadow falling across Val's face.

Alex shrugged off the thought, turning to follow Bregnest.

"So," Bregnest began as they entered one of the smaller rooms in the back of the shop, "how's your training going?"

"Fairly well. I still haven't been able to meet with Whalen, but I write to him quite often." Alex answered, and then quickly told Bregnest about his studies, and as much as he could about Whalen's advice and instruction.

"So, tell me about this new adventure," Alex said.

Bregnest nodded, settling down to business. "It seems that a cousin of mine has run into a bit of trouble. He is a king in Alusia, and some questions have come up about whether he is the *true* king."

"If he's king, how can there be any questions?"

"Well, the true kings of Athanor—that's the area he rules—have traditionally carried the Horn of Moran as a sign of their nobility and right to rule," Bregnest explained. "Unfortunately for my cousin, the Horn was lost about a hundred years ago."

"Lost? How was it lost?"

"A young prince foolishly took the Horn with him on an adventure. He never returned from his travels, and since then, the kings of Athanor have been without the Horn," Bregnest answered. "Now another family is claiming the throne, and my cousin needs the Horn of Moran to prove his true kingship."

"Can anyone with the Horn claim to be king?" Alex questioned.

"Not exactly," Bregnest replied in a thoughtful tone. "You see, the Horn will only sound if the true king uses it. A false king will not be able to get any sound from the Horn at all. At least, that's what the legends claim."

"So your cousin, being the true king, wants to prove himself by using the Horn."

"Indeed, yes. And he has offered to pay a great deal for the Horn's return."

Alex thought about what Bregnest had told him. People making trouble about who should be king was a problem—a problem that might start a war. Returning the Horn of Moran might stop the trouble, but there was no way to be sure.

"May I ask, what adventure was the young prince on when he lost the Horn?"

"I had to ask Mr. Clutter for that information," answered Bregnest. "He told me that the prince was searching for the Tower of the Moon in Norsland. The tower is supposed to contain a fairly large treasure, and I believe that is what he and his company were after."

"I take it that the Tower of the Moon is not easy to find."

"There are maps showing how to get there. Though as far as I know, nobody has tried since the time of the prince."

"Why?"

"Well, the path is supposed to be well-guarded. Stories suggest that a sphinx and possibly a griffin guard the tower."

"It must be an important treasure to require *both* creatures as guardians." Alex knew that griffins were extremely loyal and dedicated to the jobs they were given. In fact, griffins were rumored to be the best guardians to be found anywhere, unless you counted dragons.

"The Tower of the Moon was once a place of great knowledge and learning. It is said that many wizards lived there long ago, and there are legends about at least one wizard coming to live there again someday. We'll be able to learn more about the legends once we arrive in Norsland."

"All right then," said Alex. "What has the king offered for the Horn's return?"

"The king has offered one hundred thousand gold coins and a thousand of the finest horses in Alusia," answered Bregnest. "You should know that Alusian horses are considered the cleverest horses in all of the known lands."

"Then they must be impressive creatures."

"Indeed they are. In fact, Shahree is from Alusia, and you know what she is like."

"Shahree is from Alusia? If she is an example of Alusian horses, then a thousand like her would be worth far more than the gold offered."

"Well, Shahree does seem exceptional, even by the standards of Alusia," said Bregnest with a small grin. "And I think perhaps your own opinions about her may confuse your thoughts on value."

"If the horses the king is offering are anything like Shahree, I would find it difficult to sell any of them," Alex said firmly.

"We have not won the horses or the gold yet," Bregnest replied in a stern tone, though his smile remained. "And if we do, you may not need to sell them. I own some fairly large lands in Alusia and would be more than happy to keep the horses there for you, if you wish."

Alex nodded. "Tell me about the bargain. How many of us will there be?"

"There will be six of us on this adventure. Some of the

company you already know. Your friends Andy and Halfdan have already agreed to come along."

"Andy and Halfdan. We'll have good company at least."

"Also an elf named Sindar, who you do not know, though he knows a great deal about you. And Master Valenteen who is waiting with Mr. Clutter," Bregnest went on.

"And how is it that this Sindar knows about me?" Alex questioned.

"Sindar comes from the dark forest of Vargland. When we were there on our last adventure, he was away on an adventure of his own. He has heard about you from the other elves, however, and from our friend Calysto, of course."

"Then it should be a merry group," said Alex, remembering the elves of the dark forest.

"Yes, it should be," agreed Bregnest. "Now, regarding the shares of the primary treasure, since you are both a wizard *and* a warrior, I can offer you five shares out of twenty."

"I'm only a wizard in training," Alex corrected.

"So you say. Though I know more than you might guess. After all, you're not the only one Whalen has written to."

"Very well," said Alex. "What about secondary treasure?"

"Most of the secondary treasure will be divided equally between the company," Bregnest replied. "Any treasure found in the Tower of the Moon will be divided into seven shares. The extra share will be given to the finder of the Horn, or, if we find the Horn as a group, divided according to merit as I see fit."

"It all sounds good to me," said Alex. "But it also seems

you have left out a share somewhere. Shouldn't the primary treasure be divided by twenty-one?"

"I haven't left out a share. Since this quest is to aid my kinsman, I am only taking one share as a warrior and three as the leader."

"Very well then," said Alex, nodding. "I accept the bargain and will gladly sign the agreement."

"Before you accept, I need to impress on you how important this quest is. If we do not return the Horn, and soon, there could be war. We are in a race, and it is a race we must win."

"A race?" Alex questioned. "Are there others looking for the Horn?"

"No, not that I know of," Bregnest answered. "But we will be in a race against time. We must find the Horn and return it to the rightful king. If war begins before we can return the Horn . . . Well, then our adventure would be a failure."

"And there will be trouble in Alusia," Alex added. "But we should be able to do this quickly enough. The magic of the great arch will allow us to return at almost the same moment we leave."

"If only that were true." Bregnest sighed.

"What?"

"The magic you speak of—the same magic that let you return home after your first adventure on the same day you left—does not apply here."

"Why not?"

"Because both Norsland and Alusia are part of the known lands," Bregnest answered. "Time is constant in the known lands. It has to be or nothing would ever get done."

"Oh," said Alex. "I suppose that makes sense. I mean, well, I don't really understand."

"And I'm not sure I'm the one to explain it," said Bregnest. "All I can say is that for the known lands, time is constant. Ten days in Norsland is ten days in Alusia. The magical change of time only works for lands that don't interact with the known lands. Your world has little or nothing to do with the known lands, so it's easy for the magic to change time a bit."

"I see," said Alex. "And people are traveling and trading in the known lands all the time, so the magic can't do the same thing here."

"Exactly."

"Well, that's all right," Alex went on. "I'm still sure we can get the Horn back in time."

"Excellent. The company will be delighted to have you along."

"There are a couple of things I'd like to discuss with you," Alex added.

"Not trying to give away treasure again, are you?"

"No, nothing like that," said Alex. "But one of the six lost bags that I recovered during our last adventure belongs to someone in Norsland. I would like to return it if at all possible."

"We will make time for that," said Bregnest.

"And secondly, you said something in your letter about Skeld and Tayo both finding wives."

"It seems they have." Bregnest laughed. "Andy knows the whole story, so I'll let him tell you when we reach Telous. Attending the weddings won't interfere with our adventure at all. In fact, it's on our way to the Tower of the Moon, so that works out well."

"Well then, where do I sign? I can't wait to hear about Skeld and Tayo."

Bregnest showed Alex where to sign the agreement and slapped him on the shoulder in a friendly way. Alex thought Bregnest looked almost as happy as he felt, and he was sure that this adventure would be a great deal of fun.

"Val," Bregnest called as they entered the main room of Mr. Clutter's shop. "I want you to meet Alexander Taylor, our sixth member. He goes by Alex. Alex, this is Sedric Valenteen. He goes by Val."

"Pleased to meet you," Val replied.

"The pleasure is mine," said Alex, his eyes searching Val's face. There was no sign of any bruises, and Alex felt certain that what he had seen before had been a trick of the light and shadows.

"We should be off to Telous," said Bregnest. "The rest of the company will be waiting, and the midday meal will be ready soon."

"Gentlemen," said Mr. Clutter, entering the room. "All set and ready to go, are you?"

"Everything is ready. Will you file this for us, please?" Bregnest handed the adventurers' agreement to Mr. Clutter.

"Yes, yes, of course. And I hope this adventure turns out as well as your last. Oh, your last adventure was very good indeed."

"Which way then?" Bregnest questioned, cutting Mr. Clutter off before he could really get going.

"Through the wardrobe, I think," said Mr. Clutter. "That will put you just inside the Swan."

The Golden Swan was the finest tavern in Telous and the favorite of most adventurers. Alex had never traveled through Mr. Clutter's wardrobe, however, and he wasn't at all sure how it worked.

"Oh, I almost forgot," said Mr. Clutter, as Bregnest moved across the room. "Master Taylor, would you like to change your age at all?"

"My age?" Alex asked before he remembered what Mr. Clutter was talking about. "Oh, I, well . . . If I could go at the same age I was when I returned from my last adventure, that would be nice."

"Right you are," said Mr. Clutter. "I'll make a note of that. I see you're already wearing comfortable clothes, very wise that, but you might want to loosen your belt before going, just in case."

"Yes, of course," said Alex, reaching down to undo the buckle on his belt. "Wouldn't want things to be too tight."

"It's time to go," said Bregnest, walking to a large wardrobe that stood against the wall between two bookshelves.

"Enjoy yourselves," said Mr. Clutter, as Bregnest opened the wardrobe door and stepped inside.

Val followed Bregnest, but Alex stood by the door for a moment, a strange feeling of doubt in the back of his mind. He decided it was just nervous excitement and pushed the feeling aside, hurrying to follow Bregnest and Val into the darkness.

The trip through Mr. Clutter's wardrobe was, to say the least, very strange. Alex thought he knew what to expect, having gone through Mr. Clutter's back door on his last adventure. This journey, however, was something entirely different. When he first stepped into the wardrobe, everything seemed to go dark around him. Then, before he knew what was happening, he found himself sitting in a chair inside the main room of the Golden Swan. He shook his head and looked around in disbelief. He had no idea how he'd suddenly gone from walking to sitting, and he laughed at his own surprise.

"A bit strange, isn't it?" said Val from the chair next to him. "I've always preferred the back door myself."

"I think I do too."

"About time you lot showed up," said a voice that Alex recognized as his dwarf friend Halfdan. "Been wondering if you'd be here in time for the midday meal."

"I see your patience has not improved," replied Alex, as he fastened his belt once more.

Halfdan gave a grunting laugh, and pulled Alex into a friendly hug. Alex laughed as well, but before he could say anything else, he heard another voice calling his name.

"I see you've grown a bit, Master Goodseed," said Alex as his friend Andy hurried over.

"Oh, not so much," answered Andy.

Alex, Andy, and Halfdan all started talking at the same time. They all had a great deal of news to share, and even more questions to ask.

Bregnest stood behind them, finally clearing his throat to get their attention.

"If you three can contain yourselves for a moment," Bregnest began. "Alex, you need to be introduced to Sindar, and the rest of you need to be introduced to Sedric Valenteen."

"Our apologies, Master Bregnest," said Halfdan with a deep bow. "We were overcome with joy. We won't let it happen again."

Bregnest laughed and led them all into a private dining room in the back of the Swan. The introductions were made, and then Bregnest rang a golden bell that had been sitting on the table. At the sound of the bell, servants brought their meal into the room and then the adventurers were left alone to dine and discuss their plans.

To Alex's surprise, Bregnest didn't start talking about the adventure they were about to begin. Instead he let the group talk about whatever they wanted to talk about, while listening to what they had to say.

"We will discuss the adventure later," Bregnest said, noticing Alex's questioning look. "And your friends here can tell you about the rest of our former company—that is if you can get them to stop asking you questions."

They all laughed at his comment and were soon lost in conversation. Alex told his friends about his studies and about his father being an adventurer. He learned that his elf friend Arconn was on another adventure, and that Halfdan's cousin, Thrang, had been made a minister in the dwarf realm of Thraxon. It was only when they were finishing their meal that Alex was finally able to ask about his friends Skeld and Tayo.

"When did they find wives?" Alex questioned. "They've only been gone for six months. And part of that time was spent getting home, wasn't it?"

"It was on our way home," answered Andy. "We were all traveling through Norsland together and along the way we had to pass through Oslansk, one of the bigger cities in the area. While we were there, the two of them met a pair of sisters."

"Sisters?"

"Sisters," Andy confirmed. "We stayed in Oslansk for a week, and before we left, Skeld asked the younger sister—Lilly—to marry him. That would have been surprising enough, but just as we were leaving, Tayo asked the older sister, Indigo, if she would marry him."

"And they're both settling down in Oslansk?" Alex questioned.

"Perhaps not settling down, but I don't think Lilly or Indigo will let them go on an adventure for awhile."

"It seems their wealth has caught up to them," said Bregnest. "Perhaps they will be less frivolous on their next adventure."

"They've planned the weddings so that we could all be there when we pass through Oslansk," Andy continued. "And Bregnest has agreed that we should stay for the week of feasting that will follow the weddings."

"It's early spring, and the road we must follow is still covered in several feet of snow," said Bregnest. "Besides, without Thrang to cook for us, I thought we'd better enjoy as much feasting as we can. Though I'm sure he has taught his cousin here a thing or two about cooking."

"Indeed he has," said Halfdan. "And I will endeavor to live up to my cousin's reputation."

"You're cooking for us on this adventure, Halfdan?" Alex asked.

"Yes, I am."

"That's good," said Alex, elbowing Andy in the ribs. "I was afraid Bregnest would ask me to do the cooking, and then our whole adventure would be in terrible peril."

Chapter Three

Norsland

Once the questions were answered and news shared, Bregnest suggested that Alex go and check his saddle and gear that he had left in Telous.

"Shahree will be in high spirits to see you again," Bregnest added as Alex moved toward the door. "Though your separation has been longer for you than for her."

Alex knew time ran differently in the world he had lived in for almost sixteen years than it did here in the magical lands he had discovered. He wondered exactly how long it had been since he left Telous.

When Alex entered the stables of the Golden Swan, a loud whinny welcomed him. Smiling, he walked over to a familiar silver-gray horse and started rubbing her neck.

"Well, Shahree, it looks like you have been well cared for."

Shahree snorted loudly and shook her head up and down in answer.

Alex laughed and continued to rub the horse's neck. "Looks like we'll be off again soon. I hope you're ready for another adventure."

Shahree nuzzled his shoulder, and Alex could feel her excitement to be on the road again.

"I see that Calysto did not say enough," a voice commented behind Alex.

He turned around and saw Sindar standing at the stable door.

"The two of you are close," Sindar went on as he crossed to stand by Alex. "Closer than any horse and man I have ever seen."

"We have shared a lot," said Alex, turning back to Shahree. "And there is great trust and understanding between us."

"So I see. And I think Calysto must be right about you."

"In what way?"

"She told me that you were more like an elf than any human she had ever met," Sindar answered, reaching out and rubbing Shahree's forehead. "And she said that I would be lucky to go on an adventure with you."

"How long has it been since you last spoke with Calysto?"

"The new moon has appeared five times since I left the dark forest."

"She showed our company great kindness," said Alex. "Myself most of all."

"I have heard the story, though Calysto would not tell me everything that had passed between the two of you."

Alex remained silent.

"I will not ask you to tell me what she would not; it is not my place. I only thought it strange."

"If you knew what happened, you would not think it so strange," said Alex, patting Shahree's neck and turning to go.

"Already you learn to speak as a wizard."

"Perhaps . . ." A strange feeling suddenly came over Alex, and he stopped short at the door of the stable. His eyes moved to the crowded streets and buildings of Telous, searching for something he knew he would not find.

"You felt it as well," Sindar whispered. "A feeling of being watched, of a watcher with purpose."

"Yes."

"It is gone now."

"But what—or who—could it have been?" Alex questioned. "It wasn't just a feeling of being watched, it was something more. I just don't know what."

"I think there is little danger," Sindar replied slowly. "The feeling is gone, and I felt no evil in it."

Alex and Sindar returned to the Golden Swan where they spent the rest of the day talking with the other members of the company, but Alex wasn't as enthusiastic as he had been. The strange feeling of being watched troubled him, and he couldn't seem to shake his unease.

"How far is it to Oslansk?" Alex asked.

The company was sitting down to their feast, and Alex thought it would be a good idea to ask some questions.

"Perhaps a week's ride," answered Andy. "It may take a bit longer, depending on the snow."

"Snow?"

"Spring is slow to come to Norsland," said Andy. "The

snow was clearing when I rode to Telous a week ago, but we may still find some during our travels."

"I've heard that summers in Norsland are short," Halfdan commented thoughtfully.

"Not as short as stories tell," said Andy. "There are almost always six months without snow, and heavy winter lasts only for perhaps three months."

"Though even the light part of winter in Norsland may seem heavy to us," commented Sindar.

"We should be fine," said Bregnest, standing and drawing everyone's attention. "Tonight we seal our bargain and our adventure begins. You are all experienced adventurers, so there is little I need tell you. You all know what we seek, and you also know the rules of adventurers."

"We do," said Halfdan, scowling at his empty mug.

Bregnest smiled at Halfdan. "I know how great your thirst can be, and I would not wish to keep you from quenching it."

"I beg your pardon," replied Halfdan in an overly serious tone.

"There are a few things I do need to say, however," Bregnest continued. "The first is that we will buy most of our provisions when we reach Oslansk. If anyone is looking for a new adventure to start, they will certainly keep an eye on the shops here in Telous. I don't know if anyone will be looking for us, but it is always better to be a little careful early than to be very sorry later."

"There's wisdom in that," Val commented with a nod.

"You all know that we are in a race against time, but this race is not a sprint," Bregnest went on. "We have some time, and we will not go charging off wildly to reach our goal. When I left Alusia, the harvest was about to start. Fall and winter are wet, muddy months, and the ground often freezes. Winter is never a good time to go to war, so I believe we will have at least eight months before any real trouble starts in Alusia. With luck, we will find success—and the Horn—quickly.

"Finally, as some of you know, Master Taylor carries several lost bags from his last adventure. We will make time for him to return one of those bags as we travel in Norsland. I believe the heir to the bag lives near our planned course of travel, so this should not be an inconvenience to us, or cause any great delay. And so, we will drink to our agreement, our adventure, and for luck."

Bregnest rang a golden bell that was sitting on the table. At the sound of the bell, servants entered the room, filled mugs for the company, and then departed.

"To the agreement, the adventure, and for luck," Bregnest repeated, lifting his mug.

"The agreement, the adventure, and for luck." The others stood and lifted their mugs as well.

"Now, let's eat," said Bregnest, ringing the bell once more. "We will depart at daybreak and begin our adventure."

With the second ringing of the bell, more servants arrived, bringing large platters of roasted meats, bowls of vegetables and gravy, and everything else the company might want. They ate and talked and even told a few stories about past adventures. Alex was soon pleasantly full, but to his surprise Val continued to eat like a starving man.

"Can't see where you're putting it all," Halfdan commented

after pushing his own plate away. "Never seen anyone eat so much at one time."

"You sound like my wife," Val joked. "She always comments on how much I eat, and then complains that I don't ever gain weight. She says my being so skinny makes her look bad."

They all laughed at Val's words, and after some time, Bregnest suggested that they should all go to bed.

"Sleep well, my friends," said Bregnest, as he opened the door to the room he was sharing with Val. "We may be in a rush to finish our adventure, but I hope we have many happy times in front of us, and little danger."

As Alex climbed into his own bed, he noticed that Sindar was simply lying on top of the covers.

"May I ask you something?" Alex questioned.

"Certainly," said Sindar, rolling onto his side so he could look at Alex.

"Well, I was thinking about my friend Arconn and a question I never asked him. I don't ever remember seeing him sleep, and I was wondering if elves ever sleep, or if you don't need to."

"We can sleep," said Sindar. "We remain watchful and alert, but our minds rest. And remembering things long past is like sleep for us."

"Oh," said Alex, pulling his blankets around him. "So you don't dream?"

"We dream as well. I suppose I should have said that we do not sleep like men, and that men may not consider our rest to be sleep."

"That sounds like an elf reply," said Alex. "Thank you for telling me."

"Not at all."

Alex put out the lamp next to his bed and closed his eyes. Sindar started humming softly in the darkness. It was a pleasant tune—one Alex had never heard before—and he soon fell asleep listening to it.

Before sunrise the next morning, Alex and Sindar made their way to the company's private dining room. Bregnest and Val were already there, eating; Halfdan and Andy turned up shortly after Alex and Sindar sat down. There was little talk as they ate, and as soon as they were finished, Bregnest led them to the stables.

"Are you ready to go?" Alex asked Shahree as he settled the saddle on her back.

Shahree snorted loudly and stamped her hoof on the floor of the stable in answer. Alex patted her neck and smiled. He was fond of his horse and being with her again made him feel good.

When the company was ready, Bregnest led them out of the stable and into the streets of Telous. Sindar fell in beside Bregnest, while Alex and Halfdan followed them. Andy and Val were last, which made Alex feel a little awkward because on his last adventure he had always ridden at the back of the group.

They traveled south, following the well-marked path to the

great arch, the magical gateway that would allow them to enter another land. Alex watched the landscape slip by, thinking that it had changed little since he had last been there. Alex thought it felt good to be back in the saddle and riding again, then, remembering something from his last adventure, he turned to Halfdan.

"Did you happen to bring some of that ancient dwarf remedy for stiffness?" Alex asked.

"I did," replied Halfdan. "And I hope it works as well this time as it did the last time we used it."

"Why wouldn't it?"

"It's a new batch," Halfdan answered. "I'd just finished brewing it when Bregnest's message about this adventure arrived."

"Does the remedy grow more potent with age?"

"Oh, yes. Truth be told, what you had last time was almost fifty years old," Halfdan answered. "Takes a long time to get all the ingredients. Some you have to pick in the moonlight, others on the first day of winter. Course, even if you *can* get everything else, there's always the problem of moogosh berries."

"Moogosh berries?" Andy questioned.

"They're very rare," Halfdan said. "And even if you know where a moogosh plant is, it might take years to harvest the berries. Only plants that are a hundred years old produce berries, and even then, they appear only once every twelve to fifteen years."

"Perhaps I should learn to brew your potion myself," said Alex in a thoughtful tone. "But I would guess the recipe is a well-guarded secret, and I don't know where I'd be able to find things like moogosh berries."

"We do keep the recipe secret," Halfdan answered seriously. "Though that rule might be bent for a wizard like yourself."

Both Alex and Andy laughed at Halfdan's reply. The laughter sounded good in the cool morning air.

Alex wondered if all new adventures would be as bittersweet as this one seemed to be. He was happy to be on another adventure and glad that some of his friends were traveling with him, but he missed the friends who weren't here.

They reached the great arch easily before midday, and as they filled their water bags and containers, Halfdan prepared a meal.

Halfdan's cousin, Thrang, had been the cook on their last adventure together, and he was a good cook. Alex noticed Halfdan's nervous look as they ate and suspected the dwarf was worried he wouldn't measure up.

"Thrang has taught you his secrets," Bregnest commented, smiling at Halfdan.

"Indeed, you are a master cook," Andy added.

"Most excellent," said Alex. "Thrang will have a hard time getting his job back."

Halfdan bowed, blushing slightly at their comments.

Alex smiled, knowing that Halfdan took a lot of pride in his cooking skills and was pleased by their words of praise.

"And now, some final instructions before we arm ourselves," said Bregnest, getting to his feet as they finished eating.

"We will follow the standard rules for adventures. If anyone becomes lost, the company will search for the lost person or persons for thirteen days. During that time, the lost member or members will also search for the company as best they can. After thirteen days, the company will suspend the search and continue toward their final goal, and the lost member will be on his own to do what seems best to him."

Bregnest looked around at his companions, making sure they all understood what he was saying.

"I would remind each of you not to speak of our final goal to anyone," said Bregnest. "The details of our goal are not to be shared—not even with our friends or families in Norsland."

Alex noticed that Andy blushed slightly when Bregnest mentioned family, and he wondered if they would have a chance to meet Andy's family.

"I do not think we will run into any trouble between here and Oslansk, but we should arm ourselves and be prepared. Better to be cautious then to be dead," Bregnest concluded.

Once he had finished speaking, they all began taking their weapons out of their magic bags. Alex retrieved both his magic sword, Moon Slayer, from his bag and the true silver dagger that had been given to him on his first adventure. Fastening Moon Slayer to his left side and his dagger to his right, he looked around at the rest of the company.

Bregnest carried the same weapons as before: a sword at his side, a two-handed sword across his back, and a round shield with a red dragon's head painted on it. Andy carried a round shield along with his other gear, and Halfdan's ax had some fancy gold inlay added to the handle, but other than that, their weapons were the same as last time. Val carried a broadsword and a dagger, much like Alex's own. Sindar, however, had a long knife hanging from his belt, and across his back were a pair of scimitars that looked extremely deadly. Sindar also had a helmet of black steel, which Alex saw him return to his magic bag.

"Ah," said Sindar, glancing at Alex's weapons. "I see you wear the ancient sword Moon Slayer. My people have said much about your sword. I hope that, if time allows, you will show it to me."

"Gladly," Alex replied. "But I hope you will not need to see it in battle."

"A wise hope," answered Sindar. "Though I must confess, I have wondered if the stories I have heard are true."

"I can tell you that they are," Alex replied in a low tone, so only Sindar would hear him. "And though there is something of joy when I use the sword, I would prefer to keep it sheathed."

"I understand," said Sindar with a nod.

Alex was impressed. There was something about Sindar that reminded him of Arconn, but he seemed much older than any other elf Alex had ever met.

After storing their water bottles in their magic bags, they mounted their horses once more and rode toward the great arch. Alex remembered being disappointed the first time he had seen the great arch. He had expected a beautiful stone arch, but it was only two large hills topped with white towers. Andy had explained that the hills were the sides of the arch and the sky was the top, which had only made Alex wonder why it was called an arch at all.

As soon as they passed through the arch, the landscape around them changed completely. Now they were riding along a road that cut through a green meadow lined with tall pine trees. There was still a fair amount of snow and ice in the shadows of the trees, but the air was pleasantly warm.

"A large company has passed this way in the last day or two," Sindar commented as they rode forward.

"How many, do you think?" Bregnest questioned.

"Thirty or forty riders. Perhaps five or six pack animals," said Sindar. "No wagons, and nobody was walking with them."

"Do you think it might mean trouble?" Halfdan asked, his eyes moving to the trees around them.

"They might be traders," said Andy. "A lot of people come to trade for wool in the spring."

"Perhaps," said Bregnest. "As they are ahead of us and not following us, I don't think there is anything to worry about."

They moved on without saying anything more. The sun was warm and bright above them, but the occasional gusts of wind were much colder than expected, and Alex wished he had worn heavier clothes. He could tell from the chill in the air that spring had only just arrived and that winter wasn't completely gone. They followed the road south for about an hour before coming to a crossroad. Bregnest halted the company and looked at the three pathways before them.

"Well, Andy," said Bregnest, "which of these will lead us to Oslansk the quickest?"

"The eastern road." Andy pointed. "If we follow it, we will turn northeast and reach Oslansk in six days or less, barring any bad weather."

"Then east we go," said Bregnest with a nod.

It was obvious that Bregnest had known which way to go and had asked Andy out of courtesy. Alex tried to remember what Whalen had told him in his letters about courtesy and honor due to people during adventures in their homelands. It had all been interesting at the time, but Alex was finding it difficult now to recall all of the rules for Norsland. He promised himself that he would reread Whalen's letters as soon as he could.

They continued to ride until the sun began sinking behind the tall pines. A steady cold breeze was blowing now, chilling them as they set up their camp. Once everything was in order and Halfdan was busy cooking, Alex took the opportunity to show his magic sword to Sindar.

"An ancient weapon," Sindar commented, looking closely at the sword but not touching it. "I have long studied these weapons and their making. I can tell you that Moon Slayer was one of the greatest swords ever made by the dark elves."

"Do you know a great deal about the dark elves?" Alex asked.

"I do," Sindar answered. "Their ways of magic have always been of great interest to me. My own swords are also of their making, though not as old nor as powerful as yours."

"Can you tell me about Moon Slayer and how it was made? I mean, about its power? And how it chooses its master?"

"I can tell you some things, but not all. There are none now alive who know everything about the great swords and how they were made."

"The knowledge was lost with the dark elves then," said Alex sadly.

"I believe that most of the information was lost, though there are some who say it is not lost, but only forgotten."

"Do you know how the great swords choose their masters?" Alex pressed.

"I do not," said Sindar in a thoughtful tone. "I do not think even the makers of the swords knew how the masters would be chosen."

"They were foolish to make such swords then," Val commented, looking over Sindar's shoulder at Alex's sword. "To make a sword that you cannot use—that is foolish."

"Perhaps," Sindar agreed. "But when the dark elves made these weapons, they were made for a specific person or a specific reason. The first masters were known, so making the swords was not foolish. It was when these first masters died or passed on their weapons that the swords began choosing their own masters."

"And what would happen if someone the sword had not chosen tried to use it?" Val questioned.

"If the master were still alive, I believe it would be dangerous for anyone else to use the sword. I think the magic of the sword would turn it against anyone who tried to use it," Sindar answered. "If the sword had no master, it might work as a normal sword, without giving its magical powers to the user. I'm not sure."

"Did the dark elves make other weapons as well?" asked Alex.

"Yes, they made all kinds," Sindar answered. "Many have

been lost or destroyed. I believe that most of the weapons that remain are swords."

Halfdan called out that their meal was ready, so Alex put Moon Slayer back into its scabbard and accepted a plate of food. He wanted to learn more about his magic sword, and the other magical weapons the dark elves had made, but he pushed his thoughts aside, thinking that he would have time to ask his questions as they traveled.

"Will your family be in Oslansk for the weddings?" Alex asked Andy as they ate.

"Yes. And they are excited to meet you all. My little brother, Michael, seems almost ready to burst with excitement."

"How old is he?" Alex asked.

"He'll turn thirteen the day after the weddings," Andy answered. "He keeps hoping I'll buy him his own horse for his birthday."

"And will you?" Halfdan questioned.

"I'd like to, but Father isn't happy with the idea," Andy said.

"And why would your father be unhappy with such a gift?" questioned Sindar.

"Oh, well," Andy began slowly, as if considering his answer. "The horse Michael wants is not as tame as the horses we already have. Father thinks it might be too much for Michael to handle."

"And what do you think?" Alex asked.

"I think Michael will get his wish," said Andy with a sly grin.

"Perhaps we should consider getting him a saddle to go with his horse," said Halfdan.

"Oh, no," said Andy, suddenly looking nervous. "You don't need to get him a present, that would be too much."

Halfdan winked at Alex, and Alex understood that he and Halfdan would be buying a saddle when the company reached Oslansk.

They finished their meal with a great deal of talk, and they stayed sitting around the fire for a long time. The night was growing colder, but the fire was warm and comfortable. Alex wondered if they should set a watch, but Bregnest said nothing about it.

"So tell us about Norsland weddings," said Halfdan as the fire burned down. "What customs should we know about? What kind of gifts should we give?"

Andy paused to think. "I suppose the most important thing for you to know is that friends of the groom give gifts to the bride, while friends of the bride give gifts to the groom."

"Nobody gives gifts to them both?" Alex asked.

Andy shook his head. "It's an old custom all over Norsland. Though to be honest, I've never asked why nobody gives gifts to both the bride and the groom."

"So now we have to find presents for brides we've never met," Halfdan grumbled.

"You don't have to give anything expensive or extravagant," said Andy defensively. "It's more of a thank-you for the invitation to the wedding sort of gift."

"What type of gifts do strangers give?" Sindar questioned.

"Oh, well, I don't know. I mean, I don't think there is any need for you to give anything," Andy stuttered.

"It is a poor wedding guest who gives nothing," said Sindar. "Perhaps, when we reach Oslansk, I can learn more about your customs and discover what sort of gift to give."

Alex knew that, while Sindar and Val had not been formally invited to the weddings, they would both be included as part of the company in all the feasts and parties that went along with the celebrations.

"We had best put blankets on the horses," said Bregnest as the fire turned to glowing embers. "It may be spring in Norsland, but the nights are still cold."

They all tended to their horses and then went to their tents for the night. Alex was still a little concerned about not setting a watch, but he decided that Bregnest knew what he was doing. Letting his worries drift away in the darkness, he soon fell into a restful sleep.

The next morning Alex was grateful that Halfdan had brought along his dwarf remedy for soreness. All his muscles and bones ached when he woke up. Halfdan's remedy quickly cured his pains, though it didn't work quite as fast as it had the last time he had used it.

Turning, Alex saw Andy tumble over with a surprised yell. Andy had taken the remedy just before Alex, but it appeared that the potion had not worked for him.

"I can't feel my left leg," Andy shouted.

"Oh, that's wonderful!" Halfdan exclaimed as he rushed to Andy's side. "No feeling at all?"

"What do you mean?" Andy yelled. "My leg won't move at all."

"It'll wear off in a few minutes," Halfdan answered with an unconcerned wave of his hand. "Try wiggling your toes, and pay attention to which toe you feel moving first."

"What?"

"This is important, Andy," Halfdan said in excitement. "After drinking from a new batch of potion, if a person loses feeling in part of their body, their fortune can be told by which parts start feeling things first."

"You didn't mention anything about losing the use of our body parts before giving us the potion," Val commented with a sour look.

"It doesn't happen that often," Halfdan replied, blushing slightly. "To be honest, I didn't think it would happen, but now that it has . . . Andy, are you wiggling your toes like I said?"

"How should I know?" Andy snapped. "I can't feel anything."

"Well, keep trying. It should only take a minute or two."

Halfdan's prediction was correct. After a few minutes Andy's leg started to move, and before long, he was back on his feet. Halfdan continued to ask questions about which toe Andy could wiggle first, but Andy was in no mood to answer.

"I'm trying to be helpful," Halfdan finally said. "If you'll tell me which of your toes moved first, I could tell you a lot about your future."

"The little one," Andy replied as his anger cooled. "My little toe was the first one I felt. So what can you tell me about my future?"

"Oh, that's good, that's very good," said Halfdan. "If the little toe moves first, you'll have a long and happy life, filled with good fortune."

"What if his big toe had moved first?" Bregnest questioned.

"Ah, well, if the big toe moves first, you'll live to a ripe old age and have a happy marriage," Halfdan answered.

"Do all the toes have something to do with long life and happiness?" Sindar questioned.

"Hmmm, now that I think about it, they do," said Halfdan in a serious tone. "Still, it's considered very lucky to have this happen with a new batch of potion."

"Lucky that the loss of feeling doesn't last for long," Val commented quietly.

"Come," Bregnest said before Halfdan could reply to Val. "We've got places to be and things to do. We can talk about dwarf fortune-telling another time."

The short journey from the great arch to Oslansk was a pleasant one. The weather remained fair as they traveled, though the nights continued to be cold. Most mornings there was frost on the ground when they woke up, and Alex knew that Shahree was grateful for the heavy blanket he put on her at night. More than once he thought about conjuring a magical fire to keep everyone warm at night, but he always remembered Whalen's warning about using his powers.

Each night after their evening meal, the company would sit around the fire, talking and telling stories of past adventures.

Alex was beginning to feel as if he had never gone home at all, but had simply continued his last adventure.

On their sixth day away from Telous, Alex and his companions reached the city of Oslansk. Alex was impressed with the city's appearance, even from a distance. Oslansk looked like it had been carved completely from white marble. The large city sat on a hillside and was surrounded by high walls. The white buildings of Oslansk shimmered in the afternoon sunlight, looking both inviting and friendly to travelers.

"My father has invited us all to stay with him and the rest of my family," Andy said as they rode toward the city.

"Will there be enough room for all of us?" Bregnest asked in a slightly worried tone.

"Yes," Andy answered. "In fact, he rented a large house where we will be able to stay."

"Then we will accept your father's kindness and give him our thanks," said Bregnest.

"I should have told Bregnest that my father is rich," said Andy in a lowered voice to Alex. "After all, he went on many adventures before settling down in Norsland."

"Going on many adventures does not always mean great wealth," Val commented with a sly grin.

"Perhaps not," replied Andy. "But he has done very well since he retired from his adventures, and I know he can afford whatever we may require."

Alex didn't say anything in reply to Andy's words. He knew that Andy could easily pay for anything they or his family might need. After all, Andy had a huge amount of treasure from their last adventure together, and Alex was sure he hadn't spent very much of it yet.

The gates to Oslansk stood open as Alex and his companions rode up to them. The guards at the gates nodded and waved them through without questions. They were apparently expecting many guests to arrive for the upcoming weddings, and they didn't seem to think there was any danger to worry about.

As they rode through the narrow and busy streets of Oslansk, Andy joined Bregnest at the front of the company. When they reached the gates of the house Andy's father had rented, Alex saw that it was more of a mansion than a house, with its own stable and gardens inside a high wall.

"Welcome to Oslansk," said Andy, as they entered the courtyard and climbed off their horses.

Chapter Four

Oslansk

Alex and his companions looked up at the impressive house that had obviously been built with great care and attention to detail. They were just turning away to lead their horses to the stables when an excited voice shouted behind them.

"Andy!"

They all turned around to see who had yelled, and they all smiled as a tall, skinny boy came racing out of the house toward the company.

"We didn't know you'd be back so soon," Michael said, throwing his arms around Andy and almost knocking him over. "Father and Mother will be so pleased. Father was worried that you'd have trouble, you know, finding the members of your company. He was afraid it would take some time and that you wouldn't be back in time for the weddings."

"Well, we are back in time," said Andy. "And with a week to spare." He grinned. "We were lucky to find our company quickly. And if you'll let us put our horses away, I'll introduce you to my friends."

Michael let go of Andy and looked around at the rest of the

company, his eyes growing wide. Alex could tell that Michael was glad to see his brother and that he was also impressed that his brother had so many adventurers with him.

"My apologies, sirs," said Michael, bowing to the company. "I have forgotten my manners. Please, allow me to care for your horses. My father will wish to greet you and welcome you to our house."

"We can tend to our own horses," Bregnest replied. "And you need not be so formal with your brother's good friends."

Michael blushed bright red at Bregnest's words, but his face showed how pleased he was. The company all laughed quietly to themselves as they led their horses to the stable. Michael stayed close by Andy, but his eyes watched the rest of the company.

"Come, my friends," said Andy, once their horses were taken care of. "My brother is correct in saying that my father will wish to greet you all."

Andy put his arm around Michael's shoulders and led the group toward the house. Michael almost tripped as they went along because he kept looking at the company over Andy's arm.

Before they had reached the house, Andy's parents appeared in the doorway. Andy's mother seemed almost as delighted as Michael to see Andy home again, and she rushed forward to hug him and kiss him on the cheek. Andy blushed but continued to smile. Andy's father, however, simply patted his son on the shoulder and then turned to face his guests.

"Perhaps, when my son can break free, he will introduce us all."

"There is little need for formal introductions among friends," said Bregnest, stepping forward.

"No, I suppose not," Andy's father agreed. "I am Argus Goodseed, and I welcome you all to my house."

"I am Silvan Bregnest. Your kindness overwhelms us, Master Goodseed."

"Well said, Master Bregnest," Argus replied. "Please, let us do away with all formality if you will. I am simply Argus, and that should be enough between friends."

Bregnest laughed softly and nodded his agreement. He turned to the company and introduced each of them to Argus. As each man was named, he stepped forward and bowed slightly to Andy's father.

"Alexander Taylor," said Argus, when Alex was introduced. "Andy has told us a great deal about you. And Michael has been dying to meet you."

"I'm afraid that Andy has said too much," Alex replied. "I hope I can live up to whatever he has told you."

"I'm sure you will," said Argus. "And I doubt that Andy has said as much as you fear. He's been very secretive about some of the things that happened on your last adventure together.

"Now, my friends, let me introduce my wife, Azure," Argus went on. "And it seems that you have already made the acquaintance of my youngest son, Michael."

"We have indeed made young Michael's acquaintance," said Bregnest. "And I'm sure I speak for all of us when I say it is a great pleasure to meet Mistress Goodseed."

The six companions all bowed to Andy's mother, who

blushed slightly. Michael, however, suddenly became shy and looked down at his shoes.

"I regret that my eldest son, Lazarus, is not here to greet you," said Argus, in a slightly harder tone. "He's off wandering the city with his friends, but he will be here this evening to offer you a proper welcome."

"I should think that it would be hard to keep him at home, with such a wonderful city to explore," said Bregnest.

"Oslansk is indeed wonderful," Argus agreed. "I suppose we should come here more often, but our lands are several days' ride to the west and north."

Argus continued talking as he led them into the house. Rooms had been prepared for each of them, away from the busy and noisy parts of the estate. Once Alex and the others had been shown to their rooms, Mrs. Goodseed excused herself, but Michael remained next to Andy.

"May I offer you some refreshment?" Argus asked. "We can have a bite and a drink or two, and perhaps swap tales of adventures past."

"A pleasing idea," said Bregnest. "Though I think a few of my company would like nothing better than to go looking for their friends Skeld and Tayo."

"Ah, yes," said Argus with a nod. "Andy, you know where those two troublemakers are. Take your friends and show them the way."

"Can I go too?" Michael asked in a pleading tone.

"Not right now, Michael," Argus answered in a kind but firm tone. "Perhaps tomorrow they will take you with them, but not right now."

Alex and Halfdan both bowed to Argus as they prepared to follow Andy into the city. Alex made a point of asking both Sindar and Val if they would like to come along, but they both said they would rather stay behind and share stories with Bregnest and Argus.

Andy led Alex and Halfdan back into the streets of Oslansk, almost bouncing as he walked. The city was large, but he seemed to know exactly where he was going, and he led his friends quickly through the narrow, busy streets.

"Well, if it isn't Anders Goodseed," commented an unpleasant-sounding voice as Andy, Alex, and Halfdan walked into a large square. All three of them turned to see who had spoken.

Standing in front of a booth that sold sandwiches was an extremely fat and unpleasant-looking young man. Alex wondered who he was, and how Andy knew him.

"Been off fighting dragons again, have you?" the fat young man sneered. The two companions behind him chuckled.

"Hello, Otho," Andy replied pleasantly. "I see you're still trying to eat everything in the city."

Otho didn't say anything, but turned red as he stuffed his half-finished sandwich into his mouth.

Andy turned and walked away, and Alex and Halfdan followed after a slight delay.

"Who is that overweight windbag?" asked Halfdan once he and Alex had caught up to Andy.

"Otho Longtree," said Andy, his voice tight with anger. "He's the heir of Osgood Longtree."

"And who is Osgood Longtree?" Alex questioned.

"He's the city magistrate," said Andy, slowing his pace and softening his tone. "Osgood is a good man, but Otho . . ."

Andy didn't finish and started to walk faster again.

"Otho seems to be a bit of a bully," Halfdan observed thoughtfully.

"He is," said Andy shortly. "He thinks that just because his father is the magistrate, he's a big deal around here."

"I really don't like bullies," said Alex, looking back over his shoulder at the fat Otho Longtree.

"Nobody does," said Andy, a slight smile returning to his face. "In fact, it would be hard to find anyone the people here in Oslansk like less than Otho."

"Then why hasn't someone put him in his place?" Halfdan questioned.

Andy paused for a moment. "It's because his father is such a good man and an excellent magistrate. Nobody wants to tell Osgood that his son is a bully—or worse."

"Someone should," said Halfdan in a serious tone.

"I suppose so," said Andy. "But I think the news would break Osgood's heart. Most people think that Osgood's sorrow would be worse than putting up with Otho, so no one says anything."

"What was his crack about fighting dragons?" Alex asked.

"I told Michael about our last adventure," Andy answered with a shrug of his shoulders. "It seems he's been telling the story to anyone who will listen—you know, about Slathbog and all."

Alex knew that Andy was proud of his little brother and pleased that Michael believed the story about Slathbog. It didn't seem to matter very much to Andy that Otho didn't believe any of it.

They continued across the square until they reached a large tavern on the far side. The sign in front read The Dragon's Keep. The three of them laughed when they saw the poor replica of a dragon painted above the name.

"Skeld and Tayo have been staying here," said Andy as they entered. "They've both bought houses, of course, but tradition won't let them move in until they're married."

"This isn't what we ordered," they heard Skeld say loudly. "If you can't get it right, we'll just have to find someone who can."

"And who might that be?" Alex asked in a loud voice, spotting Skeld and Tayo standing at the bar next to a nervous-looking man.

"What?" said Skeld, turning to see who had spoken. His eyes widened, and he poked Tayo in the side, making him turn around as well.

"Alex?" Skeld said in amazement.

"Halfdan?" Tayo echoed.

"What—didn't you think we'd show up?" Halfdan asked with a grunting laugh.

There were no more words for several minutes as Tayo and Skeld rushed across the room and started hugging Alex, Halfdan, and Andy.

"We didn't expect to see you so soon," said Tayo.

"Andy said he was going to join Bregnest's new adventure and that he hoped you would both be joining as well," said

Skeld to Alex and Halfdan. "But we weren't sure either of you would be coming."

"Well, we have come," said Halfdan. "So why don't you finish your business and then we can talk in peace."

"What? Oh," said Skeld. "All right, Oscar, I suppose you'd better try again."

The nervous-looking man at the bar nodded, looking relieved. He bowed to both Skeld and Tayo before moving swiftly away from the bar and hurrying toward the door.

"What was all that about?" Alex questioned as Oscar ducked out of the tavern.

"He's doing a bit of cooking for the weddings," said Tayo. "We thought we'd try to get some of the food we tried in Techen, but Oscar can't seem to manage it."

"Small wonder." Halfdan laughed. "It's not easy to duplicate Techen food."

"No, it's not," said Skeld, looking sad. "But enough of this, let's get a drink and have a good long talk."

Soon the five of them were seated around a table set off to one side of the room. They all had a great many questions to ask, and Alex found himself answering the same questions that Andy and Halfdan had asked only a week before.

"What I want to know is how you two found women—sisters, for that matter—who would put up with you long enough to agree to marry you," said Halfdan, shaking his head in wonder.

"It wasn't easy," said Skeld.

"And Andy didn't help at all," added Tayo.

"What did I do?" Andy asked in a stunned tone.

"It's what you *didn't* do," Skeld commented. "You didn't make yourself scarce. Where love is concerned, two is company, three is just annoying."

"Well, if that's all my company is good for . . ." said Andy in mock fury.

"It seems to me that Andy was trying to help you two," said Alex. "Or maybe he was trying to help your future wives."

They all burst into laughter at this comment, and it was some time before any of them could speak again.

"It's good to see you all again," said Tayo. "We haven't laughed so much since . . ."

"Since we got Andy drunk and he fell off his horse," Skeld finished for Tayo, and they both started laughing again.

"What did they do to you?" Halfdan asked Andy in a concerned voice.

"Oh, it was nothing really," said Andy, his face turning bright red. "After Skeld asked Lilly to marry him, we were celebrating a little, and I had a bit too much to drink."

"More than a bit," Tayo corrected.

"Much more than a bit," added Skeld.

"Well, anyway," Andy went on, "for some reason I thought I'd ride around the square, and I just fell off my horse."

"Fell off and landed in a water trough," Tayo burst out.

"And because it was still winter, when he got back inside, he was covered with icicles and frost," Skeld added.

"We thought a snow beast was coming into the tavern," said Tayo. "I've never seen so many people run for the doors so fast."

"It seemed like a good idea at the time," said Andy in a defiant tone. They all burst into laughter once more.

"It is good to have you all here," Tayo said, recovering his voice. "Especially you, Alex."

"Why me?" Alex questioned.

"Because Tayo and I have something important to ask you," said Skeld, becoming more serious than Alex had ever seen him.

"What might that be?"

"We would like to ask you to be our ring bearer," Tayo answered.

"What would I have to do?" Alex questioned.

"You bring the rings to the wedding and present them to us at the proper time," said Skeld.

"You'll have to wear special clothes," said Tayo. "But Skeld and I would be honored to buy them for you."

"What kind of clothes?" Alex questioned.

"Oh, they're normal clothes—just all of one color," Skeld said, seeing the suspicious look on Alex's face.

"Yes, dark blue is the customary color for a ring bearer's clothes," Tayo explained. "You would do us a great honor if you would accept. Having a wizard as a ring bearer is considered good luck and a promise for a long and joyful marriage."

"Well, if that's all there is to it, I accept," said Alex, feeling slightly relieved that his friends hadn't asked him to do anything strange or magical. He also hoped that, for his friend's sakes, that a wizard in training would be just as lucky as a real wizard.

"You do us a great kindness," said Skeld, standing and bowing to Alex.

"We are once more in your debt," Tayo added, also standing and bowing.

"Now we must arrange for you all to meet our ladies," said Skeld, taking his seat once more.

"Bregnest must come as well," Tayo added.

"And the rest of your company," Skeld went on.

"The two of you have lost your minds," said Halfdan loudly. "I never thought I'd see you two acting this way. Thrang won't believe me when I tell him."

"What way?" Skeld asked with a wicked grin.

"The way you're both acting now," Halfdan answered, waving his hand at them. "It's as if you are both bewitched, and I don't mind saying that it scares me."

"Bewitched by love," said Tayo.

"Bewitched by beauty," Skeld added.

"Andy, you should have thrown them both in that water trough," said Halfdan, letting out a loud huff and then taking a long drink from his mug.

Alex could see what Halfdan meant, but he didn't let his friends' strange behavior bother him. He thought perhaps they were both more alive and more serious than they had been before, and the mix seemed to fit them.

Over a second drink they all agreed to meet the next morning. Tayo and Skeld would take Alex to buy his new clothes, and then they'd make arrangements for the entire company to come and meet their wives-to-be. With their plans made, Alex,

Andy, and Halfdan left their friends at the tavern and started back to the Goodseed house.

"They've changed," said Halfdan as Alex and Andy followed him out of the tavern. "And I'm not at all sure it's for the better."

It had been a joyful reunion, but now the sun was setting and it was time for their evening meal. As they walked back through the square, Alex kept an eye out for Otho Longtree. He'd decided that he didn't like Otho, and if the opportunity to put him in his place arose, he might just take it.

During dinner with Andy's family, Halfdan was quick to tell Bregnest how strangely Skeld and Tayo were acting and how different they seemed to be. Bregnest listened to everything Halfdan said, but didn't comment.

Andy's older brother, Lazarus, was at dinner as Argus had said he would be, and he was almost as excited to meet them all as his little brother Michael had been. It was clear, at least to Alex, that Lazarus was as proud of Andy as Andy was of Michael.

After dinner they all sat around the table talking. Argus Goodseed was interested in their stories of adventures and news from distant lands. Both Lazarus and Michael sat still as stone and hardly moved a muscle while Bregnest told a story from one of his adventures. They all clapped loudly when he finished his tale. Then Mrs. Goodseed told Michael it was time for bed.

"But, Mother," said Michael, in a desperate and pleading voice. "Just one more story, please."

"Your mother is quite right," said Bregnest, standing up.

"It is time for all of us to seek our beds. We have traveled far in a short time, and we have a great deal to do before we will be ready to continue our adventure."

They all said goodnight to Andy's family and made their way to their own rooms. Alex, however, did not go to bed, but sat up for some time reading his magic books and going over one of his father's old notebooks. He also wrote a short letter to Whalen, letting him know that everything was fine. He climbed into his bed, still thinking of how oddly Skeld and Tayo had been acting. Halfdan's comment about them both being bewitched made him smile, and he soon slipped into a deep sleep.

When Alex woke up the next morning it wasn't because he wanted to. Halfdan was shaking his bed wildly and laughing at the shocked and confused expression on Alex's face.

"Come on then," said Halfdan. "We've got to get your new clothes, and you and I have a bit of shopping to do as well."

"I feel like I've only just gone to sleep," Alex complained, rolling off his bed and onto his feet.

"Norsland nights are short in the spring and summer months," Halfdan said.

Alex didn't reply as he staggered sleepily toward the basin to wash his face. The ice-cold water was a shock, but it woke him up better than Halfdan had. Looking out his window, Alex could see sunlight already spreading over Oslansk.

"What's for breakfast?" Alex asked, stamping on his boots and following Halfdan out of the room.

"Mrs. Goodseed has seen to it, so come on," Halfdan answered.

In fact, Andy's mother had prepared a large breakfast of fried potatoes, eggs, pancakes, bacon, sausage, and several other dishes that were clearly Norsland specialties. Alex tried some of everything and had second helpings of a dish that was made up of rice, some kind of meat, cheese, and a sweet sauce.

Michael was full of questions that morning, and he couldn't seem to keep himself from asking them. The members of the company tried to answer him as well as they could, but it seemed that every answer brought new questions from Michael.

As they were finishing their breakfast, Skeld and Tayo arrived to take Alex to get his new clothes. They spent several minutes talking to Bregnest and teasing him about his being on another adventure so soon after the last one. Bregnest endured their teasing good-naturedly. Then he introduced Val and Sindar to Skeld and Tayo. Skeld and Tayo were pleased to meet them both and asked them to come to a feast that evening with the others. The new members of the company accepted the invitation and thanked Skeld and Tayo for their kindness.

As soon as the arrangements for the evening feast had been made, Skeld, Tayo, Alex, and Halfdan were on their way out the gate. Andy said he had things to do as well and left with Lazarus.

Once the company had separated, Halfdan asked Skeld

and Tayo where they could buy a saddle as a present for Michael's upcoming birthday. Skeld and Tayo thought it was a wonderful idea, but they also thought it would be very funny if Andy didn't buy his brother a horse after all.

"That would be terrible," said Alex. "A saddle but no horse—what kind of birthday present would that be for Michael?"

"It might give him something to look forward to next year," said Tayo.

Alex stopped dead in his tracks, looking at the shops and people around him. For the second time on this adventure, Alex felt like he was being watched. There was a strange intensity to the feeling, as if he were waiting for some unseen person to appear or speak.

"What's the matter, Alex?" Halfdan questioned as he turned to see what Alex was looking at.

"Oh, sorry. I just had a feeling. It's nothing to worry about."

"A feeling?" Skeld asked, a note of concern in his voice.

"I just felt like someone was watching us," said Alex. Then he waved his hand in a dismissive way. "I'm sure it's nothing. I don't think I had enough sleep last night."

Alex was glad that the others didn't ask any more questions. He didn't think he could explain the feeling that he'd had, and he was more than happy to let the subject drop.

Their conversation returned to Michael's saddle. Halfdan suggested that they buy the saddle but keep it in his magic bag. If it turned out that Andy didn't buy the horse, they wouldn't have to say anything at all about a saddle.

"Ah, dwarfs and their cunning ways," Skeld teased.

They soon arrived at the tailor's shop, and it wasn't long before Alex found himself dressed in a fine dark blue set of clothes with silver buttons. The shopkeeper approved of the fit, and Skeld and Tayo began arguing over which of them would pay for the new clothes. To settle the argument, they simply bought Alex a second set of clothes, this time all in dark silver-gray.

"You can wear the gray ones to the party the day after the weddings," said Tayo.

Alex thanked Skeld and Tayo for their gift and joked with Halfdan about how odd their friends were acting. Skeld and Tayo shrugged off any comments on their strange behavior as they led the way to a shop where Alex and Halfdan could buy a saddle. Halfdan had an eye for quality work, so Alex let him choose the saddle they would buy. Once the saddle was safely in Halfdan's magic bag, the four friends wandered back into the streets of Oslansk.

"Are there any dwarf smiths here in Oslansk?" Alex asked offhandedly.

"Well, there's old Elwig—but he does jewelry more than weapons," Tayo commented.

"Perhaps he can help me," said Alex, winking at Halfdan.

"Help you with what?" Skeld questioned.

"Oh, nothing really," said Alex. "Now I suppose Halfdan and I should leave you two, as we still have gifts to buy for the wedding."

"There is little need for that," both Skeld and Tayo protested.

"Little need for you perhaps," Halfdan answered. "Andy told us of the customs here: that friends of the grooms give gifts to the brides."

"Well, yes, that's true," Tayo agreed. "But you are both honored guests. And Alex is already acting as our ring bearer."

"That doesn't matter," said Alex. "I think your ladies deserve a gift. Perhaps something magical that will keep you two in line."

They all laughed at Alex's words, though Halfdan, seeing the nervous look that Skeld and Tayo exchanged, laughed harder still.

"I don't suppose you really do know a spell that would keep those two in line, do you?" Halfdan asked Alex as they walked in the direction of Elwig's shop.

"No, I don't. But it will be something for them both to think about, at least for a little while."

The people of Oslansk were both friendly and helpful, and it didn't take long for Alex and Halfdan to find Elwig's shop. The shop was a large one, and it was filled with hundreds of beautiful items.

Elwig was delighted to see Halfdan. Few dwarfs ever came to Oslansk, and Elwig was almost overcome with joy at seeing a kinsman. It wasn't long before he was showing Alex and Halfdan everything in his shop that might be used as a wedding gift, as well as several things that could not.

"Brooches are a popular gift," said Elwig, bringing out a large tray of brooches from behind his counter. "They're functional and practical, and you don't have to wear them every day."

Alex looked at the brooches on the tray. Most were made of silver, though there were a few made of gold as well. Suddenly Alex had an idea, and he asked Elwig for a piece of paper and a quill. He carefully drew a picture and showed the drawing to Elwig.

"Can you make a brooch like this?" Alex asked hopefully.

Elwig studied Alex's drawing. "An interesting idea. Yes, I think I understand what you want, but what would you like it made of?"

"True silver," said Alex in a low tone.

"Oh, well," Elwig stammered, "in that case, I don't think that I can do that. I haven't seen a bit of true silver in Norsland for years and years."

"I can solve that problem easily enough," said Alex, reaching for his magic bag. Alex had received a large amount of true silver on his last adventure, when he'd returned the first of seven lost magic bags he had recovered.

Elwig was stunned when Alex produced a large bag full of true silver, and for a moment he could not speak at all. He rubbed his eyes in disbelief, and then finally said that he could make what Alex wanted.

"And if your work is acceptable, you may keep the remaining true silver as payment," said Alex.

"Oh, no, sir," Elwig protested. "The payment is far too great."

"If your work is acceptable, the payment will be as I have said," Alex repeated firmly.

"You are most generous, sir," Elwig said with a deep bow.

"The work will be done as you request. I will have the brooches ready for you the day before the weddings."

Halfdan and Alex left Elwig's shop, agreeing to return the day before the weddings to collect the gifts. Halfdan had a slightly troubled look on his face as they left, and Alex asked him what was wrong.

"I think you may have offered too much for his work," Halfdan answered.

"Perhaps."

"Elwig will work night and day to make what you've requested. I hope he doesn't overdo your design."

"I did say the work had to be acceptable," said Alex. "And I think he'll do a fine job."

"Let's hope so."

"Now, what about you?" Alex questioned. "What gifts will you be giving?"

"Ah, well, I've already got mine. Thrang and I had some things made before I left for Telous, so I'm well-prepared."

"Then I suppose we should find our way back to the Goodseed house and see what the others are doing."

Halfdan and Alex worked their way back through the busy streets, asking directions every now and then from people who were passing by. Everyone seemed to know where the Goodseed family was staying, and they were all eager to help the adventurers find their way.

When Alex and Halfdan were almost back to the house, however, Alex heard a voice he recognized. He held up his hand for Halfdan to stop and remain silent. From around the corner came the unmistakable voice of Michael Goodseed.

"You don't know anything," Michael said loudly.

"I know that he's not a wizard," the voice of fat Otho Longtree replied. "He doesn't even have a staff."

"He *is,*" Michael insisted. "My brother says so, and he was on an adventure with him before."

"Balderdash. If he's a wizard, I'm an ox—and if he's even seen a dragon I'll eat my hat."

"He is a wizard," Michael repeated, his voice sounding close to tears.

Alex motioned for Halfdan to stay still as he stepped around the corner.

Otho and four of his large companions were circled around Michael, cornering him against the wall. Alex saw at once that Otho was trying to make Michael cry, and he saw Michael's desperate attempt not to do so. For an instant, Alex saw himself in Michael's place, alone and too small to fight off his tormentors.

Alex had never been bullied in his life—his stepbrother, Todd, had made sure of that—but he had seen others suffer the humiliation. He remembered how his insides had twisted when older and stronger students had tormented friends at school, and anger began to rise in him as the memories returned.

"What's all this?" Alex asked, his eyes locking onto Otho.

"No—nothing," Otho answered, his eyes narrowing.

"Then I should ask if you'd like sauce with your hat," said Alex, staring directly into Otho's beady eyes. "Or perhaps it will taste better if I turn you into an ox first. Though you don't seem to have enough brains to be an ox."

Otho's face grew bright red, and for a moment it seemed that he didn't know what to say, but he soon found his voice once more.

"You—you wouldn't dare," said Otho nervously. "I'm the heir of Osgood Longtree, magistrate of the city."

"And I'm a wizard who dislikes pompous bullies," Alex spat back at him. "And I don't really care who your father is. I think it's time for you to be taught a lesson."

"You're no wizard," answered Otho, but his tone was uncertain and laced with fear. "You don't even have a staff."

Alex felt magic building up inside of him as his emotions ran wild. A strange ringing sound filled his ears and mind, blinding him to everything but Otho and his words. He would prove who and what he was and silence this overstuffed bully once and for all.

Control your emotions, boy, a commanding voice echoed inside Alex's head.

For no more than a second Alex lost track of what was happening. The anger drained out of him as quickly as it had come, and when he blinked, he saw Otho and his friends running up the road away from him. The feeling that someone was watching washed over Alex like a wave and then vanished like the wind.

"Are you all right, Michael?" Alex asked after several silent moments.

"Ye—yes," Michael stuttered.

"Well, you'd better come along with us," said Alex. "We're just going home to see what there is for a midday meal."

Michael moved slowly, and then with a few hurried words

about making sure lunch was ready, he ran ahead of Alex and Halfdan.

Alex watched him go, worried that he might have scared him.

"Clever bit of magic that," Halfdan commented as the two of them started off once more.

"What?"

"The white flames that sprang up around you as you spoke—very impressive. No heat, no damage, but very bright and surprising nonetheless."

"I . . . I didn't . . ." Alex stammered and then stopped, shaken by what Halfdan had said. He had almost lost control of his emotions, and if he had, he wasn't sure what would have happened.

"I'd guess that Otho and his friends will stay well clear of you from now on," Halfdan went on. "They ran away like a dragon was chasing them!"

Chapter Five
Two Weddings

For the rest of the day Michael continued to stare at Alex. Whenever Alex looked at him, however, Michael would look away. Alex wondered what he could do to take away the boy's fear.

Alex had other things to worry about, too. He'd almost lost control of his emotions and let loose his magic. Some of his magic had slipped away before the strange voice inside his head had stopped him. The voice, however, had also come with the feeling of being watched. Something was going on—something important—but Alex had no idea what it could be.

It was late afternoon before Skeld and Tayo appeared, ready to lead the company to the feast. Alex followed his friends into the street, trying to be cheerful and not worry about what had happened.

"Michael told me about your run-in with Otho," Andy commented, breaking Alex's train of thought. "Did you really threaten to turn him into an ox?"

"I did," said Alex. "And I'm sure he believed I was about to do it too."

"But you wouldn't really do it, would you?" Andy asked, sounding slightly concerned.

"Well, it would help if I knew how," Alex admitted. "After all, I'm only a wizard in training, but Otho doesn't know that."

"Wizard in training or not, I reckon you could have done it if you really wanted to," Halfdan said from Alex's other side.

"As long as Otho believes that I was going to . . ."

"I wish I'd seen the look on his face," said Andy. "I think you're the first one to ever stand up to him."

"I think Michael might be a little scared of me. You know, after what happened this afternoon," Alex commented.

"Oh, no," said Andy. "I think you're his new hero."

As soon as the company reached the feasting hall, Skeld and Tayo made the introductions. Alex met Lilly and Indigo, his friend's future wives, as well as a horde of relatives he was sure he wouldn't remember. There was one person, however, that caught his attention. Cara, Lilly and Indigo's mother, had a soft golden light around her, a light that only Alex could see.

Alex didn't have time to think about this new mystery, though, because as soon as the last introduction was made, the feast started. Even with all the distractions, Alex's thoughts kept going back to earlier that day. He tried to pay attention to the conversations around him, and nod or comment at the correct times, but questions continued to pop into his mind. Who or what was watching him? Where had the voice in his head come from? And why had it come? Why couldn't he see what was happening around him?

"You seem troubled," a soft voice said from Alex's left.

Turning, Alex saw Cara standing next to him.

"Yes," Cara said, seeing the look on Alex's face. "I have magic. Have you not seen a person's magic before?"

"No, I haven't," Alex answered. "I'm fairly new to magic, and I was told by my teacher that it would take some time before I would be able to see magic in other people, or at least see it clearly."

"I remember the first time I saw the magic of another person," said Cara. "Seeing what others are, what powers they have, is not always an easy thing. You see the light around me—my magic—and you have many questions."

"Yes, I do," said Alex. He suddenly remembered Halfdan's words: *"It's as if you are both bewitched, and I don't mind saying that it scares me."* Could Cara have used magic on Skeld and Tayo so they would fall in love with her daughters? "And I wonder what you use your magic for."

"I did not use magic on your friends, if that is what you fear," Cara said after a moment of silence. "I would not do that."

"I see no magic in either of your daughters," Alex said, feeling relieved by Cara's statement.

"Lilly will never have any magic of her own," Cara said, nodding toward her daughters. "Indigo may have some magic one day—it is hard to tell. The magic of my family does not begin to grow until after the daughter has a child of her own."

"Then how do you know that Lilly will never have any magic?"

"Because only girls with dark hair receive and pass on the magic. It has always been that way."

"Always?"

"My family is an old one, and we have kept records," Cara answered. "In all of our history, only those girls with dark hair have the magic and pass it on. It is part of the legend."

"Legend? What legend?"

"Of course, forgive me," Cara said with a smile. "You are from a distant land and are unfamiliar with the legends of Norsland. There is an old legend about a wizard and the Tower of the Moon. From my family line a wizard will be born, the son of an adventurer. There are many details to the story, things that have been added over the years, so I don't know how much of the legend is true. What I do know is that one day a true wizard will come to take control of the magic that lives in the Tower of the Moon and use it to save his people."

"What magic lives in the Tower of the Moon?" Alex asked with interest.

"Why, all magic. The tower is the center of magical power for all of Norsland. Without a wizard there to control it, the magic will become weaker and start to fade."

"Does the story say when the wizard will be born?"

"It would hardly be a legend if it gave such useful and specific details," Cara sighed. "But I am hopeful that one day the wizard will come."

Alex's thoughts slipped away from Cara and the party around him, racing off to a distant tower and an unknown point in time. Somehow he knew there was trouble in Norsland, trouble caused by an unseen evil that wanted to take control and rule all of the land and its people. But to do that, it had to control the magic of the Tower.

His thoughts shifted to a frozen plain where two figures carrying staffs struggled to move forward against a howling storm. His vision zoomed in on the figures, and in his mind's eye, Alex found himself looking into his own eyes. The face was an older version of himself, the older Alex from his dreams.

"Alex?" Cara said softly. "Is everything all right?"

"I will hope with you for the wizard's appearance," Alex answered as he forced his thoughts back to the present. "However, if this legend is to come true, there is something you must do."

"Oh? What is that?"

"You must tell Indigo and Lilly about this legend. And you must tell Indigo that she may one day have magic of her own," Alex answered. "You must also tell Skeld and Tayo about this. Now, before the weddings take place."

"Why trouble them with this, now?" Cara asked in a slightly alarmed tone. "They are in love, they want to be married—why disturb their happiness?"

"Because they have a right to know," said Alex. "Cara, I can't really explain why. I know you don't want to upset them, but I must insist. They must know about the legend, or I will be forced to stop the weddings from taking place."

"You would do that? You would take this happiness from your friends?"

"You see only a hope of having a wizard in the Tower of

the Moon, but I see more. You said the wizard would take control of the magic and save his people. If the people need to be saved, there must be some great danger they need to be saved from. I will not let my friends walk into that danger blind."

"You saw something," Cara said slowly. "As I told you the legend, you saw something."

"Yes."

"I . . . I never thought about the danger." She paused, then nodded. "You are right. They should know. I will do as you ask."

"Don't worry," Alex said in a reassuring tone. "I'm sure the weddings will still take place. I just think it is for the best to let them know what their futures might hold."

That night, when he was alone in his room, Alex wrote a second letter to Whalen. He explained what had happened with Otho, including his feelings of being watched and the strange voice inside his head. He wondered if Whalen would be angry with him for threatening to turn Otho into an ox, and he worried about what Whalen would say about his near loss of control.

It was a longer letter than normal, and Alex had a lot of questions that he hoped Whalen would have answers for. He asked about any legends that Whalen might have heard or read about the Tower of the Moon and about the magic of Norsland. Alex knew that there were centers of magical power in other lands, but he didn't know much about them. When he'd finally finished writing his letter, and had sent it with a geeb, he lay awake on his bed. His mind was still looking for answers, but until Whalen wrote back, he knew the answers would not come.

The days leading up to the weddings passed swiftly, and they were not all full of fun and parties. Bregnest ordered the company to pack items for their journey, and he insisted that they not spend all their time wandering around the city. Luckily, packing the food didn't take long, and there was little to discuss about the road they would be following. Alex tried to find as many maps of Norsland as he could, but sadly none of the maps he found were any better than the map in his Adventurer's Handbook.

The day before the weddings, Alex and Halfdan returned to Elwig's shop to collect Alex's gifts. Elwig was delighted to see them again, and even more pleased when Alex praised the work he had done. His smile flickered only when Alex insisted that Elwig keep the rest of the true silver as payment for the work.

"You are too generous, Master Taylor, I cannot," said Elwig with a deep bow.

"Perhaps you would consider a trade," Alex suggested. "After all, I'm sure you could craft wonderful things from the true silver, and it does me little good in my bag."

"If it's a trade, perhaps we can make an arrangement," said Elwig, stroking his gray beard.

After a long debate, and Alex's continued praise of Elwig's work, they finally settled on a price. When Alex and Halfdan left the shop, Alex had five hundred gold coins in his magic bag and a beautiful golden brooch to go along with his other gifts. Alex planned to give the new brooch to Andy's mother for her kindness to the company during their stay.

"You drive a hard bargain, my friend," said Halfdan. "And I'm afraid you bargain against yourself."

"It's a fair price," Alex replied. "And I'm sure Elwig will make beautiful things with the true silver, so that's good enough for me."

Halfdan shook his head as the two of them made their way back to the Goodseed house. It was obvious that he thought Alex was far too generous, but Alex didn't mind. His mother and stepfather had taught him about generosity, and he knew that it had little to do with money. It was more about helping others, and giving Elwig some true silver to work with would only help the smith improve his craft.

That night at dinner Alex showed Elwig's work to the rest of the company and Andy's family. They were all impressed by the brooches Elwig had made and with the design Alex had come up with. The two brooches were almost identical and were made of true silver in the shape of a dragon's head. The head was edged with gold and each brooch had a large gem set as the dragon's eye. Lilly's brooch had a large white diamond, while Indigo's had a dark blue sapphire. Around the edge of each brooch were eight small rubies, which Alex explained represented each of the members of the adventure they had been on.

"I may have to find a wife myself if you give such fine gifts," Andy joked, his voice lowered so his parents wouldn't hear him.

That night in his room, Alex took some time to put a spell on all three of the brooches he'd received from Elwig. The spell was a simple one designed to protect the brooches from loss or theft. When that was done, Alex took the two true silver brooches in his hands and focused his mind and his magic on them. He formed a link between the two brooches, a magical connection that would let him know if his friends needed him. He hoped the spell would let him know if Cara's story ever came true.

When the wedding day arrived, Alex felt a bit nervous and out of place in his new blue clothes as he walked along the streets of Oslansk toward the main town square where the ceremony would be held. It seemed as though the whole city had been invited.

Fortunately the wedding ceremony was simple, and all Alex had to do was offer the rings to Skeld and Tayo when they asked for them. It was after the ceremony, as the festivities were about to begin, that things got interesting.

Just as Alex was sitting down, the feeling that someone was watching him came once more. Trying not to be obvious, he scanned the crowds, hoping to find the source of the feeling but there were too many people and too much excitement and movement for Alex to really see anything. Whoever—or whatever—was watching him had chosen the perfect time and place to do so.

"I hope you can dance," Sindar commented.

"Wh—what?" Alex asked, his eyes stopping on a figure on the far side of the square. Alex thought there was something suspicious about a man wearing a heavy cloak on such a warm spring day.

"Dance," Sindar repeated and paused. "What is it?"

"I need to check something. I'll be right back."

"But the festivities are just starting."

"This won't take long. Enjoy yourself. If anyone asks for me, tell them that I'll be back shortly."

Alex moved away before Sindar could ask any more questions. The figure he'd spotted was also moving, walking slowly to the edge of the square. Alex tried to keep the dark cloak in sight, but with so many people it was difficult.

Alex was certain that whoever was watching him was under that dark cloak. He feared that the watcher had noticed his gaze. Did the watcher know that he was trying to follow him? There was no way for Alex to be sure, so he readied his magic, just in case.

As he emerged from the crowds, Alex caught sight of the person he was trying to follow. He was leaving the square, heading down one of the narrow roads that led deeper into the city. Alex quickened his steps, trying to close the distance between himself and the cloaked figure. He could feel his magic growing as he hurried forward, and he let a little of it move ahead of him, looking for possible traps.

His magic didn't find anything, and Alex relaxed a little. The watcher must not know he was being followed. Alex wondered if he should try to catch the stranger, or simply follow him to see if there was something more to discover.

"Do you have a reason for following me?" A deep and strong, yet oddly soft, voice questioned.

Alex spun around. The figure he'd been following was behind him, and even with his magic at the ready he hadn't noticed until it was almost too late. Without thinking, Alex summoned up his defensive magic to protect himself from both physical and magical attacks.

"Oh, very good," said the stranger, a smile in his voice. "So fast to defend, yet holding back any attack until you know what you face. You've learned a great deal, young man."

"Who are you?" Alex demanded, a spark of anger igniting inside of him. "Why have you been watching me?"

"For the obvious reasons of course," the figure answered. "I wanted to see you, to see what magic you have, and to get some idea of what you might become."

"Who are you?" Alex asked again. He didn't like being watched, and the answers the cloaked figure had given weren't answers at all. Alex hated it when adults gave meaningless answers: "Because I said so"; "That's how it is"; "You'll understand when you're older." Alex had heard all those answers many times before. But today that kind of answer would not be enough. Today Alex wasn't just another teenager asking questions. Today he was a wizard in training. Today he would get a real answer, whatever the cost.

"Then again, you may get no answer at all."

"Wh—what?" Alex asked in surprise.

"Control. That is your weakness. You let your emotions run wild, and you lose all focus."

With a wave of his hand, the cloaked figure brushed away Alex's defensive magic as easily as brushing away old cobwebs.

For a moment Alex was too stunned to react, but then the figure started to laugh.

Rage surged though Alex like an electric shock. His anger blinded him, and his magic went wild. Without thinking, he attacked the figure in front of him, attacked to make the laughter stop. It felt like a thousand little needles poking him, a thousand little voices jeering and making fun, but anger was all Alex could feel.

"Enough!" The cloaked figure said, and Alex's magic shattered like glass.

Alex felt as if he'd been doused in ice-cold water, water that simply washed away his rage. He shivered and stumbled forward, only to be caught by the strange man.

"You had better learn some control if you want to survive," the figure whispered, lowering Alex to the ground. "If you can't control your own emotions, how can you ever hope to reach your full potential?"

"Who . . . who are you?" Alex asked once more in a desperate tone.

"Another time, young one. When you are ready."

"It was you. It was *your* voice I heard when I confronted Otho."

"Yes," the figure answered. "You were about to let something terrible happen, and I could not allow that—even if that fool deserved it."

"I don't understand . . . Why?"

The figure turned and started to walk away, but Alex still wanted answers. He focused his mind, pushed away all of his emotions and questions, and reached out with his magic alone.

"Wait!"

It was a demand, not a request. Alex's emotions were completely under control as he focused all of the magic he could muster toward the stranger. He tried to capture the figure with his magic, just as he might capture an object in his hand, but again he was surprised. There was nothing there, nothing at all for his magic to hold. The cloaked figure stopped dead, however, and turned slowly to face Alex once again.

"The day may come when you can hold me with a word, but it is not this day. Learn your lessons well, young wizard. If you manage to survive long enough, we will meet again."

"But . . ." Alex started, stopping short.

The figure that had been so solid only a moment before suddenly changed to smoke. As Alex watched, the smoke began to drift away, and when he blinked, it was gone. There was no sign of the stranger he had followed, not even the smallest trace of magic. Then a soft whisper came to Alex's ear, a whisper that seemed to come from all around him and inside of him at the same time.

"Be careful, young one. Evil is already close to you. If you do not learn to control your emotions, they will destroy you. When you send word to Vankin, tell him the Watchers have seen you. He will try to explain."

It was a long time before Alex was even able to move. He felt completely drained. Slowly he got to his feet and leaned against a nearby wall. He closed his eyes for a moment as he tried to recover his strength. The sound of hurried footsteps forced his eyes open once more, and he turned to see Val heading toward him.

"Alex, are you all right?"

"A bit winded, but no harm done."

"Sindar said you were checking on something, and he seemed worried," Val explained. "I told him I'd come find you. You don't look so good."

"The emotions of the day," said Alex.

"Yes, of course. I've heard that wizards often feel the emotions of others, and with so many people in the square and emotions so high . . ."

"I haven't learned enough to control it all yet," said Alex, not bothering to correct Val's assumption. "I'll be fine now. We should return to the party."

Val nodded and walked with Alex back to the main square. The dancing appeared to have ended, and the wedding feast was about to begin. Alex wondered how long he'd been gone. He couldn't seem to remember.

The feast was grand and long, and Alex's strength slowly returned. He was glad that Sindar didn't ask any questions when he sat down beside him. It had been a far more interesting day than Alex had thought it would be, and there were far too many things for him to think about. Besides, he already had enough questions of his own.

As the sun began to set, the wedding guests formed a line to present their gifts to the new couples. Alex suddenly worried about what Skeld and Tayo would think of his gifts. Tayo had been badly injured when they had fought Slathbog, and he hoped his gifts would not bring back bad memories for his friends now.

To Alex's relief, Skeld and Tayo were pleased with the brooches and impressed by his design. Both Lilly and Indigo beamed at Alex as they pinned their new brooches on. They each took a turn to kiss him on the cheek in thanks. Alex was glad that he had been able to make his friends—and their new brides—happy on their wedding day.

That night before Alex went to bed, he wrote another letter to Whalen to let him know what was going on, but the more he wrote about his encounter with the cloaked figure, the more worried he became. Alex thought about everything the cloaked figure had said, including the promise that Whalen would try to explain who or what the Watchers were, but Alex felt certain that no explanation in a letter would be enough.

Alex felt even more unsettled about the fact that the cloaked figure had been able to brush away his magic with no real effort. The warning about evil being close was easy enough to understand, but not at all comforting. Alex didn't know where the evil was coming from, and even worse, he still didn't know how to control his emotions.

Whalen will know, Alex thought as he drifted off to sleep. *Whalen will have the answers I need.*

Alex woke early the next morning to a familiar dinging noise. Sitting up, he saw a geeb standing on the edge of his bed. He paid and thanked the geeb, then swiftly opened the letter from Whalen.

Dear Alex,

I must apologize. I should have prepared you better and pushed you harder to learn more than you have. I also should have taught you to control your emotions before now. I am truly sorry. I hope that you can forgive an old fool for trying to teach you as he would any other apprentice. But you are not a normal apprentice, Alex, and I must remember that.

You will, of course, have dozens of questions about the Watchers. Sadly, they are more myth than fact, and it is unclear how many of them there are. What little I can tell you is that they are known to appear from time to time to give warnings and advice, so you should pay attention to what was said.

I can also tell you that the Watchers are known to work for good, and to help where they can. They are incredibly powerful, but seldom use their magic directly. The fact that a Watcher actually let you see him—let alone spoke to you—is very impressive. Sadly, you will have to do as he said and wait for the answers to your questions, as only the Watchers can really answer them for you.

Regarding the Tower of the Moon. There are many stories and legends about the Tower, and once Bregnest told me that you would be going that way, I've been asking questions. You are correct that the Tower is the center of magical power for Norsland. But it has been more than two thousand years since a wizard has lived there. I'm sorry I do not have more information, but I'm still looking, and I have sent several letters to friends. As soon as I learn anything that might be helpful to you, I will send it along.

Now, as for your training, I've included some exercises to help you control your emotions. I want you to do them every night before you go to sleep and every morning when you wake up. They may seem boring or a bit odd, but they will help you more than you might think.

I've also included a list of books for your future reading, including instructions for transfiguration, which I believe you are ready to attempt. Start with small things at first—leaves, small rocks, things like that. If you have difficulty with the magic, let me know and I'll do what I can to help.

Keep me informed on how your adventure is going. Keep your eyes open and study hard. I will hope for your success.

Yours in fellowship,
Whalen

P.S. You might ask Sindar about how to control your emotions. He knows a great many things, and he might be able to help you even more than I can.

Alex considered Whalen's letter for several minutes. It seemed that Whalen didn't have all the answers he wanted, but he did have some good advice. Worrying about the Watcher wouldn't do any good, but learning self-control would. Alex thought Sindar might be able to help him control his emotions, but he would have to wait until later to ask—the list of things he was supposed to start reading was surprisingly long.

Alex promised himself that he would do Whalen's exercises every night and morning, even though they seemed strange to say the least. Most of what Whalen wanted him to do was concentrate and breathe slowly, but there were other things as well. Count backward from a thousand while controlling the speed of his breathing. Recite the alphabet backward as fast as he could in one breath. Even balancing objects on top of each other with his magic while reciting the alphabet backward and breathing slowly were part of the list. It didn't make any sense to Alex, but he knew he would have to try.

Alex and his companions joined the Goodseed family for breakfast as usual the next morning, but there was a strange tension around the table. Michael seemed painfully excited, but nobody mentioned his birthday at all. At first Alex thought that Michael's parents didn't want to say anything in front of their guests, but then he saw Bregnest and Argus exchange knowing looks and he couldn't help but smile at Michael's impending surprise.

"Well, it should be an interesting day," Argus said enthusiastically. "More feasts and parties with the wedding couples."

"Perhaps you can tell us of the lands east and north of

here," said Bregnest. "It won't be long before we are on our way once more."

"Oh, yes, I can tell you a great deal about the lands you will cross," said Argus. "But, you know, I seem to be forgetting something—something important."

"That's odd, I have the same feeling," said Bregnest thoughtfully.

"Oh, stop it, both of you," Mrs. Goodseed snapped, clearly unhappy with their teasing of Michael. "You both know very well that it's Michael's birthday, so you might as well say so."

Alex and the rest of his companions laughed at Mrs. Goodseed's outburst, and Michael laughed loudest of all.

It seemed that the entire company had bought birthday presents for Michael, despite Andy telling them not to. Val gave Michael a magical flute that played songs by itself. Sindar gave him a large book of stories that included many beautiful illustrations. Bregnest produced a fine new bow and a quiver of arrows, and he was quick to help when Michael couldn't quite manage to string the bow by himself.

While everyone was wishing Michael a happy birthday, Andy slipped away from the table and out of the house. Mrs. Goodseed seemed to know what Andy was up to because she soon made a point of asking where Andy had gone.

"I believe he stepped outside," said Halfdan, winking at Alex.

"Outside?" Mrs. Goodseed questioned, though she didn't look at all surprised. "What in the world is he doing outside?"

"Perhaps we should go and see," Halfdan suggested.

They all filed out of the front door and saw Andy standing in the courtyard with a beautiful black horse.

"I hope he's the one you wanted," Andy said as Michael ran toward him.

"Oh, he is," exclaimed Michael, hugging Andy. "He's perfect."

"A fine-looking horse," Halfdan commented. "And Alex and I have something that belongs to him."

"What's that?" Andy questioned, though it was obvious he knew what Halfdan was talking about.

"We decided a horse was little good without a saddle," said Alex, smiling at Andy.

When Halfdan produced the saddle from his magic bag, Michael looked as if he were about to burst with joy. He looked around at all the adventurers and at his family, not sure what to do or say. It seemed as if he'd been given more than he'd ever dared to hope for.

"Well, come on then," said Andy. "You'd best go for a ride."

Michael didn't need to be asked twice, and he was soon saddling his new horse with Andy's help. Alex and his friends watched for a short time, and then went back to the house to finish their meal.

"You have all been extremely kind to my son," said Argus to the company as he took his seat in the dining room once more. "I am very much in your debt."

"It is a little thing compared to the kindness you and your family have shown us," said Bregnest. "It is not easy having so many adventurers around the house."

"Oh, it's no trouble at all," said Mrs. Goodseed. "You are all welcome, any time."

After breakfast, Alex pulled Bregnest aside for a quiet chat. He told him about the golden brooch he'd received from Elwig and how he had thought about giving it to Mrs. Goodseed. He felt that it should come from the company, as a thank-you gift to Mrs. Goodseed for taking such good care of them. Bregnest thought it was an excellent idea, and insisted that Alex present the brooch on behalf of them all.

"We will compensate you for the cost," said Bregnest.

"Oh, there's no need for that," said Alex. "It was part of a trade I made with Elwig. I have no idea what it would cost by itself."

"Still, we should make some compensation," Bregnest insisted.

Alex waved his hand. "It's a small thing between friends, and the cost is little enough."

Bregnest didn't reply, but simply nodded his acceptance.

Alex knew that Bregnest wasn't pleased with his answer, but also knew he would not argue the point.

That afternoon there was another feast, and Alex was asked to join the wedding table, as he had been the ring bearer. He sat between Lilly and Indigo, answering their questions about his last adventure with Skeld and Tayo.

Alex answered all the questions that were asked, careful to always point out Skeld and Tayo's parts in the adventure. Skeld and Tayo beamed at him, and would occasionally interrupt to point out something he had done as well. Alex was grateful that no one asked about Tayo's wounds or how he had magically called Tayo back from near death. He didn't think either of those subjects would go over too well at a wedding feast.

"You have done well," said Bregnest, walking beside Alex as they returned to the Goodseed house. "You have shown great kindness to your friends and increased their honor. In doing this, your honor grows as well."

"It seems a small thing," said Alex. "Though little things are often the most important of all."

"I see that Whalen has taught you a great deal in a short time," said Bregnest in a thoughtful tone. "You have changed much since our last journey together."

"Yes, I believe I have," Alex admitted. "But I'm still the same person, and I still know who my friends are."

Bregnest chuckled softly at Alex's reply and said no more.

Alex knew he had changed during the six months he'd been at home. He had learned more than he had ever thought possible in so short a time. He also understood a great deal more about almost everything having to do with adventures. And now he was learning more and more about magic, and what he might one day become.

Their remaining days in Oslansk passed quickly, full of both work and fun. Each day there were more preparations to be made for their journey and long discussions about what might be ahead of them. Each night there was another feast, another party, and more questions for Alex to answer.

In the little time that Alex had to himself, he began reading the books Whalen had assigned to him. He was relieved to find that simple transfigurations were not too difficult for him to do. On his first attempt, he managed to change a small rock into a white mouse. The magic didn't take a lot of energy, but it did require him to focus his thoughts and picture the mouse clearly in his head. He hastily changed the mouse back into a rock, however; he didn't want it to escape into the house and scare Andy's mother.

He also practiced Whalen's breathing exercises. Yes, they were a bit silly, as Whalen had said they would be, but already Alex could see how they could help him gain control of his emotions. They made him think about his emotions more than he normally would have, and that alone was a great benefit.

On the night of the final wedding feast, Skeld, Tayo, and their wives said good-bye to the company. They thanked them all for coming and wished them a safe and profitable journey. They all thanked Alex once again for being their ring bearer and made him promise to visit again as soon as he could.

Chapter Six

The Second Bag

The next morning the company gathered for breakfast with the Goodseed family for the last time. There was a touch of sadness in all of their faces. They would miss the fun and feasting they'd had in Oslansk, but they knew that their quest was ahead of them.

As the company gathered in the courtyard with their horses, Bregnest nodded to Alex. He grinned and retrieved the golden brooch from his pocket, stepping forward before speaking.

"Mistress Goodseed," said Alex, in the most official voice he could manage. "May I present you this gift on behalf of our company, as a token of our thanks for your great kindness."

Andy's mother blushed as Alex bowed and presented her with the golden brooch. Argus Goodseed smiled at the company but said nothing, and Alex wondered if Bregnest had mentioned the gift to him.

After several seconds of silence, Mrs. Goodseed found her voice. "I thank you all for your kind gift," she said, her voice shaking slightly. "If ever any of you are near our home, you will be most welcome."

The company bowed to the Goodseeds and then mounted their horses. Andy looked stunned and surprised by Alex's gift, but he didn't ask any questions in front of his parents. Alex wondered if Bregnest had told everyone except Andy about the gift; he could see that Andy was a little upset.

"May luck be with you," Argus called as the company rode out of the gate and away from the house.

Once they were moving through the city, Andy demanded to know why he had not been told about the gift to his mother.

"The gift was Alex's idea," Bregnest said.

"It seemed like the right thing to do," said Alex sheepishly. "After all, your family has been very kind to us."

"Why didn't anyone tell me?" Andy asked again.

"We thought you might spill the beans," said Halfdan, winking at Alex.

Andy frowned, but when the others started laughing, he joined in as well.

When they reached the city gates, Bregnest headed east, following one of many well-used roads. Argus Goodseed had told them it would take about twelve days to reach the town of Ollvi, if the weather stayed fair. From Ollvi there was a good road leading north and east to the Mountains of the Moon, where they hoped to find the lost Horn of Moran.

Not only would the trip to Ollvi allow the snow to melt off the northern roads, but Alex had a lost bag to return, and the bag's heir supposedly lived in Ollvi.

As they rode, Alex wondered what kind of trouble might be waiting for them on the road. He remembered his first adventure when the company had met both bandits and a troll.

He hoped that they would meet neither as they traveled here in Norsland, but he knew there would probably be trouble of some kind as they moved into wilder lands.

Clouds started to fill the sky as they went along that first day. By the time they had set up their camp and finished eating, a cold rain had started to fall. They put blankets on their horses, and then quietly went to bed.

The rain continued for most of the next day as well, making them all less than comfortable. Alex wondered if there was some magic he could use to push the storms away, and if his own magic would be strong enough to change the weather.

"Spring rains don't often last more than a day or two," Andy said as they went along. "But they can be heavy and cold."

"If it was much colder, it would be snow," replied Val as he tried to pull his cloak closer to him.

"I'm glad it's not snow," said Halfdan, tucking his beard into his shirt. "If it was cold enough to snow, we'd be stuck in Oslansk for some time to come."

"We're not going north yet," Bregnest said from ahead of them. "And I don't think the rain will last much longer."

Bregnest was right, and the rain stopped falling as they made their camp. They all changed into dry clothes once their camp was set up, and then Halfdan started working on their evening meal.

"Can't get a spark to catch," Halfdan huffed as he stood over a pile of twigs. "Everything is soaked through."

"Perhaps I can help," said Alex.

"No doubt you can. Why don't you magic up a fire while I go and get some water."

"As you wish," Alex replied.

Halfdan nodded, then picked up a large, cast-iron cauldron and started off for a nearby spring. Alex watched him go and then turned his attention back to the wet pile of wood in front of him.

"It will take some real magic to get that burning," said Andy.

"Not often that a dwarf can't get a fire started," Val added.

"True enough," said Alex. "There's a spell I've been wanting to try. I think it should do the job."

Alex focused his thoughts on the pile of wood and started moving his right hand in a circle. This was a new spell, and he wasn't sure how well it would work. For a few seconds nothing seemed to happen, and then a bright yellow flame sprang up in the middle of the wet wood.

"Amazing," said Andy as the flames continued to grow.

The flames didn't just catch hold on the wood, but seemed to be burning alone in the air as well. Alex kept moving his hand in a circle, and the flames grew into a four-foot-tall tornado in front of him.

"An impressive bit of magic," Sindar commented as he joined them.

"You've learned some new tricks, I see," added Bregnest. "Not simply conjuring fire anymore, but making it do as you wish."

"I've been studying—" Alex started but was interrupted.

"What the—!" Halfdan said loudly.

Alex looked toward his friend, and immediately the whirlwind of flames moved away from the burning logs and darted toward Halfdan.

"Agghh!" Halfdan yelled in fear.

Dropping the water he was carrying, Halfdan dove behind one of the tents. Alex could hear him crawling wildly away from the flaming whirlwind that was racing to the spot where his friend had been standing. Alex lowered his hand to break the spell, but he wasn't quick enough to save Halfdan's cauldron. The flames hit the half-full cauldron of water and sent up a cloud of steam. There was a loud, sharp hiss, and an even louder bang as the flames vanished.

"Halfdan, are you all right?" Alex questioned as he ran toward the tent.

"Hardly," said Halfdan, getting to his feet. "Stars and stones, Alex, what was that?"

"Just a bit of magic to light the fire," said Alex, trying not to laugh at the look on Halfdan's face.

"I thought for a minute that you'd conjured up a fire demon or something worse," said Halfdan, brushing mud off his pants.

"I'm sorry," said Alex, forcing the smile from his face. "I didn't know the whirlwind would go where I was looking."

"It's a good thing you are so quick on your feet," Sindar said to Halfdan from the other side of the tent.

"What do you mean?" Halfdan asked.

"Come and see."

They moved around the tent to see that the cauldron

Halfdan had been carrying was lying on the ground, bone-dry and shattered into a dozen pieces.

"Oh, no," said Halfdan in a pained voice. "That was my best cooking pot. It's been in my family for three generations."

"I'm sorry," said Alex. "I didn't mean to . . ."

He felt terrible for destroying Halfdan's cauldron, and worse now that he knew it had been in Halfdan's family for so long.

"Perhaps I can mend it," Alex offered as he bent down to pick up the broken metal pieces.

"Careful. It's still hot," said Sindar as he caught Alex's hand.

"No, it's no good," Halfdan said sadly. "Not even the best dwarf smith could repair it now."

"I'm really sorry," said Alex, looking from the broken metal to Halfdan. "I'll be happy to buy you a new pot, and pay you for your loss."

"No, no—that's not necessary," said Halfdan, his eyes lingering on the broken metal fragments. "I have other pots, and it's no good crying over spilled milk."

Alex didn't say anything else, but he continued to feel bad about what he had done even though Halfdan tried to make light of it, as if the pot wasn't all that important. Alex knew it wasn't the broken pot that really mattered to Halfdan; it was the memories that the pot brought back. There was nothing Alex could do to replace those memories, and that made him feel even worse about what had happened.

There was little talk as they ate that night. Finally, when the rest of the company started for their tents to get some sleep, Alex went back to the broken bits of metal. They had cooled off, and he picked them up and put them inside his magic bag. He had read something about repairing broken objects, but he didn't remember exactly how the magic worked. He did know, however, that he had to try to repair the broken pot, even if Halfdan thought it was hopeless.

On their third day away from Oslansk, Alex asked Andy about returning magic bags in Norsland. On his last adventure, Alex had returned a bag to a dwarf in Vargland, and there had been a large ceremony. Alex had learned quite a bit at the time. Now he wondered if he'd have to go through another ceremony, and if so, he wanted to know about it in advance.

"Oh, it's very simple here," said Andy. "You and one other person you choose as a witness meet with the heir and his witness. You agree on a reward for returning the bag, which is almost always a share in whatever treasure the bag holds. Once you agree on the reward, the heir will tell you the password for the bag and you both go into the bag and see what's there."

"We both go in?" Alex questioned.

"Of course," said Andy. "Normally the bag holder goes in first and the heir follows him."

"And then what happens?"

"Then, after looking at what's in the bag, you both come out again. The heir will restate the reward you've agreed on, and the witness will say that they are witnesses," Andy replied. "Then you and the heir make the arrangements for the payment to be made. That's about it."

"That's all?" Alex pressed, thinking that it sounded too simple.

"Mostly," said Andy with a shrug.

"What else is there, Andy?" Alex narrowed his eyes in suspicion.

"Well, once you and your witness leave, you tell your witness how much treasure you think the bag holds, and how much you think you should get," Andy answered. "Then when you and your witness return to collect your reward, if you, or your witness, think you've been cheated, you reject the payment. If that happens, then the magistrate has to settle the whole thing."

"Sounds fairly simple," said Alex, relaxing a little.

"It is," said Andy. "It only gets difficult if you reject payment and the magistrate has to get involved."

"Why? What happens then?"

"If the magistrate gets involved, the heir has to tell him the passwords. Then the magistrate checks the bag and the payment and decides if you're being cheated or not. If the heir is trying to cheat you, you get double the original offer, and the city gets half of whatever is left in the bag."

"And if he's *not* trying to cheat me?" Alex asked.

"Then you get half the payment and the city gets the other half," said Andy.

"That doesn't sound too bad," Alex said thoughtfully. "So all I need to know now is what kind of offer would be considered fair, and what might be considered too small. I wouldn't want to insult the heir by asking for too little."

"I've only heard about a few bags being returned," Andy said in a thoughtful tone. "I mean, it's not like lost bags get returned all the time. I think the heir will offer you something like one in four or one in five of everything the bag holds. If you think that's too much—or not enough—you can make a counteroffer."

"And how little would be considered an insult?" Alex asked, remembering the last time he'd done this.

"Oh, you might go as low as one in eight or even one in ten," said Andy thoughtfully. "Anything less would certainly be an insult, so don't let your generosity get the better of you."

It seemed that Andy also remembered the last time Alex had returned a bag. Of course, that bag had belonged to a dwarf, and dwarfs were a little touchy when it came to saying they'd offered too much.

That night, as they ate their evening meal, Bregnest said that they would start keeping watch. Alex thought Bregnest looked worried, but Bregnest was often moody, and Alex thought that the idea of keeping watch had more to do with Bregnest's own worries than any real danger.

Alex drew the last watch, which meant that he would have to get up an hour before anyone else. He thought that taking the last watch would be hard, but as it turned out, it was both easy and useful. The early morning quiet gave him time to study his books and practice his magic in peace. Alex felt lucky, too, because Sindar had drawn the watch before his, and he would normally allow Alex to study his books while he continued to watch.

On their seventh morning away from Oslansk, Alex was practicing magic and turned a large stone into a rabbit. To

Alex's dismay, however, the rabbit ran off into the tall grass before he could change it back into a stone. Sindar thought it was extremely funny, but Alex wasn't pleased at all.

"So there's one more rabbit in Norsland," said Sindar. "I'm sure there is no harm in that."

"Well, perhaps not," Alex agreed. "But the book says I should change things back into what they were, if I can."

"And why is that?"

"The book doesn't say. I suppose it's so there aren't too many rabbits all over the place."

Sindar and Alex both laughed, but then Sindar became serious.

"Could you change rocks into gold?"

"I guess so," said Alex. "Why do you ask?"

"I was just thinking that if a greedy wizard could change rocks into gold, he could make himself very rich."

"Yes, I suppose he could, if he had enough rocks."

Sindar smiled and looked thoughtful. "I have seen your generosity, so I suspect that such an idea has never entered your mind."

"No, it hasn't. But now I wonder if it would work."

"Well, a gold coin couldn't run away from you."

Alex picked up a small rock and focused his thoughts on what he wanted it to be. He felt the weight in his hand change as his magic worked, and without looking, he tossed the coin to Sindar.

"A useful trick, if ever you are in need," said Sindar as he looked at the coin. "But for me, it was better as a rock."

Alex nodded and took the coin back. He looked at it for

a moment to make sure it really was solid gold, and then he changed it back into a rock.

"You are learning quickly," said Sindar, his tone growing even more serious. "Soon, your friend Vankin will ask you to take a staff."

"Ask me to take a staff?"

"Whalen has not spoken to you about this?"

Alex shook his head.

"Perhaps I should say no more, then."

"No, please," said Alex. "At least tell me what you meant."

"To take a staff means you are willing to accept greater responsibility," said Sindar slowly. "If Whalen asks you to take a staff, you will be bound by wizard law and connected magically to your staff. The staff will be more powerful because of this connection, and so will you. I suppose you could buy a staff and use it, though it would not work as well."

"How do you know so much about wizards and staffs?" Alex asked.

"I have known many wizards in my time," Sindar answered. "I have also known many who pretended to be wizards. The pretenders are sometimes good, and some of them do great deeds. But their power is nothing—*nothing*—compared to that of a true wizard."

Alex thought about what Sindar said and it seemed to make sense. In a way, he felt like he was still pretending to be a wizard—using magic as a helpful tool, but not like a real wizard would. He knew nothing about wizard law, or staffs, or the true power of real wizards like Whalen. Alex wondered why

Whalen had never mentioned any of this to him before. He decided to ask Whalen about it in his next letter.

"Whalen said you might be able to help me learn to control my emotions," Alex commented as he put his books away.

"Control your emotions," Sindar repeated and then grinned and nodded his head.

"What?" Alex questioned, confused.

"Vankin knows things that others do not, and he has ways to use his knowledge that most would not see."

"What?"

"He knows that I was once, shall we say, hotheaded," Sindar answered as he piled wood on the fire. "I worked for many years to gain control of my temper, and he is telling me something about you without actually saying it out loud."

"I don't understand."

"You're not supposed to."

"Fine," said Alex, shaking his head. "Can you help me or not?"

"Help you control your temper? Yes, I can do that."

It was just before noon on the twelfth day when the company reached the town of Ollvi. They found the tavern where Argus Goodseed had suggested they stay, and they were soon settled in.

"Have you chosen your witness?" Bregnest asked Alex, as the company sat down in the common room.

"I've asked Andy to be my witness," Alex replied.

"Then you both should go and find the heir," said Bregnest. "We will remain in Ollvi until your business is finished."

"Even if we find the heir quickly, it might take some time for payment to be arranged," said Alex. "Perhaps I can have the payment postponed until we are on our way back to Alusia."

"The return of a lost bag is an important event," said Bregnest in a thoughtful tone. "It would be best to take care of everything at once. If it costs us a few days, or even a few weeks, then that is the price we will pay. I wish that, well . . ."

"If it would aid our quest, I can hold the bag and return it some other time," Alex offered.

"No, that would not be right. You are here, now. The bag should be returned," Bregnest said firmly. "Who knows, but perhaps it is fate that brought us here at this time. We will not tempt fate."

Alex nodded, and then motioned for Andy to join him. Alex decided that the best way to find the heir to the lost bag would be to ask the owner of the tavern if he knew the Cain family since the name on the bag was Jonathan Cain.

"Oh, yes, old Jon Cain," said the man, as if remembering something from long ago. "Been a long time since he left Ollvi."

"Do you know where we might find his family?" Alex asked hopefully.

"I expect his son is working down at the town stables," the man answered. "His name is Tom Cain, and he helps me out now and again, but I don't have enough business to keep him on permanently."

"And where would we find the town stables?" Alex questioned.

"Why are you looking for Tom?" the man asked, looking at Alex and Andy sharply.

"Our business with him is of a private nature," said Alex.

"Oh, I see," said the man, nodding and touching the side of his nose as if he knew a secret. "Got a message for him from his old dad, have ya? Well, I hope it's good news. Tom and his family could use some."

"Why is that?" Alex asked, interested by the comment.

"They've fallen on hard times," said the man, lowering his voice. "After old Jon left, things got hard for his family. They used to own a fair bit around Ollvi, you know, but they've had to sell off their land, little by little, to make ends meet."

"Well, I believe we have some good news for Tom and his family, then," said Alex. "So if you can tell us how to find the town stables, we'll be off."

The man gave them directions and wished them good luck. As Alex and Andy walked through the town, they talked about what the tavern owner had told them about the Cain family.

"I'd guess their crops failed and they've had to sell their lands and property so they'd have enough to live on," said Andy knowingly. "This part of Norsland has always been poor. If Tom Cain has a family to support, he may have to take any job he can find to make ends meet."

"If that's the case, I hope there's a lot of treasure in his father's bag," said Alex. "People who've had a hard life deserve a bit of wealth."

"Perhaps," said Andy. "But remember that there are plenty

of other reasons people might have hard times. And a lot of those reasons are because people bring hard times on themselves."

"I'll remember."

When they reached the stables, Alex asked to see the stable master. He wanted to ask a few more questions before meeting Tom Cain in person. Alex and Andy didn't have to wait long, as a large man with a full beard and a pipe soon appeared and met them outside the stable.

"You asked to see me?" questioned the man.

"Are you in charge of the stables?" Alex asked.

"I am. What can I do for you?"

"I'd like to ask you about Tom Cain," said Alex, lowering his voice slightly.

"Tom?" the man asked, looking over his shoulder to see if anyone was close by. "What do you want to know about Tom?"

"Well, we'd like to know about him and his family, and how things are with them," answered Alex. "You see, we may have a message for Tom, but we'd like to make sure we have the right person first."

"Adventurers, then," said the bearded man with a nod.

"Yes, we are," admitted Alex, slightly surprised by the comment.

"Well, I don't see no harm telling ya what I know, and it might do a bit o' good," said the man, lighting his pipe. "Been wondering if we'd ever hear about old Jon Cain again, and I'm guessing we will, from the look of you two."

Alex felt that he could trust the bearded man, though he didn't really know why.

"You have guessed correctly," said Alex. "However, we'd like to know a little more about Tom and his family before we talk to him."

"Bag holder and witness, then, is it?" said the bearded man. "Well, I'll tell you what I know, but there's probably plenty I don't know."

The man told Andy and Alex that the Cain family had once been the richest family in Ollvi. After Jon Cain had left, eleven years ago, the family started having troubles. The town magistrate at the time didn't like Jon Cain, and he used his dislike against the Cain family once Jon had left. Then their crops had failed, and the family suffered several other minor misfortunes, some from bad luck and some from other things. Now Tom Cain supported his mother, two brothers, and three sisters by working wherever and whenever he could. The rest of the family did as much as they could, but still, Tom was the one who bore the heaviest burden.

"The Cain family is the poorest family for miles around," said the bearded man in a matter-of-fact tone. "Most folks here in Ollvi remember how generous old Jon was, so we try to help out where we can. Only so much we can do though. Tom's mom has never been much on accepting what she calls charity."

"What happened to the magistrate?" Andy asked.

"Oh, him," said the bearded man, spitting into the road. "He up and died a couple of years ago. Good riddance I say."

"Well, you've been very helpful," said Alex, nodding. "Perhaps Tom Cain's fortunes will improve soon."

"I'd be glad to see that," said the bearded man with a nod of his own. "I'll just go and fetch Tom for ya, then, shall I?"

"Yes, thank you," said Alex. "And I'd appreciate it if you didn't mention our little talk."

"Not to worry."

The bearded man wandered off into the stables, and Alex and Andy looked at each other.

"He could be telling us a story."

"I don't think so," said Alex. "I feel like he was telling the truth, but I can't explain why."

"Well, you're the wizard," Andy replied.

The bearded man soon reappeared with a younger man following him closely. Alex guessed the younger man to be around twenty years old, which was a bit of a surprise. From the patched and worn look of the young man's clothes, however, Alex was sure the bearded man had been telling the truth about hard times for the Cain family.

"You asked to see me, sir?" Tom Cain asked as he approached Alex and Andy.

"I did," said Alex. "And I think I have both sad and happy news for you."

"What news, might I ask?" Tom questioned, looking slightly confused.

"Well, to be plain," Alex began and paused to consider his words. It was never easy to tell someone the news that a loved one had died.

"Yes?"

"To be plain, I must ask if you are the heir of Jonathan Cain, adventurer," Alex said.

"I . . . I am," said Tom, turning slightly pale.

"Then I must inform you that I hold the magic bag of Jonathan Cain, who is lost," Alex continued, "and that I am prepared to meet with you, if you are his rightful heir, at the time and place of your choosing."

Tom Cain stood dumbfounded for a moment, a troubled expression on his face. He looked like he wanted to cry and shout for joy at the same time, but couldn't decide which to do. It took him a moment to find his voice.

"I am honored that you have come," said Tom, swallowing hard and shaking slightly. "I ask that you and your witness come to my home this afternoon. I will be there with my witness to discuss the return of my father's bag."

The conversation seemed painfully formal, but Alex knew that he had to continue.

"At what hour would you have us come?"

"At the fourth hour after midday," Tom answered.

"We will come as you ask," said Alex with a bow.

"I thank you," said Tom, returning the bow.

Tom gave Alex and Andy directions to his house and then the two adventurers left the stable.

Alex had mixed feelings about Tom Cain and his family. Tom was obviously extremely sad to know that his father was dead, and Alex was sure the rest of Tom's family would feel the same, but at the same time, the return of the magic bag had given Tom hope for a better life—not just for himself, but for his entire family.

"You've found the heir?" Bregnest asked when Alex and Andy returned to the tavern.

"We have," said Alex.

"That is good," said Bregnest. "Perhaps payment can be made in a day or two, and we can be on our way."

"Has time become our enemy already?" Alex questioned. "We've been on the road for only a little more than two weeks."

"Time is always the enemy," Bregnest answered slowly. "I would hurry because our quest is to aid both my kinsman and my friend. I would not have him troubled longer than he needs to be."

"If all goes well, we should return before winter settles in Norsland," said Andy in a reassuring tone.

"Perhaps," said Bregnest. "But I fear we will be forced to spend the winter on the road, though I cannot say why I fear it."

"You have doubts about our quest?" Alex questioned.

"Doubts about myself," Bregnest replied in a grim tone. "But I will keep my doubts to myself until we are on the road again. Then perhaps I will share them with the company."

"As you wish."

Alex and Andy remained at the tavern, talking and joking with the rest of the company until it was time for them to meet with Tom Cain. Excusing themselves, they left to find the Cain house and arrange for the return of Jonathan Cain's bag.

As they approached the Cain house, they could plainly see that it had been a fine home once. Now the large house looked worn and hard used, but not at all shabby or uncared for. And the garden, which took up most of the yard, was ready for planting the spring vegetables.

A middle-aged woman opened the door when Alex and

Andy knocked. Her eyes were red from crying, and she wiped at her nose as she led the adventurers into a large room where Tom and his witness were nervously waiting for them.

"Please, be seated, my friends," said Tom, trying hard to smile but unable to manage it. "Let me introduce my witness—my brother Jonathan Cain, Junior."

"A pleasure," said Alex, bowing slightly. "I am Alexander Taylor. This is my witness, Anders Goodseed."

"Yes, well then," said Tom nervously. "I suppose we should get started."

"Yes, we should," replied Alex.

"All right," Tom began, still sounding and looking nervous. "I will offer one in four of all treasure in my father's bag for the bag's return."

Alex was taken aback by Tom's offer; he knew how poor the Cain family was. He rubbed his chin for a moment as if considering the offer before speaking.

"You are too generous. I will ask but one in ten."

"Now you are too generous," Tom answered. "I will offer one in five."

"I will make an offer that I hope you won't refuse," Alex replied after a moment. "If the bag holds more than ten thousand gold coins and ten thousand silver coins, I will ask one in seven of all. But if the bag holds less than that amount, I will accept only one in ten."

"You are very kind and generous, Master Taylor, and I will accept on one condition. If the bag holds more than the number you have stated, I will give you one in seven of all gold and silver, but one in five of all gems."

Alex thought for a moment, and then nodded his acceptance of Tom's generous offer. Tom leaned forward and whispered the passwords in Alex's ear. Alex nodded again, and then he retrieved Jonathan Cain's lost bag from his own magic bag. Speaking softly into the mouth of the lost adventurer's bag, Alex vanished from the living room.

When Alex entered the bag, it was completely dark. He lit the lanterns and torches with the password Tom had told him and waited. It wasn't long before Tom Cain was standing beside him inside the bag, his legs shaking and his face pale.

"I've never been in a magic bag before," Tom said nervously.

"First time for everything," Alex replied with a reassuring smile. He remembered how he had felt the first time he'd entered a magic bag. "Come on, let's look around a bit, shall we?" Alex could see that this first room contained a large desk and several comfortable-looking chairs, but no treasure at all.

They soon discovered that the bag had five rooms. In addition to the first room they had entered, there was a bedroom, a bathroom, a large storage room, and the treasure room. Alex was relieved to see that the storage room still held a great deal of food and supplies, which were still fresh and new, and that the treasure room was even larger than he'd hoped.

"Your father seems to have had some success as an adventurer," said Alex, as he watched Tom's jaw drop.

The treasure room was the size of a large banquet hall, and it was full of neatly stacked treasure. Alex was pleased to see that most of the treasure was in gold and silver coins. He really didn't want to accept any reward for returning this bag, but he knew he would have to.

"I don't . . . I don't believe it," said Tom, walking around the treasure room, his eyes wide in amazement. "I just don't believe it."

Alex managed not to laugh at Tom's enthusiasm. He thought there was enough treasure here to keep Tom and his family comfortable for the rest of their lives, and that was all anyone really needed.

Once Alex managed to calm Tom down, he began explaining how the bag worked and how Tom could get things in and out of it. Tom caught on quickly and didn't need Alex to repeat very much.

When they emerged from the bag they found Andy talking with the rest of the Cain family. Tom rushed to his mother and began telling her what was in the bag.

"You have done us a great service in returning this bag," said Mrs. Cain, bowing to Alex. "My family is forever in your debt."

"It was my duty and my honor to return the lost bag," said Alex, also bowing. "And I hope that the contents of this bag will aid and comfort your family for many years to come."

"And now for payment," said Andy.

"Yes, of course," said Tom. "It will take us some time to count the treasure and separate one in five of everything."

"One in five of gems, only. One in seven of the gold and silver," Alex reminded him. "And you should know, Tom, as I see my friend Andy has already told your family, I am a wizard, and if you try to pay me one coin more than our agreement, I may become very angry."

"Of course, Master Taylor," replied Tom. "The payment will be exactly as we've agreed. If you will give us two days to sort and count, your payment will be ready."

"Then we shall return in two days' time," said Alex with a bow.

Once they had left the Cain house, Andy asked how much treasure was in the bag. Alex told him how much he thought there was. Andy was pleased with what Alex told him, and his step had a bit more bounce in it than usual.

"You were very generous," said Andy. "But I'm glad you were. They're nice people, and they deserve better than they have."

Alex didn't say anything as his mind was already thinking ahead to the adventure. Only two days until the payment would be made, that would please Bregnest. Two days, and then they would be off into wilder lands, lands where things could become dangerous in a very short time.

Two days later, Alex and Andy returned to the Cain house and saw immediately that repairs were already being made. There were stacks of lumber and buckets of paint piled neatly in the yard, waiting for the workmen to arrive. The entire Cain family welcomed Alex and Andy at the front door when they knocked, and Alex was quick to notice they were all wearing new clothes. Tom led them to a large room at the back of the house, where he and his brothers and sisters had gathered Alex's reward.

Alex accepted the reward with a bow and swiftly stored it in his magic bag. Then Alex pulled Tom aside for a private word.

"I know your newfound treasure looks like it has no end," said Alex in a serious tone. "But I would advise you to be both careful and generous with your gold. You never know what tomorrow may bring."

"You are wise as well as generous," said Tom, bowing to Alex. "I will heed your words and always remember your kindness."

Alex and Tom bowed once more to each other in front of their witnesses, and the return of the lost bag was done. As Alex turned to leave with Andy, Tom's younger brother Jonathan asked the question Alex had been expecting.

"Are you . . . are you really a wizard?"

"I am," said Alex with a wink.

Without saying anything more, Alex picked up an old piece of cloth that was lying on the floor. With a wave of his hand he changed it into a beautiful silk scarf, which he presented to Mrs. Cain with a smile.

"An impressive bit of magic that," said Andy, as they walked back to the tavern where their companions were waiting. "It seems you're becoming more of a wizard all the time."

"It was a simple gift for a kindhearted lady," said Alex. "Besides, it's good practice."

Chapter Seven

Goblins and Elf Blades

As Alex was getting dressed the next morning there was a sudden pop and a ding as a geeb appeared on his bed. He quickly paid for the message and then pulled on his boots. Once the geeb had vanished, Alex opened the letter, which was from Whalen.

Dear Alex,

I understand you have been talking to Sindar about staffs and about what your future may hold. Sindar was correct in what he told you about the difference between buying a staff and being asked to take one. That is one of the reasons I've told you not to buy a staff. For now, I will tell you this: a staff is a tool, and nothing more. As you seem to be getting along without this tool, I see no reason to burden you with it, at least not yet.

Let me know about the return of the second lost bag in your next letter. Also, don't worry about the rabbit that got away. You are quite right in your guess—it wouldn't do to have too many of something left running around.

I'm glad to hear that you are gaining more control over your emotions. I'm also pleased with the progress you have made in your studies. I've included more reading for you to do, and I will be sending you a few new books in the next day or so.

Keep your eyes open, and take care of yourself.

Yours in fellowship,
Whalen

Alex joined the rest of his companions in the common room for breakfast, and then they all headed for the stables, ready to continue their journey.

He wondered if he should mention Whalen's letter to Bregnest, but decided not to. Bregnest knew that he was writing to Whalen regularly, but he hadn't mentioned anything about it to the rest of the company.

Bregnest seemed to be in a better mood this morning, more relaxed than he had been for the past several days. Perhaps it was because they had spent so little time in Ollvi returning the lost bag, or perhaps he had overcome his own doubts. Alex didn't ask why, but he was glad to see that Bregnest was back to his old self again.

As Alex and his friends rode out of Ollvi, they passed the Cain house, which Alex pointed out to the rest of the company. He was pleased to see a large number of workmen at the house, and he hoped that the Cain family would find joy in their newfound wealth.

"It appears you've done them a great kindness," Halfdan commented to Alex.

"I believe that I have."

"I suppose you know what this means?"

"What?"

"It means your legend will continue to grow," Halfdan joked. "The kind and generous Master Taylor, who refuses to accept the rewards due him."

"Well," Alex snorted, "I know one dwarf who won't be writing my life's story."

"There is some truth in what Halfdan says," Bregnest commented from in front of Alex. "Your generosity increases your honor, though it does little to increase your wealth."

"Generosity where it is needed," Alex answered after a moment's thought. "If they'd been rich and snobby, I might have asked for more than the heir offered."

"Which also shows your wisdom," Bregnest replied.

Alex didn't say anything more. He was much too happy to worry about being too generous or about having stories told about him. He knew that most people would think what they wanted to think no matter what he said. It was like how everyone believed he was a wizard when he was still only a wizard in training. He had tried to explain the difference so many times that he'd finally just given up.

The road they were following led almost due north, though slightly to the east from time to time. Alex wondered how far it was to the Mountains of the Moon, and how long it would take them to get there. He'd studied several maps of Norsland, but none of them showed distances. If the distance from Oslansk to Ollvi was any indication, he thought it would take them at least a month to reach the mountains, maybe longer.

That night, as the company ate their evening meal, Bregnest shared his concerns with all of them. He told them about his fear of having to remain in Norsland over the winter, and about his doubts of finding the Horn of Moran quickly. Alex thought this was strange because Bregnest had always been confident in the past. He wondered if Bregnest might be worried because this quest was to help one of his relatives, but he didn't think that was the real reason.

"The guardians of the road could be difficult to pass," said Andy in a thoughtful tone once Bregnest had finished speaking. "I've never seen a griffin, but I've been told that they can look inside a person and see what's there."

"That is true," said Sindar knowingly. "Griffins can read a man's heart, and if you carry evil of any kind, they will bar your path. They can be deadly enemies, so it is best to stay on their good side."

"And a sphinx as well? I don't know . . . " Halfdan mused, shaking his head and stroking his beard in thought.

"What about sphinxes?" Alex asked, knowing almost nothing about the creatures.

"They always speak in riddles," Halfdan answered. "If we don't answer its riddle correctly, it will attack us."

"That is true," said Sindar. "However, if you don't answer the sphinx at all, it will let you withdraw."

"Have you met a sphinx then?" Val questioned.

"I have," Sindar answered. "And I am relieved to say that I did not have to fight it."

"So you guessed its riddle correctly," said Val, sounding impressed.

"No," answered Sindar, shaking his head. "I couldn't answer the riddle, so I departed without speaking."

"If a sphinx can out-riddle an elf, we may be in for some serious trouble," said Halfdan.

"We do not know how far along the road the prince went, so our worries may be groundless," Val commented.

"We don't know if the prince even stayed on the road," Bregnest added grimly. "The road is just the starting point. Though if we meet the guardians of the road, they may be able to tell us where to look for the Horn of Moran."

They all agreed that it was pointless to worry about the guardians, at least until they reached the Mountains of the Moon.

They continued to ride north, and the days passed by with little to tell them apart. The ride was enjoyable and the landscape was pleasant, now that summer was coming to Norsland. Three days out from Ollvi they left the open fields of the settled lands and continued through large pine forests, mixed with wide areas of rolling grasslands.

The company continued to keep watch at night, and Alex continued to read and practice his magic in the early morning hours. Sindar seemed to enjoy watching Alex practice his spells, and he would sometimes make comments on how well Alex was doing. Alex also continued to update Whalen about the adventure, and about how his studies were going.

After three weeks of traveling, they could see distant snow-capped mountains ahead of them. Alex guessed they were the

Mountains of the Moon, and he also guessed that it would take at least another three weeks for the company to reach them.

Late one afternoon, the company came to a sudden halt. The pine forest they had been riding through had ended, and in front of them was a steep, rocky hillside that dropped into a wide valley below. The road leading into the valley was badly damaged and worn by the weather, and it was overgrown with bushes and small trees in several places.

"We'll wait for morning before trying it," said Bregnest thoughtfully. "We've traveled far today, and the horses are tired."

"Best to rest," said Sindar, looking down the hillside at the broken and overgrown road. "It will take some effort to get down this safely."

They all agreed that it would be best to wait for better light, and they moved back into the trees a short distance to set up their camp. They didn't talk much as they ate their evening meal, and everyone seemed to have their own thoughts. After dinner, they sat quietly around the campfire, not even sharing stories as they normally did.

Without warning, Sindar suddenly jumped up and moved away from the fire. The others got to their feet as well, their hands moving to their weapons as they looked into the darkness. Alex wondered what had alarmed Sindar, but he didn't have long to worry before Sindar reappeared.

"Alex, put the fire out. Quickly," whispered Sindar. "There are goblins moving down the valley."

Alex magically put out the fire so that there would be no smoke, and looked around at his friends' faces. They all gathered around Sindar to find out what he had seen and how much trouble they might be in.

"Goblins are rare in Norsland," Bregnest whispered.

"Rare, but not unheard of," Andy added.

"I count perhaps threescore of them in the valley," said Sindar. "Though they will have scouts out as well."

"Do you think they are aware of us?" questioned Val, looking in the direction of the valley.

"I don't think so. Our fire was small and hidden in the trees. And we are downwind of them, so they can't have smelled us."

"Threescore may be few for goblins, but more than enough for the six of us," said Halfdan, fingering the ax at his side.

"We have a choice to make then," said Sindar, looking at Bregnest. "We can remain where we are and hope they don't discover us, or we can move back the way we have come, which might be the wisest thing to do. There is also a third choice, though I doubt any of us would like it—we could stand and fight."

"All you say is true," said Bregnest. "Battle, however, is the last thing we want."

"If the goblin scouts are any good, they'll find us here for sure," said Halfdan.

"The horses are too tired for us to make a run for it," Val added. "I doubt we would make it more than a mile or two."

"Gather your gear," Bregnest ordered. "We can't stay here and we can't run, so we'll do what we can. We'll walk the horses back the way we came, and hope for the best."

"There was some rocky ground two, maybe three, miles

back," Andy whispered. "We'd be out of the trees but able to see anything coming toward us."

"I remember some large rocks on the east side of the road," said Alex. "If we can reach them, we would have some cover as well."

"Two or three miles is a long walk, so we'd best get moving," said Bregnest. "Keep your horses quiet, and no talking. Sindar, scout ahead of us, but not too far. If we are attacked, I want you close."

They moved into the darkness as quietly as they could. The night air was still, and every sound they made seemed incredibly loud to Alex. He wished there was some wind to help cover the noise they were making, but his wish went unanswered.

Alex didn't know much about goblins, but what he did know didn't make him feel good. Goblins were warriors, and they could see in the dark. If the goblins found them, they would have to fight for their lives. And with sixty or more goblins so close, Alex wasn't feeling too confident.

Without thinking about it, Alex rested his hand on the hilt of his sword. The touch of the cold metal calmed his mind, just as it had in the past, but this time he could feel the magic slipping into him, and with it came the desire to destroy the goblins. They were evil after all, and the world would be better if they were destroyed. In fact, they should be thinking of how to kill the goblins, not looking for a way to escape them.

"Take your hand off the sword," a voice whispered. "Don't touch it unless you are attacked."

Alex jerked his head around to see who had spoken, but nobody was there. Slowly he let his hand fall to his side, his mind focusing on the path ahead of him. His desire to kill the goblins had been strong, but now it seemed foolish. Six against sixty? The company wouldn't stand a chance in a fight; they would all be killed.

Time seemed to slow down. The rocky place Alex remembered seemed to be further away than he'd guessed. Troubled thoughts filled his mind as the group continued to walk, and the thoughts weren't all about goblins. This wasn't the first time he'd heard a voice that seemed to be coming from inside his own head.

Alex was starting to think they had gone too far, that they'd missed the rocky place in the darkness, when Bregnest came to a sudden stop. Without speaking, he motioned for the others to follow him off the road, pointing to a high spot a few hundred yards away where four stones, each one nearly as tall as Alex, formed a rough square, giving them some cover. They started forward once more, moving slower than they had before and unavoidably making more noise. Some of the rocks on the hillside were loose, and they clacked loudly against each other as the horses walked over them.

"This will have to do," Bregnest said quietly when they reached the standing stones. "We'll tie the horses between the rocks, and—"

His words were cut short as Sindar dove forward, knocking both Alex and Andy to the ground. Alex heard a loud crack, and then what sounded like a stick being dropped on the rocks.

"Arrows," Halfdan growled. "We're in trouble now."

"Let the horses run," Bregnest yelled. "Get into the square."

Alex let go of Shahree's reins as he tried to get to his feet. He could hear the other horses already running across the stony ground, but Shahree stood still, waiting for Alex to command her.

"Go!" Alex yelled, afraid that an arrow would hit his horse at any moment. "Guide the others to safety. I will call you when the danger has passed."

Shahree snorted and dashed into the darkness, vanishing in seconds. Alex stumbled over loose gravel and crashed into one of the large stones, falling to his knees. His mind raced with fear, and he tried as hard as he could to focus and control his emotions. The goblins had them trapped, and he couldn't see any way for them to escape.

"Is anyone hit?" Sindar questioned.

"Thanks to you, no," Andy answered in a shaky voice.

"They will be coming soon," said Bregnest. "I'll take the north side. Sindar, the south. Alex and Val, the east. Halfdan and Andy, the west. Stay near the rocks, and don't let them draw you away."

Stay near the rocks, Alex repeated to himself as he drew his sword.

The magic of Moon Slayer flooded him, and just in time. As soon as the sword was in his hand the goblins came from all directions. Alex's fear disappeared, and the desire to destroy the goblins was stronger than ever. Taking one quick step forward, he drove his sword through the first goblin warrior and was back behind the rocks before an arrow could find him.

Two more goblins appeared, one of them tripping over the body in his rush to reach the rocks. Alex brought his sword down on the goblin's head, while Val took care of the other one with several quick slashes from both his sword and his dagger.

"Everyone still all right?" Bregnest questioned in the darkness.

"That was only a test," Halfdan commented after everyone had said they were fine. "They're testing our defenses. They'll come in greater numbers before long."

"First they will give us some time," Sindar added. "In case we decide to run for it and make ourselves easy targets."

Sindar was right. The night was silent for a long time; Alex could hear his friends breathing around him. He knew the goblins were still there, just out of sight, waiting for the right time to attack again. The magic of his sword urged him to move forward, to go out and hunt down the evil in the darkness, but he resisted.

Alex tried to relax, but it wasn't easy. Taking several deep breaths he focused his thoughts on something other than the trouble they were in. At first he couldn't think of anything at all, and then he thought about the goblins. Why were they even here? The goblins had been moving down the valley, but where were they going? The more he thought about the goblins, the more he felt his magic moving outward, away from him.

Unsure of what he was doing, Alex let his magic flow. He felt the emotions of his friends for a moment—their worries and fears—but then his magic moved on. Hoping that his magic could somehow help, Alex focused on every thought and feeling that came into his mind. There was nothing for a time, and then a mix of hate and fear crashed into his mind.

He pressed himself against the rock he was standing next to so he wouldn't fall down. A wave of thoughts washed over him, and as he struggled to sort them out, he suddenly understood.

"They will come from the north in force," Alex said softly. "One or two from each of the other sides, but at least a dozen from the north."

"How do you—" Val questioned, but stopped short when he saw Alex's face.

"Magic?" Bregnest asked.

"Yes," said Alex, pushing himself away from the rock. "They will be here in a few minutes."

"Alex and Sindar with me on the north," Bregnest ordered without asking any more questions. "Sindar, keep an eye on the others, just in case."

They had barely moved into position when the goblins appeared, howling and yelling like demons. Alex let the magic of his sword guide him as he fought, but he continued to resist the urge to rush out and slay every goblin he could find.

The battle was short and bloody, and near the end, Alex looked around in time to see a huge goblin hit Halfdan with a hammer-like weapon. Halfdan went down hard, and Sindar quickly drove both his swords into the goblin's chest. The elf reached down to check Halfdan for wounds, and Alex was glad Halfdan hadn't been killed.

"Take more than a little tap to keep me down," Halfdan growled in defiance.

"Why don't they come in larger numbers?" Val questioned. "They could easily overwhelm us if they sent more warriors."

"A game," Sindar answered softly. "It is a game to them.

Goblins love to gamble, and we have given them the perfect opportunity."

"What do you mean?" Alex questioned.

"They gamble on who will come against us," Sindar answered. "They place bets on how many will return, on how many of us they will kill or capture. The lives of others, even others of their own kind, mean little to goblins. They will gamble all night if they can."

"And when morning comes?" Bregnest questioned.

"If we can hold until morning, we may have a chance to escape," said Sindar. "If we try to run now, we have no chance at all."

"Then we'd better build up our defenses," said Halfdan. "We can pile up their dead and make a wall to funnel their next attack into a smaller space."

The night seemed endless, as did the number of goblins that came out of it. Alex and his friends would fight for a few minutes, killing eight or ten goblins. They'd move the dead goblins to form grotesque walls around the small square of stones, and then Alex and his friends would rest and wait for the next attack.

Alex always knew when the goblins were coming, and where the most goblins would be, and Bregnest never questioned how he knew. Alex's knowledge was keeping them alive, but he wasn't sure it would be enough.

At first his magic let him know which direction the main attack would come from, but as the night wore on, Alex's magic showed him more. He knew there were more than the sixty goblins Sindar had originally estimated. Several hundred goblins encircled the hilltop, and at times he could even hear what they were saying.

"It will be dawn in about two hours," Sindar said after another short battle.

"A long time to hold our ground," said Val. "Perhaps we should try to cut our way through. Head south. The goblins are less likely to follow us toward a city, and—"

"No," Alex interrupted. "We can't fight our way out to the south."

"Why not?" Bregnest questioned. "What do you see?"

"I . . . I don't know," Alex answered. "Someone has arrived, someone in charge. He's not happy that we are here. The goblins need to be someplace else, and we are slowing them down. The leader is sending something to put an end to this problem—to us."

"Sending something?" Halfdan questioned.

"I don't know what it means," Alex went on as if he hadn't heard the question. "A hand, a fist . . . I don't understand."

"A fist," Sindar repeated in a worried tone. "That's what goblins call their shaman. Goblin shamans have powerful magic, and they are normally escorted by a hundred of their fiercest warriors."

"Then our troubles just got worse," said Val. "We need to make a run for it, before this goblin shaman gets here."

"But without horses, how far can we run?" Halfdan questioned.

"We can't stay here," said Andy.

"Alex," Bregnest said softly, "can you tell where their lines are the weakest? If we can hit them where and when they don't expect it, we might be able to break through."

Alex didn't answer for several seconds as he let his magic search around them. Most of the goblins were to the south, expecting them to run. He wasn't sure where the shaman and his escort would be, but the leader of the goblins was to their west.

"North and east," Alex finally said. "That's where the fewest goblins are."

"Then we move, as soon as their next attack is defeated," said Bregnest. "If we head out as soon as the attacking goblins are down, the noise of our movement might go unnoticed."

"If we are attacked before we can make our escape, do we stay as a group, or is it every man for himself?" Val questioned.

"A coldhearted question to ask, but one that must be answered," said Sindar. "Some of us must escape to take a warning to the people of Norsland if nothing else."

"The words are bitter, but it is every man for himself," said Bregnest. "Sindar, Halfdan—you are both able to see better in the dark than the rest of us. You two will lead. Alex, Val, and Andy will follow you. I'll bring up the rear."

"As soon as the next battle is over then," said Sindar, bowing to Bregnest. "May fate smile on us all."

"They are coming from the north," Alex said after a few minutes of silence. "Only from the north this time. There are no other goblins approaching."

No one said anything as they all prepared for the fight and the desperate flight that would follow. Alex didn't like the idea of leaving his friends behind if they couldn't escape, but Bregnest had said the words. "Every man for himself" meant exactly what it sounded like. Each of them was to try to escape, not stopping to help their friends or to fight off the goblins. They were to escape at any cost, and then take a warning to the people of Norsland.

"Here they come," Sindar whispered in the darkness.

Alex and the others didn't wait for the goblins to reach the rocks, but charged out to meet them head on. The goblins were taken by surprise, and it didn't take long for the company to finish them off. Sindar and Halfdan headed northeast at a trot as soon as the last goblin was down. Alex let Val and Andy move ahead of him as he followed, hoping to keep as many of his friends as safe as he could.

They went on for a time, and Alex searched the land around him with his magic. He couldn't feel any goblins near them, and for a moment he felt relieved, but then he realized his mistake. Something was hiding the goblins from his magic, something he had never encountered before, and that could mean only one thing. The goblin shaman was close by, working his own magic to hide his warriors and trap the party on open ground.

He had to warn the others, but Alex knew that calling out would be a mistake. He looked behind him, but Bregnest was nowhere to be seen. Cursing himself for not noticing the shaman's magic sooner, Alex raced after his friends. Bregnest would catch up in a few minutes—he couldn't be that far behind—and then they could make a new plan for their escape.

Running as fast as he could and still being silent, Alex sent his magic out ahead of him. He couldn't see far in the darkness, but he knew his magic would lead him to the others faster than his eyes could.

Alex hadn't run far before he stopped short. His magic didn't feel anything ahead of him, not even the empty land. It was as if a cloud of darkness had covered him, smothering his magic and leaving him blind. He was completely helpless, and his friends were running into a trap.

A flame of anger came to life inside Alex's chest and he started forward once more. He had failed his friends, and he was angry with himself. He had been foolish, trusting magic that he didn't understand and had never used before. It must have been easy for the shaman to use him, to turn his confidence against him. Now he would die—worse, his friends would die—because he hadn't been smart enough to see the trap.

He drew Moon Slayer and the magic of his sword flowed into him, joining with his own anger as it came. Alex didn't try to hold back his anger or his desire to destroy goblins; he let the feelings grow inside of him. The goblins would pay for the lives of his friends before this night was over. He would kill them all if he could, and he would destroy the shaman that had used him.

He started running once more, letting the magic of his sword guide his steps. It wasn't long before Alex saw three dead goblins lying near a narrow path. His friends had put up a fight; perhaps there was still hope. When at last the path came to a meadow, he found what he was looking for.

The first three goblins never knew he was there, and the six who were close to them only had time to scream in fear before

Alex hacked them down. The screams alerted other warriors, but that didn't save them. Goblin weapons and armor shattered under the force of Moon Slayer as Alex drove headlong into his enemy. Broken steel and goblin blood fell like rain in the clearing, and then the unexpected happened.

Alex felt something powerful and as cold as ice hit him from behind. Pain filled his mind and drove him to his knees. He lifted his head and saw his sword on the ground a few yards in front of him, but he couldn't remember dropping it. A great weight seemed to be resting on his back.

"Your sword is no match for my magic, boy," a rough, jeering voice said from Alex's left. "Take him. Put him with the others. We'll have some good sport with this lot once we get home."

Take him.

Those two words burned into Alex's mind, igniting his anger once more. *Take him*—as if he were no threat, as if he were a piece of baggage to be carried away. He would not be taken, not by these foul creatures, and he would not submit to the magic that held him down. His friends might already be lost, but he would make the goblins pay for that loss.

As his anger rose up inside of him, the weight on his back grew lighter. Alex pushed himself to his feet, turning to look at the goblin who had spoken. Even in the shadow-filled meadow Alex could see the shaman clearly. A strange black mist filled with purple and blue streaks seemed to float around his enemy like a lightning storm at night. In his right hand the shaman held a staff with what looked like a human skull attached to the top of it. Seeing the skull sent Alex into an even greater rage, but instead of letting the anger take control, he used it to focus his thoughts and his magic.

The goblin's eyes grew wide as Alex stood up. The purple and blue flashes around the shaman grew brighter and spun around him with dizzying speed. He was terrible to look at, but his voice was full of fear when he started to yell.

"Kill him! Kill him now!"

Alex reached out for his sword and it flew through the air to his hand. Even as his fist closed around the hilt of the sword, the dark blade was moving, becoming a blue-white flame. Three warriors stood between Alex and the shaman, but the flaming sword passed through them without slowing, instantly turning them to ash.

The shaman raised his left hand to cast a spell, but he wasn't fast enough. The world seemed to slow down around Alex, and for a moment he could hear no sound at all. He didn't move forward to kill the shaman with his sword, he only moved his own left hand in a small circle.

Flames exploded from the shaman's chest, rising fast and hot and spinning wildly around the rest of his body. The shaman screamed in agony as a whirlwind of flame consumed him. Alex poured all of his anger into the fire, letting it grow larger and hotter with each passing second. The tornado of blue-white flame was more than thirty feet tall when it started to move with deadly speed and accuracy.

Goblins ran in every direction, yelling and screaming words that Alex didn't hear. Wherever the goblins went, the flames followed, burning them like dry grass on a windy day. Rocks and trees exploded when the heat of the flames touched them, the debris tearing apart any goblins that were nearby. Soon it looked as if the entire forest was on fire, and Alex did nothing to slow the flames.

Once more he let his magic flow outward, searching for the cursed creatures he wanted so much to destroy. There were a few goblins left in the forest around him, but most were running away in panic. He could feel more goblins in the distance, but they were too far away for the flames of his anger to reach them. They would live for now, but sooner or later he would find them and destroy them, just as he had destroyed their shaman.

Slowly Alex's anger faded. With his rage spent, the tornado of flame flickered and died out, leaving only the burning trees to light the meadow around him. He was tired, worn out, and terribly sad. His friends were lost, he was alone, and all he wanted to do was sleep.

Dropping to the ground, Alex tried to think. The shaman had said something about the others, but in his anger he hadn't been listening. It was something important, something he needed to remember, but it wouldn't come to him. Before he could force the answer out of his tired brain, Alex collapsed into unconsciousness.

Chapter Eight

Hostages

It was a few seconds before Alex realized he was awake and that the feeling of something approaching was more than just another bad dream. He didn't move a muscle as he waited, letting his magic tell him what he needed to know. He tightened his grip on Moon Slayer, ready for whoever or whatever was creeping up on him.

In a flash of speed Alex was on his feet, his sword raised and ready to strike. Sindar jumped back in surprise, his own swords coming up in defense. For a second the two of them looked at each other, unable to believe what they were seeing.

"Alex! You survived," Sindar almost shouted.

"Sindar, you're alive," Alex said at the same time.

They threw their arms around each other like long lost brothers, and for a minute nothing else in the world mattered.

"The others?" asked Alex, as they broke apart. "Have you seen any sign of them?"

Sindar shook his head "I thought . . . I thought you were all dead because of my foolishness."

"Foolishness? What are you talking about?"

"I should have known this was a trap," Sindar answered

slowly. "I have fought goblins many times before. I know how cunning they can be. I should have known that an open path would lead to a trap. Forgive me, Alex. I've failed."

"It's not your fault," Alex said softly. "If anyone is to blame, it's me. I should have noticed the shaman's magic sooner. I shouldn't have been so confident in my own abilities. If I hadn't believed everything my magic told me, this never would have happened."

"You are not to blame," Sindar replied. "And perhaps neither am I. Enough of doubts and blame—there will be time for that another day. What about the others? I've seen no sign of them, and I've searched the dead between here and the rocks we took cover behind last night."

"I haven't seen anyone," said Alex. "What happened to you during the battle?"

"Halfdan and I were in the lead," Sindar said. "Fifteen or twenty goblins attacked us, and we were separated in the fight. I tried to get back to the rest of the group, but more goblins appeared. I thought it best to lead as many of them away from the company as I could, so I killed a few to make sure they would follow me and I led them west."

"He said to put me with the others," Alex said suddenly. "'Put him with the others. We'll have some good sport when we get home,' that's what he said."

"Who said that?" Sindar asked in alarm.

"The goblin shaman. He was here when I entered the meadow. He hit me with some kind of magic that pinned me to the ground. I don't remember everything that happened, but I know he said to put me with the others."

"The shaman? Did he escape with the other goblins?" Sindar questioned in a worried tone.

"No, I destroyed him," Alex answered, sitting down on a large rock.

"It would have been better if our friends had died with him," Sindar said slowly. "Death is better than being hostage to a goblin."

"Hostage?" Alex questioned in alarm.

"You are sure the shaman said to put you with the others?" Sindar asked, ignoring Alex's question.

"Yes, I'm sure that's what he said."

"Then the others have been captured, probably with the help of the shaman's magic. The goblins will take them back to their caves, and then . . ."

"If our friends are alive we have to go after them," Alex said. "If there is any chance at all of saving them we must try."

"Yes. It will be difficult, but we must try."

"Let's get started," said Alex, standing up once more. "The goblins have been running for hours, we need to hurry if we are going to catch them."

"Rest a little longer, Alex," Sindar answered. "You've had a long night and used a great deal of magic. You will need all the rest you can get if we are to chase the goblins on foot."

"We won't be on foot for long," said Alex. "The horses may have run, but I can call Shahree back to me. She'll bring the other horses with her, and then we can go."

"Then call to your friend, and rest while she comes to you," Sindar said, his voice little more than a whisper. "I will search for any signs of a trail, and try to find our friends' weapons while you gather your strength."

Sindar hurried off as soon as he had spoken, leaving Alex alone.

Alex stood for several minutes, trying to relax and letting his feelings melt away. His mind became clear, and he focused his thoughts on Shahree, trying to picture her as clearly in his mind as he could. He knew that Shahree would not go far and that she had only run becuse he had told her to. For a long moment he held his breath, concentrating on his horse.

"Shahree," Alex called softly. "Shahree, come to me."

For a moment he stood listening, hoping that his magic had worked. There was no reply to his words, though he had not expected one. And then his magic told him that Shahree had heard him and that she was already gathering the other horses and galloping back to him.

"I have found our friends' weapons," said Sindar when he returned to Alex a short time later. "And I have found the trail of the goblins who have our friends. Now we must consider how best to pursue our enemy."

"What do you mean?" Alex questioned, thinking that they would simply ride out as soon as the horses returned.

"Goblins will not travel in sunlight unless they absolutely must," said Sindar. "They are unsteady on their feet while the sun is up."

"So if we catch them in sunlight, we will have a great advantage."

"I doubt that we will catch them during the day," said Sindar, rubbing his face in thought. "These goblins will move at night. They will find a hiding place when the sun starts to rise and not move again until it begins to set. Our advantage is that days are long in Norsland during the summertime, so we will have more time to pursue them and they will have less time to flee."

"And when we overtake them?"

"Then we will rescue our friends, or at the least avenge their deaths. Rescue will be difficult, as goblins would sooner kill their captives than let them go."

"Then we have a great disadvantage in trying to save them."

"We may find a way," said Sindar. "Much will depend on where and when we find them."

"How many goblins do you think there are? I mean, how many are we going to have to kill to free our friends?" Alex questioned.

"Fifty—maybe sixty of them," Sindar answered. "From the trails I could find, it appears that they have broken into smaller groups and are all running for their holes. I would guess the loss of their shaman has them scared. Whatever trouble they were on their way to make, it will not happen now."

"At least we have done some good," said Alex. "The horses will be here soon, and then we can start after the goblins."

"They will know you for a wizard and a warrior, and they will fear you," Sindar commented. "You have used a lot of magic; perhaps you should rest a little longer before we start."

"Their fear may drive them to kill our friends," said Alex in a worried tone. "I can rest once we have rescued the others."

"Their fear will drive them to run, but not to kill the

others. They will keep them alive as hostages, and use them to drive you away, if they can."

"How could they use my friends to drive me away?" Alex asked.

"They will make threats and promises. They will promise to let them go if you will promise not to attack. Their promises will be lies, of course, but as a wizard, you would be bound by your promise."

"I would not feel bound by anything I promised to goblins," said Alex defiantly.

"They are clever and wicked. They will make you promise by something that matters to you greatly. I have seen others caught in such traps before."

"I do not know what promise goblins would ask that I would feel bound to keep, but I do not wish to find out. Perhaps we should start walking now, the horses can catch up."

"Your magic needs time to recover," Sindar said slowly. "And we may need all the magic you can summon to save our friends."

"My magic is fine," Alex answered. "I will be able to do whatever needs doing when the time comes."

"Are you so sure?"

"I—" Alex started and stopped. "No, I guess I'm not. Whalen explained how there is only so much magic a wizard can do before it runs out. He told me that magic is like a bowl catching raindrops. Every bit of magic used takes some of the water out of the bowl, and it sometimes takes a long time for the bowl to fill up again."

"From the looks of this meadow, I would say you poured a

great deal of water out of your bowl," Sindar said in a worried tone.

"Whalen also said that different wizards have different sized bowls," Alex answered, not wanting to think about what might happen if his magic ran out. "He told me I would know when the bowl was nearly empty, and right now, it doesn't feel very empty."

"Very well," said Sindar. "We will begin our chase as soon as the horses return."

Shahree and the other horses appeared in less than an hour. Sindar and Alex checked them all to make sure they were unhurt before they started off after the goblins. Alex was worried for his friends and what the goblins might do to them, and his worries made him eager to be moving.

Sindar led the way, and Alex followed close behind him. The goblin path was easy to follow. The creatures had hacked at trees as they passed and stomped the grass flat; Alex could have followed the path in the dark if he had to.

"How do you know that our friends were captured by this group of goblins?" asked Alex.

"Boot prints," Sindar said. "The goblins trample everything, but here and there I see prints from leather boots."

"But how do you know they belong to Bregnest and the others?" asked Alex.

"Goblins don't wear leather boots. They either go barefoot, or they wear square-toed boots with iron soles."

Alex didn't ask any more questions, trusting that Sindar knew what he was doing. They rode without stopping until the sun was down and the only light was the deep red of the western horizon. Sindar insisted that they rest for a few hours and get something to eat. It had been a long time since Alex had eaten, and he was hungry, but he didn't feel at all sleepy.

"You are still hot with anger, though you seem to have your emotions under control," Sindar commented. "You should rest, even if you don't feel the need. When we overtake our enemy, you must be fresh and ready for battle."

Reluctantly Alex tried to sleep, but his dreams were full of goblins and he kept waking up. He finally managed to slip into a light but restful sleep. His mind remained alert as his body relaxed, and he let his thoughts search for a way to free his friends.

Before the sun was up the next morning, Alex and Sindar started following the goblin's trail. "I would guess from their tracks that only fifty or so of our enemy remain," said Sindar. "If no others join them, we may have a good chance of killing them all."

"Fifty goblins against the two of us?"

"I know. It seems unlikely that we could kill them all and save our friends at the same time."

"It is a difficult problem," Alex commented, seeing how troubled Sindar was. "First things first, however. We must find the goblins, and then we can decide how best to destroy them and rescue our friends."

"You are correct. These tracks are only hours old. I think if we ride hard, we may catch the goblins tonight. Though I would prefer finding them while the sun is up if we can, since that is when they will be the weakest."

"That would be best. If luck is with us, we may find the goblins tomorrow and free our friends by tomorrow night."

"And if luck is against us, we will slay the goblins before the third day arrives," Sindar said softly, his voice deadly cold.

All that day Alex and Sindar followed the goblins' trail through the forest and open meadows. Alex was surprised that the goblins had traveled so far so quickly, and their speed made him worry.

As darkness was covering the land, Sindar halted once more. He looked at the ground and then at Alex.

"These tracks are fresh," Sindar whispered. "We should rest here for a time. If the goblins discover that we are following them, they will move faster tonight, and our hopes of catching them tomorrow will be lost."

"Will they be watching the road behind them?" Alex questioned, climbing off Shahree.

"Probably. They know that you were left behind and that you may follow. They do not know that there are two of us—or at least I don't think they know. It would be to our advantage if they think you are alone."

"Have you thought of a way to rescue our friends?" Alex asked hopefully.

"I have an idea, but it is not yet clear to me. Much will depend on where we find the goblins hiding tomorrow."

Alex nodded his understanding and loosened Shahree's saddle. They might need to ride fast at a moment's notice, but he wanted to make her as comfortable as possible. Alex gently stroked Shahree's neck, whispering softly that he was sorry for her burden. Shahree nuzzled his shoulder but made no sound, and Alex knew that she understood.

Sindar let Alex sleep until midnight and then woke him to continue the chase. Alex felt completely refreshed and was glad to be back in pursuit of his friends. He didn't want to leave them in the goblins' hands any longer than he absolutely had to. And with Sindar's help and a little luck, they might be able to rescue them in less than a day now.

As dawn came once more, Sindar made Alex rest again. Alex was vexed by the delay, but he did as Sindar asked. Sindar, after all, knew a great deal more about goblins than he did. Alex slept for about an hour and then was up again, ready to carry on the chase.

Sindar looked troubled as they moved forward, however. This was the second full day of hunting, and soon the chase would be at an end, one way or another. Alex hoped that Sindar would find a way to rescue their friends, because he had no ideas at all.

Shortly after midday, Sindar stopped and motioned for Alex to remain where he was. Alex watched as Sindar jumped from his horse and moved into the trees without making a sound. Alex knew they must be close to the goblins, and he was starting to feel nervous. He had trusted to luck before, but he didn't like doing it when his friends' lives were on the line. When Sindar returned, he motioned for Alex to follow him back the way they had come. After about a mile, he spoke.

"The goblins are in a narrow gully," said Sindar. "The back of the gully is steep and they aren't watching it. That is where our friends are, with only a few guards watching them. There are three other men tied up as well. They appear to be soldiers, but I don't recognize the design on their uniforms."

"Three others?" Alex questioned, then shook his head. "Three or thirty, it doesn't matter if we can't get down the gully to them. If we had bows we might be able to kill the guards and then climb down to our friends and the others, but as we are . . ."

"We don't need bows. The mouth of the gully opens into a wide meadow, and on the far side of the meadow the trees are thick."

"How will that help us?" Alex questioned.

"My plan is this: Tonight, when the sun touches the tops of the trees, you start dozens of fires on the far side of the meadow. The goblins will think that a large number of men or some other enemy has camped there, and they will be worried. While they are distracted, I will climb down the back of the gully and free our friends."

"They will see you," Alex protested. "And even if you make it down, you'll be trapped in the back of the gully."

"Perhaps," Sindar agreed. "However, I should be able to kill the guards and free our company. I doubt they will be in any shape to fight, at least at first. That won't matter because once they are safe, I will attack the goblins from behind. Then you can ride forward and attack from the front."

"A risky plan at best," said Alex, shaking his head as he tried to think of a better way to rescue their friends. "There are fifty or more goblins, Sindar. I know they fear our swords, and I know Moon Slayer can help us kill them, but—fifty of them?"

"We have no choice," Sindar insisted. "It is unlikely that we will catch them in a spot like this again. In another day or two they may reach their own caves, and all hope will be lost. The goblins are afraid, and the fires you conjure will add to their fear. Those who let fear govern them often make mistakes."

"You're right," Alex agreed reluctantly. "We have no choice. We must do what we can and hope for the best. Perhaps I can find another way to add to their fear. I might be able to cast an illusion or two that will help us."

"Rest now," said Sindar. "There are still several hours before we need to move, and you have slept little in the past two days."

"I'm fine. I will have time to rest when this is finished."

"Try to rest your mind at least," Sindar persisted. "You will need all your power and all your luck this night."

Chapter Nine

Rescue

Alex managed to sleep for perhaps two hours before he was up and moving around once more. He was nervous and worried and even a little scared. The plan he and Sindar had agreed on was terribly risky and almost sure to fail. Unfortunately, it was the only plan they had, and Alex knew this might be the only chance they had to save their friends.

Alex knew Sindar was tense as well, but neither of them spoke about what was going to happen. They simply waited for the sun to set and hoped that their plan would work.

Alex tried to think of something he could do to scare the goblins even more. He had thought of using illusions to add to their fear, but for a long time he couldn't think of anything that would make the goblins want to run instead of fight. When the answer finally came to him, Alex almost laughed out loud. It was an illusion he was sure he could create and one that was sure to make the goblins run away as fast as their legs could carry them.

"A dragon?" Sindar questioned when Alex presented his

idea. "Indeed, there are few creatures that would not run away from a dragon, but can you do it?"

"I can create the illusion of a dragon," Alex answered confidently. "I might even be able to make it breathe fire."

"Then perhaps one large fire on the hillside," said Sindar. "As if the dragon is just waking. Have your illusion fly out of the fire toward the gully. And if you can manage to ignite a few trees along the way, it would help."

"I'll do all that I can," said Alex. The sun was already dropping into the west, and he walked to Shahree and tightened her saddle. "Let's get moving. It's time."

"When the sun touches the trees and the meadow is covered with shadow," Sindar reminded Alex.

"Be careful," Alex said. "I don't want to come to the wall looking for you."

"You will not find me there. If your dragon does not drive the goblins off, I will attack. If you hear the sound of battle, come quickly, my friend."

"As fast as I can," Alex answered, turning Shahree into the trees.

Alex rode in a great loop around the goblin camp, making his way to the far side of the meadow. He had studied the land as they had waited and knew exactly which path to take. Sindar rode in the opposite direction, and Alex hoped that he would arrive quietly at the back of the gully, unnoticed by the goblins below.

Alex tried to clear his mind as he rode, but his worries persisted no matter what he did. Absentmindedly he patted

Shahree's neck, knowing that he might have to ride her into battle for the first time.

"I must move swiftly, my friend," Alex said softly to the horse. "I do not willingly take you into this fight, but it seems I have no choice."

Shahree snorted at his words, as if unconcerned by the thought of battle. Alex patted her neck again. He was glad that she at least didn't seem worried about what was coming.

Reaching the place above the meadow where he would create his illusion, Alex dismounted and looked toward the gully where his enemy was waiting. He couldn't see much except for an occasional flash of sunlight on steel. Obviously the goblins had set a watch at the mouth of the gully, and Alex hoped they were paying attention.

As the last rays of sunlight left the meadow and the sun touched the treetops, Alex mounted Shahree once more. He was still nervous and worried, but it was time to set their plan into action.

"Let us hope for the best, my friend," Alex said to Shahree.

Shahree snorted in excitement, and Alex let loose his magic, sending an entire grove of pine trees into flames. The trees burned like matchsticks, and as the flames reached into the sky, Alex created his illusion.

A huge red dragon exploded out of the burning trees. Alex let loose a thunderclap spell that sent flaming branches flying in every direction. He let his thoughts slip into the illusion, which allowed him to control it and see the world through the dragon's eyes. A wild sense of freedom filled him, taking his breath away as the illusion lifted into the darkening sky.

For a few seconds the dragon hovered over the meadow, and in those seconds Alex fought to keep himself from becoming part of his own illusion. He had known that creating illusions could be dangerous, but he had not known how dangerous. The beauty and power of the dragon filled his mind, and he longed to have the complete freedom that the dragon shape offered.

Shahree snorted and reared slightly, shaking Alex from his thoughts. Alex could still see through the eyes of his illusion, but the desire to become part of it was gone. Refocusing his mind, he sent his dragon diving toward the meadow and the unsuspecting goblins.

The dragon breathed out a ball of flame as it dropped toward the gully, and in the firelight Alex could see that his idea was working far better than he'd expected. Goblins ran wildly out of the gully, fighting past the slower goblins in front of them. The dragon flew over the gully before lifting back into the air and turning slowly toward the meadow.

"Now, my friend," said Alex as he urged his horse forward. "We need to reach the others before any more trouble finds us."

Shahree whinnied loudly and galloped down the hillside. As they reached the open meadow, Shahree broke into a run.

Alex set his illusion to circling the meadow, allowing the circles to grow larger and larger with each pass, as though the dragon was hunting.

As Alex rode into the gully he called out to Sindar, "Are they all right?"

"They are alive," said Sindar. "Though they've had a rough time of it, and were treated none too gently."

Alex jumped from his saddle and ran forward to help cut the ropes from the rest of the company. He left the unknown three men tied up for the time being. His friends all looked pale and tired, but unhurt, and that was a huge relief. Alex wanted to cheer, but then he saw the fear in his friends' eyes. He turned to see what they were looking at and realized that they could see his illusion flying past the gully.

"Didn't you tell them about the illusion?" Alex asked.

"I tried," Sindar answered. "But a few of the goblins were still in the gully when I arrived—trying to hide from your creation, I suspect. I dealt with them quickly enough, but there hasn't been time to explain the mischief of a clever wizard."

Alex sent his illusion into a wider circle, using it to search the land for any possible enemies while he and Sindar explained things to their friends. It took some time for all the questions to be answered, and while they talked, Alex started a campfire. He knew that it was safe for them to stay here, at least for tonight, and he thought a meal would do everyone some good.

"Our weapons?" Bregnest asked.

"We recovered them before starting after you," said Sindar, reaching for his magic bag. "We had great hopes of returning them to you."

"And your hopes have proven true," said Bregnest, taking his weapons from Sindar. "We are all very much in yours and Alex's debt."

"We did what we had to do," Sindar answered, handing

out the rest of the weapons. "But there are other matters we need to discuss." Sindar's eyes moved to the three men who were still tied up.

Bregnest turned to look at the men and nodded. Alex saw his friend stiffen in the firelight, and without asking, he knew that Bregnest recognized the uniforms the men were wearing.

"You are a long way from home, brothers," Bregnest said slowly. "What brings soldiers from the house of Domina to Norsland?"

"Lord Bregnest," one of the men answered, bowing his head slightly. "Our lives are in your hands, so it would seem an honest answer is the only one that will do. I fear, however, that honesty may cost us what little we still have left."

"Speak freely," Bregnest answered calmly. "If there is any way to repay your honesty, I will find it."

"So be it," said the man with a sigh. "We were sent by Lord Kappa to follow you and your company. In following you, we ran into a host of goblins. I fear the rest of our men were destroyed, and we three were unlucky enough to be captured by the foul creatures."

"How many men were with you?" Bregnest questioned. "And what were your orders concerning myself and my friends?"

"There were forty of us—a full company," the man answered. "Our orders were to follow you at a distance and not interfere or help you in any way. If you and your company appeared to be returning to Alusia before the spring festival, we were to detain you and escort you back to Kappa at a relaxed pace."

"The spring festival," Bregnest repeated. "Yes, that makes sense."

"What is the spring festival?" Alex asked.

"It is the end of the rainy season in Alusia and the start of the planting season," Bregnest answered as he rubbed his nose.

"And how long before the festival starts?" Sindar asked.

"Almost seven months from now," said Bregnest. "So it appears we know how much time we have to finish our quest."

"That's all fine and well," said Val, "but there are more important matters to consider. The goblins may have run off, but they'll be back soon enough. We have a long way to travel and little time to watch after prisoners. It would be foolish to take these three with us, and reckless to simply let them go."

"You would have us kill defenseless men?" Sindar questioned.

"They've told us a bit about why they are here, but I doubt they've told us everything," Val replied. "I think they were sent to waylay us on our journey, like bandits. I think they would have killed us if the chance had appeared."

"That is not true," one of the bound men said hotly. "We were ordered to capture you, not to kill you. We are soldiers, not scum."

"Capture or kill, it comes to the same thing," Val said coldly. "But there is no need to risk our honor by killing these three. We can simply leave them for the goblins to find. That would be a much more fitting punishment than a quick and simple death."

Alex was concentrating on his illusion and searching for danger, but when he heard Val's suggestion, he turned his attention back to his friends. The idea of killing the men turned his blood cold, but the thought of leaving them tied up for the goblins to find was even worse.

"Your words are cold and cruel, Val," said Bregnest. "I hope it is only your anger talking. There are few enemies I would give willingly to goblins, and these three are not among them."

"We have to do something with them," Halfdan commented in an uneasy tone. "And we really can't take them with us."

"I will think on it," said Bregnest. "For now, we should eat and try to rest. Alex, is it safe to camp here for the night?"

"There are no goblins or any other enemies for many miles," Alex answered as he looked to the sky. "We are safe enough for the time being."

"Then we will stay here for now," said Bregnest. "A normal watch will do. These three will remain bound for now. In the morning we will decide what is to be done with them."

Alex's friends started setting up camp, and Alex watched his illusion as the dragon made one last large circle around them, and then hovered over the empty meadow. Val was right when he said that they couldn't take the three men with them on their quest, but Alex felt there had to be some other way to deal with them, a way to free the soldiers without putting the company at risk. If they let the soldiers go, they would return to Alusia and tell their story. The man named Kappa would send more soldiers and that would mean more trouble in the future. There was no simple answer, and Alex stood looking up at the dragon for a long time without seeing it as he tried to think.

"It is amazing, but it is time to let it go," Sindar commented from Alex's side.

Alex jumped slightly at the sound of Sindar's voice.

"Yes," Alex answered, lifting his hand and moving it back and forth as if erasing something from the sky.

The dragon remained still for a moment before it disappeared into a cloud of red and gold sparks. Alex stared into the darkness, and after a few minutes Sindar spoke again.

"How is your magic holding up? Are you getting close to the bottom of the bowl?"

"No, I don't think so," said Alex.

"You are sure that you will know when you are near your limit?"

"I believe I will know. Whalen explained it clearly to me, and I haven't seen or felt any of the signs yet."

"You have done a great deal of magic in a very short time, Alex. I would not press you on this, but I fear we may need more of your magic soon. If you are near your limit, things could become very difficult."

"Things are already difficult," said Alex. "Sindar, we can't kill those soldiers. And we can't leave them here for the goblins. We have to find something else to do with them."

"Their fate is not decided," Sindar said calmly. "If there is a way to set them free, Bregnest will find it."

"I am tired," Alex said after a long pause. "Perhaps something to eat and some sleep will help me think."

"Perhaps," Sindar agreed. "But Alex, this is not your

decision to make. Bregnest has the final word about what we do with those men. You may give your opinion, but you are bound to do as he decides."

"I know. I just hope the decision is something he can live with."

Alex turned and walked back to the campfire. Halfdan was already cooking, and the others looked almost too tired to eat. It was only after they had finished eating and Halfdan had taken some food to the three soldiers that anyone said anything.

"I should keep watch tonight," Sindar said. "The rest of you need to sleep, but I can rest and watch at the same time."

"A kind offer," said Halfdan, trying to hold back a yawn.

"Not a bad idea," said Bregnest. "We have a long walk ahead of us, and a good rest will help us on our way."

"Not as long a walk as you think," Sindar replied. "Our horses are tied up about a mile away. Alex was able to round them up the morning after we were attacked, which is why we were able to rescue you as soon as we did."

"A story I would like to hear, but now is not the time," said Bregnest. "Sindar, can you get the horses now? I think most of us can stay awake while you are gone."

"As you wish," Sindar answered, getting to his feet.

Once Sindar was gone, Alex looked around the campfire. His tired friends looked as if they were about to fall over, and he didn't believe any of them could stay awake until Sindar returned.

"Why don't you all lie down," Alex suggested. "I've had

more rest over the last few days than you have. I'll keep watch until Sindar returns."

Bregnest nodded his agreement with Alex's suggestion, and Andy, Halfdan, and Val got to their feet without comment and moved off to find their blankets. Bregnest, though, sat with Alex without speaking, his eyes locked on the campfire and his forehead wrinkled in thought. Alex didn't say anything, not wanting to interrupt Bregnest's thoughts. Finally, when Alex could hear Halfdan snoring softly, Bregnest spoke.

"Can you magically change what a man believes?"

"I'm not sure I understand what you're asking," Alex answered.

"Can you make them believe that they escaped from the goblins themselves?" Bregnest nodded his head toward the three soldiers. "Can you make them forget that we were with them, and that you and Sindar rescued us?"

"It is possible," Alex answered slowly. "I have never tried to do anything like that, Bregnest. I'm not sure I can. But if that is the only way to save their lives, I will try."

"There may be another way, but I'm not sure the others will accept it."

"They will accept your decision, whatever it is," said Alex. "I would like to set the soldiers free. I do not believe you would leave them here for the goblins to find, and I know you don't want to kill them. If there is another way, please use it."

Bregnest didn't reply, but simply nodded. They sat in silence, watching the fire burn down, until Sindar returned with the horses. Patting Alex on the shoulder, Bregnest thanked him for speaking his mind, and then went to get some sleep.

"He seems less troubled," Sindar commented as he sat down beside Alex.

"I think he is," Alex replied.

"Perhaps you should get some sleep as well," said Sindar.

"Sleep does sound like a good idea," said Alex as he rubbed one ear. "I don't sense any danger close to us, but wake me if you need me."

If Alex had any dreams that night, he couldn't remember them when he woke. Slowly he rolled out of his blankets and pulled on his boots. Sindar was still sitting next to the campfire. Bregnest was already awake, pacing back and forth beside the fire with a troubled look on his face. Without speaking, Alex took a seat beside Sindar and waited. It wasn't long before the others started to wake up and gather around the fire as well. No one said anything as they waited to hear what Bregnest would say.

"A decision must be made." Bregnest stopped pacing and turned to look at the company. "But before that decision is made, I would like each of you to speak your mind concerning our captives. Sindar, your thoughts, please."

"I will not leave them for the goblins to find," Sindar answered without hesitating. "I would prefer not to kill them if possible, but if our adventure is in danger from them, then I will do what must be done."

"Alex?" Bregnest questioned as Sindar fell silent.

"I would like to set them free," Alex answered. "I will not leave them for the goblins, and I will not kill them. If you decide they must die, I will not stand in your way, but I will not take part in their deaths."

"Val?"

"I would take back my rash words," said Val. "I spoke last night without thought, and I can see that my words have troubled you all. I would leave no man for goblins to take, but I cannot see how we can set them free. We are trying to save the kingdom of Athanor from war, and if three men must die for the greater good, then I say let them have a quick and clean death."

"Andy?"

"Like the others, I would not leave them for goblins," Andy answered slowly. "But I don't see how killing them would help us. Yes, they might tell others that we are still alive and searching for the Horn, but I don't see what harm that can do us. It might make it harder to return to Athanor when we are done, but that's going to be difficult anyway."

"Halfdan?"

"I see you've left me for last. I've had some experience with this kind of thing," said Halfdan with a sigh. "I was on an adventure once where we faced a similar problem, and I'm not proud of how we solved it. I did not vote to kill our prisoners, but I did not speak up to set them free either. I still see their faces in my nightmares. I would save the rest of you from living with the regrets and doubts that I live with. I say let them go. Let them go; we will face whatever trouble may come of it. If we kill them, we will have to live with it for the rest of our lives."

"You would risk our adventure and possibly our lives to set these men free?" Val questioned.

"I would," Halfdan answered firmly. "I know the price that must be paid for killing without cause."

"Enough," said Bregnest. "I have heard what you have to say, now I will hear what our captives can say for themselves. Halfdan, Andy, cut them free and bring them here."

Halfdan and Andy hurried to do as Bregnest said. Alex hoped that Bregnest would choose to set the men free. Bregnest had said something about another way, a way that the other members of the company might not accept. After hearing what his friends had to say, Alex hoped that Bregnest's other way would work.

"Well," Bregnest said when the three soldiers were standing next to the fire, "you've heard us talking. You know the decision we are trying to make and what your fate might be. Do you have anything to say that might influence our decision?"

"Lord Bregnest," one of the soldiers said, taking a step forward. "We have also talked. We all know you by name and by reputation. We have heard the stories of your adventures, the tales of what you have done for Athanor, and the rumors of good deeds you have done in secret. We can offer little to convince your friends that we mean you no harm, but we are soldiers of the house of Domina, sworn to protect the people of Athanor. As men of honor we offer to you, Lord Bregnest, the *rowshak el cal*."

"A great offer," Bregnest replied. "And the only one that could save your lives. As a lord of Athanor, I will accept your oath and call on the members of my company to witness it."

"What is a *rowshak el cal*?" Sindar questioned as the three soldiers dropped to one knee in front of Bregnest.

"The words are as old as Alusia," Bregnest answered. "I'm not sure of the exact translation, but it means a soul oath. They will take an oath on their souls not to betray us and to do as I ask. If any of them break their oath, the other two will hunt him down and kill him in the most painful way possible. If the others fail, then their family will take up the task, hunting the betrayer and his family to extinction."

"A powerful oath," said Halfdan. "I will be honored to act as witness."

"Words," Val said in a sour tone. "They may mean the words now, but will they remember them when they are free and safe?"

"Words are what make a man," Bregnest replied. "What is honor, Val? It is saying you will do something and then doing it. Honor is keeping your word, and adventurers are not the only people with honor."

"I . . . I'm sorry. I've trusted before and been betrayed," said Val. "I do not trust so easily anymore."

"Form a circle around us," Bregnest commanded the group.

Alex and the others obeyed, and Bregnest held out his left hand, palm up. Each of the soldiers placed his right hand on top of Bregnest's left, and then Bregnest put his right hand on top of them all.

"Make your oaths," said Bregnest.

The soldiers spoke softly in unison. Alex understood most of what they said, except for the words from the ancient language of Alusia. As the soldiers finished speaking, Bregnest said a few of the ancient words as well, accepting their oaths.

But before Bregnest could release the soldiers' hands,

Alex stepped forward. He put his own right hand on top of Bregnest's, and the words came to him as if he had always known them.

"I bind your oaths to you with a wizard's seal of magic and with hope. For as long as you keep the oaths you have sworn this day, good fortune will follow you and yours. In the instant you betray this oath, all that you hold dear will wither and rot before your eyes."

Alex felt a surge of power rush through him as he finished speaking, and he knew that Bregnest and the soldiers felt it as well. Alex lifted his hand and returned to the circle.

"So be it," Bregnest said after a moment of silence. He released the soldiers' hands.

Alex thought he should feel tired or dizzy because the magic he had just done was powerful, but he didn't. If anything, he felt more alert and awake than ever, full of energy and magic, ready for whatever lay ahead of them.

After a few minutes, Halfdan started cooking breakfast. The three soldiers sat to one side of the fire while Alex's friends put away their blankets and tended to the horses.

"Alex, are you all right?" Sindar questioned in a soft voice as he walked up beside him.

"I feel wonderful," Alex answered. "Maybe too good."

"That was some powerful magic," Sindar said. "Vankin told you that magic was like a bowl catching water and that there are limits to how much magic you can use. I would think you are getting close to your limits after sealing the oath like that."

"So would I," said Alex. "I've done less magic before and

felt dizzy or tired afterwards. The morning I lost the rabbit—the one I'd created out of a rock—I felt a little tired then. It didn't last long, but after using my magic, I felt like sitting for a bit, like I needed to catch my breath. But this time I don't feel tired at all. I feel like the bowl has instantly been refilled and I'm ready for anything."

"Strange," Sindar said in a thoughtful tone. "I think, before you use any more magic, you should send a message to Vankin. He might be able to explain what has happened, and I'm sure he will want to know about your bowl being filled again so rapidly."

"You are right," said Alex. "I'll write to him tonight when we make camp."

The rest of the morning was spent putting packs together for the three soldiers to take with them. Having no horses, they would have to walk, and it would take them some time before they would reach a town or city. Bregnest gave each of them a small bag of money so they could buy more food when they reached a town.

"What would you have us tell Kappa when we return?" one of the soldiers questioned.

"Only that you were attacked by goblins and managed to escape," Bregnest answered.

"He will ask about you and your company, Lord Bregnest," the man went on. "How would you have us answer?"

"Tell him that you did not see us," Bregnest replied. "Tell him that you don't know how we could have escaped the goblins when most of your company was destroyed."

"As you wish," said the soldier with a bow.

After the midday meal, the soldiers said good-bye and wished the company good luck before heading south. Alex and his friends followed the goblin path for most of the afternoon, turning more to the north a few hours before the sun set. If they were lucky, Alex thought they might be able to make their way through the woods and reach the road in two or three days. But how long it would take them to reach the Tower of the Moon was still a mystery.

Chapter Ten

Centaurs' Woods

It was late afternoon on the third day when Alex and his friends found the main road, and after riding north for a few miles, Bregnest had them set up camp for the night.

Alex had started to worry as they traveled. He was worried about the time it would take them to find the Horn of Moran and return it to Alusia. He was worried about his magic, too. Was it right that he felt full of magic and not tired or drained in any way? He had written a long letter to Whalen, explaining everything that had happened and exactly how he had felt, but so far Whalen had not written back.

They followed the road northward for three more days, and Alex was relieved that there were no signs of goblins or anything else that might be trouble. Alex's early morning watch remained his favorite time of the day as well, now that the company was together again. Alex continued his studies, but thought it best not to use any magic until he heard from Whalen, and Sindar agreed. Alex enjoyed talking with Sindar as much as anything. Sindar would answer questions he had and tell him stories of times long past. Sindar seemed to know a great deal about a great many things, and Alex thought he must be extremely old, even for an elf.

On the morning of their fourth day on the road, a geeb from Whalen finally arrived just as Alex was preparing to study his magic books. He was glad that the others were still asleep so he could read the letter in private.

Dear Alex,

I was pleased with the way you handled the return of Jonathan Cain's bag. It sounds like you returned it at a time when it was most needed. Your generosity and kindness to the Cain family will both increase your honor and your fame. I'm sure your friends have mentioned this to you.

I am disturbed and troubled by the goblins you met. Goblins have always been rare in Norsland, and the fact that they had a shaman with them is alarming. I am also puzzled by the fact that the goblin shaman did not see you for what you are, at least not until it was too late. Magic knows magic, and the fact that the shaman didn't know you had magic is odd and interesting. More important is the fact that you were able to destroy the shaman. An impressive feat for any wizard, and I am pleased that you were able to do it with the limited training you have had. We will talk more about this when we meet. For now, well done.

I would hope you have learned a valuable lesson: namely, emotions can be powerful tools, so long as you control them and they do not control you. You were able to control your anger and use it as a tool. Remember that lesson.

Now, about you feeling strong and refreshed after doing a great deal of difficult magic. I can't be completely sure, but I think I know what has happened. Simply put, the magic you used to seal the soldiers' oaths did much more than just that. When magic is used for great good, it tends to energize the person using the magic. You don't need to worry, and you don't need to stop practicing your magic. I've told you how you will feel when your magic is near its limit, so please continue to practice.

I am enclosing more instructions for your reading. You are doing well, and I am impressed and pleased to hear about your increased abilities with transfiguration. I should warn you, however, not to try to transfigure any of the guardians of the tower that you may meet. Transfiguring magical creatures can be more dangerous than you know.

Yours in fellowship,
Whalen

Alex refolded the letter once he was done reading it and stored it in his bag. He told Sindar what Whalen had said, and Sindar was relieved to know that they didn't need to worry about Alex's magic anymore. Alex asked Sindar if goblins might be traveling in Norsland from some other land.

"They don't use the arch, do they?" Alex questioned.

"They have some magic of their own," Sindar answered.

"Traveling to new lands is difficult for them, but not impossible. Goblins seldom move to new lands, however, unless they are forced to."

"What about the shaman? Whalen was troubled by the fact there was a shaman with the goblins."

"True shamans are rare," Sindar replied in a thoughtful tone. "Even more rare than wizards."

"A true shaman?" Alex questioned.

"As I understand it, true goblin shamans are born with their powers," Sindar explained. "They need little training, and their power grows slowly for as long as they live. A true shaman can choose a lesser shaman and teach him to use magic. Lesser shamans have limited powers, but can still be deadly. I can see why Whalen is worried. If the goblin you destroyed was a lesser shaman, that means that a true shaman is still hidden somewhere in Norsland."

"And if I destroyed a true shaman?"

"That would be my hope," Sindar answered. "But I don't know any way we can be sure of that."

Alex didn't ask any more questions. Before the rest of the company woke up, Alex sent another message to Whalen, asking if there was any way to know what kind of shaman he had destroyed. He was worried that a true goblin shaman in Norsland would mean trouble for his friends, but he didn't know if he could do anything about it.

The company was soon on the road once more, and Alex's thoughts turned back to how little time they had. They had been in Norsland for nearly three months, and he knew that there were never more than six months of good weather here.

He hoped that they would reach the Mountains of the Moon soon and find the Horn of Moran. If they were lucky, they could make it back to Ollvi or maybe even Oslansk before winter set in. If they were unlucky . . . well, spending the winter in the pine forests didn't sound like much fun to him.

Days went by, but the distant mountains never seemed to get any closer. Alex wondered how much further they would have to go once they reached the mountains to find the Tower of the Moon when a deep booming voice called out.

"Hold!"

Alex looked around but could see no one. He looked at his companions, but they were as surprised as he was.

"State your name and your business in our woods," the voice called.

"I am Silvan Bregnest, the leader of this company," Bregnest answered. "We are adventurers, seeking the Tower of the Moon."

Alex was shocked that Bregnest had said where the company was going. He hadn't even told Skeld and Tayo the details of their quest.

"And why do you seek it?"

"We seek a treasure that was lost there."

"What treasure?"

"The Horn of Moran," Bregnest answered again, a slightly dreamy quality to his voice. "It was carried there a hundred years ago and has not returned."

It was so unlike Bregnest to talk about their final goal that Alex was certain there must be some kind of magic at work.

"Bregnest," Alex said sharply, before the voice could ask anything else.

He turned toward Alex, looking as if he had woken up from a wonderful dream and longed to return to his sleep.

"Bregnest," Alex said again, in as calm a voice as he could manage.

"What?" asked Bregnest, shaking his head.

"What are you doing?"

"We see you have a wizard with you," said the voice, before Alex could say anything more. "His wits are not so easily confused."

Bregnest and the others looked around as if they were hearing the voice for the first time. Alex was surprised and a little amused by the looks on his friends' faces. Something in the sound of the mysterious voice made him feel safe and unafraid.

"Forgive us," said the voice, as a large creature stepped out of the trees and into the road in front of them. "We are not trusting of outsiders."

Alex looked at the creature and started to smile. The lower half of the speaker was a sleek black horse, but where the horse's head should have been there was the torso of a man.

"I am Usel, leader of my people," the centaur said proudly. "I ask your forgiveness, and swear that neither I nor my people will repeat what you have said."

"There is nothing to forgive, Usel," Bregnest replied, slightly shaken by the centaur's sudden appearance. "You must look to your own security. We know that you and your people will not share what you have learned."

"You are most kind, Silvan Bregnest. Will you do us the honor of dining with us? We have much to talk about."

"The honor is ours, and we will openly speak of our plans and goals with you and your people."

"Come then," said Usel, turning and starting off down the road.

The company followed Usel, and Alex saw several more centaurs move out of the forest and into the road behind them.

Usel led them a short distance, and then turned into the forest. They rode single file behind the centaur, but even so the path was difficult to follow. After a mile or so, they entered a clearing with several enormous dome-shaped huts in it.

"Welcome to our village," said Usel, as he turned to face the company. "First we will eat, then we will talk. I will have a table made ready for you."

Usel trotted off as soon as he finished speaking, leaving the adventurers alone. Alex and the others climbed off their horses and gathered together, waiting for Usel to return.

"You don't remember anything?" Alex asked the others in disbelief.

"Not until Usel said we had a wizard with us," said Andy.

"I remember," Sindar commented. "It was strange, as if I were in a memory of another time. I could hear what was being said, but I could not speak. And it didn't seem to matter. All that mattered was the memory."

"And you weren't affected at all?" Bregnest asked Alex.

"No," said Alex. "I was a bit confused when you started answering all the questions and telling Usel about our goal. That's when I asked if you knew what you were doing and you all seemed to wake up."

"Do you think we can trust them?" Halfdan asked quietly, looking around the clearing.

"Centaurs are very trustworthy," said Alex, remembering what he had read about them. "They are both honorable and noble. We needn't worry."

"You speak kindly of us, master wizard," said Usel, trotting back to the company. "I hope your words will put your companion's minds at ease."

"I meant no offense," said Halfdan, bowing to Usel.

"Then none is taken, master dwarf," replied Usel. "Come, let us share a meal, then we will talk."

"What of our horses?" Alex asked, looking around for a stable.

"Leave them," Usel answered. "My people will care for them."

Alex patted Shahree's neck and followed his companions. Usel led them to the center of the village where a long table had been set up for their use. Large, round logs had been rolled up to the table for the company to sit on, and several centaurs were already carrying wooden trays full of food to the table for them to eat.

"I hope you like our food," said Usel. "We seldom have guests of any sort. We are little prepared for, well, people like yourselves."

"You are most kind," Bregnest replied. "We are grateful that you and your people would make such an effort for our comfort."

Usel bowed his head slightly without comment and trotted away, leaving the company alone with their table full of food.

The centaurs, it seemed, preferred not to eat with their two-legged guests.

"Strange creatures," commented Halfdan, taking a seat and looking at the food. "Though they appear to be excellent cooks."

The company agreed and joined Halfdan at the table. The food was very good in fact, and not at all strange. Alex quietly ate his meal, wondering what Usel might be able to tell them about the Mountains of the Moon and the tower they were looking for.

"We should talk now," said Usel, returning as Alex and his friends were finishing their meal.

Usel led them to a large fire a short distance away from the village. More logs had been placed around the fire for the company to sit on and an open space had been left for Usel to stand. Alex could sense the other centaurs nearby and wondered why they were remaining out of sight.

Usel lowered himself to the ground and looked around at the company. He seemed to be studying their faces. After several minutes, he took a deep breath and began to speak.

"You are looking for the Tower of the Moon."

"We are," said Bregnest. "We are looking for the Horn of Moran. We wish to return it to its rightful owner."

"This horn you speak of—you said it was carried to the tower a hundred years ago."

"It was," Bregnest answered. "A young prince carried it on an adventure to this land. The prince never returned home, and now the Horn is needed."

"This prince—was he a relative of yours?"

"Distantly."

"Oh, well," Usel began, sounding a bit uncomfortable, "I'm not sure how to say this . . ."

"Do not be troubled," Bregnest said. "I know that the prince was a fool, and possibly worse."

Usel laughed. "I remember this prince of yours, and you are quite right to call him a fool."

"So he passed through your woods?"

"He did. Perhaps that is one reason why we are less friendly than we should be."

"How so?" Bregnest questioned. "If he has done any harm to your people, I will try to repair the damage."

"No, nothing like that," said Usel, waving away Bregnest's offer. "It's just that he was . . . well, to be honest, he was a little full of himself."

"Pompous and insulting perhaps," Bregnest added.

"That too," Usel agreed. "We have so few visitors here. I'm afraid the prince and his attitude put us off being friendly to two-legged company."

"We cannot blame you for that."

"Perhaps things will change, now that you and your company are here," Usel went on in a hopeful tone. "We are quick to forgive, though perhaps not so quick to forget."

"You are most kind, Usel. I hope that my company and I will help ease your caution toward visitors."

"As do I," said Usel. "Now about this goal of yours. I should tell you that the prince never returned from the tower, and neither did any of his company."

"Yes, we were fairly certain of that already," said Bregnest, becoming more businesslike again. "Though we do not know if he ever reached the tower, or if he even stayed on the road."

"I can't tell you if he reached the tower or not, but I'm sure he stayed on the road. What I know of the tower and the road to reach it I will freely share with you."

"Whatever you can tell us will be most helpful, and if we can in any way compensate you for your troubles, we will be happy to do so."

"You are kind, but there is no need for anything like that," said Usel. "Now about the road. Let me see, I suppose the best place to begin is on the far side of our woods. Not far from here is the frozen waste, a wide strip of land that separates our woods from the enchanted woods on the other side."

"Enchanted woods?" Bregnest asked.

"Perhaps that's not the best way of putting it," Usel replied thoughtfully. "Though there is some kind of magic there to be sure because the trees are always green, even in winter."

"Do you know what sort of creatures live in those woods?"

Usel shook his head. "I doubt there is anything dangerous because your foolish prince got through the woods, or at least that's what I was told. Anyway, after the woods you'll find the road that leads up the mountains. At the beginning of the road is the first gate." Usel paused for a moment to think before continuing. "The road up the mountain is steep and rocky, and very narrow at certain points. When you reach the upper end of the road, you'll come to the second gate."

"Is there anything else you can tell us?"

"Let me think, let me think. The second gate comes right before the tower, and a set of stairs leads from the gate to the tower. The torches are always lit inside the tower, or so I understand. The story is that there is a considerable treasure inside the tower as well, but I don't know if that's true or not."

"Well, we know more than we did," said Bregnest. "And we are in your debt."

"Not at all," replied Usel. "And perhaps you won't need to pass through either gate, as I don't really know if the prince made it through the first gate or not. Perhaps you will find the Horn along the way, and can return quickly."

"That is our hope as well," said Bregnest. "Though to be honest, I have doubts about a speedy return."

"Oh, one more thing," said Usel, paying no attention to what Bregnest was saying. "Unless you have a great deal of food for your horses, it would be unwise to take them into the frozen waste. Almost nothing grows there, and the mountains will have less still."

"We carry little for our horses," said Bregnest. "Though I would be unwilling to leave them behind and uncared for."

"Well, it may be more difficult for you, but leaving them would be best," said Usel, looking serious. "If we thought you were taking them to die in the frozen waste, we would not allow you to pass through our woods. Horses are kindred spirits to us, after all, and we will not see them harmed if we can stop it."

"And we would not willingly harm them," said Bregnest. "Our young wizard would not allow it, even if we had minds to do so."

"Yes, I see," said Usel, looking at Alex. "My people noticed his unusual conduct toward his horse. We see a great kindness in him."

"You see truly," Bregnest agreed. "Could we leave our horses in your care until we return? Again, if we can compensate you for this service, we would be pleased to do so."

"Yes, we will care for your horses until you return," said Usel after a moment of thought. "As for compensation, we care little for treasure, and the woods hold all that we need. Now, it is time to sleep. In the morning we will discuss your plans further, and perhaps I will think of some kind of payment."

"Very well," said Bregnest. "Where would you have us sleep so as not to disturb your people?"

"You may remain here by the fire."

Without another word Usel rose from the ground and trotted away from the company. They all sat silently and watched the centaur go. Then they all took blankets out of their bags to sleep on.

"We know more than we did," Bregnest commented, as he sat down on his blankets. "Though leaving the horses will cost us time."

"Leaving them here will save us time," Alex corrected.

"In the greater scheme of things, you are probably right," Bregnest agreed. "But the trip across the frozen waste promises to be long and hard. And on foot it will be an even longer journey."

"We've walked long, hard roads before," said Halfdan in a confident tone.

"But what about fire and hot meals?" Val asked.

"We don't need to worry about that," Halfdan commented. "We have a wizard with us."

"And we can take extra wood in our bags," said Andy with a yawn.

"Sindar, you have said nothing," said Bregnest turning to the elf.

"There is little that has not been said," Sindar answered. "And I agree with most of what has been said."

"Elves," Halfdan muttered and rolled into his blankets.

For a long time Alex lay awake, looking into the night sky. His thoughts drifted, but he could not focus his mind. He felt safe and comfortable, but there was something at the back of his mind that troubled him. Something dark, like a long-forgotten dream that he couldn't remember no matter how hard he tried.

Usel woke them the next morning and invited them to breakfast. Once again the table was made ready for them and the centaurs left them alone. Alex could see that several centaurs remained nearby, occasionally glancing at the company. He wondered if this was to see if they needed anything, or just to keep an eye on them.

While they were eating breakfast, a geeb suddenly appeared on the table in front of Alex. Val was so surprised that he almost fell over backward, which caused the rest of the company to laugh. Alex retrieved Whalen's message from the geeb and sent it away. He didn't really want to read the message in front of his friends, but he had little choice.

Dear Alex,

I received your last message, but I'm afraid I don't have an answer for your biggest question. The fact that the shaman you destroyed did not see your magic leads me to believe that he was not a true shaman, but only a lesser one. Try to remember everything you can about the shaman you fought. True goblin shamans carry a staff and wear dark colors—browns and blacks, mostly. Lesser shamans often wear bright colors—reds and greens.

Keep up the good work and keep me informed. Let me know if you can remember any details about the shaman you fought.

Yours in fellowship,
Whalen

Alex folded the letter and stored it in his magic bag without speaking, then returned his attention to his breakfast. Bregnest watched him for a moment, but did not ask any questions. As Bregnest had not said anything, no one else made any comment about the letter.

As Alex and his friends were finishing breakfast, Usel returned to the table. He looked more serious than he had the night before, and when he spoke it was in a more businesslike tone.

"You will move on then?" Usel asked, but it didn't sound at all like a question.

"We will," Bregnest answered.

"Then I shall lead you to the far side of our woods. And I hope that you find what you seek."

"As do we," said Bregnest. "But there is still the matter of our horses and compensation for your care of them."

"Yes, there is," said Usel. "And my counselors have advised me that I must ask for fifty silver coins and one large emerald from each of you, to be paid on your return to our woods."

"Is this all they ask?" said Bregnest, sounding slightly relieved.

"This is the price we ask for the care of your horses while you are away," Usel answered. "Though, between us, we would care for your horses even without payment."

"Your price is fair and we agree," said Bregnest. "And if fortune smiles on us, we may wish to pay more."

"Oh, no," said Usel, sounding slightly alarmed. "We have little need, and anything more would be, well, silly."

"As you wish," said Bregnest.

"Very good," Usel said. "I will show you the way to the frozen waste."

"Is it far?" Bregnest asked.

"On foot, it will take perhaps until midday to reach the edge of our woods."

"Then we will follow where you lead."

Alex and his friends fell into line behind Usel and started off through the forest. Alex wanted to say good-bye to Shahree and explain things to her, but he had no idea where the centaurs were keeping the horses. Somehow, Usel seemed to know Alex's thoughts, because he led the company to a large open space where their horses were grazing.

"I thought you might need to collect things from your saddlebags," said Usel, looking at Alex. "And I believe your elf friend might be able to explain things to the horses as well so they won't worry."

"You are very kind," said Bregnest.

Alex went to Shahree and patted her forehead. He was sorry to leave her, but he knew the centaurs would take good care of her.

"So we must part again for a little while," Alex said softly. "You will be safe here, and I'll return as soon as I can."

Shahree nuzzled Alex's shoulder affectionately and seemed to understand what he was saying. Sindar made his way to each of the horses as well, whispering something to them that Alex didn't understand. Once they had gathered their things and stored them in their magic bags, they all returned to Usel, ready to continue their march.

The trek through the woods was difficult for Alex and his friends, and Usel would often have to stop and wait for them to catch up. As midday approached, however, the woods around them began to thin. Alex could see that there was a great deal of sunlight ahead of them, and it was clear that the edge of the forest was near.

"It will take you two weeks to cross the waste on foot," Usel commented as they moved forward. "Perhaps a little more or less, depending on your pace. You should move as fast as you are able to, however, as summer is already growing old.

You should have six weeks before the snows start falling once more."

"Do you have any idea how long it will take us to climb the mountains to the tower?" Bregnest asked, looking troubled.

"No," Usel answered. "Much will depend on how rapidly you pass the first and second gates. If you begin your return across the waste within five weeks, you should be safe enough. If you can't start back until the sixth week from now, it would be best to spend the winter in the enchanted woods. You don't want to be in the frozen waste when the heavy snows come."

"You give wise counsel," said Bregnest. "I hope that we shall return before the snows come."

"If you wish to travel south before spring, you must return here before six weeks have passed," Usel replied. "We will keep watch on the waste while you are gone. If you are near our woods when the snows come, we will do what we can to help you."

"You have shown us great kindness," said Bregnest, looking into the frozen waste. "We will not soon forget you, or your assistance."

"I will leave you then," said Usel, looking at each of the company in turn. "I wish you luck in your journey, and a speedy return."

Without waiting for a reply, Usel turned and walked back into the woods. Alex and his companions watched him go, and then looked out into the frozen waste.

"We'll eat here and gather wood for our bags," said Bregnest. "We have little time before winter comes again, so we should use it wisely."

Halfdan began cooking at once, while the rest of them gathered dry wood to add to their magic bags. As they prepared for their long walk, Alex wondered about Usel's warning. The frozen waste looked unpleasant enough, but surely they could cross it even after the first snows of winter fell. Though he knew little of Norsland winters, he didn't think the first snowfall would be any problem for the company.

Halfdan called them all to eat, and Alex's thoughts about Usel's warning were soon lost.

Chapter Eleven

The First Gate

It didn't take long for Alex and the others to learn why it was called the frozen waste. The ground was rock hard, but some spots were slick with a thin layer of moss, which often hid glass-smooth ice that was slightly melted by the sun. The path they followed was a poor one, hardly more than an animal trail, but it led directly toward the Mountains of the Moon. Alex thought he could see a spot of green far off in the distance that might be the enchanted woods, but when he blinked, it was gone.

"Two weeks of slipping and sliding across this," Halfdan grumbled. "We'll all be lucky not to fall and break our heads."

Halfdan's prediction was all too correct. The first day of walking everyone except for Sindar fell several times. There was no talking as they traveled because all of their attention was focused on the next few steps they would take.

Sindar was light on his feet and would seldom slip, even on the smoothest ice, so he often moved ahead of the company and then stood looking across the waste until they caught up with him.

The frozen ground was uncomfortable enough to walk on,

and almost impossible to find a level spot to lie down on to sleep.

Five days into the frozen waste, Alex received another message from Whalen, which cheered him up considerably and took his mind off his sore feet and body.

Dear Alex,

As you are now approaching your goal, I need to tell you a few things. First of all, be prepared for a sphinx and at least one griffin to be guarding the road to the tower.

The sphinx will ask a riddle before letting you pass, and it might help to know that the riddle will often have something to do with the person being asked. Also, don't try to make the riddle harder than it is. Sphinx riddles are often simple—so simple that people can miss an obvious answer—and thinking about the riddle too much will only confuse your mind.

It is most important to remember that griffins are proud creatures. Do not give them any reason to think that you are insulting them. Griffins seem to have a soft spot for wizards, however, so that might be a great help to you and your friends. Griffins can also see what kind of person you are, so if any of your friends have any evil intentions, the griffins will likely bar your path. That shouldn't really be a problem, but you never know.

Once you reach the tower, if you have to go that far, there are two libraries you should know about. The upper library contains a great deal of knowledge and would be a wonderful addition for your future learning and worth far more than any treasure you might find. If possible, you should try to store the upper library in your magic bag.

The lower library is dangerous and full of dark, evil magic. You should avoid the lower library if you can. If you cannot, you must try to destroy it. In fact, it would be best all around if you are able to destroy it.

Now, some final words of advice. Control your emotions. I know you've been working hard on this, but what is coming may test your ability to the breaking point. Knowing that you will be tested will give you a chance to prepare yourself.

Finally, remember, do not try to find difficult solutions to your problems. Simple solutions are usually best and most often correct.

Take care, and let me know how things go.

Yours in fellowship,
Whalen

Alex read the letter twice, wondering why Whalen was only now telling him about the libraries. Obviously Whalen had known about them all along, but for some reason he hadn't said a word. Alex's thoughts turned to the lower library and how he might destroy it.

"I suppose fire would work," Alex said to Sindar, as they waited for their companions to wake up.

"Have you ever tried to burn a magic book?" Sindar questioned.

"Of course not."

"I don't think fire would have much effect. Magic books resist fire."

"Perhaps I could change the books into something else. That way nobody could read them," Alex suggested.

"That might work," said Sindar, getting up and stamping his feet on the cold ground. "But couldn't another wizard change them back again?"

"Yes, if he knew what they were to begin with. But what if I changed them into mice or something?"

"That could be a lot of mice."

"I don't know what else to do," said Alex. "But there must be a way, or Whalen wouldn't have told me to try."

"Perhaps. Or perhaps there is no way, and that is why Whalen did not tell you exactly what to do."

Alex frowned. "Why would Whalen ask me to do something that can't be done?"

"Perhaps Whalen doesn't know the answer," Sindar answered slowly. "Or perhaps he simply wishes to see what you will do."

As he marched across the frozen land that day, Alex's thoughts were filled with the puzzle of the lower library. Nothing he thought of seemed to solve the problem of the library, or the question of why Whalen hadn't told him what to do. The more he thought about it, the more doubts came into his mind. Could he even destroy the library? Did he know enough? Did he have enough power to work the magic?

"Try not to think about it so much," Sindar told him a few days later. "Whalen said simple solutions were best. If you think about it too much, you might miss something obvious. And besides, you may not have to do anything. We may find the Horn before reaching the tower."

Alex agreed and tried to think of something else as they continued to go north. This was easy to do, as the enchanted woods rose up ahead of them. The woods looked pleasant and incredibly green compared to the frozen lands around them.

"I'll be glad when we reach the woods," said Andy, stretching the kinks out of his back. "This cold, hard ground makes sleeping painful."

"If you wanted the comforts of home, then perhaps you should have stayed home," Sindar joked.

The others all chuckled at Sindar's comment. Alex thought about his own home, and he longed for a real bed to sleep in. There were other things he missed as well: the hot showers, Mr. Roberts's cooking, the quiet room where he could study his magic in comfort. Still, he loved being in the outdoors, traveling with his friends, and telling stories around the campfire at night. Both worlds were part of him now, and for the time being, the comforts of home would have to wait.

When the company finally reached the edge of the enchanted woods they had been walking for fifteen days. Bregnest was not pleased with how long the journey had taken. Usel had told them to start back within five weeks, and now they had less than three weeks to find the Horn and return.

"I thought we would cross faster," said Bregnest as they ate dinner.

"Perhaps the distance from the centaurs' woods to here

changes," Halfdan suggested. "That might be what Usel meant when he called this wood enchanted."

"I don't think that is what he meant," said Val nervously. "I feel as if we are being watched."

"As do I," Sindar added. "But I think the eyes are merely curious, and friendly enough. We have nothing to fear."

"Perhaps," Val replied.

The next morning they started through the woods, and they all began to feel that someone or something was watching them. Often they would hear movement in the trees, but they never saw anything at all. Once Alex thought he heard something that sounded like a giggle from some nearby bushes, but no one else seemed to notice the sound so he didn't say anything.

The path wound randomly between the trees, and the further along the path they went, the more nervous Alex and his friends became. They spoke little as they traveled and tried to move as quietly and as fast as possible. Even Sindar, who maintained that there was nothing to fear, would seldom speak or make any noise as they hurried forward.

"Whatever is in these woods, I wish it would show itself or leave us be," Halfdan complained loudly as he cooked their evening meal.

"Perhaps they are unsure of us," Sindar commented. "There are many good creatures who are simply shy of strangers."

"Sindar is correct," Bregnest added. "Even the centaurs were less friendly than other creatures I have met. I think it is because adventurers seldom come here, and they do not know about us."

"Or they might know more about us than we care to think," Sindar commented happily.

"Maybe they don't like over-jolly elves," grumbled Halfdan.

"Perhaps not," Sindar agreed.

The next day things were better. They no longer heard movement around them in the woods and the feeling of being watched had lessened. Andy claimed that the smell of Halfdan's boots had driven off the unseen creatures, but Halfdan was in no mood to be teased.

It took the company four days to make their way through the enchanted wood, and with each day that passed, Bregnest grew more tense. Alex knew that Bregnest didn't want to spend the winter in Norsland, but it was beginning to look more and more like they would have to. Ahead of them towered the Mountains of the Moon, and they could already see the outline of the first gate in the distance.

"Should we press on, or wait for morning?" Bregnest asked.

"It will be dark soon, and we may lose our way if we press on," said Andy.

"We need to rest and eat," Halfdan added.

"We should go forward as fast as possible," Val commented, looking toward the gate. "If we do not push forward, the snows may trap us here."

"I think we should move forward early tomorrow," said Alex. "We will all think more clearly after some food and a little rest."

"Sindar, do you have anything to add?" asked Bregnest.

"I agree with Alex," said Sindar, his gaze fixed on the gate.

"We will need to be thinking clearly when we reach the gate or our adventure may end there."

"Very well then," said Bregnest in a defeated tone. "We will eat and rest. When it comes time for the last watch, we will all rise and move forward to the gate."

Halfdan busied himself cooking their evening meal. Andy sat down beside the fire, still trying to loosen his stiff neck, while Bregnest, Alex, Sindar, and Val all remained standing at the edge of the woods, looking toward the first gate.

"Our time grows short," Bregnest said softly.

"Perhaps Usel was wrong. The snows may not begin as soon as he thinks," Val offered in a hopeful tone.

"Centaurs know many things that others only guess at," said Sindar. "We have time yet—at least two more weeks to find the Horn and start back."

"And the Horn may be waiting for us at the first gate," said Bregnest, sounding hopeful.

"And if it is, will we not seek the treasure of the tower?" Val questioned.

"The treasure of the tower is not our goal," Bregnest answered. "If we had more time I might consider it, but if the Horn is at the first gate, we will turn back before winter comes."

"Of course," said Val. "I only thought that the treasure of the tower would be worth an extra day or two."

"Not if it means we must remain in Norsland all winter," said Sindar.

"You seem very quiet, Alex," said Bregnest, a questioning look on his face. "Are you troubled?"

"No," Alex answered with a sigh. "Just lost in thought."

"And are your thoughts hopeful?" asked Sindar, turning to look at Alex.

"It is nothing," said Alex. "The road has been long, and my mind and body are both tired."

"Then come and eat," called Halfdan. "Eat and then to bed so your mind will be fresh tomorrow. I don't want to meet the guardian of the first gate with a tired wizard by my side."

"Wizard in training," Alex corrected. "And if you don't want me along, I will gladly wait here for your return."

"No offense," said Halfdan, winking at Alex as he handed him a plate of food.

"Tired or not, I want Alex along," said Andy. "I've seen him in action, and I don't like the idea of facing the guardians without him."

"I'll be there," said Alex. "And I hope there won't be any action to see."

"We should rest," said Bregnest as he ate. "Whatever tomorrow holds, at least we will face it refreshed."

But Alex couldn't sleep that night. For several days he had felt that there was something important he needed to remember, something that was always just out of his reach, and the fact that he couldn't remember what it was troubled him.

They started toward the first gate before the sun had risen the next morning. The night before it had looked only an hour or two away, but as they walked across the frozen land, the gate grew larger and larger in front of them. It was midday by the time they finally reached the first gate, and they all stood looking at it in wonder.

The gate was at least two hundred feet high and appeared to be made of solid granite. After a few minutes of looking at the gate, Alex realized that it hadn't been built at all, but rather it had been carved out of the mountain. The path passed exactly through the center of the massive structure. There were no doors or bars to be seen, only a great archway lined with pillars that led into the mountains beyond.

"Look at the bones," Halfdan whispered as they moved forward.

They stopped short. Broken bones littered the ground in front of them. Rusted weapons were scattered among the bones along with fragments of armor, the metal torn apart like paper.

"Come on," Bregnest said in a firm tone. "Do not speak unless you must. We don't want to give the guardian any reason to attack us."

Slowly they started forward once more, moving toward the mountainous gate and the guardian that waited for them. As they drew closer, there were fewer bones to be seen, but that did little to comfort them. They walked close together, watching for any sudden movement that might be an attack.

Climbing a wide set of stairs, they came to a flat, open space, and at the top of the stairs was the guardian. Sitting in the center of the archway, partly covered by shadows, a huge catlike creature watched them with huge, unblinking eyes.

As they moved slowly toward the shadows, the guardian moved forward toward them. To Alex it looked like a lion had grown more than twice its normal size, but where the lion's head should have been, there was a woman's face.

The sphinx made no sound as it moved forward, and its eyes followed every move that Alex and his friends made. When they reached a point that only the sphinx seemed to know, the sphinx sat down and began to speak.

"If you wish to pass this way, you must answer what I ask," the sphinx said sweetly.

"May we answer as a group, or must we go one at a time?" Bregnest questioned.

"Either," the sphinx answered. "Though if you wish to answer as a group, I will choose the one to speak. And if you wish to answer alone, I will choose the order."

"And if we can't answer what you ask?" Bregnest questioned.

"I will ask, and you must answer or withdraw."

"And if we answer wrong?" Bregnest persisted.

"If you answer wrong, you will neither go forward or back," said the sphinx, nodding to the bones scattered around the steps.

"Can you tell us if another passed this way?" Bregnest asked.

The sphinx did not answer but turned its head slightly to one side and continued to watch them.

"Will you answer our questions if we answer your riddle?" Bregnest tried again.

The sphinx remained silent.

After a moment, Bregnest turned to the company. "Together, or one at a time?"

"We should go together," said Halfdan instantly. "We are a company and should not divide."

"But if the one asked the question can't answer it, none of us may pass," Val said in a worried tone.

"And if the person gives the wrong answer, we will all be in trouble," Andy added.

"Some of us must get past or we will never find the Horn," said Sindar. "The others can wait here, or take their time to answer."

"Together," Alex said firmly, his eyes fixed on the sphinx. "We should go together or not at all."

"I agree," said Bregnest and turned back to face the sphinx. "We will pass together. To which member of our company will you ask your question?"

The sphinx looked at each of them in turn, as if considering who to ask its riddle to. For several minutes the sphinx said nothing, and they were all starting to worry.

"The young wizard," the sphinx finally said. "He will answer the question for you all."

Alex was afraid this would happen. He had never been good with riddles, and he often guessed them wrong. Now his friends were depending on him to get the right answer so they could move on. Of course, if he couldn't answer, they could still withdraw, but that wouldn't help them find the Horn. If he answered incorrectly, however, they would be in trouble, and he wasn't sure how much use his magic would be if they had to fight the sphinx.

Alex tried to remember what Whalen had told him in his letter: Don't overthink the riddle. Look for a simple answer.

"Are you ready?" asked the sphinx, as Alex stepped forward.

"I am."

"Unseen but heard, untouched but felt. Relief from the sun, a breath and I'm done. Never staying, always going, gently moving, never blowing. What am I?" the sphinx questioned.

Alex stood looking at the sphinx in wonder. He had no idea what the answer was. "Could you repeat that, please?"

The sphinx smiled at Alex and repeated the riddle. Alex listened carefully to every word. He felt like he should know the answer. It had to be something simple—something so simple that nobody would ever think of it.

"One more time, please?"

As Alex listened to the sphinx repeat the riddle the third time, he felt a cold breeze blow across his face. He wouldn't have noticed the breeze normally, except the answer suddenly came to him.

"You are a gentle breeze on a warm day," said Alex.

"I am," replied the sphinx, bowing slightly and stepping aside so the company could pass.

Once they had all passed the sphinx, Bregnest turned to see if the sphinx would answer his questions about the prince and his party.

"Others have passed this way, but none have returned," the sphinx answered and then lay down in the middle of the archway, ignoring them completely.

"Well done, Alex," said Halfdan, slapping him on the back. "I'd have never thought of that."

"I was lucky," Alex admitted.

"So you always say, though I think there is more to it than that," said Bregnest.

The others were all relieved that Alex had managed to answer the sphinx. Alex, however, wasn't sure if he was happy or not. The puzzle of how he might destroy the lower library had returned to his mind again, and he really had no idea how he could do it.

"We still have a long march ahead of us," Sindar commented.

Looking at the path ahead of them, Alex could see that it would be both long and difficult. The path from the first gate started climbing the Mountains of the Moon, winding up the mountainside like some monstrous snake, vanishing from sight high above them.

"It looks narrow in spots," Sindar continued. "Almost too narrow."

"Let's get moving," said Bregnest. "We don't know how far it is to the second gate, and time is running out."

The company began walking once more. The road was fairly wide at the bottom of the mountains, but it became more and more narrow the farther they went. Before long, Alex and his friends were forced to walk in a single file, bent with the effort of climbing. In places they had to use their hands as well as their feet to scramble up the mountainside. Now and then one of them would slip a few feet back down the path before catching themselves.

As darkness was gathering around them, they came to a wide spot that opened suddenly on the side of the mountain.

Bregnest signaled them to stop, but it was several minutes before he had breath enough to speak.

"A hard road," Bregnest finally managed to say, still breathing heavily.

None of the others spoke for some time, winded and exhausted. Alex noticed that the air felt much colder here on the mountain, colder even than it had been on the frozen waste.

"I would not want to be on this road when the snows come," Halfdan commented.

"This path would be impossible in winter," said Val. "I only hope we are well off it before the snows arrive."

"If we have not found the Horn or reached the tower within seven days, we will go back," said Bregnest in a bitter tone. "We must find the Horn and return it to Alusia, even if we are too late to prevent a war. And if we are caught on this path when winter comes, we may never return at all."

"Going back would mean passing the sphinx again," said Andy, sounding worried. "Next time it may not ask Alex to answer the riddle."

"We have not reached that point yet," said Bregnest. "We still have seven days before we must consider our options."

"And if we must go back, at least we'll have a long winter to prepare," Halfdan added.

Alex didn't comment. He conjured a cooking fire for Halfdan and sat thinking. His thoughts were not on going back or the coming winter, but on the second gate and the tower that lay beyond. He thought they would reach the second gate at least, but he didn't know if they would pass the guardians that waited at it. They needed to stop a war, or at the very least, make it a short war. And if they managed to reach the tower, he would have to try to destroy the lower library. A shiver ran through him at the thought.

Alex put out his magical fire when Halfdan had finished cooking, and they had eaten in the gathering darkness without speaking. Now they were lying half awake, uncomfortable and unable to sleep, wondering how far they had to go and how hard the trail would be before they reached the second gate.

"You seem troubled, my friend," said Sindar as he sat in the darkness beside Alex.

"Thinking too much again," Alex said softly.

"Ah, the problem of the library. I will admit, it is a difficult problem."

"There must be a way or Whalen wouldn't have suggested that I destroy it."

"To destroy is always easier than to create," Sindar replied softly. "Though to destroy completely and forever . . . I do not know if that is possible."

"How far away do you think the second gate is?" Alex asked.

"A day, maybe two. If it is much farther than that we will be going down the other side of this mountain."

A day or two to reach the second gate, and then they would have to face the griffin guards that could read a man's heart. Alex felt tired, but sleep would not come. He sat in the darkness, trying to clear his mind, but his thoughts continued to press in on him. Whalen had told him to look for simple solutions, but he couldn't think of anything simple that would work.

When morning finally came, Alex's body felt rested, but his mind was tired from all of his thinking. He was glad when they started climbing again because the hard work forced him to focus on nothing but the path in front of him.

If anything, the climb was harder than it had been the day before. They ate their midday meal at one of the few places they found where the path was wide and almost level, and then they rested for about an hour before continuing.

Late in the afternoon, just as Alex thought he couldn't take another step without resting, the trail leveled out once more. There was rock on both sides of the path, and it was far easier to move forward. They continued for a short distance and came to an open space that looked like a crater. A cold wind was blowing, but there was no sign of the second gate.

"We seem to have reached the top," said Bregnest after a few minute's rest. "Perhaps tomorrow's road will be less steep, and we will make better time."

"And perhaps the path will start down again and this is only the first mountain we will have to climb," said Val, sounding depressed.

"I do not think so," Halfdan commented. "If the builders of this road wished us to climb a different mountain, there are easier ways to lead us to it."

"It is likely that the builders of this road wished it to be hard," said Sindar.

"Why?" Andy asked. "I imagine they had to use the road as well, didn't they?"

"I do not know," Sindar answered. "But it seems they had

some purpose in mind when they built it. I would guess to keep away unwanted visitors."

After resting for several minutes, Alex conjured a cooking fire for Halfdan. His mind felt clearer here with the cold wind blowing his hair, and his thoughts about the lower library did not trouble him as much as they had.

For the convenience of his friends, Alex conjured several small balls of light, which he sent floating around the cooking fire. His friends were all impressed by this feat of magic and watched the balls with great interest.

"Your abilities have grown since the last time we traveled together," said Bregnest.

"They have," Alex agreed.

"It is most impressive," commented Sindar. "I have not seen this done before."

Alex sat watching the balls of light, his mind far more relaxed than it had been for several days. Once Halfdan had finished cooking, Alex put out the blue-flamed cooking fire, but left the balls floating around the company.

"There is no heat or flame in them," Andy observed.

"No," said Alex. "They are called weir lights."

"How long will they last?" Val questioned.

"As long as I want," said Alex. "I've read that if you catch one in a jar, you can keep it forever. If the jar breaks, however, the light will try to escape."

"Perhaps we should all get jars," Halfdan suggested. "A light that doesn't go out could be a useful tool."

"Oh, they can go out," said Alex. "But only by magic."

"If they would escape from someone who kept them in a jar, why do they remain here now?" Bregnest questioned.

"Because I'm paying attention to them," Alex replied. "If I left them alone without commanding them to stay or follow me, or if I went to sleep, they would simply float away."

"Could you capture one in something other than a jar?" Halfdan asked in a thoughtful tone.

"I've read of some weir lights being trapped in crystals or gems, but that is much more difficult to do."

"Ah, but such a light inside a gem would make a fine treasure," Halfdan said gleefully.

"Such a gem would be nice, but the lights are so much nicer floating on their own," said Sindar.

They all finished eating and lay down on their blankets, watching the weir lights floating above them. Alex would occasionally change their colors just so Halfdan would chuckle. He was pleased that the spell had worked so well and that his friends found so much joy in the small balls of light. When Alex began to feel sleepy, he put out the weir lights. He felt relaxed, and even though he knew troubles lay ahead of him, tonight he didn't care.

When daylight came the next morning, they were all feeling refreshed. Their moods had improved, and even Bregnest did not look troubled. They ate their breakfast and started forward with little talk.

The trail had rock on both sides of it, but in some places the rock was low enough they could look out across the lands below them. Alex noticed that Andy would always look away from the open spots, as if he did not wish to see how high they were.

"Are you all right?" Alex asked Andy in a low voice so the rest of the company wouldn't hear.

"I don't like high places," said Andy, his voice a bit higher than normal. "They make me feel dizzy and confused."

Alex nodded but didn't say anything more. He had never known about Andy's fear of heights, and now he felt a little sorry that he had asked.

They made good progress that day as the trail wound along the top of the mountains. There were no longer any steep spots to climb, only long, gentle ups and downs. As the sun began to sink in the west, they all began to feel restless. With each turn of their path, they hoped to see the second gate or the Tower of the Moon, but instead they saw only more of the trail. When the sun was almost gone, Alex began to wonder where they would be able to find a place to sleep.

Just then, the company emerged from the trail into a wide-open space.

"We are there," said Bregnest suddenly.

The second gate looked nothing at all like the first gate. There was no fine building or high arch, only the open space in front of them and a long stairway leading to the Tower of the Moon.

"Where is the gate?" Halfdan asked.

"Where is the guardian?" Val questioned.

"Both are before you," answered Sindar. "Look closely, just this side of the stairway, and you will see the gate and the guardians."

Looking into the gathering darkness, they could see what Sindar meant. On either side of the path sat an enormous griffin. Their wings were held high over their heads, forming a strange-looking archway. The griffins were much larger than Alex had imagined they would be, and he knew that their sharp, eagle eyes had already seen the company.

"Impressive guardians," Halfdan commented softly.

"And effective," Sindar added. "They can see right through a person and know if they are good or evil, happy or sad. They see everything."

"And how do we pass them?" Andy questioned.

"I imagine they will tell us what we need to do," said Bregnest. "But I think before we approach, we should rest. We will attempt the second gate in the morning."

Chapter Twelve

The Tower of the Moon

The company had a hard time trying to rest again that night. Their thoughts and eyes continued to wander toward the griffins, which were hidden in darkness. No one was hungry, but Halfdan prepared a simple meal just so he had something to do. They had reached the Tower of the Moon, and when the sun came up, they would have to pass before the griffins.

Alex knew the griffins would only stop them if they were evil. Evil, however, was not the right word. He had read about griffins and stories about people who had encountered them. Griffins didn't see things simply as good or evil; they looked more at intentions, at a person's conscience, at the reasons people had for doing what they did.

"It has been a long road," Bregnest commented in the darkness. "I hope we find what we came looking for."

"It must be here," said Andy. "The sphinx said the prince did not return, and there's no other path he could have taken."

"The sphinx said that others had passed and did not return," Sindar corrected. "We don't know who those others might have been."

"I agree with Andy," said Halfdan. "Usel said the prince traveled this way, so the Horn must be here. I'll feel better once we have it and are away from this place."

"Do you doubt your ability to pass the griffins?" Val questioned.

"No," said Halfdan. "But everyone may hide some evil inside of them, even from themselves."

"And few of the mortal races know themselves as well as they think they do," Sindar added.

"Is it different for elves?" Alex questioned.

"Yes and no," answered Sindar in a quiet voice. "We know ourselves far better than mortals do, but even so, evil may hide where we least expect it."

They fell silent for a time, each of them searching their own hearts and thoughts. Alex wondered if his growing pride in being a wizard might be considered evil. He wasn't sure how the griffins would judge him, or what they might consider evil that he would not.

"It will do no good to worry," said Sindar. "The griffins will judge as they see fit, and only another griffin would truly understand the judgment."

"How will we proceed in the morning?" Andy questioned. "Will we stand before them as a group? Or one at a time?"

"One at a time," Bregnest answered after a few moments of thought. "I believe we will all pass, but I think we should each stand alone before the griffins."

"And if all do not pass?" Val asked.

"The judgment of the griffins is not the same as man's,"

Bregnest answered. "If any of this company fail to pass, none here will speak against them."

They all became quiet once more, though Alex didn't think any of his companions were sleeping. He was worried about getting past the griffins, but he was more worried about what waited for him at the tower. His mind burned with thoughts of the lower library, but he still didn't have any answers about how to destroy it.

The wind picked up as the night went on, and it was getting colder. Alex thought about how long they'd been in Norsland. By his count, they were only just starting their fifth month. Andy had said there were at least five or six months of good traveling weather, so why had Usel warned them to start back so soon? Surely they had at least a month before winter would return. Faced with more questions than answers, Alex slowly fell into a light sleep.

A terrible, screaming cry snapped him awake. Alex jumped to his feet, his hand reaching for Moon Slayer at his side. He looked around to see where the cry had come from.

Everything was dark, but he could hear something large moving nearby. The griffins were awake in the darkness, and they sounded both angry and pained.

"Bregnest?" Alex called, looking around but seeing nothing in the darkness. "Sindar?"

There was no reply, only the angry sounds coming from the griffins.

Alex stood for a moment, unsure of what to do. Where were his companions? Why were they not answering his calls? His thoughts were numbed by the darkness, and fear was growing inside of him. He knew that he had to do something—anything—and fast.

With an effort of will, Alex conjured up a half dozen weir lights. As they floated gently around him, the fog in his mind began to clear and the darkness around him fled. He felt like a great weight was suddenly lifted from him.

Looking around, he saw that his friends were all still on the ground as though they had not heard the screaming pain of the griffins and were simply resting, waiting for dawn. Then he noticed that only four of his friends were there. Val was gone.

"Bregnest!" Alex shouted, bending over his friend and trying to shake him awake.

Bregnest didn't answer. Alex tried to wake each of his friends in turn, but none of them would wake up. When he shook Sindar, the elf mumbled slightly, but he, too, seemed completely dazed.

Alex didn't know what to do. He needed to help his friends, but he also needed to find Val. Where had he gone? And what had caused the griffins to cry out in such terrible pain and anger?

Simple solutions, he thought, remembering Whalen's advice. He had to think of something fast and simple that would help his friends. Fire. That might help. Fire was the adventurer's friend and ally.

Stepping away from his friends' blankets, Alex conjured a blue-white fire. The heat from the flames pushed back the cold mountain air. As fast as he could, Alex moved his companions as close to the fire as he dared, still trying to wake them. Only Sindar spoke, but his voice was a faint whisper.

"My pendant. I need my pendant." Sindar pulled at his shirt with his right hand, desperately trying to find something.

Alex pushed aside Sindar's hand and pulled open the top of the elf's shirt. There was no pendant, only a dark red line where something had been yanked from around Sindar's neck.

Alex searched Sindar's blankets and the ground around him. He forced more magic into the weir lights, changing them from gentle gold to dazzling white. The bright light glinted off something, but as Alex reached out for it, his hand stopped. Sindar's pendant was made of true silver, but there was no mistaking the design. It was shaped like a flower, the same flower as the pendant Alex's father had hidden.

Alex retrieved the pendant, but almost dropped it as it burned his hand with cold. The cold was gone almost as soon as the pendant was in his hand, the burn forgotten, and a gentle warmth seemed to flow out of the metal flower.

"Here, I have your pendant," Alex said, forcing it into Sindar's hand.

Sindar took a few deep breaths. His muscles relaxed, and his eyes fluttered open. For a second he seemed confused, and then he spoke in a desperate, pleading tone.

"Val. Some evil has taken over his mind."

"What?" Alex asked, wondering if he'd heard Sindar correctly.

"Val carries a great evil with him. He will go to the tower. You must stop him before he reaches the lower library," said Sindar, blinking slowly.

"But I can't leave you and the others," Alex protested. "The others won't wake up, and you can barely speak."

"Go, quickly," said Sindar, his tone becoming urgent. "I will recover soon. I will care for the others while you are gone."

"Sindar, this is madness," said Alex. "What evil does Val carry?"

"Go," Sindar repeated. "Go now."

Alex looked at Sindar and his other friends. If he left them, they might be lost, but what could he do for them if he stayed? If Val was carrying some evil and he reached the lower library, it could be disastrous.

Alex knew what he had to do. "Do what you can for the others. I will return as soon as I can."

Sindar seemed to nod, but he said nothing.

Alex put out the weir lights but left the fire burning, then he ran toward the Tower of the Moon with only one thought in his mind. Stop Val. Stop the evil.

"Stay," an angry voice commanded as Alex ran toward the stairs that led to the tower.

Alex slid to a stop. He had forgotten that the griffins were still there, and they were angry.

"What do you seek in the Tower of the Moon?" the griffin growled.

"I seek the evil that has gone there," Alex answered.

"The evil you seek traveled here with your company. It attacked us, blinding us with its dark magic. Why do you seek it now?" the griffin demanded.

"We did not know this evil was with us," said Alex defensively. "Now that it has shown itself, I must stop it from reaching the lower library and learning even greater dark magic."

The griffin paused. "There is no evil in you," it said finally in a somewhat softer tone. “You may pass. But know this, young wizard, your friends will remain here as hostages.”

“Hostages?”

“We will allow you three hours. You must either destroy this evil or return here with it. If you do not return before the time is up, the hostages are forfeit.”

The griffin’s words filled Alex with a cold fear, but he had no choice. “Agreed,” he said, resolved to his fate.

“Then go,” the griffin commanded. “And return swiftly—if you can.”

Alex didn’t hesitate. He rushed up the stairs that led into the tower without looking back. He had little time and no idea where Val might be. What evil Val carried with him Alex could not guess, but he knew it must be powerful in order to blind the griffins and allow Val the chance to slip past their watchful gaze.

Alex was breathing hard when he reached the top of the stairway, his heart pounding loudly in his ears. The entrance to the tower was in front of him, but there was no sign of Val. He stopped for a moment, trying to catch his breath and think. Val had carried the evil, but for how long? And why had Alex not felt the evil, as he had before when other evil had been near him? He was only a wizard in training, how could he possibly defeat this overwhelming evil?

Alex approached the tower, his worries picking at his brain. He had to try, even if it was hopeless. If he failed, he would probably die, though the thought of his own death didn’t bother him as much as the knowledge that if he failed, his friends would surely die as well. And if he succeeded, he had only three hours to return to the griffins and save his friends.

As he entered the tower, Alex found himself in a wide chamber. The torches were lit, which helped him to see, but it also helped his enemy. Looking around, he saw there were two stairways leading out of the chamber. One stairway led up into the tower, the other spiraled down into the mountain beneath the tower.

"It must be down," Alex said to himself.

Alex ran to the stairway on his right and started down. The stairs circled around the wall of the tower and were poorly lit. Carefully, Alex moved downward, keeping his eyes open in case Val was hidden somewhere, waiting to attack him. There were no hiding places along the stairway that he could see, but Alex continued to move with caution.

At the bottom of the stairs was a long hallway, and at the far end of the hallway, Alex could see what appeared to be more stairs leading down. Alex moved down the hallway as fast as he could. He watched for any sign of movement and listened for any kind of sound. He paused at the end of the hallway to listen again, but there was only silence. There were no doorways or passages leading away from the hallway, so the only thing to do was to continue down.

The second stairway ended in a narrow chamber. There were doors on both sides and a large double door at the far end. Alex moved into the middle of the room, looking for any sign that he was going in the right direction. There was something familiar about the room, but Alex couldn't remember where he had seen it before. He felt certain that he was going in the right direction, but if he had chosen wrong and the library was higher in the tower, he was wasting what little time he had.

Alex stood for a second with his eyes partly closed, listening. A cold breeze blew across his face from the direction of the large double door, and he took that as a sign. He moved to the door and reached out for the handles. His hands shook slightly, and he could already feel the evil and hate waiting behind the doors. Not just waiting, but waiting for him.

Focusing his thoughts on what he had to do, Alex pushed the doors open and stepped into the lower library. Val was standing halfway down a large empty room, looking back at Alex.

"I knew you would come," said Val in an odd-sounding voice. "I knew you would try to stop me."

"What are you doing, Val?"

"What I have been told to do," Val answered, his face twisting into what might have been a grin. "I do what my friends say because they want what is best for me."

"What friends?" Alex asked, stepping closer to Val and looking around the empty room.

"The friends that I have carried with me on this foolish quest," answered Val. "The friends who found me on my last adventure and showed me what I could be, if I listened to them."

"And what is that?" Alex asked, thinking that Val's words sounded strangely familiar.

"I will be king of the known lands. All will bow before me, and all will give honor to me."

"I have heard such promises before," Alex said softly. "They are lies, and those who promise such things are full of evil."

"So you say," Val answered with a sneer. "You threw away your chance. You refused to accept them once, and now you will pay the price of your foolishness with your life."

"I threw away only lies. I refused to accept their evil, and I have paid no price for my choice."

"Your time is over, wizard. We will destroy you," Val screamed, leaping forward, the point of his sword driving toward Alex's heart.

Alex spun away, avoiding Val's attack by dropping to the floor and rolling back to his feet. Moon Slayer was in his hand as he turned, and the magic sword began to glow softly in the darkness. Alex felt Val's next attack coming, and he spun away as he slapped Val's sword aside with Moon Slayer.

The two of them began a deadly dance around the empty library. Val spun and attacked wildly time and again, but Moon Slayer was always there to block his attacks. Several times Alex saw an opening where he could easily have killed Val, but he didn't. Val was his friend, and he was being controlled by evil; Alex felt like he had to try to save him from that evil.

"You only delay your end," Val yelled. "I can fight for hours, but sooner or later you will need rest."

"Whatever promises you have been told are lies. Evil can't give you greatness, it will only use you and then throw you away when it is finished."

Their swords crashed against each other.

"Let go of the evil, Val," Alex said in a calm voice. "Think of your friends, your wife."

"Wife?" Val shouted, diving forward to attack once more. "I have no wife. That was only a fantasy, a dream that has not yet come true. But my true friends will make that dream come true, along with all my other dreams. They want only what is best for me."

"You will be betrayed," said Alex. "Remember when you trusted before. You were betrayed before, and the evil that claims to be your friend will betray you in the same way. Let it go, Val. Let go of the lies the shadow has whispered to you and reclaim your honor as an adventurer."

"Betrayed," Val said, his voice softening. He froze in place, his sword held out in front of him, the tip wavering. There was a confused look on Val's face, but Alex could see a great struggle in his eyes.

Alex took the opportunity, hoping it was the right thing to do, hoping that Val would understand. Swinging Moon Slayer as hard as he could, Alex aimed for Val's sword. A shower of sparks filled the room as Val's sword shattered, and Val fell back as if he had been dealt a deadly blow.

"Val?" Alex questioned as he stepped closer. "Are you all right?"

"Alex? I . . . I don't know," Val answered slowly. "You could have killed me, but you did not. It might . . . it might have been better if you had."

"Nonsense," said Alex. "Let go of the evil, Val. Let go of the dreams that cannot be, and come back to your own life."

"Yes, I understand now," said Val, his voice growing stronger. "I . . . Forgive me, Alex. I have been a fool."

"There is no need for forgiveness," said Alex. "Come, we need to return to the others."

"As you wish, my master," Val whispered.

Before Alex realized what Val had said, Val lifted his hands and cast a spell. Alex's body was racked with pain and an icy cold filled his insides. The pain forced him to his knees, and for a moment he thought he was going to throw up. He had felt this sickening cold once before, and it had almost destroyed him then.

Forcing himself to ignore the cold and the pain, Alex raised his hands instinctively, drawing on his own deep magic. The spell that came to him in his time of need was nothing he had ever heard of or read about.

Val shrieked in agony, and the painful cold that consumed Alex began to fade. Alex got back to his feet and saw Val, curled on the floor, whimpering in pain. For a moment he felt pity for Val, but then Val's body began to twitch as if his pain was increasing and a strange shadow began to spread like a puddle of ink around him.

Alex watched in stunned amazement and horror as the shadow began to take shape. As the shadow took its full form, Alex recognized it from a dream he'd had long ago and from a night he could never forget. This was the evil that had reached out for him in his dream, a dream he had forgotten until now. This was the evil that had almost destroyed him on his first adventure, and now he knew it for what it was.

"So, young wizard," said an ice-cold voice. "You have forced me to leave this pathetic excuse of a man and show myself."

"And now I will end your evil," said Alex in a determined voice.

"You do not have that power," the voice taunted. "All you have done is to delay my plans. Look around you, fool. Do you not realize where you are?"

"In the lower library of the Tower of the Moon," said Alex, but he suddenly realized what the shadowy figure meant. This was the library, but there were no books here; it was empty.

"So, you see at last," said the voice. "The library is mine, safe from you in this fool's bag."

"You have done great evil, and I will stop you from doing more," Alex yelled. "I have defeated you before, and I will do so again."

"Young fool," whispered the shadow. "There is no reason for us to be at odds. Take the treasure of the tower and the Horn that you seek. And I can add to your treasures as well."

The shadow turned to look at Val. Val slowly took his magic bag and spoke into it. There was a moment when the air seemed to ripple and spark and then the empty library was filled with treasure from Val's bag.

"All this I will offer you," said the cold voice. "All this, and a hundred times more. All that I ask is that you leave us now. Leave us, and you will have your reward."

"You are the fool," Alex spat back. "This treasure is not yours to give, and even if it were, it means nothing to me."

"Arrogant whelp!" the shadow screamed, its voice echoing around the empty room. "I have made you a fair offer, and once more you refuse me. So be it. Though I cannot harm you as I am, I can destroy your hopes. The library is mine, and it will remain mine."

The shadow turned to look at Val once more. Before Alex could move, Val had spoken into his bag and vanished.

"Before you could hope to strike at me, I will join my servant in his bag and use him to become greater than you can imagine," said the voice as if reading Alex's mind.

Alex stood in stunned silence, looking at the bag on the floor. With Val in his bag, Alex would be unable to move it from where it lay on the stone floor. He didn't know what to do. He had tried for weeks to think of a way to destroy the library, but now it was out of his reach.

"Your time is short, wizard. You dare not wait if your friends' lives mean anything to you," the shadow voice mocked.

The dark shadow claimed that Alex could not destroy it, but Alex knew that was a lie. He decided he had to do something, no matter how foolish it might seem. Lifting his hands, Alex focused all his thoughts and power on Val's bag. The magic of the bag would only let the adventurer who owned it move it from the floor, but Alex didn't want to move the bag, he wanted something else.

There was a loud crack, like ice shifting on a frozen lake, and it was done. A large black stone now stood on the floor where Val's bag had been. Alex felt completely drained. Changing the magic bag had taken all the power he could summon, and now he had nothing left to fight the shadow.

"Very clever," said the shadow. "You have prevented me from joining my servant and using the library, but it is a small victory. I may not be able to destroy you in my present form, but I will find another way. There are always fools who will let me into their hearts and minds. And time is on my side."

Alex knew the evil voice spoke the truth this time. He had stopped the shadow for the time being, but another wizard could change the stone back into a magic bag. And Alex could not stay and protect the stone forever.

"So, young wizard, you have failed. I will leave you now to ponder your defeat, and I will return at my convenience to claim my prize."

The shadow figure changed as it finished speaking, becoming a misty, almost fluid, form. Alex watched it change, too tired to stop it or even to speak. A shrieking ice-cold wind blew past Alex, pushing him down until he was flat on his back. And then the shadow was gone.

Alex struggled to his knees. He was cold, sad, and defeated. He had failed completely. The shadow was still free, and, worse, it would return. For a moment he felt like crying, but then a voice he had never heard before came into his mind.

"Simple solutions are often the best," the voice said.

Alex shook his head. There was no simple solution to this problem, at least none that he could think of. Then another voice came to his mind, a kind, soft voice: the voice of the sphinx.

"Unseen but heard, untouched but felt," the voice said softly. The riddle of the sphinx returned to Alex's mind, and he felt as if a light had been turned on inside his head.

Alex started to laugh as the cold slipped away. He felt his strength return to him in a dazzling rush that almost took his breath away. The answer was so simple, so obvious, and so clever that he had never considered it. Standing up, Alex moved to the stone that had once been the magic bag of Sedric Valenteen. Alex felt sorry for Val, but he knew that Val had made his own choice, and now he had to suffer the consequences of that choice.

Lifting his hands and pulling all of his magic to him, Alex closed his eyes. A cool breeze blew across his face once more, and when he opened his eyes, the stone was gone. Worry slipped away; Alex was certain that no one would ever be able to change the cool breeze back into a stone or a magic bag. He had won in the end, and the shadow didn't even know it. Someday the shadow would return here to claim its prize and find nothing at all.

Tired, but pleased with his success, Alex looked around at the room full of treasure. If Val had an heir, all of this belonged to them. He would take it and hope to return it to Val's family sometime in the future. He took his magic bag and spoke into it. The air seemed to ripple and spark once more, and the treasure disappeared with a flash.

Alex moved back to the stairway as fast as he could, not wanting to waste another moment. He ran up the two flights of stairs, his legs burning with the effort. When he reached the main chamber, he paused for a moment. He didn't know how much time had passed, but he thought it couldn't be more than an hour. With only a moment of thought, he went to the stairway that led higher into the tower. He wanted to find the upper library and the Horn of Moran, if it was there.

At the top of the stairway was a door, which Alex opened to see another large chamber full of treasure. Ignoring the treasure, he continued forward toward another stairway at the far end of the chamber. He knew where it would lead him.

At the top of the second set of stairs, Alex found himself in the upper library of the Tower of the Moon, surrounded by shelves, tables, and thousands of books. He quickly reached for his magic bag, holding it out toward the center of the room.

"Treasure room," Alex said loudly.

With a sound like rushing wind, the entire library disappeared into his bag. Only one thing remained, and it was something Alex had not noticed when he'd first entered the room. He moved closer, looking at the strange object in wonder.

Against the back wall a single stone table remained and hovering just above the tabletop was a bright silver flame. The flames moved like a living thing, but Alex didn't feel any heat coming from them. For a few minutes he stood looking at the flames, and a strange desire to reach out and touch the silver fire filled his mind.

"Take it," a voice whispered to him. "Take the power and become the master."

Before he knew what he was doing, Alex reached out his hand toward the flame. Alarm bells rang wildly inside his head, warning him to stop, but his hand continued to move forward.

"A wizard born in Norsland must come," another voice yelled inside his head. "Only a wizard born in Norsland can take this power."

Alex's hand stopped moving, his fingers slowly curling into a fist. Cara had told him about the legend of the tower, about a wizard who would come to save his people. Alex knew he could touch the flame and become the master of all the magic in Norsland, but then the legend would fail. Worse, if he took the power, he would have to remain as the guardian of the tower for as long as he lived.

"No," Alex said softly. "This is not for me. Another will come to guard this power."

"Wise. Very wise," a deep voice answered.

Alex spun around at the sound of the voice.

A ghostly image of a man moved across the empty room, stopping a few feet from Alex. "I am sorry you had to be tested like that," he said. "All who enter the tower must face the test of the flame, but you are the first to ever pass the test."

"Who are you?"

"I am Garson," the ghost answered. "I was the last guardian of the tower. Now I wait to pass on the knowledge I have and the secrets I have kept to the new guardian."

"I am Alexander Taylor," Alex said.

"You are a wizard and an adventurer." Garson nodded. "You have come here looking for the Horn of Moran. Yes, I know. I can see your power, and I am glad you have come. The Horn is with the treasure of the tower, but it does not belong here. It must be returned to Alusia."

"Yes," said Alex. "The Horn is needed to prove the true king of Athanor."

"Oh, it will do much more than that," said Garson. "The Horn is one of three guardian objects that bind the people of Alusia together. It is the simplest of the three, and the only one that could be taken from the land. But simple or not, it is part of Alusia, and it must be returned. It has only been here for a short time, but already Alusia is breaking apart. The Horn will help unite the people once more."

"If the Horn is so important, why was the prince allowed to take it from Alusia? Why bring it here?"

"The people have forgotten what the Horn is," Garson answered sadly.

"What happened to the prince?" Alex questioned. "And to the adventurers who were with him?"

"The men who came here with the Horn were adventurers, but not wizards. They felt the same desire you did to touch the flame, but they were not wise enough to see that the power was not free for the taking. They failed the test and were destroyed. I am sorry that it happened, but I could not stop it."

"I have destroyed the lower library of the tower," Alex said after a moment of silence. "I have taken the upper library and put it in my bag. I will not restore the lower library, but I should leave the upper library here."

"The tower is more than libraries and treasure," Garson replied with a wave of his ghostly hand. "Libraries can be replaced. Take what you have won and learn from it. Take the treasure in the room below as a reward; the Horn you seek is with the treasure. I ask only that you leave some token of yourself behind to mark you as a friend of the tower. Perhaps someday you will return, and if you are a friend of the tower, the guardians will allow you free access."

"Thank you," said Alex. "I am sorry I cannot stay. The guardians gave me three hours to destroy the evil that came here, and that time is running out."

"You have other reasons to hurry," said Garson. "There is

a storm brewing. Winter is closing in; I do not think you will be able to outrun it."

"We can't wait for winter to pass," Alex said in a worried tone. "We have to get back to Alusia before the spring festival or else there will be war."

"The storms that are coming cannot be stopped," Garson answered slowly. "As I am now, I have little power in this land, and even less in others. I can, however, see some of what the future holds. I see that your friends have been touched by a curse. You will be stopped by winter, but not for as long as you fear. You will be able to move south much sooner than you might expect."

"That is something," said Alex, thinking of the ghost's words.

"Little things often make the biggest difference," Garson said softly as his image started to fade. "You should go. Move as quickly as you can, young wizard. Time is running out."

The ghost vanished before Alex could reply. Without waiting, Alex hurried back down the stairs to the chamber full of treasure. He knew the Horn was here, somewhere, but Garson was right, he didn't have time to look for it.

"Treasure room, separate," said Alex, hoping the bag would understand what he wanted it to do.

Once again there was the sound of rushing wind as the air rippled and sparked. When the chamber was emptied, Alex shifted his bag to his shoulder. He took a single gold coin from his moneybag. With a little effort, he changed the appearance of the coin in his hand. Tossing the coin toward the center of the empty treasure room, he caught it with magic before it hit the floor. The gold coin flashed as it spun in midair, held by a magical thread.

With a bit of pride, Alex looked at the token he had created that marked him as a friend of the tower. One side of the coin held the image of a dragon's head with eight stars around it, while the other side had the image of Moon Slayer on it. Alex knew that the coin would remain where it was until the next keeper of the tower came to claim the power of Norsland. And he knew from his dreams that he would also return when that time came.

Running out of the tower, Alex started down the path to the second gate and his friends. The sun was coming up, and in the dim morning light, he saw Sindar arguing with the griffins, demanding that they let him pass and allow him access to the tower.

"It's all right," called Alex. "The evil has gone."

Bowing, the griffins moved aside without speaking to let Alex pass between them. Then they moved back to block the path to the tower.

"How are you, Sindar?"

"Better now that I see you, my friend," Sindar answered.

"And the others?"

Sindar hesitated. "I don't know what's wrong with them. They seem to be stunned, but otherwise unhurt. When I ask them to stand or move, they do as I bid, but they don't seem to see what is around them. And they cannot speak at all."

"You seem to have recovered," said Alex. "Though I was worried when I first found you."

"Evil has less effect on me than on others," said Sindar.

"And I was lucky you were able to recover my pendant for me. It has taken most of the time that you've been gone for me to recover, and I still feel a deep coldness inside."

"It will pass," said Alex.

Alex and Sindar returned to their campsite and tried once more to revive their companions, but nothing seemed to work. Alex didn't know any spell that could reverse the curse, and he was tired. Changing Val's magic bag into a stone had drained him, and changing the stone into a breeze had taken even more out of him, far more than all his running up and down the tower stairs.

"We need to get out of the mountains," said Alex, dropping onto his blankets beside the fire.

"Yes, but perhaps first you should rest."

Alex shook his head. "I'll be fine. I should send a message to Whalen. He may know how to break this spell."

"Possibly, but do we have time to wait for a reply?"

"No," said Alex with a sigh. He rubbed his eyes. "I'll send a message and then we can break camp."

"Rest first," said Sindar softly. "Collect your thoughts and rest your body. You've had a long night."

Alex's eyes were already closing. He would rest for an hour or two, then send a message to Whalen.

Whalen will know what to do, he thought as he drifted off to sleep. *Whalen is a great wizard. He always knows what to do.*

When Alex woke, he felt much better. Looking at the sun, he could tell he had been asleep for almost three hours. Sindar was walking around the fire with Andy, but Andy seemed unaware of anything around him.

"Any improvement?" Alex asked.

"No. I thought perhaps moving around would help them, but they seem unchanged."

"They will be moving around quite a bit soon enough. Let me send a message to Whalen, and then we'll start back down the mountain."

Sindar nodded, but said nothing, helping Andy sit back down beside the fire. While Alex wrote his message, he noticed the blank stare on Andy's face. He hoped that Whalen would have an answer and that the answer would come soon.

Once Alex had sent his message, he and Sindar began leading the others back down the path toward the first gate. Their going was painfully slow because their companions would run into the stone sides of the trail yet continue trying to move forward. After several hours of turning their friends back onto the path, Sindar came up with a clever solution.

Fastening a length of rope to each member of the company, Sindar was able to pull their dazed companions into the correct path as they went along. But even with this improvement, their progress was incredibly slow.

What had been a day's travel going up the path took them almost three days to travel back down. Alex was beginning to worry that they wouldn't be off the mountains before the snow began to fall, and he certainly didn't want to spend the winter stuck on the mountainside.

"From here on it will be more difficult," said Sindar, dropping to the ground beside Alex. "The path is steep, and there aren't any rock walls to keep our friends from falling off the edge."

"I know," said Alex. "And they don't seem to be improving at all." He thought for a moment. "I suppose I could change our friends into mice and carry them down the mountain inside my magic bag."

"Do you think you could do that?"

"Perhaps, but I've never transfigured a human, and I'd hate to accidentally hurt one of our friends."

"Then don't think on it," Sindar advised. "We will manage, somehow."

Alex simply nodded. What he had said wasn't entirely true. When Alex had transfigured Val's magic bag, Val had been inside it at the time. It wasn't a pleasant thought and he pushed it aside. Transfiguration was a simple solution, but not one he was willing to try on his friends, at least not yet.

"Perhaps we should just put them inside one of our magic bags as they are," Alex said softly.

"A simple solution to our problem, but there are dangers. We do not know what magic Val used on them, and the magic inside the bag may trigger some greater damage."

"Yes, I suppose that is possible," said Alex. "And then there are the rules of honor to consider."

"Giving another the safety of your bag without his consent is a loss of honor for both the person being protected and the holder of the bag," said Sindar in a troubled voice. "The rules of honor are there for good reasons, but those reasons hardly apply right now."

"If things get worse and we can't get off the mountain, we may have to risk that loss of honor."

"Not yet. Not if there is another way to save our friends. We will find a way to save them, Alex. I'm sure we will."

For a long time they sat in silence. Alex felt too tired to sleep or think. He lay back on his blankets and watched the stars above him, letting his thoughts wander freely.

"You have not said what happened in the tower," Sindar said softly.

"We haven't had time," Alex replied. "And I'm not sure I can really explain everything."

"Rest, Alex. The morning may bring new hope."

"And a message from Whalen," Alex added, his mind and body finally succumbing to sleep.

Alex woke to the dinging of a geeb and was glad to find a message from Whalen had indeed arrived. He paid the geeb and tore open the letter, his hopes high that the answer he needed was here.

Dear Alex,

I will not trouble you for details now as I understand the situation you are in. I'm afraid I can't be of much help to you. There is a spell that might cure your friends, but I cannot write it here, and even if I could, I'm not completely sure you could use it. It is a difficult spell to work and can go very badly wrong if not done correctly.

My best advice to you is to get to the enchanted woods as quickly as you can. You may find help in the woods, if you can reach them before the snows block your way. I believe that time will heal your friends, but winter is coming and you can't wait.

I am sorry that I cannot be of more help to you at this time. Whatever happens, don't give up.

Yours in fellowship,
Whalen

Alex showed the letter to Sindar before storing it in his bag. He felt a little frustrated that Whalen had the answer but that he could not share it. Now he and Sindar would have to do what they could, and Alex wasn't at all sure it would be enough.

Chapter Thirteen

Brownies

Alex had managed to defeat the evil shadow, destroy the lower library, and recover the Horn of Moran, but he felt like none of that mattered. They were still trapped on the mountain, and his friends were helpless. For the first time Alex thought their adventure might be a failure, and his mood grew darker as he considered what that failure would mean.

"Comc," said Sindar. "We will do what needs to be done."

Alex agreed and tried to shake off his dark mood. Both Whalen and Garson had told him not to give up or give in to despair, but Alex felt that this was an almost hopeless situation. If Whalen had been there, he could have cured Bregnest, Halfdan, and Andy, and they could easily get off the mountains. In the end, however, Alex knew there was nothing he could do but carry on. If they were going to get off the mountains before winter set in, it was up to Sindar and himself to get them off.

They moved along the trail more slowly now, staying close to the mountain and avoiding the edge. To keep from losing one of their friends over the edge, Alex and Sindar were forced to move them one at a time. This was tiring and time-consuming because Alex and Sindar had to climb each section of the path twice and descend it three times to move the company forward at all.

After ten days of moving forward only a few hundred yards at a time, they finally reached the spot where they had camped their first night on the mountain. The wind blew constantly, and the sun hardly ever came out from behind the gray clouds that filled the sky.

"We're almost down," said Sindar. "Perhaps another two or three days and we'll finally be off the mountain."

"And then what?" Alex asked softly.

"Whalen said we might find help in the enchanted woods. At least we will find shelter there from the coming snows."

"I'm sorry," said Alex, looking at Sindar. "I've been letting myself think only dark thoughts of failure. I'm feeling sorry for myself, I guess."

"Sorry for yourself or for your friends?" Sindar questioned.

"A little of both I suppose."

"Then stop one and do what you can to help the other."

Alex knew there was no reason to be depressed. They would make it off the mountains and to the enchanted woods before it started to snow. He had the Horn of Moran in his bag, but still, he couldn't find any joy inside himself. Worry filled his mind, and not just about his friends. Alusia needed the Horn of Moran in order to know who the true king was. But even more important than that, the Horn would unite the people of Alusia and stop the different kingdoms from drifting apart and falling into an unending series of wars.

It took the company three more days to reach the first gate, and it was already dark when they got there. The sphinx watched them silently as they approached and passed through the gate.

Alex wanted to move on at once, but Sindar insisted they rest before starting for the woods. Alex reluctantly agreed. He had only slept for a few hours each day and had hardly eaten since leaving the Tower of the Moon. All he could think about was helping his friends by getting to the enchanted woods before the snow started to fall.

"All right," Alex said. "We will rest. But only for an hour or two. The snow will be falling soon, and I can rest once we get to the woods."

Alex conjured a fire to keep the company warm, and then helped Sindar wrap their companions in blankets. Sindar quickly cooked a meal for the two of them and made Alex eat a second helping. When he was finished eating, Alex lay down and almost instantly fell asleep. His dreams, however, were dark and troubled, and not at all restful. It wasn't long before Alex woke, and when he did, he found snowflakes falling on his face.

"We must hurry," said Alex, jumping to his feet. "If the snow gets too heavy, we won't be able to find the woods at all."

"I will lead," said Sindar, attaching the guide rope to his belt. "I can see better in the darkness, and it would be deadly to get lost now."

Sindar set a quick pace, and Alex had trouble keeping up. He felt tired and weak, and with each step, his feet felt heavier. The cold wind numbed his senses. At times it seemed that Sindar was pulling the entire company forward like a great sleigh horse in the snow. The ground was already white, and the air was so full of snowflakes that it was hard to see anything. They had walked for a long time when Sindar suddenly stopped.

"The snow is too thick," Sindar yelled over the howling wind. "I can't see where we are going."

"We can't stop here," Alex yelled back.

"We can't go on without some kind of guide. We could wander for days in this storm and never find the woods."

"I have an idea," said Alex, forcing his nearly frozen brain to work.

Holding his hands close together, Alex conjured up a large, bright blue weir light. Concentrating on where he wanted to go, he focused on the light that hovered in front of him and simply said, "Lead me."

The light hovered for a moment and then moved slowly forward and to Alex's left. Alex and Sindar quickly changed places in the marching order, retying the rope that held the company together. The weir light seemed to wait for Alex to follow and never moved too far ahead of him. It always seemed to move in a straight line, though it was hard to be sure in the blowing snow.

The snow was soon ankle-deep, but the weir light continued to guide them. Alex desperately hoped that his magic was working, because if it wasn't, they might be traveling in circles. After walking for what seemed like hours, Alex finally saw the dark shapes of trees ahead of him, and he let out a sigh of relief.

As they continued to move forward, the snow grew lighter, and in a few minutes they were inside the enchanted woods.

"A useful bit of magic," said Sindar. "A pity that Halfdan didn't see it, he would have enjoyed that very much."

"Perhaps another time," said Alex, conjuring several additional weir lights to guide them into the dark woods.

"It is warmer here. The air is much warmer, in fact."

Alex had noticed it as well. The change in temperature would normally have troubled him, but all he wanted now was to find a place to sleep.

After moving into the woods a short distance, they came upon a small meadow. Alex stopped the company and untied the rope from his belt. He was so tired that he could barely help Sindar with the others. He lit a fire and let the weir lights fade.

"I need to sleep," said Alex, dropping onto his blanket. "I don't think I've ever felt so tired."

"Rest, my friend," said Sindar. "I will watch and keep the fire burning. You have done a great thing, and have earned a rest."

"*We* have done a great thing," Alex corrected as he closed his eyes.

When Alex woke up, the sky was much lighter, and he thought he heard Sindar talking to someone. Alex hoped that his friends had recovered, but when he sat up, he saw Sindar sitting alone by the fire. The fire was larger than it had been, and Alex wondered why Sindar had built it up so much.

"Who are you talking to?" Alex asked.

"The brownies, of course," Sindar answered.

"Brownies?"

Sindar grinned and pointed to a large brown stump a short distance from the fire. Alex didn't remember the stump being there, and he felt a little confused. Rubbing the sleep out of his eyes, he suddenly realized that the stump was actually a small, brown-skinned creature that looked more like a miniature dwarf than anything else Alex could think of.

"Welcome, master wizard," said the creature, removing its pointy hat and bowing to Alex. "We hoped that you would be returning to our woods."

Alex blinked several times to make sure he was seeing what he thought he was seeing. The brownie giggled, and Alex recognized the sound as the laughter he'd heard when they had passed through the enchanted woods before. The brownie took a few steps closer, then bowed once more.

"I am Tip, at your service," said the brownie.

"Thank you," Alex managed to reply.

"I was just discussing our friends with Tip," said Sindar. "It seems that he and his people might be able to help them."

"If you can, we would be very much in your debt," said Alex as he studied the brownie in front of him.

"Oh yes, I'm sure we can help, but there are a few difficulties involved," Tip answered.

"Difficulties? What difficulties?"

"Well, as I was telling your friend Sindar, we don't like to show ourselves to humans or dwarfs," said Tip, turning slightly red in embarrassment.

"But I'm a human."

"You're a wizard," said Tip. "And that makes a difference."

"So, you can help them, but you don't want them to see you," said Alex, slightly puzzled.

"Not exactly," said Tip. "We can help them, but we don't want them to know we helped them, or even that we were here."

"And that is the difficulty," said Sindar, looking at Alex.

"I see," said Alex, trying to think of a way around this difficulty.

"I do have a solution," Tip said.

"And what is that?" Alex asked with interest.

"We could put your friends in an enchanted sleep," said Tip. "They could sleep all winter, and when spring comes, they will wake up and be themselves again."

"And this is your solution?"

"In part," Tip answered. "You see, the enchanted sleep will help them heal faster, and they wouldn't know we helped them. Unless, of course, you tell them."

"I see," said Alex with a soft laugh. "So Sindar and I need to promise not to tell them about you."

"Exactly," said Sindar.

"And you would be willing to take our word?" Alex asked Tip.

"Of course," Tip answered in a surprised tone. "Elves we trust very much, and wizards we know do not lie. At least good wizards don't, and we know you are a good wizard, so that's that."

"Well then, Sindar, what do you say?" Alex questioned.

"I have already given my word to tell no human or dwarf about what happens here," said Sindar. "Of course, wizards are another story, so I'm sure you could tell Whalen."

"Oh, yes, we know Whalen Vankin and we trust him very much," said Tip, his head bobbing up and down rapidly. "But you must promise not to tell your friends what happened to them here. Neither them, nor any other human or dwarf."

"I promise not to tell any human or dwarf what happens here, or about your people who live here in the enchanted woods," said Alex.

"Very good," said Tip, beaming at Alex. "Now, we will take you and Sindar to a much nicer place where you can spend the winter as our guests."

"And our friends?" Alex questioned, not wanting to leave Bregnest, Andy, and Halfdan lying in the meadow.

"We will take them to another place, near the southern edge of the woods," Tip answered. "When spring is near, we will lead you and Sindar to them, and then you can wake them up."

"Very well," said Alex. "We accept your kind offer."

Tip seemed thrilled. He gave a short, loud whistle, and the meadow suddenly came alive with brownies. Alex and Sindar both laughed as what appeared to be hundreds of brownies bowed and introduced themselves. After a moment, Tip clapped his hands three times and the brownies became almost instantly quiet. Tip gave instructions for a group of brownies to move Bregnest, Andy, and Halfdan, and then asked Alex and Sindar to follow him.

Alex was still tired, but he got up and followed Tip into the trees, still surrounded by the rest of the brownies. After a short hike through the woods, they arrived at the strangest-looking village Alex had ever seen. The brownies' houses were all between six and eight feet high and painted in every color imaginable. Some of the houses were all one color, but most were a mixture of colors and patterns. Alex particularly liked one large house that was painted with red and white stripes like a giant peppermint.

"Welcome to our village," said Tip when they reached the town square. "We have a small house prepared for you, though it is not as grand as we might hope. I thought you might want to rest a bit and take a bath before this evening's feast."

"You are most kind," said Sindar. "I am sure that my friend and I will be comfortable."

"Indeed, your kindness overwhelms us," Alex replied.

Alex and Sindar both bowed to Tip, which seemed to please him and make him laugh at the same time. Tip then led them to a small cottage just outside the brownie village. It was actually a very nice cottage, with one large room that had a table, a sink, and two beds in it, and a smaller room with a large bathtub in it.

"I'll leave you until the feast," said Tip. "If you need anything at all, just ask."

"Thank you very much," Alex and Sindar said at the same time.

Tip closed the door behind him, and Alex looked at Sindar

in amazement. He had never considered the possibility that brownies lived in the enchanted woods, though now he understood what Whalen had said about finding help here.

"Did you know they were here?" Alex asked as he tested one of the beds.

"No, but I could feel their goodness when we passed though the woods before. Though at the time, I didn't know where that goodness came from."

"I suppose we're lucky they decided to help us," Alex commented, feeling sleepy once again.

"I think we can thank your weir lights for that," said Sindar, testing the other bed.

"Why is that?"

"Because they saw the lights and decided to investigate them. Tip told me before you woke up. They were impressed by the lights; I'll be surprised if they don't ask you to conjure them up again."

"That wouldn't be a problem," said Alex as he yawned.

"Perhaps you should finish your night's sleep," said Sindar. "I'm going to take a bath."

"Wake me when you're done," said Alex, before rolling over and going back to sleep.

When Sindar woke Alex, it was several hours later. Alex felt refreshed and hungry, now that he knew they were all safe. He rolled slowly off his bed and began taking off his boots.

"I thought you might have needed sleep more than a bath," said Sindar with a smile. "And now you'll have to wait for a bit, as our hosts are bringing our midday meal."

"Excellent. I feel like I haven't eaten in days."

There was a knock on the door, and a dozen brownies poured into the room before he or Sindar could even say, "Who's there?" The brownies all carried trays of food which seemed far too large for them, but they managed somehow. The table was soon filled, and Alex and Sindar both thanked their hosts, which made the brownies burst into a fit of giggles. As quickly as they appeared, the brownies vanished, leaving Alex and Sindar to their meal.

"Why do they laugh so much when we thank them?" Alex questioned as he started filling a plate with food.

"It's their way," Sindar said. "They prefer their help and service to remain anonymous. So when we notice them doing things for us and thank them, they think it's very funny."

"As long as they're happy."

"They're always happy. And it appears that they are good cooks as well."

As they ate their meal, Alex told Sindar what had happened in the Tower of the Moon. Sindar turned pale when Alex told him about the shadow, and about having met it once before in Vargland, but Alex didn't ask Sindar if he knew what it was.

"So you turned the stone into a breeze?" Sindar asked, making sure he had heard correctly.

"I did," said Alex. "I remembered the riddle the sphinx had asked, and it suddenly hit me that a breeze could never be turned back into a stone, or a magic bag."

"And the shadow had already left when you did that?"

"Yes."

"Well, it won't be happy if it ever returns."

"I hope it never returns. But if it does, it will go crazy trying to figure out where the stone has gone."

"No less than it deserves," Sindar observed. "I do feel sorry for Val though."

"So do I. I think he was once a good and honorable man."

"But he listened to the shadow," said Sindar. "He made his own choice, and it was a poor one."

"There is something else I wanted to talk to you about," Alex said, and then paused to consider his words. "The pendant you wear—the one you so desperately wanted just after the attack."

"Ah, yes. I have worn that for many years," said Sindar. "It is an ancient talisman. There is some magic in it, as I'm sure you noticed."

"Yes, I did, but that's not what I want to ask. You see . . . Well, it might be best to show you."

Alex reached for his magic bag and called out the pendant his father had left for him. Holding it up so Sindar could see it, he noticed a strange look on his friend's face, a look that vanished as quickly as it had appeared.

"My father hid this in his own magic bag," Alex explained. "He left a note with it, telling me that I could freely trust anyone who wore this symbol."

"Your father," Sindar repeated slowly. "Yes, I should have guessed, but . . ."

"But?" Alex prodded.

"It is difficult to keep track sometimes," Sindar answered. "I should have given things more thought when we first met. Your father—his first name was Joshua?"

"Yes."

Sindar nodded but remained silent for several minutes before speaking.

"I met your father once, many years ago. I did not get the chance to know him, but he was well-respected among us."

"Among the elves, you mean," Alex clarified.

"Oh, yes, among the elves, but that isn't what I'm talking about. You see, the pendant is a symbol of the ancient order of Malgor."

"The order of Malgor? What is that?"

"Basically the order is a collection of people who gather information. We keep records about people, places, cities—all kinds of things."

"Why?" Alex asked. "What are the records used for?"

"From time to time we discover something important. I say discover, but it is more like making connections between points of information. When we do find something, we pass the information along to the people who need to know."

"I don't understand. What information? Who runs the order? Why was it set up in the first place?"

"I can tell you some things, but not everything," said Sindar after a moment of thought. "For example, I can tell you that when I return home, I will report on this adventure and the fact that there appear to be more goblins in Norsland than there once were—including the presence of a goblin shaman. The order might decide that they need more information about goblins in Norsland, or they might just let the kingdoms of Norsland know that there are more goblins."

"I see," said Alex. "Still, who is in charge? Who decides

what information is important? What else does the order of Malgor do?"

"So many questions," said Sindar. "As for the who and the why, I don't think I should say. Many people who belong to the order do not know who is in charge, and since you are not a member . . ."

"I'm sorry," said Alex. "It's just so interesting. Obviously my father was a member of this order, and he wanted me to trust any members that I might meet."

"Yes, but I think your father may have overstated his desire. I would not be so quick to trust completely if I were you. You are a wizard after all, and blind trust does not go well with that title."

"You don't think I should trust the members of the order?"

"I think you should use your own judgment," said Sindar. "Now, I think you should take a bath and get ready for the feast. It should be a merry night."

Sindar said nothing more about the order of Malgor, and Alex didn't press him for answers. He knew enough for now, and he promised himself that someday he would know more.

The brownies were thrilled that Alex and Sindar were their guests and would squeal and giggle when either of them would thank them for their kindness. Alex tried hard to remember all the brownies' names, but there were just too many of them, and the brownies all looked very much alike to him. Whenever he would call a brownie by the wrong name, the brownie would think he was making a wonderful joke, and then tell him its correct name. In the end, Alex stopped trying to sort it out.

The days passed swiftly, and the brownies never seemed to grow tired of Alex and Sindar asking them questions or thanking them. Often Alex would conjure up weir lights and send them floating around the village, changing colors from time to time as they went. The brownies seemed to enjoy the lights even more than Halfdan had, and it made Alex happy to hear them laugh in surprise whenever one of the lights changed colors.

After a week in the village, Alex sent Whalen a long message, telling him everything that had happened at the tower and how he and Sindar were now guests in the brownie village. Alex also spent a fair amount of time in his bag, sorting through the treasure he'd recovered from the tower. He was hoping to have the treasure sorted and divided before they started south once more, but that was going to take some work. A few weeks later, Whalen sent a reply to Alex's message.

Dear Alex,

You have done better than I had hoped. I am impressed with the way you've handled things. I never would have thought to change the stone into a breeze. Very clever on your part, I must say.

I do have some ideas about what the shadow is, but it will take some explaining, which I would rather do in person. I hope to meet you on your return to Telous, or perhaps in Alusia. I believe Bregnest, once he is recovered, will insist that you all go with him to complete your adventure by returning the Horn.

I was sorry to hear about Sedric Valenteen, but, as

you said, he made his choice. You did what had to be done, so don't blame yourself for what happened.

Continue to study your books, and feel free to start looking through the upper library, which you now have in your bag. I don't think you will need to update me quite so often, but feel free to write if you have questions. Also, I think you can judge for yourself when you should and should not use your powers, so don't let my earlier warnings stop you from doing something you feel needs doing. Of course, don't use your powers for just anything; use your common sense and you should be fine.

Yours in fellowship,
Whalen

P.S. Just a reminder to honor your promise to Tip. I know you would never break your promise on purpose, but you may find it difficult to keep once your friends recover. Perhaps you and Sindar should agree on a story for your friends. You still have time to think of something before they wake up.

Whalen's letter lifted Alex's spirits, and that afternoon he started working on a story with Sindar. They decided, after some debate, that the simple truth would work best. No mention of the brownies would be made, but the fact that the two of them had been stuck in the woods would be enough.

"Our adventure climbing down the mountain will be far more interesting," Sindar commented. "The fact that we spent a few weeks or even months in the woods, with nothing to do but wait, will not attract many questions."

As the days passed, Alex continued to sort the treasure from the tower and search for the Horn of Moran. Other days, he would look through the large library or visit with the brownies.

Winter continued, and Alex and Sindar both watched the weather for any sign that they could safely move on. Sometimes Alex would wander to the edge of the enchanted woods and look out across the frozen waste, thinking about the future. He appreciated Usel's warning about not being in the frozen waste when winter came. The snow was almost as deep as Alex was tall, and the wind blew wildly across the open land.

Alex used his time to study and practice his magic, and to just think. He even had time to reread some of his books and learn how to magically mend Halfdan's cooking pot. It was an odd bit of magic, but after a little practice, Alex was able to make the pot as good as new. He was pleased with his work, and he knew Halfdan would be glad to have his pot back.

"You seem strangely quiet," said Sindar, one night after another excellent feast with the brownies. "Are you troubled?"

"Not troubled. Just thoughtful."

"More like a wizard all the time."

"Or more like an elf," Alex answered and laughed. "I was just thinking about something—something I'm not likely to find an answer to."

"And why would you spend time thinking about things that have no answers?"

"Oh, there is an answer, I'm sure of that," said Alex. "I'm just not likely to find it anytime soon."

"Then I suppose thinking about it won't hurt, as long as you are prepared to wait for your answers."

"I can wait. I believe I am less hotheaded than I once was."

"I believe that you are," said Sindar.

It wasn't until Alex had sorted almost all the treasure from the Tower of the Moon that he found the Horn of Moran. It was about eighteen inches long and perhaps eight or nine inches across at its widest point. It was made of a black material that Alex had never seen before, and the gentle curve made it look like a horn from some enormous animal. True silver bands had been wrapped around either end, and there were loops in the silver where a strap could be attached so the horn could be carried. Alex showed the Horn to Sindar, who was stunned when he saw it.

"It's been carved from a Durnlow horn," Sindar whispered in awe.

"What's a Durnlow?" Alex questioned.

"They are a rare and magical creature, something like a giant goat or perhaps more like a ram," Sindar explained. "Stories say that they are even more magical than dragons, and that to see one means good fortune for the rest of your days. Their horns cannot be taken from them, but they can be given as gifts to those the Durnlow deems worthy."

"It is one of the three guardian objects of Alusia," said Alex. "It makes sense that it would be something as special as a Durnlow horn. I wonder what it sounds like. You know, when the true king blows it."

"I would not try to sound the Horn if I were you," said Sindar. "If it makes no sound, we will think it a great joke, but if it plays a note, then what?"

"It won't play a note," said Alex.

"You do not know that for sure. Would you risk adding king to your already long list of titles?"

In the end, Alex took Sindar's advice and returned the Horn to his bag. He really didn't think the Horn would sound for him, but he didn't want to risk being called a king as well as a warrior, a wizard, and a dragon slayer.

Winter held an icy grip on the land, but as time went on, there was little new snow. Alex knew that they would soon be able to leave the enchanted woods and continue their adventure, even if the temperature remained cold. Alex would be sad to leave the brownies, but he was also looking forward to meeting Whalen in Telous.

One night, after another long feast, Tip came to their cottage. He was smiling, but even with his cheery face, he seemed sadder than Alex had ever seen him before.

"It is time," said Tip. "Winter is not over, but I think you will be able to travel south without too much trouble. Tomorrow I will lead you to your friends, and you can continue your adventure."

"We will be sorry to leave your village," said Sindar. "You have been most kind to us and to our sleeping friends."

"Oh, it's nothing." Tip laughed. "We seldom have guests, and such excellent guests at that."

"Can we do anything to repay your kindness?" Alex asked.

"You can keep your promise, which I'm sure you will," Tip

answered. "And if you get the chance, you might come and visit us again."

"Then we will hope for such a chance," said Alex. "Though you will forgive us if we don't bring such sleepy friends next time."

"Oh, of course," said Tip. "Now I'll let you get some sleep, and tomorrow we will be on our way."

Tip left Alex and Sindar alone, but they didn't feel like talking. They had agreed on the story they would tell their friends and the answers they would give to any questions. They had asked each other about the story so many times that they both knew every detail by heart. They both hoped that the story would satisfy their three sleeping friends.

Alex went to bed, and as he was falling asleep, he heard Sindar humming softly to himself in the darkness.

Chapter Fourteen

Awakening

The next morning was full of mixed feelings for Alex and Sindar. The brownies made a great fuss over saying good-bye and wishing them good luck. None of the brownies would accept any kind of gift, laughing whenever Alex or Sindar offered. Alex thought it strange that the brownies would be so helpful and yet so unwilling to receive anything in return. He thought there was a good lesson in their ways, but he knew that few people would see it.

Tip led Alex and Sindar through the woods for most of the day, but there was little talk as they went along. Dozens of brownies accompanied them, and when the group stopped for the night, the brownies took care of setting up camp, and before long they were all sitting around the fire, eating.

After they had eaten, Sindar told a story about an adventure he had been on, but Alex wasn't listening. His mind was already racing ahead, thinking of the dangers they might still have to face as they returned to Alusia. He had thought that finding the Horn would be the hardest part of the adventure, but now he worried that returning it to the rightful king might be harder still.

They continued walking all the next day, and as night was falling, they came to a large meadow. Alex and Sindar spotted their three friends lying in the soft grass at the edge of the meadow. They looked as if they were sound asleep, but otherwise quite normal.

"In the morning I will tell you how to wake them," said Tip. "Then we will leave you, and you can wake your friends and go on your way."

"Where is the road back across the frozen waste?" asked Sindar.

"If you leave this meadow at the far end, you will come across the road very soon," Tip answered, pointing. "You might have trouble traveling through the frozen waste, but if you continue south, you will be safe enough."

"You have been so kind to us, is there nothing we can do to repay you?" Alex asked once more.

"Oh, no," said Tip in a serious tone. "You have already repaid us by letting us help you."

"As you wish then," said Alex with a bow.

"Now, come my friends," said Tip. "One last feast before we part."

Alex and Sindar followed Tip back to the campfire and the feast, leaving their friends to sleep. When they had finished feasting, Alex put on a bit of a show for his friends. He conjured several large weir lights and sent them rocketing into the night sky like fireworks. When the lights began to look like stars, he would have them burst into dozens of smaller lights that fell slowly, fading just before they touched the ground.

The brownies were all delighted by Alex's show and cheered and clapped well into the night.

"We will be tired in the morning if you don't stop soon. Our friends have rested for months," said Sindar. "If we do not rest, they may leave us behind on the frozen waste."

Alex nodded, and sent one last light into the sky, which burst into a rain of gold and silver sparks as big as coins.

The next morning the brownies said their last good-byes to Alex and Sindar, still cheerful and as full of joy as always. When the last of the brownies disappeared into the woods, Tip turned to look at Alex and Sindar.

"Now, to wake your friends," said Tip. "All that you need to do is sprinkle a little water on their faces, like a soft rain. They will wake up and remember everything up to the time they went to sleep on the mountain."

"You have our thanks," said Sindar, as he and Alex bowed to Tip.

Tip simply waved his hand at them, and then followed the other brownies into the woods, vanishing from sight.

Alex and Sindar took out some water and woke their friends from their long sleep.

"How did we get here?" Andy questioned, sitting up and looking around in confusion. "And where is Val?"

"What happened on the mountain?" Halfdan demanded, wiping his face.

"Did you find the Horn?" Bregnest asked in concern.

"We will explain everything," said Sindar. "And yes, Alex has recovered the Horn of Moran."

The story of how Alex and Sindar had gotten the company

to the enchanted woods was a good one, but Halfdan continued to ask what they had been doing while stuck there. Bregnest was worried about how much time they had spent in the woods and kept asking how soon they would be able to move. It took some time for everything to be explained, and it was nearly midday before the entire story was told.

"So the evil was with Val?" Bregnest asked sadly.

"He carried it with him for a long time," said Alex, choosing his words carefully. "He said something about having met the evil on his last adventure."

"The fault is mine," said Bregnest. "I asked him to join the company. It is my honor alone that will be touched by this."

"Not so," Sindar said. "You could not have known. The evil was well-hidden. Even I was fooled and blinded by it, and that is much harder to do than you may think."

"Still, the choice was mine," said Bregnest. "I have lost at least part of my honor."

"Sindar is correct," said Alex. "The evil fooled us all. It is darker and more clever than you can believe. Even I, a wizard, did not see it until it was almost too late."

Bregnest nodded, but said nothing.

"It has all turned out well," said Halfdan. "The evil was defeated, the treasure recovered, and our goal accomplished."

"To blame yourself for this is foolish," added Andy.

"I was leader," said Bregnest. "I chose Val, and I alone must take the blame."

"Enough," said Alex in a stern tone that seemed to shock his friends. "Yes, Bregnest, you are the leader of this company, but there is no blame to be taken. This evil was far beyond your abilities to see, and I won't hear any more about a loss of honor. The quest has been completed, or almost, and the honor for its success is yours. You may have chosen Val—but you chose the rest of us as well."

Even Alex was surprised by his sudden outburst, but he felt that he'd said what needed to be said. Bregnest stopped talking about his loss of honor, and the others all looked at Alex in surprise.

"Now then," Alex said in a softer tone. "We have a long march across the frozen waste and a treasure to divide. I think the treasure should wait until later, but for now, I will deliver the Horn of Moran to you, Bregnest, for safekeeping."

Alex retrieved the Horn from his magic bag, and, bowing, he offered it to Bregnest. Bregnest seemed hesitant to take it, but after a moment, he accepted it from Alex with a low bow.

"The honor of the Horn's recovery is yours, my friend," replied Bregnest. "Though I will carry it as you ask."

"I recovered it only because you chose me to come on this adventure," said Alex. "So if my honor grows, so does yours."

Bregnest nodded and after a moment, cleared his throat. "Alex is right, the treasure from the tower can wait until we have crossed the frozen waste," he said, sounding like his old self.

Without any more talk they started off into the frozen waste. They all knew how long and hard their march would be, but there was little doubt about the success of their adventure.

As they made camp that first night, Alex retrieved Halfdan's pot from his magic bag and held it out for his friend to take. "I almost forgot to give this back to you."

Halfdan looked stunned and was unable to say anything for several seconds. "How?" he finally managed. "It was broken beyond repair."

"I had time to study my magic over the winter while you were sleeping, and I found a way to repair it," Alex answered.

Halfdan gently rubbed the iron pot, his eyes filled with wonder.

Alex was pleased that he could give Halfdan something so simple, yet which meant more to his friend than a pile of gold.

The days in the frozen waste passed slowly, and it wasn't until early on the fourteenth day that they reached the centaurs' woods.

Usel was waiting for them as they entered the woods, as if he had been expecting them. "We have seen fire on the frozen waste for many nights. We knew that this must mean your return."

"Our young wizard has been practicing his craft," replied Bregnest. "His abilities—"

"One of your company is missing," Usel interrupted.

"Val was lost to evil," said Bregnest, a dark look crossing his face. "Though it was an evil he chose and carried with him."

"Then he alone can answer for it," Usel observed, and without another word, turned and led the company into the woods.

When they reached the centaur village, they found that dozens of tables had been set up around a center table with an elaborate feast laid out for them. The centaurs all seemed much friendlier toward the company than they had been before, and this made Alex and his friends more relaxed as well.

As the feast was coming to an end, Usel asked Bregnest if the company was prepared to make their promised payment. Bregnest said that they were. While the company collected the silver and emeralds that Usel had requested, Usel joined his counselors at a separate table.

"You will each make payment for your own horse," said Usel. "Though now that there is a horse without a rider, we will not hold you accountable for its care."

"I will make the payment for the extra horse," said Bregnest. "As leader of this company, it is my duty and honor to do so."

"As you wish," said Usel, bowing slightly.

Usel called each of the company forward in turn, and he and his counselors accepted the payments. The centaurs all bowed as payment was made and thanked each member of the company. Bregnest and the rest of them thanked the centaurs in turn for the excellent care their horses had received.

"I suppose you'll want to go south as soon as possible," said Usel.

"We would be honored to remain in your woods if time permitted," said Bregnest. "But we have already been on this adventure longer than I thought we would be."

"Then in the morning you shall depart. But tonight, will you share your story with us?"

"Gladly," answered Bregnest.

That night Alex and his friends sat around a large fire with Usel and his counselors. Bregnest told most of their tale, though Sindar told the parts after the company had been attacked in front of the Tower of the Moon. Alex noticed that Usel had a strange look on his face when Sindar told about their stay in the enchanted woods, as though he heard more than was being said. Usel made no comments, however, and seemed to accept the story as Sindar told it.

Later that night, as his companions slept, Alex got up and walked away from their camp. He was troubled, thinking about Val and what had happened to him. He wanted to ask Bregnest if Val had an heir, but he didn't want Bregnest to start blaming himself for Val's evil again.

"Are you in need of something?" a voice questioned from the darkness.

"No, I am not," said Alex, looking up at Usel. "I'm just restless and have too many thoughts to sleep."

"I understand. You are concerned about your friend, Bregnest, and about the adventurer who was lost."

"Yes, I am. Bregnest believes it is his fault that Val was lost."

"But surely you have spoken to him about this. He cannot doubt your word that he is not to blame."

"I don't know," Alex replied thoughtfully. "Perhaps he doesn't doubt what we've said, or even really feel that he is to blame. But I know he feels that his honor has been damaged."

"So it has," said Usel in a kind and understanding voice. "For when any man does evil, it damages the honor of all."

"True," Alex agreed. "Bregnest, however, feels this loss of honor more keenly than the rest of us."

"He is a man of deep feeling and thought. I think, in time, he will see that his honor has not been damaged greatly."

"I hope so. He is a good man, and my friend."

"You think a great deal of your friends," Usel said softly. "Such friendship speaks well of a man, and may well increase the honor that he holds so dear."

"You speak wisely, Usel. I wish we could remain with your people for a time. I would like to learn more of your wisdom."

Usel nodded his head slowly, but did not reply. For a long time Alex and the centaur simply stood in the dark woods, gazing into the night sky. As the moon was sinking into the trees, Usel suggested that Alex get some sleep. Alex agreed even though he wasn't tired. He thanked Usel for his kindness and quietly made his way back to his blankets.

In the morning, after they had eaten and said their good-byes to Usel and his people, their horses were brought to them. Shahree was eager to be on the road again, and she shook her head and stomped her hoof impatiently. Alex noticed that Val's horse was with the others, and he wondered what would become of it.

"The horse is yours, Alex," said Bregnest. "You defeated the evil, and the horse belongs to you now. Also, the treasure that Val offered you in the tower is yours to keep or give away as you please."

"Did Val have an heir or any family?" Alex asked in a hopeful tone.

"None that I know of," Bregnest answered. "I will check with Mr. Clutter when we return to Telous, if you wish. Or you might ask the bag maker."

Alex nodded and took the reins of Val's horse in his hands. The horse was a kind-looking animal, dark brown with a black mane and tail. Alex wondered what he would do with the horse, but then he thought of the reward for the Horn's return—a thousand Alusian horses—and shook his head. It seemed that he would have many horses to deal with, once they reached Alusia.

Usel and the other centaurs waved good-bye as they rode into the woods, and they were soon lost to sight in the maze of trees.

Alex and his friends continued forward without talking, each of them thinking his own thoughts, and all of them relieved to be heading south once more.

The winter days were short, and the weather remained cold as they traveled. It sometimes snowed a little at night, but never enough to slow them down for long. Alex continued to send messages to Whalen, though not as many as he had before. He had finished studying the books Whalen had sent him at the end of his first adventure, and now he was looking through the books of the upper library. He decided he'd ask the bag maker to modify his library to expand as needed.

It wasn't long before the company was back in the valley where they had first seen the goblins. It was midday, and there was no sign that goblins had been using the valley since the last time they had been here. They hurried on, however, not wanting to linger so close to the place where their adventure had nearly come to an end.

"How much time do you think we have left?" Alex asked that night as they sat around their campfire.

"If all goes well, we should reach Alusia well before the spring festival," Bregnest answered. "The road from Athanor to the arch took me nearly three weeks, so it will probably take us three weeks to return to Athanor with the Horn. And once we get there, we may still have trouble reaching the king. If Kappa has men watching the road with orders to stop us, things could become difficult."

"I'll be glad to get to Alusia," Halfdan commented. "Don't remember what it's like to be properly warm."

"We can travel across the country if we have to," Sindar said to Bregnest, ignoring Halfdan's comment. "We will fight our way there if we must."

"Let's hope we don't have to fight our way from the arch to Athanor," Bregnest replied. "We won't know anything until we get to Alusia, so it's pointless to worry now."

They continued south along the road to Ollvi, meeting no trouble as they traveled. Bregnest seemed more relaxed than he had been, but he still urged the company forward as much as possible. Alex knew that Bregnest's concern was for his cousin, and he could understand his desire to hurry.

They reached Ollvi just after midday. They found rooms at the same inn where they had stayed before, and then gathered in the main bar to talk. Bregnest thought they should move on early in the morning, but their discussion was cut short by the arrival of Tom Cain.

"Master Taylor," said Tom. "I heard that you and your friends had returned. I have come to invite you and your company to join my family for your evening meal."

"You are most kind. However, such a request should be

made to our company's leader," replied Alex, motioning to Bregnest.

Tom seemed confused, but he soon recovered. "Sir," he said to Bregnest. "Would you be so kind as to honor us?"

"The honor is ours," said Bregnest. "My company and I will be pleased to join you."

Tom, in his excitement, bowed several times before making his way out of the inn. Bregnest chuckled slightly at Tom's behavior and then returned his attention to the company.

"Well," said Bregnest, "a fine meal tonight and the road again tomorrow."

That evening, Alex and Andy led the company to the Cain house. They were both pleased to see that the house looked much better than it had the last time they were in Ollvi. Tom had obviously spent a fair amount of his father's gold to restore the house to its former glory, and he had done a good job of it.

The Cain family greeted the company at the front door of the house, and Mrs. Cain led them into a large dining room where an excellent meal had been prepared for them. At Mrs. Cain's request, Bregnest told them the story of how Jonathan Cain's bag had been recovered. Alex listened to Bregnest's retelling of the story, both pleased and relieved that his own part in it had not grown with time. After Bregnest had finished the tale, Alex asked Tom how his family was getting along.

"I have managed to regain quite a bit of what my family once owned," said Tom. "If I could buy some horses for our southern fields, I think we may begin to see some profits."

"Are horses hard to find here in Ollvi?" Alex questioned.

"They are not so common as they once were," Tom

answered. "I was hoping to breed horses, but the cost here in Ollvi is high. I suppose I'll have to buy at least one and ride to Oslansk, or maybe even further south, to get a better price."

"What price do people here ask for horses?" Alex asked.

"If you can find a horse for sale, which is rare, the price is at least fifty gold coins, usually more. Those who own horses seldom sell them, and so they can demand whatever price they desire."

"But you need a horse," said Alex.

"I do," answered Tom, a slightly confused look on his face.

"Well, you never know, something may turn up."

After they had finished their meal and thanked Mrs. Cain for her kindness, the company returned to the inn. After his friends had gone to bed, Alex sat down at a table and wrote a short letter to Tom. He explained that the horse was a gift from the company, a thank you for having them all to dinner. Once he finished the note, he went to find the innkeeper. Alex quickly explained what he wanted the innkeeper to do, and the innkeeper seemed to be pleased with Alex's plan and accepted the letter for Tom Cain. When Alex offered to pay, the innkeeper refused, but bowed to Alex, saying that it was his honor to help.

The next morning, as they prepared to leave, Alex didn't saddle Val's horse. Halfdan was quick to question Alex about it, and he seemed stunned by Alex's answer.

"What do you mean you're leaving it here?"

"A small gift to a friend," Alex answered with a grin.

"But this horse has great value here in Ollvi," Sindar commented. "You could sell it for a high price."

"Perhaps," said Alex. "However, he reminds me too much of Val, and I would like to leave that memory behind. Besides, I'm sure he'll have a good home with the Cain family."

"You'll give away all you have one of these days," said Andy with a laugh.

"That would take some doing," Alex answered.

Chapter Fifteen

Otho's Wish

The trip from Ollvi to Oslansk was cold, and for the most part, uneventful. On the third day, Alex received a short message from Whalen saying that he would not be in Telous when Alex and the company returned from Norsland, but that he felt sure he would be there after their trip to Alusia.

Alex tried hard not to show his disappointment at learning his meeting with Whalen would be delayed by at least six weeks. He wanted to meet Whalen face-to-face as soon as possible.

A few days before they reached Oslansk, Andy suggested that they stay in the city for at least a week. He said something about needing a good long rest in a nice warm city, but he didn't sound very convincing to anyone.

"Lilly and Indigo don't have another sister, do they?" Halfdan asked suspiciously.

"As a matter of fact, they do," said Andy, turning bright red.

"And I suppose she is as pretty as both of her sisters," said Sindar.

"Well, she is rather pretty," Andy admitted. "But we're only friends, and that has nothing to do with my wanting to spend some time in the city."

The entire company burst into laughter at Andy's denial, and Andy was soon beet red, but laughing as well.

"Perhaps we should ride south now and avoid Oslansk all together," Halfdan suggested.

"I think the sooner we get Andy away from here, the better off he'll be," Bregnest added with a slight chuckle.

"Every man has a right to fall in love," said Sindar.

"I think Andy will be safe enough. As long as we keep an eye on him," Alex commented. "Besides, I think I may have some business to take care of in Oslansk as well."

"What business is that?" Bregnest questioned, turning to look at Alex.

"Oh, nothing of great importance," said Alex. "I'd like to check on Skeld and Tayo. I'm afraid they may be itching for another adventure, and I might be able to cure them, at least for a little while."

For the rest of the evening they joked and told stories and tried not to think about the danger that waited for them in Alusia. Halfdan kept insisting that he wasn't going to let Andy out of his sight when they reached Oslansk, no matter what Andy said.

"Next thing you know, he'll be talking about retirement," complained Halfdan as they all rolled into their blankets. "He's far to young for that."

They reached Oslansk the next day at sunset. Once again, the guards waved them into the city without questions. Andy suggested they stay at the Dragon's Keep as it was by far the nicest tavern in Oslansk. Bregnest agreed, and Andy led them through the streets to the tavern.

The company had only just finished ordering their evening meal when Skeld and Tayo arrived at the tavern. They were both happy to see their friends again and keenly interested in how their adventure was going.

"But wait," said Tayo suddenly, his smile fading. "Where is Val?"

"He is lost," Bregnest answered in a troubled tone.

Bregnest reluctantly agreed, after some persuasion, that Alex and Sindar could tell the story of what happened at the Tower of the Moon. Alex didn't really want to tell the story, so he let Sindar explain things to his friends.

"It is a sad thing that Val brought this evil on himself," Tayo commented, looking at Bregnest.

"And sadder still that he refused to give it up, once Alex had caught him," Skeld added.

"He was deceived," Alex said softly. "The shadow has great power and can tempt even the strongest of men to do evil."

"But you were not tempted by it," said Tayo confidently.

"Not this time," said Alex. "But this is not the first time we have met."

"What? When have you met this shadow before?" Bregnest asked in surprise.

"In Vargland," said Alex, looking at Bregnest. "That night at the ruins of Aunk. I did not recognize the shadow then, but it was there."

"Ah, but you defeated its plans then, and you have done so again," said Halfdan.

"Yes," Alex agreed. "But I fear it will try to tempt me again. It is not vanquished or destroyed."

"Enough," said Bregnest so suddenly that they all looked at him in surprise. "You had the victory then, Alex, and you have had another now. We do not know what the future holds, so let us not be troubled by it."

"Quite right," Sindar added.

The conversation soon turned to other matters, and Alex was glad that it did. He didn't like thinking about the shadow and its tempting words, or the terrible cold he felt inside himself both times he had fought it.

"You'll be staying for a few days then?" Skeld questioned, winking at Andy.

Alex noticed that Andy blushed slightly, but he said nothing.

"We thought to move on quickly," said Bregnest. "We must still complete our adventure, and we have little time to waste."

"A few days won't make a great difference," said Tayo. "And besides, you must dine with us at both of our houses before you leave."

"He's right, of course," Skeld added. "Lilly and Indigo will skin us alive if you don't."

"Very well," said Bregnest. "We will remain for three days and leave the morning of the fourth. On the third night, however, I will host a banquet to repay your kindness."

"Then tomorrow you will dine at my house," said Skeld.

"He won the toss," said Tayo. "We flipped a coin before coming to see you."

Skeld and Tayo remained with the company until it was late, talking and laughing and telling bits of stories from past adventures. As they were leaving, they promised to return the next day at four hours past midday to lead the company to Skeld's house. Alex and his friends made their way to bed that night looking forward to at least a few happy days in Oslansk.

The next morning Bregnest was busy arranging for a feast. Halfdan and Sindar had decided to look around the city together, and Andy said he'd go with Alex to visit Elwig the dwarf.

Elwig was delighted to see Alex again and instantly started showing him the items he'd made from the true silver that Alex had left with him. Alex was pleased to see everything, but he had other thoughts on his mind. While Andy was busy looking around the shop, Alex pulled Elwig aside for a quiet word.

"I have another bargain for you," said Alex.

"Anything at all," Elwig agreed.

"I would like you to make six more brooches, exactly like the last two," said Alex in a lowered tone so Andy wouldn't overhear him. "Don't set a stone for the dragon's eye, though, as I don't know which stones will be required."

"I can make them as you desire, but it will take time," said Elwig, matching Alex's low tone.

"That is all right. I will be leaving the city soon, so please hold the brooches until I send for them," Alex said. "If you will do this for me, and set the eye of each dragon when I ask for it, I will provide you with the true silver to do the job."

"I will do as you ask," Elwig said with a bow. "And if I cross the wall before you require these brooches, my heir will hold them for you."

"You are most kind," said Alex. "As payment for your work and your holding of these items, you shall keep the remainder of the true silver I give you." Alex produced another large bag of true silver from his magic bag and put it in Elwig's hands.

"Again, you are too generous, Master Taylor," Elwig said. "Your payment is too great, even if my family must hold these things for a thousand years."

"I will not take no for an answer," said Alex.

"Very well then," said Elwig, bowing. "It shall be as you request. And a blessing on you for your kindness."

His business finished, Alex joined Andy near the back of the shop. Andy said he was looking for a present to give to Lilly and Indigo's youngest sister, Kate. Alex smiled, but decided not to tease Andy about it—at least not until they were on the road again.

Andy soon found a brooch that was to his liking, and Alex was not surprised when Elwig asked a surprisingly low price for it.

"Your friend has been such a good customer and so generous that you deserve a discount," said Elwig when Andy asked about the price.

"Halfdan will be angry with me," said Alex as he and Andy left Elwig's shop.

"He should have come along then," said Andy. "After all, I thought he said he wasn't going to let me out of his sight while we were here."

They both laughed as they started back toward the Dragon's Keep. As they walked, Alex asked Andy how serious he was about Kate. Andy blushed and explained that he wasn't ready to get married just yet.

Suddenly Alex heard a voice he recognized and did not like. Holding his hand up so Andy would stop talking, he moved closer to the voice, listening.

"Oh, they're adventurers all right, but what does that mean?" Otho Longtree said loudly, a pompous tone to his voice. "They come back with stories about oracles and dragons and bandits, but how do we know the stories are true? For all we know, they may go off to a secret land where gold can be picked up like pebbles and diamonds like sand."

"I don't think it's as easy as that," said a girl's voice.

"That's Kate!" Andy whispered to Alex in surprise.

Alex nodded and held up his hand again for Andy to remain silent.

"You only believe the stories because you're in love with Anders Goodseed," Otho sneered. "I suppose you believe everything Andy and his little brother say. Well, let me tell you, I've seen this supposed wizard friend of theirs, and he looks like a very unpleasant fellow. Why, when he was here before, I confronted him but he couldn't even do a simple magic trick."

As Otho spoke, Andy moved forward angrily, but Alex caught his arm and shook his head in warning. Otho's words would have enraged him the last time he had been here, but now they didn't bother him at all. They did, however, give him an idea.

"And all this talk about the Oracle of the White Tower and

dragons and all. I'll bet the Oracle is some old witch who lives in a cave, and the dragon was just a little lizard in the sun. And the company they keep—elves and dwarfs! Why, if I were Andy Goodseed, I'd wish to be anything—even an ox—instead of an adventurer."

Alex smiled at Andy and motioned for him to follow, but remain silent. They turned the corner and came face-to-facc with Otho and his group of unfriendly looking companions.

"Your wish is granted," said Alex.

"What?" said Otho, turning to see who had spoken.

"I said, your wish is granted."

Otho looked as if he was going to be sick, and the crowd of mostly young women all took several steps back.

Alex tried to look grim, and with a wave of his hand and a small popping sound, he changed Otho Longtree into a fat and bewildered-looking ox. The entire crowd gasped, but Alex took no notice.

"You there," said Alex, pointing to one of Otho's companions. "Run and tell this windbag's father that his son's wish has been granted."

The boy seemed unable to move. He simply stood where he was, looking at Alex, dumbfounded.

"You two," said Alex, pointing to two more of Otho's companions. "Lead this fat animal home, as I don't believe he has the brains to get there by himself. Tell his father that I'm staying at the Dragon's Keep for the next few days. He can find me there if he wishes to discuss his son's change of appearance. I can't see why he would, however, as this seems a great improvement to me."

As soon as Alex finished speaking, he turned and walked away. The crowd parted in front of him, and Andy came running up behind him, a stunned look on his face.

"I can't . . ." Andy began, then stopped. "I can't believe you did that."

"It's better than he deserves," Alex replied.

"But his father—"

"It's time his father learned the truth about his son," said Alex. "And if his father won't see the truth, I'll have to leave Otho as he is."

"Yes, but . . ." Andy began and stopped again.

Alex tried to look stern and wise as he met Andy's eyes, and then they both burst into fits of laughter.

That night, as they ate dinner at Skeld's house, Andy kept looking at Alex and trying, unsuccessfully, to hide his chuckles with his napkin.

"So," said Skeld, trying to keep a straight face. "I understand you had a run-in with Otho Longtree today."

"A small one," Alex replied.

"Did you really turn that fat bully into an ox?" Skeld burst out suddenly, laughing so hard that tears came to his eyes.

"Yes, I did," said Alex in a serious tone, but he had a hard time keeping a straight face.

"But his father is such a good man," Lilly protested, giving Skeld a disapproving look.

"So I have heard," said Alex. "However, a father's goodness will not excuse a son's bad behavior."

"But surely you will change him back?" Indigo questioned. "I mean, he's Osgood's heir."

"I see that you are both concerned for Osgood Longtree and this tells me that the father is worthy of some consideration," said Alex. "Rest easy. I have sent word to Osgood and told him if he wishes to discuss his son's appearance, he can call on me at the Dragon's Keep."

"Surely Osgood will come," said Lilly.

"I don't know," Tayo commented. "I think Otho might make a wonderful ox—once he's had some training, that is."

Even Indigo and Lilly laughed at Tayo's comment, but Alex could see they were both still concerned. As for his own feeling, Alex would be only too happy to let Otho remain an ox for the rest of his days. He knew, however, that Osgood would come and he would have to tell him something, but he hadn't decided what he would say.

The next morning, shortly after the company had finished their breakfast, a sad-looking old man entered the Dragon's Keep. Alex watched him ask the innkeeper a question and saw the innkeeper point in his direction.

"Do I have the honor of addressing Master Alexander Taylor?" the man asked nervously as he approached Alex.

"You do," Alex answered, bowing slightly.

"I am Osgood Longtree, magistrate of Oslansk. I have come to discuss the . . . Well, the wish of my son, Otho."

"I would be honored to talk to you," Alex replied, motioning for Osgood to take a seat.

"I am told that Otho has in some way offended you, Master Taylor," Osgood began, "and this is the reason for the, um, the change that has come over him."

"Master Longtree, I do not know what you have been told,

so allow me tell you why I have changed your son into an ox. Had your son's insults been directed at me alone, I would have let them pass with perhaps a warning."

"I am sorry if Otho has insulted you and your friends," Osgood said quickly. "I'm sure that I can compensate you all for anything that Otho may have said or done. I'm sure—"

Alex held up his hand, cutting off Osgood's words. "My dear sir, I have heard nothing but good about you from everyone in this city, which makes my current task very difficult. You see, you are well-loved and none of your people wish to see you miserable. So now, as a stranger, I must inform you of what others will not."

"And what is that?"

"I must tell you, sir, that your son is a pompous blowhard and a bully," said Alex. "He is most unpopular in this city and is only tolerated because the people of this city hold you in such high regard."

"He is a bit headstrong, but I don't think that—" Osgood began, and then stopped as Alex held up his hand again.

"Sir, if you do not face the truth in this matter, I will be forced to leave Otho as he is. For too long the honor of the father has protected the son, and the son has dishonored the father."

"I see," said Osgood, looking even sadder, though he no longer sounded quite as nervous.

"I hope that you do," said Alex. "Because I have heard so much good about you, I am prepared to change your son back to his natural form."

"Will you?" Osgood asked in a hopeful tone.

"I will," Alex answered. "However, I have some conditions I must insist on."

"Anything. I'm sure that Otho has learned his lesson and will do whatever you ask."

"Perhaps he has," Alex allowed. "Unfortunately, I will only be in Oslansk for a few days, and he may return to his old ways once I am gone."

"I will not allow that," said Osgood, in a tone that sounded like he meant it.

"I am sure that you will not," said Alex. "Now, for my conditions. I require a public apology from Otho. He has slandered myself and many of my friends, and worst of all, he has slandered the Oracle of the White Tower. After the public apology, he must take an oath before the people of this city that he will never speak against myself or my friends again."

"Of course," Osgood agreed. "It is only right that he should make public amends for public insults."

"This may seem a simple thing to you, but you are a man of honor," said Alex. "I am not so sure of Otho or his honor, so I have one more condition."

"And what is that?"

"I require a written copy of his apology and oath. This written copy will be signed by Otho and witnessed by yourself and any others you may wish," answered Alex. "It is to be kept on record here in Oslansk. If Otho ever breaks his oath, he is to be banished from this city—forever."

"Banishment seems a harsh punishment," said Osgood in a sad and troubled tone.

"Do you doubt your son's ability to keep his oath?"

"I must confess that I do," answered Osgood. "I may have lived in darkness where my son is concerned, but I have not been completely blind."

"Then if not banishment, what would you suggest?"

"I can think of nothing else that would keep Otho from breaking his word, except perhaps the threat of being turned back into an ox."

"The threat is there, but I will not be here to carry out such a punishment if it is needed," said Alex.

"Then it shall be as you ask," Osgood agreed. "I see that you have considered this matter far more than I ever have."

"Perhaps, as a stranger, I can see things more clearly."

"I hope Otho has not put you off," Osgood added. "I mean to say, that I hope you will return to our city in spite of my foolish son."

"I would like that very much," said Alex. "I have many friends here in your city, and in Norsland as well."

"Then you will surely hear if Otho breaks his oath."

"I will," said Alex. "A fact you may wish to remind Otho of from time to time."

"When would you like the apology and oath to take place, Master Taylor?"

"Tomorrow, I think," said Alex. "Talk this over with Otho; even as an ox he will be able to understand you. If he agrees to my demands, bring him to the square tomorrow, one hour before the midday meal."

"It shall be as you wish," said Osgood.

Alex and Osgood shook hands, and Alex thanked him for coming. Osgood was in much better spirits when he left the tavern than he had been when he arrived. Alex watched him go and hoped that this ordeal had not been too hard on the old magistrate.

That night at dinner, Alex told everyone what Osgood had agreed to. Lilly and Indigo looked relieved, Tayo simply nodded, but it was Skeld who put into words what most of them were thinking.

"You couldn't leave him with a tail, could you?" Skeld chuckled. "Might do him some good, and—"

Skeld's words suddenly turned into a hacking cough as Lilly elbowed him sharply in the ribs. Alex grinned, glad to see that Skeld had met his match in Lilly.

The next morning, the square in front of the Dragon's Keep was overflowing with people. Alex guessed that most of the city had heard about what he had done to Otho, and they had all turned up to see him change Otho back into his normal self. Alex also guessed that most of the people wanted to hear Otho's apology and oath.

As Alex walked out of the tavern, the crowd parted in front of him. Osgood had arranged for a raised platform to be erected so everyone would be able to see Otho take his pledge. Alex was quick to notice that Andy was standing next to Kate in the crowd; she was wearing the brooch Andy had bought from Elwig.

Osgood seemed to be in good spirits and greeted Alex like an old friend. Otho, the ox, was standing close by and looked as if he wanted to run away when Alex approached. Alex tried to look stern, leaning forward to speak to Otho in a lowered voice.

"I'm only changing you back because of your father," Alex said firmly. "If I ever hear that you've dishonored him in any way, or broken the oath you take today, I will return and change you into something far worse than an ox."

Alex stood up and focused his thoughts. He had never actually changed a human before, or at least not this way, and he was hoping for Osgood's sake that he could do it. With a wave of his hand and a loud popping noise, Otho suddenly appeared where the ox had been standing.

As soon as the change happened, Otho took several steps away from Alex, stumbling and falling backward into a water trough. The crowd roared with laughter, but Alex was unmoved. He simply indicated that Otho should proceed to the raised platform to make his apology and take his oath, dripping wet.

Once the conditions Alex had insisted on had been fulfilled, Osgood came forward and shook Alex's hand again. Alex bowed to Osgood and thanked him for everything he had done. Osgood turned to his son, who, because it wasn't yet springtime in Norsland, was covered in a growing layer of ice.

"Come," Osgood commanded. "We have a great deal to talk about."

"A pity," said Skeld, stepping up beside Alex. "He did make a fine-looking ox."

"Don't insult oxen," Alex answered.

That night they had their farewell feast, which Bregnest had arranged for. They all joked and talked as they ate, but there was a bit of sadness mixed with the laughter. When the feast was over, there were many sad good-byes to be said. Alex noticed that Andy said his good-byes quickly and left the inn in a hurry. He knew that Andy had another good-bye to make, and he felt happy for his friend.

They left Oslansk the next morning as planned, and Alex was happy to see that almost everyone they passed in the streets waved and wished them good luck. He liked Oslansk, and he hoped that he would be able to return here someday.

Chapter Sixteen

Alusia

The journey back to the great arch was a short one, and the company remained in good spirits as they traveled. Bregnest told them that they would be staying in Telous for three days, once they'd left Norsland, so he could arrange for them to travel to Alusia. Plus, that would give them time to divide the treasure from the Tower of the Moon.

Alex was pleased with the short stay. He wanted to find out if Val had an heir or any family as soon as he could.

They arrived in Telous in time for their midday meal, and after they had eaten, Bregnest hurried off to arrange for their journey to Alusia. Alex and his friends had the afternoon unexpectedly free, and Alex visited the bag maker in order to modify his library to expand as needed. He also added a second treasure room to his bag. Sadly, he also learned that the bag maker didn't know about any heir to Val's bag.

That night the company ate together at the Golden Swan, and Bregnest looked grim as they took their seats. Bregnest told them that he had received word that the situation in Athanor had grown worse.

"There have been some fights in the streets, and several disputes about land rights, but no open fighting," Bregnest explained. "Not yet."

"We can't move any faster," Halfdan observed. "But we have recovered the Horn and that will prove your kinsman's right to be king."

"It may be beyond the Horn's power to do so now," Bregnest answered grimly. "It seems that open war is not far off in Athanor."

"Then we will aid your kinsman in retaining his crown," said Sindar. "We are still in his service and will defend him and his throne if we must."

They all agreed with Sindar's words and pledged to defend the rightful king of Athanor, whatever the cost. Bregnest did not comment, but he nodded his understanding of their pledge, a grateful expression on his face.

After they had finished their meal, Alex followed Bregnest to a large room at the back of the tavern. He retrieved the treasure he had taken from the Tower of the Moon, which he had already sorted, and then bowed to Bregnest.

"A sizable treasure," Bregnest commented, looking around the room. "I see how most of your winter in the enchanted woods was spent."

"There was little else to do," said Alex. "I thought it might save time, and I was looking for the Horn anyway. I'm sure you will want to check my sorting, however, as I may have miscounted."

"Nonsense. I am sure you have sorted fairly. In the morning, I will divide the shares."

Alex wanted to say something hopeful, but the possibility of war in Athanor had him worried. This adventure had seemed so simple when he'd first heard about it, but it wasn't just about returning the Horn—not anymore. Now it looked as if he and his friends would have to help fight in a real war.

And if war started in Athanor, there was no telling where it might spread to. It had to be stopped before it got out of hand.

In the morning, before the others woke, Alex took some time to write to Whalen about the possible war and his fears that it might spread. He mentioned his own pledge to defend the rightful king of Athanor and explained that he knew that it was not required for adventurers to defend the people who were paying for their adventure, but that this felt like the right thing to do.

After breakfast, Bregnest led the company to the back room where the treasure waited.

"There are seven piles of treasure, as our agreement called for," said Bregnest. "One for each of the company who signed the agreement, and one for the finder of the Horn. Since Alex was the one who found the Horn, these two piles are for him." Bregnest pointed to the two stacks closest to Alex.

They all cheered until Bregnest held up his hands for quiet.

"The pile for Val must be decided on," said Bregnest, his tone changing. "As Alex and Sindar have twice saved us on this adventure, I say the pile should be divided between them. Do any disagree with this decision?"

The company remained silent and Bregnest nodded after a moment.

"Then the treasure is divided," said Bregnest, smiling for

the first time in several days. "We should store our treasures and then prepare to ride to Alusia."

They cheered once more and started storing their treasure as fast as they could.

They were on the road to the great arch less than an hour later, leaving Telous a day earlier than planned. They rode at a gallop, hoping to make the journey to Athanor in as short a time as possible. Things may have changed in Alusia, but they were ready to do whatever they had to do in order to make their adventure a success.

Alex hoped that Whalen would reply to his last message soon, and maybe offer some advice about how to deal with the situation in Alusia. Whalen's home was in Alusia after all, and Alex thought he might know a great deal about both Bregnest's cousin and the family that was causing problems in Athanor.

When they reached the great arch, the company paused for a hurried meal. They said little, though Andy and Halfdan did try to cheer up Bregnest from time to time. He accepted their attempts in a good-natured way, but Alex could tell that his friend's thoughts were already miles ahead of them, worrying about what they might find at the end of the journey.

As they rode through the great arch, Alex found that he instantly liked Alusia. The land was made up of gently rolling hills and the air smelled fresh and clean. Tall grass waved in the gentle breeze, looking like a vast green sea. Clusters of tall oak trees dotted the grasslands and the hilltops, adding a darker shade of green to the view. The temperature was warm, but not too warm; it felt like a pleasant spring day.

"Is the weather always like this?" Alex asked.

"For the most part," answered Bregnest. "In high summer it is not so green and in the winter it rains most days."

"And the temperature remains so agreeable?" Andy questioned.

"It is a little colder in winter," answered Bregnest. "Though it is never as cold as Norsland in spring. It seldom snows here, except in the far north and south."

They continued until it was too dark to see more than a few yards in any direction. They set up their camp quietly, and Bregnest asked Alex to conjure a cooking fire for them. There were no stories or jokes that night. A harsh but determined mood settled over them.

The next day, as they moved forward once again, Alex's worries began to grow. Whalen had not written back to him since his last letter, which was odd. Surely Whalen would be as worried as Alex was and want to do anything to prevent a war in Athanor.

"We still have almost three weeks before we reach Athanor," Alex whispered to himself. "Whalen will write back soon, I'm sure of it."

The days seemed to pass slowly despite their attempts to move as fast as possible. They were all becoming as tense and nervous as Bregnest was. Alex tried to calm his worries by imagining Whalen turning up in Athanor and setting things right in the nick of time. These thoughts were of some comfort, but the need to hurry still pressed in on him.

Early on the morning of their tenth day in Alusia, Alex and his friends crested the top of a large hill and saw trouble.

"Bandits," Bregnest said angrily. "They have surrounded a company on that small hill."

"The company are adventurers," said Sindar, shading his eyes from the sun. "I count seven standing. One down."

"The bandits have taken their horses," said Bregnest without replying to Sindar's comment. "See there—away from the group—some of the bandits are waiting with the horses."

"We must assist the adventurers," said Halfdan, pulling his ax from his belt. "We are honor bound to give them aid, as you well know."

"But how best to do that?" Bregnest questioned. "If we attempt to save them, we may lose their horses. Or do we try to recapture the horses and then save the party?"

"I have an idea," said Sindar.

"Explain," said Bregnest.

"Bregnest, you go with Halfdan and Andy to recover the horses," said Sindar, still looking toward the encircled company. "Alex and I will attack the bandits around the hill. The magic of our swords will scare them, and I think they will try to flee. If they do, they will most likely flee in your direction."

"Where we will be waiting for them," said Halfdan in a grim tone.

"And Alex and I will be behind them, pressing them forward to their doom," Sindar added.

"Very well," said Bregnest. "We have no time to make other plans. Come, Halfdan, Andy, we will ride behind this hill and take the bandits holding the horses from behind."

"Alex and I will ride the opposite way in order to reach the hill unobserved," said Sindar.

The group split up without another word, and Alex and Sindar made their way along the back side of the hill, moving closer to the bandits. They had more than a mile to go before they could launch their attack, so they moved as fast as they could. It wasn't long before they entered a cluster of large oak trees only a few hundred feet from the attacking bandits.

"They are not goblins, but they are just as evil," said Sindar, looking at Alex and drawing his scimitars.

"Then they will fear us as goblins do, or they will never fear anything again," said Alex, pulling Moon Slayer from his side.

Alex and Sindar charged out of the trees, yelling like wild men.

The bandits spotted them before they had covered half the distance between the trees and the hill, and they let out several loud yells of their own.

The power of Moon Slayer filled Alex as he charged forward, riding Shahree into battle. Shahree moved so fast that the bandits nearest the trees had no time to run or fight before Alex had cut them down.

The bandits, as Sindar predicted, wheeled their horses away, breaking into a run as they tried to escape. Alex and Sindar pursued the bandits without slowing, hacking them down from behind as they went.

When Alex had fought the goblins, he had been filled with rage and the desire to destroy, but now there was only the heat from the magic sword, and his desire to do what had to be done.

The fleeing bandits came to a sudden stop, turning and

screaming madly at each other. Bregnest, Halfdan, and Andy blocked their path; there was no easy escape. Several of the bandits charged forward toward Bregnest and the others, preferring to take their chances there rather than face Sindar and Alex. The fight was short and bloody, and few of the bandits made it out alive.

The last three bandits, having been knocked off their horses, dropped their weapons and fell to the ground. Alex jumped from his saddle, his sword at the ready. There was no sorrow or pity in his mind as he advanced on the three evil creatures before him, only a need to finish this work.

"Alex, no!" yelled Sindar sharply, rushing forward to block Alex's path.

Alex paused and looked at Sindar in confusion. Sindar had put away his swords, and Alex could see that their magic was already fading.

"They have surrendered, Alex," said Sindar. "They have given up and are begging for mercy."

"And would they have shown mercy if we had not arrived?" Alex asked, the power of his magic sword flowing through his veins like fire.

"No," Sindar answered honestly. "But they have no honor, and we do."

Alex paused, thinking about Sindar's words but still wanting to finish what he'd begun. He knew that Sindar would not try to stop him from killing these three bandits, but he also knew that Sindar was right.

Alex stepped away from the bandits, returning Moon Slayer to his side. The heat began to fade as soon as he let go of the sword, and he was glad that it did. He had nearly killed three unarmed men who were begging for mercy, and, while they were bandits, it still would have been a dishonorable thing to do.

"Bind them," Bregnest said to Halfdan. "We will deliver them to those they attacked."

Halfdan hurriedly tied the bandits' hands together and then tied them to each other with a long piece of rope. While he was doing this, Alex helped Andy gather the horses that had not run off. Once they had collected all the horses that were close by, Bregnest led the company back to the adventurers they had rescued. Halfdan rode at the back of the company, pulling the captured bandits along behind him on foot.

"Well met," a voice called from the hill as Alex and his friends approached.

"Well met," answered Bregnest.

"We are in your company's debt," said a tall, thin man, stepping forward. "Had you not arrived when you did, I fear we would all have been lost."

"We saw from the hill that one of your company was down," Bregnest commented. "Is the wound serious?"

"The wound is small, though we fear that it may be poisoned," answered the thin man. "Have you a healer among you?"

"We do," said Bregnest. "He has some considerable skill and will do what he can for your comrade."

"Please, hurry then. Our fallen member is of some importance to us."

"Formal introductions can wait," said Bregnest, nodding for Alex to proceed.

Alex climbed out of his saddle and hurried forward. The thin man looked slightly troubled when he saw that Alex was the healer, but Alex took no notice. The other adventurers had gathered around their fallen comrade, and Alex was surprised to see that it was a young woman.

Trying to hide his surprise, Alex bent down to look at her wound. There was a long, jagged cut across her upper left arm, but it wasn't very deep. Alex asked the young woman if she could hear him, and she said she could, but her voice sounded weak and slightly dreamy.

"Boil some water," Alex ordered. "Now."

While Alex waited for the water, he removed a black steel helmet from the young woman's head. He looked at her closely and thought she didn't quite look like a human, but not really like an elf either. Putting these thoughts aside for the time being, he retrieved the dragon's bane plant and some other ingredients from his bag.

Alex was amazed to see that the plant had grown quite large since he had found it during his last adventure. He knew that the dragon's bane plant could cure most poisons as well as have a healing effect on wounds. He hoped that the poison had not traveled too far in the young woman's bloodstream.

As soon as the boiling water was brought to him, Alex poured a small amount into a cup, setting it aside. Then he pulled two leaves from the plant and crushed them in his hands. He added the powder to the water still in the pot. A clean, fresh smell filled the air instantly, lifting Alex's spirits and giving him hope.

"Wash her wound with this." Alex handed the potion to one of the adventurers who was watching him.

Alex took the remainder of the water and started brewing a second potion. He added two more leaves to the cup, along with several other things. When the potion was ready, he asked the young woman to drink it. She tried, but was unable to hold the cup by herself, so Alex held it for her as she drank.

"What is it?" questioned one of the adventurers.

"A simple potion with healing powers," said Alex. "The dragon's bane plant can cure most poisons."

"What do we do now?" asked another adventurer.

"Now we wait," Alex answered. He set down the empty cup and then returned the dragon's bane plant to his magic bag.

"I believe introductions are in order," said the thin adventurer. "My name is Nellus. And the young woman is Tara."

Alex didn't catch the names of the other adventurers or even pay much attention when Bregnest introduced himself and his company. He knew there were certain ceremonies between adventurers that had to be observed, but his thoughts were on Tara. He hoped that his potion would work quickly, but she didn't seem to be responding to it at all. Alex had to remind himself that potions often took some time to do their work.

"Well, Master Bregnest," said Nellus, "we are in your company's debt, though I fear we will see no profits from our adventure."

"And why is that?" Bregnest asked, interested.

"Young Prince Varson asked our company to seek the Horn of Moran and return it to him."

"You have abandoned this quest already?"

"Not abandoned. We have learned from Mr. Clutter that another company has undertaken the same quest," said Nellus, his eyebrows rising slightly. "However, this other company has undertaken the quest for the king of Athanor, and we thought we should end our quest and tell the prince that the king had already sent for the Horn."

"If the prince wishes the Horn, it is not to prove himself king," Bregnest commented in a grim tone.

"Then my guess is correct: you are the king's company. Do not take me wrong, Bregnest. We mean no disrespect to you, your company, or the king."

"I understand you, Nellus," said Bregnest. "I see that you are an honorable man and would not undertake the quest in competition with the king's requested company."

"Let us speak plainly," said Nellus, looking troubled. "I believe that Prince Varson wishes to use the Horn to prove his own kingship."

"But he is not the true king."

"I believe you are correct, but I fear Varson now believes himself to be the rightful king. His adviser, Kappa, has convinced him that he should be king, and all of his thoughts are bent on taking control of the kingdom."

"Surely the Horn will prove him to be a false king."

"I doubt Varson has considered that," said Nellus. "And I also doubt that Kappa will allow him to try to sound the

Horn. Kappa only wishes to keep the Horn from King Trion so that he cannot prove that *he* is the true king."

"Kappa will be disappointed, I think," Bregnest replied softly.

"I believe he will. However, Kappa may try to prevent you from returning to the king. I have heard rumors of war, though we are still too far from the city of Athanor to know if the rumors are true."

"We also have heard these rumors," said Bregnest. "As for myself and my company, we will defend the king, whatever Varson and Kappa do."

"A good choice. Sadly for myself and my companions, we must return to Prince Varson and renounce our quest. I fear that Kappa will not be pleased with us."

"Could you perhaps delay your return?" Bregnest questioned. "If you did not return too quickly, Varson may be shown the error of his ways, and Kappa may decide to flee."

"A good idea, and I wish we could. Unfortunately, we have all sworn an oath that we will return as swiftly as we can. Even if we renounce the quest, we must fulfill our oath."

"Then perhaps we can travel together," said Bregnest. "Varson's palace is close to Athanor, so our paths go the same way."

"We would be most honored to travel with your company, though it appears it may be a few days before we can move on."

"Yes," said Bregnest, looking at Alex. "I doubt very much that my friend Alex will leave Tara until he is sure she is out of danger."

"Then we should set up camp in the oak trees," suggested Nellus. "That is, if the healer thinks Tara may be moved."

"She can be moved," Alex replied. "Though I feel that more troubles her than her wound, or the poison in it."

"You see many things," said Nellus, a surprised look on his face. "We will not speak of this now. Let's move Tara and set up camp. Then we will discuss payment for your services."

"We must also discuss captives," said Bregnest. "Three of the bandits chose surrender, and we must decide what is to be done with them."

Nellus nodded but didn't reply. The two companies moved to the nearby grove of oak trees and set up their camps slightly apart from each other. Once this was done Andy, Halfdan, and Sindar went to search the dead bandits for any treasure. Bregnest remained talking with Nellus, and Alex remained beside Tara.

Alex felt a great need to hurry to Athanor, but he felt an even greater need to help Tara. There was something strangely sad about her, something that he couldn't put his finger on.

Alex's friends returned with a small amount of treasure the bandits had been carrying, and Bregnest offered the treasure and the captured horses to Nellus.

"We are in debt to you and your company," Nellus said in a businesslike tone. "You shall keep what the bandits had, and we will make some payment to you for your assistance."

"And what payment do you offer?"

"I offer five thousand gold coins from each of my company," said Nellus. "Also, I will ask that each of my company deliver to you one in ten of the primary treasure from their next adventure."

"You are most generous, Nellus. Perhaps too generous," said Bregnest. "My company and I have had the honor of assisting you, so I will ask for something less."

"That is your right, Bregnest, though I think the offer is not over generous," said Nellus, looking slightly worried.

"I will ask but two thousand gold coins from each of your company, and one in twenty of their next primary treasure," said Bregnest. "Your current adventure has cost you much already, and may cost you more when you reach Prince Varson."

"You are both kind and generous, and your honor is great," said Nellus. "I agree to your request."

"And the prisoners?" Bregnest questioned.

"We will not kill them, though it is our right," replied Nellus. "We will take them to King Trion, and there they will receive their punishment."

"As you wish."

Nellus called his company together. The adventurers all agreed to Bregnest's terms, and they each came forward to make payment to Bregnest and swear the requested oath.

Bregnest accepted their payments and their oaths, bowing to each member in turn. Then he called Alex and the rest of their company together, dividing the payment among them.

Once the ceremony of payment was over, Alex returned to Tara's side. He hoped she would show signs of improvement, but she remained unchanged. Sindar came to see how Alex was, and he paused to look at Tara. Alex thought Sindar looked slightly alarmed, and he was quick to ask his friend why.

"She has elf blood in her," Sindar answered in a whisper.

Chapter Seventeen

Back to the Wall

Alex remained next to Tara as night fell over Alusia. He ate little and said less as he tried to think of a reason why Tara was still sick. The dragon's bane potion would remove the poison from her system, but he felt that she did not wish to be healed and perhaps that was the reason she had not improved.

Alex did not sleep at all that night. His mind was full of questions that he could not answer, and his heart longed to press forward to Athanor. Nellus and the other members of his company came to check on Tara from time to time, but Alex had nothing to tell them.

When morning finally came, Tara was pale, and it seemed that she had little life left in her. Nellus asked Alex if he knew what was wrong, and Alex nodded.

"I fear that she does not wish to be healed," Alex said slowly. "I can feel a great sorrow in her. A longing for something that is lost."

"You see many things, healer," said Nellus. "I will tell you what I know of Tara. Perhaps that will aid you in healing her."

"She has moved closer to the wall in the night. I do not know what I can do for her."

Both companies gathered around Alex and Tara as Alex talked to Nellus. They all looked troubled, and Alex wished he could tell them something to comfort them.

"You have an elf in your company," said Nellus, looking at Sindar. "Perhaps he can call her back from the wall?"

"I have been to the wall before," Sindar replied, a pained look on his face. "I do not wish to return there and would do so only if Bregnest commanded me to."

"I will give no such command," Bregnest was quick to reply. "I know you would go if I asked this of you, Sindar, but I will not put you through that trial. I would not command you to do such a thing, not even if Tara were my own child."

"My apologies, Sindar, Bregnest," said Nellus, bowing. "I do not know much about the wall, and I asked before thinking."

"There is no harm," Sindar replied. "I can tell you that to call someone back from the wall requires great power. The one time that I attempted to do so, it nearly destroyed me."

"Then we have a sad journey ahead, and must carry sadder tidings to Tara's family," said Nellus with a deep sigh.

"She has not crossed the wall yet," said Alex defiantly. He shook his head to clear his thoughts and pushed away the sorrow that had built up inside of him. "Nellus, tell me all you can about Tara."

"What do you wish to know?' Nellus asked, looking shocked and surprised by Alex's sudden outburst.

"Tell me about her family, her adventures, what she was like—everything you can think of."

"As you wish," said Nellus, pausing for a moment to collect his thoughts. "Tara is the youngest daughter of King Nordal from the land of Kess. She has two older sisters and three older brothers. She is greatly loved by her family and by all in the kingdom. She was only allowed to undertake this adventure because her father thought it sounded fairly safe. She has a great talent with animals and can calm even the most angered or fearsome of beasts."

Alex asked Nellus a few questions from time to time as he continued to talk, trying to understand what Tara was like and why she was so sad. He learned that she had gone on three other adventures and had found some success as an honorable adventurer.

Once Nellus had finished, Alex asked each of his company to tell him their own impressions of Tara. They all spoke highly of her. They agreed that she had a temper and that she had definite ideas about things. She would argue her point of view as far as she could without offending her companions, and then would accept whatever decision Nellus made without argument.

The information was interesting, but none of it seemed to answer the questions that Alex had. He wondered what Tara's great sorrow was and what the reason for it could be. He could feel the depth of her sorrow as if it was his own, but he could not see any reason for it in what Tara's friends told him.

"Does she have elf blood in her?" Alex asked, remembering Sindar's comment.

"She does," Nellus answered. "Her mother was half-elf."

"Was?"

"Her mother was killed several years ago when Tara was young. I don't think she can even remember her mother, so I didn't mention it before."

"How was her mother killed?" Alex questioned.

"Bandits," Nellus replied slowly, looking toward the three bandits they still held captive. "She was traveling to see an oracle and her company was attacked. Only one of the company survived, and he died of his wounds after telling the story of what had happened."

"Very well," said Alex, deciding in his own mind what he must do for Tara.

"I don't see how anything we said could help you heal her," said Nellus sadly. "I had hoped that it might, but . . ."

"Your hopes are not in vain. Your words have cleared my own thoughts and driven out my doubts."

"Then you know of a way to heal her?" Nellus questioned.

"Yes," said Alex in a determined tone. "I will call her back from the wall. I will free her from the sorrow that drags her down, if I can."

"But you are not an elf."

"No, I'm not," said Alex. "But I am a healer, and I have been to the wall before. The shadow lands hold no fear for me. I will go."

"Alex," said Bregnest looking worried. "I know more than perhaps anyone about your journeys to the wall. I must warn you against returning there again."

"I thank you for your concern, Bregnest. However, this is

a burden that I must carry," Alex replied. "You know a great deal about my journeys to the wall, but you do not know all."

"Then be careful, my friend," said Bregnest with a slight bow. "We will await your return."

"Journeys?" Nellus asked, stunned. "You have been to the wall more than once?"

"I have been to the wall three times," said Alex. "Twice I went before I knew about the wall and the shadow lands beyond. Those times friends of great power called me back. The third time I went by my own choice, knowing what I would find there. I went to call back a friend and free him from a terrible burden."

"And you are willing go there again—for a stranger?"

"I will help Tara, though I have never met her," Alex answered firmly. "This is the burden I carry now, and I will help in any way that I can."

"Then go, Master Taylor," said Nellus, looking almost as worried as Bregnest. "We will watch and hope for your success."

Alex nodded, sitting for a moment, gathering his thoughts and working his magic. He knew what he would find at the wall, and he knew that the shadow lands would call to him as they had before. He focused his mind on his friends, the people he cared for on this side of the wall, and on what the future might hold for him. Alex thought of his hopes and dreams, everything that would keep him anchored to this side of the wall and to life.

Once he was ready, Alex took Tara's right hand in his own

left hand. Pausing for a moment to focus his magic, he placed his right hand on top of Tara's hand. Softly, he called her name.

It happened much slower than the last time he'd worked this magic. Alex called Tara's name three times before he felt himself moving away from his friends under the oak trees. Slowly his vision cleared, and once more he found himself climbing a grass-covered hillside in a shadowy land.

Tara was not standing at the top of the hill. Worried, Alex hurried to the hilltop, and looking down the far side, he could see the stone wall that divided the land of the living from the land of the dead. There, about halfway down the hill, stood Tara. She looked confused and afraid, as if unsure which way she should go or what she should do.

"Tara," Alex called softly, moving down the hill toward her.

"Have you come for me?" Tara asked as Alex approached. "Am I to go over the wall then? Does my mother wait there?"

"Calm yourself, Tara. I have come for you, yes, but not to take you across the wall."

"But my mother is there," Tara protested.

"Your mother is not beyond the wall, Tara. Your mother was half-elf and has gone to the halls of waiting with her people."

"How . . . how do you know this?" Tara questioned as she searched the wall with her eyes.

"I know many things, and I know that if your mother was beyond the wall we would see her there now, waiting for you," Alex answered. "Let go of your desire to find her there, before it is too late."

"I . . . I do not remember my mother," said Tara with a

sob. "I can't even remember her face. I hoped to see her here, but . . . there is nothing."

"Your mother is alive in you, Tara. To see her, all you need to do is look in a mirror, or at your sisters and brothers. Your mother is alive in all of you."

"Who . . . who are you?" Tara asked, looking away from the wall and sounding tired and confused.

"I am a friend. I have come to help you, but you must also help yourself."

"I do not know you. Why should I trust you or believe anything you say?"

"We have never met, that is true. But your friends, Nellus and the rest of your company, have told me about you, and I feel that I know you."

"Perhaps you know something of me, but that is no reason for me to trust you," Tara pointed out.

"You speak truly, so to win your trust, I will tell you something of myself and how I came to know you."

Alex told the story of how he and his friends had rescued Nellus and his company from the bandits. He also told Tara about his attempt to cure her and Nellus's request that Sindar call her back.

Tara listened to all that he said, but she did not speak.

"Last of all I will tell you this," said Alex. "I am a warrior and a healer. I am also a wizard. Because of this, I know and feel your sorrow. I have felt your sorrow as if it were my own. I know how much you wish to see and remember your mother. I know what it means to lose a mother, Tara, as I have also lost my mother."

"You know much and say many things," Tara replied slowly as Alex paused. "I feel that I should trust you, and I hope that you can help me. I feel so lost, and I don't know what to do."

"I will help you," said Alex. "Seeking your mother here will do you no good, and your sorrow only weighs you down. You must let go of your sorrow, but remember your mother. Seek joy and fulfillment in life, Tara, as your mother would wish you to."

"You speak well," said Tara, turning to look back at the shadow lands. "I will do as you ask."

"Then come," said Alex, taking Tara's hand. "We must return to the world of light and leave the shadow lands behind us."

"They look so pleasant," Tara said softly as Alex led her up the hill.

"Those beyond the wall find them so. Your time to cross over the wall is far distant. Now you must return and look for happiness in life."

"I will try," said Tara, her voice almost a whisper. "It will be difficult, but I will try."

"Then you have already won a victory," said Alex as they reached the top of the hill. "I hope that you will have many more."

Alex opened his eyes and looked up at the concerned faces around him and gave them a weak smile. He turned, and after a moment, he spoke to the young woman by his side.

"Tara," Alex said softly, squeezing her hand. "Tara, can you hear me?"

"Yes," Tara replied weakly. "Where are we?"

"We have returned."

"Returned? Returned from where?" Tara asked as she sat up, her voice growing slightly stronger. She looked at Alex in wonder and confusion. Her expression changed suddenly, as she looked wildly around for the bandits she remembered had attacked. It took a few minutes to calm her down, and as her fears vanished, the confused look returned.

Alex smiled at her and leaned forward. He whispered a few words in her ear, and then, sitting back, he spoke a single word.

"Remember."

Tara looked puzzled for a moment, and then she burst into tears. She clung to Alex's hand as she cried, as if afraid to let go. The members of both companies quickly busied themselves about their camps. For a long time, Tara continued to cry, and Alex did his best to comfort her.

"Thank you," Tara said at last. "Thank you for helping me."

"It was . . ." Alex began and stopped. "It was my very great pleasure to help you."

Tara smiled and kissed Alex's hand before letting it go.

Alex felt slightly embarrassed by the attention, but he said nothing. He felt sure that, in time, Tara would be able to let go of her sorrow and look forward to all that life had to offer. Alex gave Tara some privacy so she could recover herself to face her friends. He was relieved, even relaxed, and it felt like a great weight had been lifted from his own heart as well.

"You are most kind, Master Taylor," said Nellus when Alex joined the others at the campfire. "We are even more in your debt."

Alex nodded. He knew that Nellus and his company would honor him, but it seemed like a small thing. What mattered most to him was that Tara had returned by her own choice, and that he had been able to help her.

"Once again, you risk your own safety for others," Sindar commented softly.

"What safety did I risk?"

"You went to the wall of your own free will," Sindar answered. "There is danger there, even for elves, yet you went to help a woman you do not know and to whom you owe nothing."

"I went because I could help. I chose to help Tara rather than let her cross the wall alone and before her time. There was little risk to myself."

"So you say," said Sindar, looking troubled. "But the wall is always a dangerous place for the living, no matter how strong they are."

That night the companies ate together, and Nellus's company made a point of thanking Alex many times for what he had done for Tara. Alex smiled and returned their bows, though after a while he thought it was all a bit too much. None of them knew the simple pleasure he found in helping Tara, and to him, that was reason enough to do what he had done.

The next morning, Tara was feeling much better, and the two companies rode forward together. Bregnest, insisting that they move quickly, had tied the captive bandits to their horses. Alex thought that was exceptionally kind, considering they were bandits.

They still had several days to ride before reaching Athanor, however, and the companies became friendlier as they went along. It turned out that members of both companies had common friends, and there was a great exchange of news and stories between them as they rode.

Alex welcomed the new friendships he made, though he noticed Tara seemed somewhat shy of him. He thought it might have something to do with his calling her back from the wall so he said nothing about it.

When they were two days away from Athanor, Alex noticed that several riders passed them on either side, well away from the road. None of the riders approached them, but Bregnest seemed troubled by their presence. The riders worried Alex as well, and he hoped that some evil had not already happened in Athanor.

Alex also wondered why Whalen still had not replied to his last letter. He had hoped to meet Whalen when they returned to Telous, but now doubts had entered his mind. If Whalen couldn't reply to messages, what did it mean?

Chapter Eighteen

The Horn of Moran

When the two companies of adventurers were only one day away from Athanor, a group of soldiers met them on the road. The leader of the soldiers called them to a halt, riding forward to speak with Bregnest and Nellus.

"What business do you have here?" questioned the soldier.

"Our business is our own," answered Bregnest. "Why do soldiers bar the road to Athanor?"

"No one's business is their own these days," said the soldier. "We are here by Prince Varson's decree."

"The prince cannot bar the king's road," said Bregnest, sounding surprised.

"Prince Varson has made a claim to the crown. Until the matter can be settled, we have been ordered to bar the road to keep aid from reaching Trion."

"*King* Trion," Bregnest corrected in an angry tone. "Trion is still king of Athanor, no matter what Varson claims."

"You speak truly, Trion is king—at least for the time being," the soldier replied, bowing slightly. "However, we have our orders. Now, give me your names and tell me what business brings you to Athanor."

"I am Nellus, son of Norson, adventurer," said Nellus. "My company and I are on a quest for Prince Varson."

"Silvan Bregnest, adventurer," said Bregnest, still sounding angry. "My company and I are on a quest for King Trion."

"Very well," said the soldier, looking troubled. "You may all ride with us to Prince Varson's camp. I am sure the prince will wish to meet with Nellus and his company."

"And what of myself and my company?" Bregnest questioned.

"You will remain near the camp of Prince Varson as"—the soldier paused for a moment, choosing the proper words—"guests of the prince."

"Very well," said Bregnest. "We will ride to the camp, but if we remain, it will be because we wish to remain, not because Varson orders us to."

The soldier bowed slightly to both Bregnest and Nellus and returned to his company. He barked out some orders and the soldiers broke into two smaller groups. Ten soldiers rode in front of the adventurers, and the other ten rode behind. Alex thought the armed guard was unnecessary; if he and his friends wanted to ride away, there was little the soldiers could do to stop them. But Bregnest and Nellus seemed content to follow the soldiers, and Alex thought it the best course to take, at least for the time being.

It was early afternoon when they reached Prince Varson's camp. The leader of the soldiers asked Nellus and his companions to follow him to Prince Varson's tent. He also asked

Bregnest and his company to wait where they were for the time being.

"I fear great trouble lies ahead for us all," Nellus said to Bregnest in a lowered tone as they shook hands. "But we will not speak to Varson or Kappa of your company or your quest for any reason."

Bregnest nodded to Nellus, who then departed with the soldiers. Alex and his friends dismounted and gathered together to discuss what had happened and what they should do next.

"It is worse than I feared," said Bregnest softly. "If Varson has already made a claim on the crown, then there is nothing to stop open war."

"We still have the Horn of Moran," said Halfdan softly, looking at the company of soldiers surrounding them.

"Kappa will never let Varson try to use the Horn," said Bregnest. "I'm sure he'd rather kill us all than let us take the horn to Trion."

"We could cut our way through," said Sindar. "Though I don't like the idea of killing innocent men."

"How innocent can they be?" Andy asked. "They are supporting Varson. They are all traitors."

"No, they are not traitors," said Alex. "They are deceived by Varson and Kappa. Even the captain of the soldiers we followed here seemed to be unsure of Varson's claim."

"We must do something," said Halfdan. "If we wait here, we are no good to anyone."

"Not necessarily," said Alex, his mind racing with excitement as he thought his plan through. "If we wait here, someone will come to question us about our business—perhaps even Kappa himself. He knows about our quest; after all, he sent men to stop us in Norsland. I don't think he will want anyone else to know about the Horn."

"An accurate guess," said Bregnest sourly.

"Suppose he makes us an offer for the Horn," Alex continued. "He'll want the Horn where he can protect it, and he'll want us to go away."

"That, or he'll try to put us in prison or worse," said Sindar.

"I don't think he'll try that—at least not until he's tried to buy the Horn or bribe us away from the king," said Alex. "If he makes us an offer, we should ask for time to consider it. We can tell him we'll give him our answer in the morning."

"So we buy one more night of freedom," said Bregnest. "I don't see how that helps our situation."

"I'm coming to that," said Alex. "Once he agrees to give us the night, he will leave us under guard. We wait awhile, and then I will ask the guard for an audience with Prince Varson and Kappa."

"And what will you say to them?" Halfdan questioned eagerly.

"Well, if I can get them both together, I think I can convince the prince to try to use the Horn. I might even be able to arrange it so he will set up a competition between himself and Trion. That would be better."

"Kappa will never allow it," said Bregnest, shaking his head.

"You forget that I am a wizard," said Alex. "If I get Kappa

and Varson alone, I'm sure I can make Kappa say or do something to anger me. Once that happens, I'll change him into a pig or something. Then I'll be able to convince Varson to an open and fair—well, competition seems like the best word for it."

"Clever," said Bregnest, nodding his head. "And if your plan fails, we can still force our way through to Trion."

"I hope that my plan will work," said Alex. "I agree with Sindar—I would hate to have to kill so many innocent men."

"It is agreed then," said Bregnest. "We will try your plan, and use force only as our last resort."

Alex was relieved. He hoped that the prince was as big a fool as he seemed to be and that Kappa was as evil as it appeared he was.

They waited through the afternoon, and, as Alex had suspected, Kappa appeared just before sunset. He was dressed in fine, blue robes and wore a long, golden chain around his neck. Alex could see in Kappa's face that he was nervous and worried by Bregnest's sudden and unexpected arrival.

"So, Silvan Bregnest, you've returned," said Kappa with a sneer in his voice. "And you've brought friends with you as well."

"I have returned," answered Bregnest. "We wish to speak with King Trion about a matter that is important to him."

"I am not surprised to hear that you would like to see Trion," said Kappa. "But I'm afraid that won't be possible, at least not for a little while."

"So we are to remain here as prisoners?"

"As guests," Kappa answered with a wicked grin. "Prince Varson does not wish to make you or your friends prisoners."

"But we are not free to go."

"And if you were free to go, would you?" Kappa asked. "Or would you try to reach Trion in his castle?"

"We are on a quest for the true king of Athanor," answered Bregnest. "We would take him our news."

"Ah, yes, of course. However, there is some question as to *who* the true king of Athanor is. Perhaps your news can wait while this question is settled."

"Perhaps it can," said Bregnest, his tone softening slightly. "Though waiting is often a tiresome and costly business."

"Of course it is," said Kappa with a nod. "I'm sure that some accommodation might be reached, if only I could be sure that you would not do anything foolish."

"Your words hold some wisdom, Kappa. I would not wish to act the fool, nor lead my friends on a fool's errand."

"You have never played the fool, Bregnest," Kappa said in a sickly sweet voice. "Perhaps, if you and your company would make a pledge or take a simple oath . . . ? Nothing serious, just something to protect your honor from a moment of rash thinking."

"Perhaps," said Bregnest. "It would be foolish to rush off with so many questions unanswered. Truly, Prince Varson is fortunate to have you as his adviser."

"You are most kind. Would you and your company be willing to take such an oath?"

"I can answer only for myself in this matter," said Bregnest.

"Let me discuss this with my companions who are not of this land. I think I can show them the wisdom in what you say."

"And how long would such a discussion take?"

"The sun is now setting, and we have ridden far," said Bregnest, looking toward the west. "Let us have until morning. I am sure the new day will bring you the answer you desire."

"As you wish," said Kappa, bowing stiffly. "I will return when the sun rises, with great hopes for our future understanding."

"You are most kind," said Bregnest, bowing in return.

Kappa hurried away from the camp, and once he was gone, Bregnest spat.

"If I had not agreed to your plan, Alex," said Bregnest, shaking his head and scowling.

"You did well," said Alex. "Now, as long as Kappa doesn't try something foolish, we should be fine."

"What do you think he'll try?" Andy questioned, looking confused.

"I don't think I'll give him the chance to try anything," answered Alex.

"How long will you wait before seeking your audience?" Bregnest questioned.

"At least two hours. Kappa needs time to think about your conversation, and I wouldn't want to rush him. We might as well have our evening meal while we wait."

"Very well," said Bregnest. "Be careful of Kappa, Alex. He is little more than a well-dressed goblin."

"That is exactly what I'm counting on," said Alex with a grin.

Halfdan prepared a meal for them, but only Alex seemed to have any appetite. Alex was fairly sure Kappa would do nothing until morning, and by then there would be nothing at all that he could do.

After eating, Alex lay down and considered exactly what he would do and say once he'd arranged his audience with Varson. He wanted to make the prince believe that the idea of a contest with the Horn of Moran was his own. The prince's pride would be his most effective weapon, and he knew that he would have to play up to the prince if he wanted to win the day.

After two hours had passed, Alex got to his feet and prepared for the next part of his plan. With a nod to his friends, he walked toward the guards who stood around them.

"I wish to speak to Prince Varson and his adviser, Kappa," Alex told the guard in a low voice.

"The prince and his adviser are not to be disturbed," the guard answered sternly.

"If you will send a message to the prince or to his adviser, it will be to your great advantage," said Alex, producing three gold coins and slipping them into the guard's hand.

The guard looked at the coins and then at Alex. Alex could see he had judged the man's price correctly, and he soon found himself being led to the elegant tent of Prince Varson. Before entering the tent, Alex removed his weapons and placed them inside his magic bag.

"You're a member of Bregnest's party," said Kappa, as soon as Alex entered the tent.

"I am," said Alex, bowing first to Prince Varson and then to Kappa.

"And what do you wish to speak to us about?" Kappa questioned angrily.

"About the Horn of Moran, of course."

The color drained from Kappa's face, but the prince seemed to come alive with excitement.

Alex tried not to smile, though it was exactly the reaction he had hoped for.

"And what do you have to say about the legendary Horn?" Kappa snapped.

"As you may have guessed, our company was searching for the Horn at the request of King Trion."

"And are the legends true?" Prince Varson questioned, moving closer to Alex. "Does the Horn exist?"

"The legends are true, my lord," Alex answered with a bow. "And I can assure you that the Horn of Moran does exist."

"Do you carry this Horn?" Kappa asked before the prince could ask another question.

"I do not, but one of our company does," said Alex. "And I am sure that the Horn could be produced, if the proper reasons were given."

"Bah! You are a trickster hoping to play us as fools," said Kappa. "What reasons do you need to produce the Horn? What proof do we have that your company even has the true Horn? This could all be some story you've made up in hopes of receiving a reward."

"The reasons are obvious," said Alex calmly. "I do not wish to see war in Athanor. The proof, of course, is in the Horn itself because it will only play a note for the true king of Athanor. As for more proof, I can give only my word that I speak truly. And as for rewards, I will leave that decision to the true king of Athanor." Alex bowed to Varson, which seemed to please the prince, but Kappa looked worried.

"You are full of lies," Kappa yelled. "You seek only to deceive us and ruin our hopes."

"Silence, fool!" Alex yelled back at him.

With a wave of his hand and a blinding flash, Alex turned Kappa into a donkey. "Forgive me, my lord," Alex said to Varson in an apologetic tone. "I have lost my temper. Your adviser's claim that I had lied to him was really too much."

Prince Varson seemed almost as stunned as the donkey, and he looked from Alex to the donkey and back again, not knowing what to do or say.

"As you can see, my lord, I am a wizard," Alex continued. "My only wish is to see peace in Athanor and the true king on the throne."

"Yes, yes, of course," said Varson in a shaky voice.

"Your adviser's doubts about your kingship troubled me, and I beg your forgiveness for my rash actions."

"Not . . . not at all," said Varson, recovering from his shock. "He did sound rather doubtful, didn't he?"

"Yes, he did, my lord. But I assure you that I have no such doubts."

"You are most kind," said Varson, trying to sound more businesslike.

"It is no great kindness to serve a true king. However, I am troubled by your preparations for war."

"Oh, yes," said Varson, waving his hand in a dismissive way. "It's because Trion won't accept me as the true king."

"Of course," said Alex understandingly. "I suppose you are as troubled by all of this as I am."

"Why, of course I am. I . . . Oh, I'm sorry, I don't know your name."

"I am Alexander Taylor, my lord. I am an adventurer and a wizard, and I am at your service."

"Thank you, Master Taylor, that's very kind. You know, to be honest, I don't think Kappa believes I am the true king. He didn't seem at all interested in my recovering the Horn of Moran."

"How could he doubt you?"

"Well, he's been acting very funny, I must say," Varson continued, obviously pleased with the sound of surprise in Alex's voice. "You know, he didn't even want me to send another party of adventurers in search of the Horn."

"Why would he oppose such a brilliant and well-conceived plan?"

"I don't know," said Varson, looking at his adviser thoughtfully. "You know, I think you should leave him as a donkey. At least until I've proven my true kingship."

"As you wish," said Alex. "However, how will you convince Trion to accept you as the true king?"

"Well, as you said," Varson explained as if Alex was a bit slow. "I'll play a note on the Horn and that will be that."

"Very wise, my lord. You will prove yourself to be king and remove the threat of war from the kingdom at the same time. A bold move. Might I make a small suggestion to enhance your plan?"

"Of course, you may speak freely."

"Would it not prove your kingship to all of Athanor if you challenged Trion to a contest?"

"An excellent idea! Yes, most excellent. In fact, that is what I'll do. I'll insist that the people of Athanor gather, and then I'll compete with Trion. I'll ask him to play the Horn, and when he fails, he will look a total fool. Then I will play the Horn, and everyone will know that I am the king."

"A most inspired plan. However, my lord, perhaps *you* should play the Horn first. There is no need to make Trion look like more of a fool than he already is. And such a gesture will show your people your great kindness and win many hearts that may not otherwise be yours."

"Yes, of course," said Varson. "The true king should be kind to fools like Trion. That is what I'll do."

"And how soon will you be able to prove yourself and claim your throne?"

"Tomorrow at high noon, I think," said Varson with a satisfied tone. "There are a lot of people in Athanor, and I will have messages sent to the nearby towns as well. We will march forward in the morning, and before tomorrow night, I will be king. That will end the threat of war quickly, and everything will be as it should be."

"Wonderful," Alex gushed.

"You have been most helpful, Master Taylor. I would be pleased if you would accompany me to the contest."

"A great honor," said Alex. "If I may be so bold, perhaps you will allow me to hold the Horn. That way Trion won't be able to use any magic to make himself appear to be more than he is."

"Another grand idea. You are a wonder. If there is anything I can do for you tonight, please don't hesitate to ask."

"There are two small matters," Alex said slowly. "I hate to bring them up at a time like this, so perhaps I should not."

"No, no," said Varson, waving his hand. "Please, let me do what I can for you."

"You are most kind, my lord. The first matter concerns some bandits that my company and I captured on our way here. No doubt you will wish to judge them, once your throne is secured. In the meantime, if a few soldiers might be spared to guard them, it would be helpful."

"Of course," said Varson, trying to look and sound like a king. "I will have some men sent right over to take these bandits off your hands. Now, what else would you ask?"

"The second matter concerns the fate of the adventurers traveling with Master Nellus. Our two companies have several friends in common. It would be, shall we say, awkward if anything unpleasant were to happen to Master Nellus or his companions."

"Yes, I can see that clearly enough," Varson agreed. "That fool Kappa has had them placed in chains, but I can remedy that. In fact, I think they did me a great service in attempting to find the Horn, so I am in their debt. I will have them freed at once and returned to your camp. That way your company will see how kind the true king can be."

"You are generous and kind, my lord. Now I suppose we should both get some rest, tomorrow promises to be an important day."

"Yes, yes, it does," said Varson, almost falling over in his excitement. "I will send an honor guard for you in the morning, and you will ride beside me to Athanor."

"You do me a great honor," said Alex.

When Alex reached the door of the tent, he turned to look back at Varson and Kappa the donkey.

"Shall I ask your guards to remove this donkey?" Alex asked.

"Yes," said Varson in a definite tone. "Send them in at once. And thank you again, my friend."

"Not at all, my lord, not at all."

Alex had a hard time controlling his laughter as the guard led him back to his friends. As they approached Bregnest and the others, Alex slipped the guard three more gold coins for his service. The guard bowed to Alex, and then hurried back to his post.

Before Alex could tell his friends what had happened in Varson's tent, more guards arrived, escorting Nellus and his company to the campsite. The guards bowed to Bregnest, removed the chains from Nellus and his friends, and then took the three captured bandits away with them.

Once the guards had departed, Alex told his friends everything that had happened. He had a hard time keeping them all from laughing too loudly as he told the story. Once, when a guard seemed to take too much interest in the noise they were making, Halfdan quickly praised Varson loudly. This seemed to satisfy the guard's curiosity, and he soon returned to his post.

"He actually thanked you for turning Kappa into a donkey?" Andy asked, wiping tears off his cheeks.

"He did," said Alex. "And he's also asked that I ride beside him to Athanor in the morning. I will be holding the Horn so Trion can't play any magic tricks with it."

"You are a genius," said Bregnest, slapping Alex's shoulder. "This will be far better than anything I had hoped for."

The following morning, before everyone was awake, Alex asked Bregnest to send a short letter to his cousin, King Trion. Bregnest explained to Trion what would be happening that day and asked him to go along with it. Bregnest also told Trion that Alex was a member of his company and that his only goal was to prevent all-out war in Athanor.

With his message sent, Bregnest returned the Horn of Moran to Alex with a bow, and Alex stored it safely inside his bag. Shortly after Alex and his friends had finished their breakfast, the prince's personal guards appeared to escort Alex to Varson. Alex said good-bye to his friends with a bow and a wink, then followed the guards to Varson's tent. Holding Shahree's reins behind him, Alex waited patiently outside the tent for the prince to appear.

Varson arrived, wearing his finest clothes and looking excited and pleased with himself. He grinned at Alex as he awkwardly mounted his own horse and prepared to lead the entire company toward Athanor. Alex felt a little sorry for Varson; he wasn't an evil man after all, only a very foolish one.

As Varson's army moved forward, Alex acted his part as well as he could. Varson seemed confident that he would be king before the day was over, and he made several promises to Alex and to the rest of the adventurers, including offering to pay whatever price Trion had promised for the return of the Horn and add to it. Alex simply smiled and said Varson was far too generous. When they approached the city of Athanor, Alex leaned toward Varson and spoke in a lowered voice.

"Before we begin, perhaps I should remind the people that the Horn will sound only for the true king," said Alex.

"Yes, I think that would be best," agreed Varson. "In fact, you may say that you are there to judge the contest fairly and announce to the people who their true king is."

"You honor me, my lord. But surely there are others more qualified than I who can judge this competition. I am not from this land, so perhaps someone who lives here should act as judge."

"You make a good point," said Varson after some thought. "I will have the captains of my army act as witnesses, and if Trion wishes, the captains of his army as well."

"An excellent solution, my lord. Then there will be none in Athanor who can doubt the true king."

"That is correct, my friend," said Varson with a nod. "After all, I don't want war any more than you do. I can't blame Trion's soldiers for his mistakes after all."

"You are most wise," Alex replied.

Varson seemed lost in his thoughts of becoming king, and he didn't say anything more as the company approached the gates of Athanor. A messenger rode into the city with a request for Trion to meet Varson at midday to prove once and for all who was the true king. The rest of the army assembled outside the city walls. The messenger was only gone for a short time before returning with Trion's answer.

"The fool has accepted," said Varson, waving the message in front of Alex. "He must actually believe he has a chance."

"Men will often do foolish things to prove what they believe."

"Yes, I suppose they will," said Varson, sounding almost sad. "I wish that Trion would simply accept me as king. I really hate to embarrass him this way."

"You are kind, my lord. Perhaps Trion will concede the contest once you have blown the Horn."

"Yes, that would be better than seeing him try hopelessly to sound the Horn. Then at least some of his honor might be saved. You know, he is an honorable man, and he has run the kingdom very well over all."

Alex did not reply but simply nodded.

As midday approached, Varson's soldiers set up a large, raised platform so everyone would be able to see Varson and Trion compete with the Horn. Alex commented on what a good idea it was and praised Varson for thinking of it.

At midday the gates of Athanor were opened wide, and Trion and his captains emerged from the city, followed by a large crowd. Even more people gathered on the city walls to watch the competition. Alex was pleased that there would be so many witnesses. No one in all of Athanor would be able to question the true king after today.

Varson and Trion met at the foot of the platform and bowed to each other. Varson's captains lined up on one side of the platform, while Trion's captains lined up on the other. Varson then led Trion and Alex onto the platform, looking at the crowds confidently.

"If you will, Master Taylor," said Varson once the three of them were on top of the platform.

Alex bowed to Varson and then to Trion. He noticed that Trion looked stern, but that his eyes were shining brightly. Trion looked a great deal like Bregnest, and Alex was glad to be able to help him secure his throne.

"People of Athanor," Alex called loudly. "This competition will be to determine the true king of Athanor. I have been asked to serve as the judge, along with these assembled captains of the armies of Athanor. I have brought with me the legendary Horn of Moran, which will only sound for the true king of this people. I call upon all of you to act as witnesses this day."

Alex turned to Varson and Trion. He bowed once more to each of them and then produced the Horn of Moran from his magic bag. He held the Horn up and turned in all directions so that all the soldiers and all the people could see it. The bands of true silver flashed like fire in the sunlight, and the watching crowds fell silent.

Then, facing Varson and Trion once more, Alex spoke in a softer tone. "My lords, if you are both prepared, we will proceed."

"I am prepared," Varson answered eagerly.

"As am I," said Trion, still looking stern.

"Which of you will go first?" Alex questioned.

"I will," Varson answered quickly. "As I have made a claim on the crown, I will go first."

"As you wish," Trion replied in a grim tone.

Varson stepped confidently to the front of the platform and stood beside Alex.

"Prince Varson has asked to make his attempt first," Alex called out loudly.

Alex held out the Horn of Moran to Prince Varson. Varson put it to his mouth and blew until he was red in the face. But no sound came out of the Horn at all. Alex felt a mixture of amusement and pity. When Varson finally quit blowing, he was gasping for air. He looked shocked and completely dumbfounded.

"Prince Varson's attempt has failed," Alex called out. "Now King Trion will make his attempt."

Alex motioned for Trion to come forward. Trion bowed to Alex with just a hint of a smile on his face.

Once again Alex held the Horn steady. Trion took a deep breath and put his mouth to the Horn. As he began to blow, the Horn began to sound a long, loud note, which grew louder and louder. The sound filled Alex with a fierce and overwhelming joy. After the sounding of the Horn, Trion stepped back, his stern look softening.

"King Trion is the true king of Athanor," Alex proclaimed to the waiting crowds. "Let none here doubt, the Horn of Moran has spoken."

Turning, Alex bowed and presented the Horn of Moran to Trion, who accepted it with a bow and a quick wink.

Trion turned to look at Varson, who was pale and shaking, looking around as if he didn't know what to do. As Trion moved toward him, Varson dropped to his knees and begged for forgiveness.

"Forgive me, my lord. I have been a great fool. Kappa convinced me that you were not the true king, and I believed his lies."

"You have been a great fool," Trion agreed. "And you have

brought your own land to the very edge of war and ruin. Once you had great honor and you served Athanor well. I will remember your years of good service now, as I name your punishment. As punishment for your actions, I confiscate your lands and properties. I take away all your titles and honors. I name you as the lowest servant in the king's house."

"Better than I deserve," said Varson, remaining on his knees. "You have been too kind, my lord."

"Perhaps so," said Trion, looking stern. "But I will say this: in time your honor, your titles, and your lands may be restored to you. Of course, much depends on how well you serve Athanor from this day forward."

"I will serve you as best I can, my king," Varson replied, looking slightly relieved.

"Now, for the root of all this evil," said Trion. "Bring Kappa forward that I might proclaim his punishment."

There was a slight delay, but in a few minutes, two of Varson's soldiers led a nervous-looking donkey forward. They stood the donkey in front of the raised platform and stepped back.

"What is this?" Trion asked, a stern but slightly confused look on his face.

"Lord Trion," said Alex, stepping forward. "The soldiers are not trying to fool you. This is, in fact, Kappa. I'm afraid he was attempting to prevent us from returning the Horn of Moran to you. To overcome the difficulties he was putting in our path, I was forced to change him into his present form."

"I see," said Trion. "Then this is the punishment I name for Kappa. He shall remain as he is. Perhaps in this form he will better serve the kingdom of Athanor, which he has tried so hard to destroy."

"A most fitting punishment," said Alex.

"And a most interesting tale, I would guess," replied Trion. "Come, I will call Bregnest and the rest of your company to us. We will share a midday meal, and I will hear the story of your adventure."

Alex walked with Trion back into the city of Athanor, where the crowds were all cheering for Trion's success.

Bregnest and the rest of Alex's friends soon arrived at the city and were given seats of honor at the king's table. Bregnest told his cousin about the adventure they had been on and all the troubles they had faced in finding the Horn of Moran. Trion and his court listened to the story with great interest, and when Bregnest reached the end of the story, the entire court broke into joyful cheers once more.

Alex and his friends could now laugh openly about everything that had happened. Halfdan insisted that Alex retell the story of changing Kappa into a donkey once more, and they all laughed again.

"You have all done a great service, both to myself and to my kingdom," said Trion when the cheering finally stopped. "I fear that the promised reward is too small."

"The payment was agreed to," said Bregnest. "Everything we have done has been part of our agreement with you."

"Very well then. I will have the payment made ready, and you shall have it tomorrow morning."

"As you wish," answered Bregnest, bowing to the king.

"I will, however, use my right as king to award special

honors to each of you," Trion continued. "And I will not forget the noble efforts of your fellow adventurers, who renounced the quest that Varson sent them on."

After they had eaten, Nellus and his company came to say good-bye to Alex and his friends. They would be leaving for their homes in the morning and wanted to thank Bregnest's company once more for their rescue.

"My friend," Tara said to Alex, taking his hand in both of hers. "I owe you a great deal more than thanks."

"Your friendship and happiness are a greater payment than any treasure," Alex replied. "I am sure of your friendship, and I have great hopes for your happiness."

"You are very kind. If ever you come to my father's kingdom in Kess, you will be well received."

"I look forward to that time," said Alex with a bow.

Before the companies parted, Tara kissed Alex on the cheek and slipped a small silver brooch into his hand. Alex nodded to Tara as she left with the others, slightly embarrassed by her kiss.

"Now Alex will be looking to retire," said Halfdan, shaking his head.

"Not any time soon," Alex replied softly.

The next morning, Trion presented the adventurers with their gold, and Bregnest commanded that Alex should take the two shares that would have gone to Val. Alex accepted without argument, though he would have much preferred dividing the shares with the others. Once the gold was divided and stored in their bags, Trion led the company to a large field where their horses were grazing.

Alex was delighted to see so many wonderful horses in one place at one time. The only problem he could see was deciding what to do with the three hundred and fifty horses that were his. Bregnest laughed and said that he would gladly care for Alex's horses on his own lands. Trion overheard what Bregnest said, and in gratitude for Alex's service, he also offered to care for Alex's horses on his lands.

Sindar and Halfdan both decided that they had no need for so many horses and offered to sell their horses to Alex. After some debate, Alex paid fifteen gold coins for each horse and promised a free horse to either of his friends whenever they needed one.

Andy, thinking about his future, made arrangements to return his share of the horses to his home in Norsland. He said he thought his family might try raising horses because horses were not overly plentiful in any part of Norsland. He was also sure that Michael would be angry if he did not return home with the horses. This last remark made everyone laugh, including Andy.

Alex and his friends remained as Trion's guests for a week. Each night they ate with the king, and at each feast at least part of their story was retold.

One evening during the week, when things were quiet and not many people were around, Alex had a long talk with Trion and his most trusted lords. He explained that the Horn of Moran was more than just a symbol of the true king, it was a guardian object for all of Alusia.

"Guard the Horn well," said Alex, looking Trion in the eye. "Sound it at each spring festival and again at the harvest festival so all will know there is a true king in Athanor. If you do this, your kingdom will be united and grow larger as the years pass."

Trion thanked Alex for explaining what the Horn really was and promised he would do as Alex had said.

"The people of Alusia have slowly been breaking apart for many years," said Trion. "There are disputes and bitter rivalries in many places. Perhaps, with the Horn's return, our people can come together once more."

At the end of their week in Athanor, the company said their farewells to Trion and started off once more toward Telous.

"Why are you returning to Telous?" Alex asked Bregnest as they left Athanor behind.

"I have to pay Mr. Clutter," Bregnest answered. "I also need to update the files on each of you. And I'd like to talk to Whalen, if he's around."

Alex had almost forgotten that Whalen had never replied to his last message. He hoped that Whalen would be in Telous when they arrived so they could finally meet, and he decided to send another message to him, just in case.

"Another adventure is almost over," said Halfdan as they ate dinner that night.

"Only this chapter of the adventure is over," said Sindar. "With luck, there are still many chapters to come."

Chapter Nineteen

A Wizard's Staff

Alex and his friends rode away from Athanor in high spirits. Their adventure had turned out well, and they had managed to prevent war in Athanor. Alex felt a little sorry for Varson and hoped that someday his honor would be restored. On the morning of their third day away from Athanor, Alex received the long-awaited letter from Whalen.

Dear Alex,

I must apologize for not replying to your previous message. To be honest, I decided to use the situation in Athanor as a test for you. I know that may seem like a foolish decision on my part, but I did not believe your company was in any great danger. If things had gone wrong, I would have been there to assist you in a matter of days.

I will be arriving in Telous in a few days' time and will wait to meet you there. You have done far better than even I expected, and I am both proud of and pleased with your success.

We will have a great deal to talk about when you arrive.

Yours in fellowship,
Whalen

"So, Whalen was testing you," said Bregnest when Alex told him about the letter. "Wizards have their own ways, I suppose, and their own reasons for doing things."

"But if the plan hadn't worked there could have been a war," said Alex, not at all happy about the test.

"But your plan did work," said Sindar. "War was avoided and the true king remains on his throne. Whalen was correct to trust you."

"That doesn't matter," Alex said. "What if I hadn't thought of the plan? Or what if Kappa had done things differently? There were all kinds of things that could have gone wrong."

"Do you think it would have been your fault if war had broken out in Athanor?" Bregnest questioned.

"Well, yes," Alex replied.

"Was it you who talked Varson into making a claim on the throne?" Sindar asked.

"No, I didn't do that."

"Was it you who brought armies to Athanor to try to take the throne?" Bregnest asked.

"No, I didn't do that either," Alex admitted again.

"So, if there was a war, why exactly would it have been your fault?" Sindar questioned.

"All right, so it wouldn't have been my fault," said Alex with a grumpy sigh.

"You've done a great deal of good and you're unhappy about it," said Bregnest with a smile.

"I'm not upset about that," said Alex, starting to feel foolish. "I'm upset because Whalen took a terrible risk and a lot of people might have had to pay for it."

"And there is the lesson of your test," said Sindar. "Sometimes others may have to pay for our actions, or our inaction. The difference for you is that wizards can do great things, and if they are wrong, many more people have to pay for their mistakes."

Sindar's words reminded Alex of something he'd learned on his first adventure. Accountability and responsibility went with power, and even more so with great power. It made perfect sense now that he thought about it, and he felt that Whalen had been right to test him.

Their journey continued without interruption, and Alex's mood improved as they rode toward the great arch. Bregnest entertained the company with stories about his own lands, some of which they passed on their journey to Telous. Alex was impressed with Bregnest's descriptions of his lands and thought Alusia would be an excellent place to live, if he ever decided to move away from his stepfather's tavern.

They spent their last night in Alusia camping a short distance from the great arch. They had decided to ride to Telous the next morning so that they would arrive in time for their midday meal. Alex hoped that he would be able to return to Alusia soon, both to see his friends and to see his many new horses.

"Perhaps you should have chosen a horse or two to take

back to Telous with you," Bregnest commented as they sat around the campfire that night.

"I have the only horse I need," Alex answered. "Though I suppose someday Shahree will grow too old for adventures."

"Most horses only make it through three or four adventures," said Sindar in a thoughtful way. "Adventures are harder on the horses than on the adventurers who ride them."

"And they don't get to change their age on adventures like we do," said Andy.

"I'm quite happy with my present horse," said Alex, hoping to change the subject.

"And I'm sure she is happy with her present owner," said Halfdan.

Alex grinned at Halfdan's comment, but did not reply. He didn't want to think about going on an adventure without Shahree. He knew that someday he would have to, but he hoped that day was far, far away.

"Tomorrow you will meet Whalen," said Bregnest with a twinkle in his eye. "It has been a long time coming."

"It has," Alex agreed, trying to hide his excitement.

"Perhaps he will ask you to travel with him," Andy commented. "That would be an adventure worth going on."

"And perhaps Whalen will ask something else of you," said Sindar, catching Alex's eye. "He may no longer think of you as an apprentice."

"I believe Master Vankin still has a great deal to teach me," said Alex. "As I've been telling you all for this entire adventure, I'm only a wizard in training."

"It seems you've had a fair bit of training then," Halfdan laughed. "You'll be taking a staff soon, I would guess."

"I will wait until Whalen says I am ready before taking a staff," Alex replied.

"And only time will tell when that might be," said Sindar softly, as if reading Alex's mind. "Though for all that is good in the known lands, I hope that it is sooner rather than later."

The following day, as the company approached Telous, Alex's nervous feelings grew to a new high. Soon he would be meeting Whalen for the first time in person. He felt like he already knew Whalen from all the messages and letters they had exchanged and from the stories he had heard about Whalen, but this was different. Whalen was known as the greatest wizard alive, and more than anything else, Alex hoped that Whalen would ask him to go on an adventure with him so that he could continue his training in person and learn by watching him work.

When they finally reached the Golden Swan, Alex was so nervous he could hardly move. He had some trouble getting off Shahree, and he stumbled on the steps of the Swan. He knew he was being silly, but he couldn't help it.

"Bregnest," a voice called as the company entered the Swan. "Good to see you again, my friend."

Alex looked over and saw that Whalen was both everything and nothing at all like he had expected. Whalen looked old, but not too old; thin, but not too thin. He was almost six feet tall with shoulder-length silver-gray hair and a neatly trimmed goatee. Alex could also see that he had a great deal of magical power.

"Whalen," answered Bregnest. "It has been too long, my old friend."

"And this must be Alex," said Whalen, approaching Alex with his hand outstretched. "So good to meet you face to face at last."

"A great honor," Alex managed to say, shaking Whalen's hand.

"Oh, perhaps," said Whalen with a mischievous look on his face. "Though perhaps the great honor is mine."

"Sir?" Alex asked, not understanding what Whalen meant.

"Now then, Bregnest, introduce me to the rest of your fine company," Whalen continued, not taking time to answer Alex. "Alex has kept me up with your adventure, of course, but now I can ask all those little questions that are best asked in person."

Bregnest introduced the rest of the company to Whalen, and Whalen greeted them all as if he knew them. Alex was relieved to see that his friends were nearly as nervous as he was. In fact, Whalen had to take Andy's hand and shake it before Andy would stop bowing to him.

"Well, now," said Whalen. "I do hope you'll allow me to join you for your midday meal."

"It would be both our honor and our pleasure," Bregnest replied.

Whalen nodded and waved his hand toward a small dining room set at the front of the Swan, where arrangements had already been made for their meal. As soon as they were seated, servants appeared with trays of food.

Whalen was interested in everything Alex's friends had to

say. He seemed to be almost overflowing with energy as he asked all kinds of questions about what had happened on their adventure. He seemed most interested in the minor points that Alex had neglected to mention in his letters, and he listened closely to every answer.

"You turned old Kappa into a donkey?" Whalen laughed. "Exactly what he deserved. I'm pleased that Trion saw it that way as well, and chose to leave him in that form."

"It seemed the most fitting thing to turn him into," said Alex.

"Of course it was. You have become very good at reading people, Alex. I am impressed with your judgment on this adventure."

"Thank you," said Alex.

"Now, to business," said Whalen in a slightly more serious tone. "Bregnest, I take it you have not had your final feast with this company or declared your adventure at an end?"

"That is correct," said Bregnest. "I thought perhaps tonight or tomorrow we would take care of that final part of our agreement."

"Tomorrow night would be better," said Whalen, looking at Bregnest with his eyebrows raised.

"Then tomorrow night it shall be," said Bregnest with a slight bow.

Alex thought it was odd that Whalen wanted them to wait; he wasn't a member of the company, after all.

"Now then, with your permission, Bregnest. I would like to have a good long talk with Alex," said Whalen.

"He is free to do as he wishes until tomorrow night's feast."

"Very good," said Whalen with a nod. "If the rest of you will excuse us. Alex, we have a great deal to discuss."

Alex was puzzled, but decided that Whalen had his reasons. With a quick nod to his friends, Alex followed Whalen out of the dining room and toward the back of the Swan.

Whalen led Alex to a small room with two comfortable chairs, a small table with a lamp, and a large fireplace. The curtains in the room were pulled shut and the lamp and fire were both burning brightly.

"Have a seat," said Whalen, closing the door behind them.

Alex sat down in one chair, and Whalen sat in the other chair, looking at Alex for what seemed like a long time.

"I suppose you know what I want to talk to you about," said Whalen in a serious tone.

"No," Alex answered nervously.

"I want to ask you to do two things, and then to let me do a third," said Whalen. "First of all, I want to ask you to take your staff."

"A . . . a staff?" Alex asked in shock. "But I'm still in training, I still have so much to learn."

"Exactly. You have learned that you still have much more to learn. That is perhaps the hardest thing for any wizard to discover."

"I . . . I don't understand."

"Of course you don't." Whalen chuckled. "Thinking that you know everything you need to know and that you understand everything that is said is what keeps most wizards from ever becoming really great."

Alex was confused by the statement, but then felt like a

small light suddenly came on in his head as he understood what Whalen was saying.

"The second thing I want to ask you is to swear an oath to obey wizard law," Whalen said.

"The staff and the oath don't go together?"

"Oh, no. Most people who find out that they're wizards, or I should say potential wizards, run right out and buy a staff. Some wait until they've had an adventure or two, and some wait for an oracle to tell them to buy a staff."

"But you told me not to buy a staff," said Alex, confused.

"Of course I did. Any fool can buy a staff, and some can even manage a good deal of magic with one. You, on the other hand, managed a good deal of magic without a staff, which makes your deeds far more impressive."

"When do most wizards take the oath?" Alex asked.

"Many never do," said Whalen sadly. "You see, the oath is only given to true wizards—those who have managed at least four great wizard tasks."

"What four tasks have I done?" Alex questioned, thinking back over his adventures and wondering what Whalen would consider to be a great wizard task.

Whalen smiled. "Your interest in this matter shows good sense and humility, both things that help make a truly great wizard."

"But what four tasks have I done?" Alex asked again. "I mean, I know I've done some good things, but nothing great."

"Don't be too sure about that," Whalen replied. "The first two tasks were completed during your first adventure. Bregnest told me about them after your return, and I've done some checking since then to make sure he was right."

"What did I do?"

"First, you defeated the wraiths at the ruins of Aunk. Few wizards could have done that at all, and fewer still without a staff."

"But I didn't know what I was doing," Alex protested. "And besides, I was only able to defeat the wraiths because of Moon Slayer."

"Ah, yes, your magic sword. Personally, I thought having the sword choose you should have counted as a task, but the council didn't agree with me."

"The council?"

"I'll explain that in a minute," Whalen replied with a wave of his hand. "Your second task was killing the dragon Slathbog and destroying his carcass."

"Again, that was mostly because of Moon Slayer."

"The sword helped, of course," agreed Whalen. "However, you looked into the dragon's eyes. I know of only one wizard who has ever done that and lived to tell the tale. You, however, broke the dragon's magic and his will—a great task indeed. Then you turned him to ash with a single command, which I believe should also have counted as a separate task."

"Yes, but—" Alex began.

Whalen held up his hand. "Your third task should have been destroying the goblin shaman in Norsland, but I think it best that we keep that quiet for the time being. So, your third official task was destroying the lower library of the Tower of the Moon and driving away the evil shadow that was trying so hard to get it. And your fourth task was stopping a war in Athanor, which could easily have spread to other kingdoms in Alusia, as well as to other lands."

"But in Athanor I hardly did any magic. It only worked out because I tricked Varson into doing what I wanted him to," said Alex before he could stop himself.

"You may not have used much magic, but you did display a good deal of cunning and common sense. You came up with a plan and made it work."

"All right," said Alex after a few moments of silence. "If you say these are great wizard tasks, I will believe you."

"Excellent! Now, for the council I mentioned. There are nine wizards on the council—myself included—who work to fight evil, help train young wizards, and uphold wizard laws."

"And this council has decided I've managed four great tasks and they want me to take an oath?"

"Yes, we have and we do," Whalen answered. "As your teacher, I would like you to take a staff, and the council would like you to take an oath to obey the wizard laws."

"And what are these laws?" Alex questioned, worried he might have already broken some of them.

"Oh, they're simple rules, nothing too difficult to do or too hard to remember. The most important part is that you promise not to do evil and that you try to do good whenever and wherever you can."

Alex sat thinking about everything Whalen had said, and he felt unsure of himself. If he accepted his staff, he would be considered a true wizard, and he wasn't sure he was ready for that. He had hoped to continue learning with Whalen, but maybe that wasn't a possibility.

"I know this is a lot to take in all at once," said Whalen in a kindly tone. "Perhaps you were hoping to continue your studies, or undertake an adventure as my apprentice. I, however, believe you are already a true wizard and that it is time for you to take your staff. I will always help you if I can. And as your sponsor, I will expect you to keep me updated on what you're doing."

"Sponsor?" Alex questioned.

"Since I'm the one asking you to take a staff, by wizard law, I am responsible for you to some degree."

Alex didn't reply, thinking quietly for a time. Whalen and the council considered him a wizard. All his friends thought he was a wizard and would never listen when he said he was still in training. And he had also called himself a wizard several times on this last adventure, so somewhere inside he must believe that he was a wizard.

"You said there was something else," Alex said slowly. "Something I had to let you do."

"Yes, if you agree to take a staff and swear the oath, I would like to place a spell on you—the Rel O'Gash," said Whalen.

"What kind of spell is it?"

"One that will help you control your O'Gash," Whalen answered and then smiled at the puzzled look on Alex's face. "O'Gash is an ancient name for a wizard's inner eye—his sixth sense. A wizard's O'Gash helps him know things, like when someone is lying to him. It also gives you warnings when something is wrong, and sometimes can give you knowledge that you didn't have before. You've already used your O'Gash, Alex. The spell will simply help it grow stronger and help you understand it better."

"I have found magic when I needed it," Alex said slowly. "I've used spells that I've never read or heard before. They just came to me when I needed them."

"That is your O'Gash helping you. I would have explained this to you sooner, but I honestly didn't think your O'Gash would grow as strong as it is so quickly. In fact, you are something of a surprise to the council."

"I am?"

"It doesn't often happen," Whalen said slowly, "but every now and then a person is born who, like you, can use a high level of magic, even without training. You have learned everything I've given you much faster than any normal apprentice would, and you have found magic when you needed it most. The council and I agree that you may, in fact, be wizardborn."

"Very well," said Alex, taking a deep breath. "I will do as you ask—I will take a staff. I will also swear the oath and agree to obey wizard law. And whenever you are ready, I will let you put the Rel O'Gash on me."

"Well done, well done indeed. I am pleased with your decision."

"What now?"

"Now we go to Blackburn's so you can summon your staff," replied Whalen.

"Summon a staff?"

"Of course," said Whalen, getting up and moving to the door. "You could take just any staff, of course, but if you summon one, it will work better for you. We'll take care of the Rel O'Gash later tonight, once you have your staff."

"I'm not supposed to talk about the Rel O'Gash, am I?" Alex asked, already knowing the answer. "I mean, not with anyone but you or another wizard."

"I see your O'Gash is already teaching you," Whalen replied with a nod.

Whalen led Alex out of the Swan and into the streets of Telous while he explained about summoning a staff. There was a simple spell that would call forth the staff best suited for Alex. It was also a useful spell to know, Whalen explained, in case you dropped your staff and needed it in a hurry.

"Master Vankin. Master Taylor," said Mr. Blackburn as Alex and Whalen entered his shop. "A great honor to have you both here."

Alex had been to Mr. Blackburn's shop once before when he had bought Moon Slayer. He liked Mr. Blackburn, and he liked looking around his shop even more.

"We've come to get my friend a staff," Whalen said enthusiastically.

"'Course you have," said Mr. Blackburn with a nod. "Knew he'd be back for one. Said so in the book."

"May we see the staffs you have?" Whalen asked.

Mr. Blackburn bowed and led Alex and Whalen to a back room of the shop. Alex was surprised to see at least a hundred staffs lined up, all made of different woods and metals, and all giving off a little bit of their power. He could feel the magic in the room. He looked around the room with wide eyes, wondering which staff might be the best one for him.

"Whenever you're ready, Alex," Whalen said quietly.

"Are you sure there's one here for me?" Alex asked.

"Oh, yes, I'm sure of it."

"What if there's more than one?" asked Alex, imagining all the staffs in the room suddenly landing on top of him.

"That would be unlikely," Whalen said thoughtfully. "There have been a few cases where two staffs were summoned, but that was a long time ago."

Alex nodded and stood for a moment without moving. He knew without being told that this was one of the most important moments of his life. He was about to summon his staff and become a true wizard. Slowly he raised his hands and repeated the spell Whalen had taught him.

To Alex's shock and surprise, the moment he finished the spell, three staffs jumped from the wall and moved across the floor to stand directly in front of him without any support.

"Oh, my," said Whalen, sounding almost as surprised as Alex felt. "Well, this is something, isn't it?"

"Did I do something wrong?"

"No, you did it exactly right," Whalen replied. "Let me see what we have here."

Whalen began walking back and forth, looking at the three staffs. Alex's nervous feeling reached a new high, and he wondered for a moment if he should change his mind about taking a staff.

"Oak and gold," said Whalen. "A fine-looking staff. And yes, holly and silver, an excellent staff. Well, ironwood and true silver, a strange combination, but another wonderful staff."

"Should I try again?" Alex questioned.

"No, there won't be any need for that. It looks as if the staffs will have to compete."

"Compete?"

"Yes," Whalen replied in a thoughtful tone. "You will use each staff to do the same magical act. The staff that does the best job will be the one for you."

"And if they are all the same?"

"Well, that's hardly likely," said Whalen. Then he stopped to consider the question for a moment. "Of course, if they do, that will be interesting, won't it?"

Alex didn't answer, afraid to ask what Whalen might mean by interesting.

"Well, come along," said Whalen. "Bring the staffs. I think we'll step outside for this. I'll ask Mr. Blackburn to help me judge."

Alex collected the three staffs and followed Whalen outside. He wondered what kind of magical act Whalen would ask him to do and how Whalen and Mr. Blackburn would judge the results.

Whalen turned to face Alex. "Pick one staff and lay the others aside for now."

Alex kept the oak and gold staff in his hand and leaned the other two against the wall of Mr. Blackburn's shop.

"Now, Alex, I want you to use your staff and change this large rock here into solid gold," said Whalen, as if his request was perfectly normal.

Alex looked at the rock. It was nearly three feet tall and almost as long. He wondered how Whalen would know if it was solid gold or not. Putting the thought out of his mind, he concentrated on the task at hand. After a few seconds, he touched the rock with the bottom of the staff.

"Oh, well done," said Whalen. "Mr. Blackburn, what do you think?"

"Well, I don't know if it's gold all the way through," Mr. Blackburn replied. "But it looks like it's all gold on the outside."

"All right, Alex," Whalen continued. "Now use your staff to change the gold into a dog."

Alex was surprised by the request, but he didn't ask any questions. Once more he focused his mind, and after a moment, he touched the rock a second time with the staff.

"A golden retriever, how fitting," said Whalen with a chuckle. "Mr. Blackburn, what do you think?"

"Looks all dog to me," said Mr. Blackburn, patting the dog on the head.

"All right, Alex," said Whalen. "Now turn the dog back into the original rock."

Once more Alex did as he was told. Even though he liked the dog and didn't really want to change it back, he knew that it was really a rock.

"Now use your staff to send a large red fireball into the sky," Whalen ordered. "Have it explode and vanish when it reaches about a hundred feet up or so."

Once more Alex did as he was told, and after a few moments of thought, an enormous bright-red fireball shot from the head of the staff. When the fireball was a hundred feet in the air, a tremendous explosion shook the ground under his feet and rattled the windows of Mr. Blackburn's smithy.

"Very well done," said Whalen. "That should wake up the people of Telous."

Whalen asked Alex to change staffs and repeat the process. To Alex's surprise and confusion, he managed the exact same results with both of the other staffs.

"I never seen anything like this before," said Mr. Blackburn, rubbing his head. "There's no difference between them and that's a fact."

"I agree," said Whalen, smiling but sounding slightly troubled.

"Perhaps some other task would work better," Alex suggested.

"No, I believe it would be the same," said Whalen. "This is strange, but it has happened at least once before."

"It has?"

"Well, once that I know of," Whalen answered. "Of course that was before my time, but the incident is well-documented."

"What do we do now?" Alex questioned, hoping the answer would be simple.

"Conflagration," Whalen answered, and Mr. Blackburn let out a loud gasp.

"What's that?" Alex questioned.

"It's a magical command that will combine all three staffs into one," Whalen said slowly. "I've never seen it used, of course, but I'm quite sure you can manage it."

At this point Alex wasn't sure he could manage anything at all. He didn't comment on his own doubts, however, but listened closely as Whalen whispered the command in his ear.

"Concentrate on all three staffs joining together," Whalen added as he took a step back.

Alex summoned all three staffs once again so they were standing in front of him. He closed his eyes for a few seconds, trying to focus all of his energy. Opening his eyes, he looked at the three staffs and, when he was ready, he thought of the command Whalen had whispered to him.

The three staffs moved slowly toward each other until they touched. Alex could feel heat coming from the staffs, but he continued to concentrate as hard as he could. The heat continued to grow, and Alex thought he could smell smoke. Suddenly there was a blinding flash of pure white light and only one staff remained.

"Amazing," said Mr. Blackburn, a look of wonder on his face. "Never thought I'd see such a thing in all my days."

"Few people have," said Whalen. "In fact, my dear Mr. Blackburn, we three are the only ones to have seen something like this in more than a thousand years."

Alex's thoughts remained fixed on the staff in front of him. It looked completely different from any of the three staffs he started with, though strangely the same. The new staff was made of some black and shiny wood with interwoven patterns of true silver and gold wrapped around it.

"Go ahead," said Whalen, looking at Alex. "Take your staff, my friend."

Alex reached out and took the staff in his hand. A strange feeling of warmth filled him, and the staff seemed to shiver slightly at his touch. He looked at Whalen, then at Mr. Blackburn, then back at the staff. This was something he'd never expected, but something he was very happy about just the same.

"Don't forget to pay Mr. Blackburn," Whalen reminded Alex.

Alex nodded and asked Mr. Blackburn how much he owed him.

Mr. Blackburn, who seemed even more shocked than Alex, had some trouble deciding on a price. In the end, with a little help from Whalen, they agreed on a price, and Alex paid Mr. Blackburn for his wonderful new staff.

"Well, the council will certainly be interested in this turn of events," said Whalen as he and Alex walked back to the Golden Swan. "A most impressive feat indeed. It may count as your fifth great wizard act."

"I don't think taking a staff should count as a great wizard act."

"Well, perhaps not," Whalen agreed. "But that decision will be up to the council."

"When do I take the oath?" Alex asked as he and Whalen entered the Golden Swan.

"Tomorrow night, during your company's final feast," said Whalen. "I will ask them all to be witnesses for you. It will put a nice end on your latest adventure."

Alex nodded. He was eager to take the oath to obey wizard law. After all, he was one step closer to being a true wizard.

Chapter Twenty

A New Beginning

So, you've taken your staff," said Sindar when Alex and Whalen entered the main bar at the Golden Swan.

"I have," said Alex, grinning from ear to ear.

"It's about time," Halfdan added, stepping forward to shake Alex's hand. "I've been wondering when you'd get around to it."

"And I've been wondering why Whalen made him wait so long," said Bregnest, shaking Alex's hand as well.

"All things in time," said Whalen.

Andy was too amazed to even speak, and he simply shook Alex's hand.

"It's all right," Alex said. "You don't need to say anything." He was still having a little trouble believing he had taken a staff. He couldn't stop smiling.

"A real wizard," Andy finally managed to say. "Imagine—me being friends with a real wizard."

Alex laughed. He knew Andy had always considered him a real wizard, but it seemed that Alex's taking a staff had finally allowed Andy to say the words out loud.

"Well now," said Whalen after the congratulations had

ended. "I have something to ask each of you, and I hope you will all agree."

"How may we be of service?" Bregnest asked.

"Tomorrow night, at your company's final feast, I would like you all to be witnesses for Alex," answered Whalen. "I will be taking Alex's oath as a true wizard."

"We would be honored," said Bregnest, bowing to both Whalen and Alex.

"I know you can answer for your company, Bregnest, but still I must ask each of you to answer for yourselves," said Whalen. "After all, it's not a simple thing to be a witness."

"Do they have to do something?" Alex questioned, surprised by Whalen's comment.

"Nothing difficult," Whalen answered. "They will sign a document saying that they are witnesses, and their files will be updated to show as much."

"Why would that be important?" Alex asked, puzzled.

"So other adventurers will know that they are your witnesses, of course," said Whalen as if that explained everything.

"Witnesses for a wizard are often given greater preference for adventures," Sindar explained. "Your honor will shine on us because we have ridden with you."

After all of Alex's friends agreed to witness for him, Whalen turned to Bregnest. "I suppose it's time for our evening meal. I'll need to speak with Alex again once we are done."

The company and Whalen enjoyed a long and somewhat rowdy meal. Later, Whalen led Alex to the back room of the Swan. Once they were seated, Whalen told Alex more about the wizard laws and about the responsibilities that went with being a wizard. They talked late into the night, and Alex learned a great many new things.

At one point when Whalen had paused in his explanation, Alex asked him a question that had been on his mind for some time. "Do you remember the ring I recovered on my first adventure?"

"Yes, you've told me about it," said Whalen.

"Iownan said she couldn't tell me what the ring was. When I asked if she didn't know what the ring was or if she just couldn't tell me, she said she couldn't tell me."

"That is common with oracles," replied Whalen. "They always know more than they are willing to say."

"Can you tell me what the ring is?"

"I'm sorry, Alex, I have no idea what it might be. However, if Iownan advised you to keep the ring safe, but not use it, I would heed her instruction. She has her reasons."

"I'm not in any rush," said Alex. "I've wondered about it and thought that you might know something about it."

"I understand completely. Perhaps someday Iownan or some other oracle will tell you what the ring is. When that happens, you might let me know as well."

Alex felt that Whalen was the only person he'd ever met who truly understood him. It seemed strange in a way, as the two of them had only really met that day.

"Oh, yes," said Whalen suddenly. "You'll want to keep your staff in your bag while in Telous, and of course when you're at home."

"Why?"

"Well, in Telous, you really have no need of the staff and

carrying it around is considered a bit showy, if you know what I mean."

"And at home?"

"Well, I think you'd look very odd walking around your stepfather's tavern with a staff," Whalen laughed. "And your stepfather might faint if you came home carrying one. You've only been on two adventures, after all."

That night, Alex thought about what Whalen had told him about wizard law and being a wizard. Whalen had also given him a lot of advice on how to choose his adventures in the future. Whalen had also worked the Rel O'Gash spell, and Alex could already feel it working. His mind seemed more organized than it had been, and he could recall the things Whalen had said with ease.

The next morning after breakfast, Whalen once again took Alex to the back room to talk. Whalen taught Alex several more things, including the spell he had been unable to share with Alex during his journey down the Mountains of the Moon. By midday Whalen was finishing giving Alex instructions and advice.

"You should spend the afternoon thinking," said Whalen as they left the small room together. "You need to consider what the oath means and be sure that you're ready to accept it."

Alex nodded. Whalen was right, of course; he had a lot to think about. Whalen had explained so many things in such a short amount of time that Alex wanted some time to sort them all out. He needed some time alone, time to think about what he was and where that might lead him.

After eating the midday meal with his friends, Alex

returned to the small room alone. He considered what it meant to be a true wizard, wondering if he was really ready for the burden. He had only been on two short adventures. Wizards were revered; they were expected to know things and to be wise. In the end, he decided that all wizards had to start somewhere.

Alex was surprised when Whalen knocked on the door to tell him it was time for the company's final feast. The afternoon had slipped away, but Alex had made up his mind. He would take the oath, and do everything he could to keep it, whatever his future held.

As Alex entered the dining room with Whalen, his friends stood and bowed to both of them. Alex felt slightly embarrassed by the attention, but he didn't say anything. Whalen led him to the head of the table and indicated that he should remain standing.

"Alexander Taylor," said Whalen, turning to face him. "You have taken your staff and agreed to take the wizard's oath. Do you do this of your own free will?"

"I do," Alex answered.

"Will all those gathered here as witnesses acknowledge that he takes this oath of his own free will?" Whalen asked, turning to the company.

"We will," Alex's friends all replied.

"Present your staff," Whalen commanded.

Alex took his new staff from his magic bag and held it out toward Whalen. Whalen did not touch the staff, but looked at it closely.

"Alexander Taylor, do you swear by your staff that you will obey the wizard laws?"

"I swear by my staff," answered Alex, a tingling sensation running through him as he spoke.

"Will the witnesses testify?" Whalen asked, continuing to look Alex in the eye.

"We will," his friends answered

"As a member of the council of wizards, I, Whalen Vankin, accept the oath of Alexander Taylor," said Whalen, his eyes shining with happiness. "I name you a true wizard and a friend of the council of wizards."

Alex smiled and bowed to Whalen. Whalen returned his bow, and the company all cheered. Alex was now as much a wizard as any wizard could ever be.

"A fitting end to this adventure," said Bregnest as Whalen and Alex took their seats. "If there are no questions or disputes, I will call our agreement fulfilled."

None of the company spoke so Bregnest went on.

"Our agreement is complete, and another first-class adventure is over."

"And a new adventure begins for our wizard friend," said Sindar.

Alex and his friends laughed, and Bregnest rang the bell to call the servants. Their final feast was long and full of conversation and storytelling. Alex knew he would soon be leaving his friends once more, but he hoped he would see them all again soon.

As they were finishing their meal, Alex learned that most of his friends would be leaving for home the next morning.

Halfdan, Andy, and Sindar would all be riding to the great arch together. Bregnest would be going to Mr. Clutter's shop with Alex. Whalen said he would wait at the Swan for Bregnest's return, before traveling to Alusia.

"You know," said Whalen looking at Alex. "You might want to start thinking about moving to one of the known lands."

"Moving?" Alex questioned.

"You won't be staying with your stepfather forever," said Whalen in a kindly tone.

"But I've only visited three of the known lands, and then only for a short time."

"It's only a thought. You don't have to move right now, or even decide on a land this minute. And you can always move again, if and when you feel like it."

"I did rather like Alusia."

"As do I," Whalen replied. "It would be nice having you close as well. If you like, I'll keep an eye out for a suitable place for you. You know, a small farm or something."

"Would you?" Alex thought the idea sounded wonderful. Of course, he would have to talk to Mr. Roberts about it, but he felt sure that his stepfather would accept whatever decision he made.

"I'd be happy to," Whalen said. "As I said, it would be nice having you close."

They finished their feast but none of them wanted to say goodnight or good-bye. They remained at the table for a long time, talking about what they would do next, and eventually their good-byes were put off until the following morning.

"Thrang will be pleased when I tell him you've taken your staff," said Halfdan the next morning at breakfast. "Though he'll be disappointed that he wasn't here to see it."

"It's his own fault for trying to retire," Alex answered. "Though I'd guess he's not completely retired yet."

"He's got an adventure or two left in him," said Halfdan with a wink.

"Skeld and Tayo will be green with envy," said Andy. "This might put an itch in them to go on another adventure."

"Tell them they'd better get permission from Lilly and Indigo first," said Alex. "Give my best to your family, will you, Andy?"

"I will," Andy promised. "And Michael will be pleased to hear about your staff, I'm sure."

"And you, Sindar," said Alex. "Are you returning to the dark forest?"

"I am. And I'm sure Calysto will be pleased with all I have to tell her."

"Give her my best," said Alex. "And greetings to Iownan and Osrik if you happen to see them."

"I'm sure I will," Sindar replied. "Take care, my friend. May we ride together again one day."

"As long as there aren't so many goblins next time," Alex laughed.

Sindar smiled, and then leaned close so that only Alex could hear what he said. "I've been thinking about our discussion—the one about the pendant I wear. If you like, I can try to find out what your father did for the order."

"Would you?"

"I can try," Sindar answered. "Such questions are not often asked, and even less often answered, but I can try."

"Please do," said Alex. "And let me know if there's anything I can do to help."

"Until we meet again, my friends, be well," said Sindar, winking at Alex.

With those final words, Halfdan, Andy, and Sindar climbed onto their saddles and rode away from the Golden Swan. Alex waved to them as they went, and then turned to look at Bregnest.

"How are we getting to Mr. Clutter's?" he asked.

"Through the wardrobe," Bregnest sighed.

Alex said good-bye to Whalen, promising to keep in touch with him as often as he could. He felt sad at the parting, sadder even than leaving his friends behind. He had only been face to face with Whalen for two days, but he felt like he'd known him all his life.

Whalen smiled and promised to keep an eye out in Alusia for Alex's new home. As he took Alex's hand to say good-bye, he spoke in a lowered voice. "We will meet again, my friend. And perhaps we will even share an adventure some day."

Alex bowed to Whalen, and then followed Bregnest back into the main lobby of the Golden Swan.

Bregnest sat down and said, "Clutter's adventure shop." He vanished.

Alex followed Bregnest's example and as soon as he had repeated, "Clutter's adventure shop," everything went dark around him. For a minute he felt confused, and then he saw the open door of the wardrobe in front of him.

"Back again," said Mr. Clutter as Alex stepped out of the wardrobe. "And another successful adventure, if I do say so myself."

"Very successful," replied Bregnest. "We've completed our quest, and Master Taylor has taken his staff."

"How wonderful," said Mr. Clutter, beaming at Alex. "I knew he would one day, but after only two adventures, that is outstanding."

"You are most kind," said Alex.

"Not at all," Mr. Clutter went on. "This is truly amazing. I'm sure you'll be in great demand for future adventures."

"Perhaps," Alex allowed.

"I suppose you'll want to change, then," said Mr. Clutter. "I'll just let you get on with it. And I'll collect the files for you, Master Bregnest."

Alex watched as Mr. Clutter hurried from the room, just as he always seemed to do. Alex changed back into his old clothes and looked at himself in the mirror. He had to laugh at his strange appearance. He had gotten so used to being in his adventurer's clothes that his reflection looked odd to him.

"Heading back to your stepfather's tavern?" Bregnest asked as Alex emerged from the changing room.

"For now. Though Whalen did suggest I think about moving to a known land."

"Did he suggest which land?" Bregnest questioned with interest.

"I rather liked Alusia," answered Alex.

"You would be most welcome there. And it would put you closer to Whalen."

"It would, if he stays home," said Alex. "But he did say he'd keep an eye open for me."

"Then I will also keep an eye open," said Bregnest. "I would like to thank you for all you did on this adventure, Alex."

"You have thanked me enough already. You've thanked me so many times that I'm starting to think I did something extraordinary."

"You did several extraordinary things on this adventure, just as you did on your last adventure."

"I did have some help. I was lucky enough to have some good friends along with me."

"I hope that we will ride together again someday," said Bregnest, looking a little sad.

"As do I, my friend. And I hope that day is not too far off."

"Well then," said Bregnest awkwardly, "I suppose you'd best be off."

"Yes," said Alex, shaking Bregnest's hand. "And if Whalen finds me a new home, I'll be sure to let you know."

"You had better," Bregnest laughed.

Alex said a final good-bye to Bregnest and left the shop before Mr. Clutter could return. He had a great deal to think about, and Mr. Clutter's fast talking would only confuse his mind right now.

Alex wandered back up Sildon Lane, wondering how Mr. Roberts would react to everything he had to tell him. He knew his stepfather would be pleased with the story of his adventure. Alex hoped that Mr. Roberts wouldn't be too upset about his plans to move to Alusia, but there was no rush to discuss that.

Alex turned the corner that led back to the Happy Dragon and laughed out loud. He had all day to decide what to tell Mr. Roberts; he had returned on the same morning he had left. For now, he was happy to simply go home and take some time to think about his future.

Reading Guide

1. At the beginning of the story, Mr. Roberts talks to Alex about teamwork and the importance of being part of a team. He reminds Alex that he doesn't have to do everything, and that other people on the team need to help out as well. How important is teamwork in your life? How important is it to include everyone on your team?

2. Early in the adventure Alex runs into a bully named Otho. Have you ever had problems with a bully? Later in the story, Alex turns Otho into an ox, but we can't do that to bullies in our world. How can we deal with bullies in our own lives? How can we help other people who are being bullied?

3. Alex sometimes has a hard time controlling his emotions. He almost loses his temper several times even though he knows something terrible could happen if he does. Do you ever have trouble controlling your emotions? Have you ever lost your temper and then later regretted what happened?

4. Alex is given a list of things to do that will help him control his emotions, including his temper. What kind of things can you do to control your emotions? Are there other emotions besides anger that need to be controlled?

5. Sedric Valenteen tells the others that he has a hard time

trusting people because he was once betrayed. Have you ever been betrayed by someone you trusted? Does a bad experience like being betrayed make it harder for you to trust other people now?

6. Bregnest tells Val that honor is saying you will do something and then doing it. What do you think Bregnest means? What other ways are there to be honorable? What do you think honor really means?

7. The brownies in the enchanted woods refuse to accept any kind of payment for their help. They say that because Alex and Sindar let them help they have already been repaid. What do you think they mean? Have you ever helped someone and felt that being able to help was the best payment you could ever get?

8. Bregnest feels that his honor has been damaged because of the choices Val made. Have you ever felt that your honor or reputation was damaged by something other people have done? How do the actions of your friends and family affect you? How do your actions affect your friends and family?

9. Alex is willing to fight a war for what he believes is right. What would you be willing to do for something you believe is right?

10. Pride is mentioned several times in the story. Alex fears that his growing pride about being a wizard might be considered evil. The bully Otho thinks he is better than others because of his father's position in the town. Varson's pride makes him believe that he is the true king. How can pride help us? How can pride hurt us? Are there different kinds of pride?

11. Whalen Vankin tells Alex that he is responsible for him to some degree, because he is the one asking Alex to become a true wizard. Are there people who are responsible for you and the things you do? Are you sometimes responsible for other people and what they do?